Death, Despair
&
Other Happy Endings

An Anthology of
Short Stories, Flash Fiction,
Poems and Plays

Bunbury Writers Group

Edited by Mary Elgar
Elgar Editing Services

For our families and friends
who have been our critics,
psychologists, supporters,
but most of all, our sounding boards.

Thank you for giving us time and space
to write, for understanding our need to
take ourselves into our own world
and let our imaginations run wild.

*'There is no greater agony
than bearing an untold story inside you.'*
Maya Angelou

*'People say, "What advice do you have for people who want to be
writers?" I say, they don't really need advice, they know they want to be
writers, and they're gonna do it. Those people who know that they really
want to do this and are cut out for it, they know it.'*
R.L. Stine

*'And by the way, everything in life is writable about if you have the
outgoing guts to do it, and the imagination to improvise.
The worst enemy to creativity is self-doubt.'*
Sylvia Plath

Contents

Flash Fiction (Stories less than 1,000 words)

Poems

Plays

About the Authors

Preface

It was hot and I was drinking beer after hearing Robert Drewe speak at the Perth Writers Festival, when I told my friend that I'd looked for and failed to find a writer's group in Bunbury. I can't remember how long I whinged for, or what exactly I said, but it was along the lines of 'Regional area ... no literary culture ... backwards ...'

I won't forget his response.

'Can I challenge you ... why don't you start up your own?'

Thus, The Bunbury Writers Group was conceptualised.

I'd never started a community group before, so I was operating from instinct. I created a Facebook page and flooded Bunbury Community pages until I was kicked out or silenced by the administrators. The requests to join the group dripped in and the first meeting was set for the Bunbury Library. From memory, eight or so said they were coming, and only two other people showed up. It was awkward. We were self-conscious. Maybe this wouldn't work? Or had I made a tactical error?

The next week I set it at the Parade Hotel. Perhaps it was the availability of alcohol, but more people showed. We met in the late afternoon, trying to spot each other by our shirts, like pointing out dolphins gliding through the estuary, only we were more graceful (Nina probably said she'd be holding a bottle of wine, Mark might've said he'd be wearing a Stephen King shirt). It was the first meeting in which we shared our work – faltering voices, double-handed grips tensed on either side of the A4, and then the innumerable seconds of silence when finished. It was supportive, constructive and exhilarating; virtues and feelings that have come to define the ethos of our group. The sky was black, and it was cold when we left, ear to ear grins on our faces.

Five people who attended that meeting are still members of the group today; four of them – Mark, Nina, Suzi and myself – are founding members. We stepped up to share the workload; social media administrators, making decisions, organising meetings, posting and advertising and getting people to come in and talk to us, etcetera.

Much of the initial format sticks to this day – a meeting every two weeks where we share work we've written.

One issue we needed to sort out was a permanent meeting location. We needed a consistent space that would allow us the privacy to share our own writing. The venues we tried around town, while supportive and accommodating, couldn't meet our rock star desires. *Why can't they give us our own space? Why do they have the music turned up so loud? Are the other customers deliberately talking loudly? Why are there other customers?!*

Enter Caf-fez, our self-appointed spiritual home. I'd become mates with Bianca and Matt because I basically had my own writing desk up the back. I can't remember if I asked, or Bianca offered, but she said she'd open up for us rent-free every two weeks for two and a half hours. Since then our meetings have thrived. We have developed an intimacy that allows us to concentrate and communicate deeply, not to mention that we're catered for by Bunbury's best barista.

It was Suzi who brought a crime writer and Executive Director of Leschenault Press and Book Reality, Ian Andrew, to come and speak with us. It's fair to say that Ian's interest in the group has been vested from the beginning, so keen is he to see a flourishing literary community in the South West. When the idea of an anthology was floated, I'm not sure Ian would have let us do it any other way, than with his company. Apart from being a mentor to the group, Ian's company has hired out the rooms for our writer's retreat, given cost-price workshops, and held our hand through the production process of this anthology.

Why would anyone want to join a writing group? Despite literature being produced and consumed solitarily (in the most part at least), writing is unmistakeably social in nature – you write so that others can read, and you write because you want to repay the joy of reading others. To write art that means something to someone else, you have to write with feeling. As such, when we share our art, we are sharing a little bit of our soul. I can't describe the thrill of reading someone else's work when they've nailed it. I can't describe the elation when you share something that you've worked hard on, and you witness the unabashed enthusiasm glowing on the readers' faces, and you're doing internal fist pumps because you've nailed it. On the flipside, after you share the first chapter of your perceived masterpiece and you realise through the shifty glances and crossed arms of the others that you've missed the mark. It is devastating. You can get indignant. *They just don't get it. Maybe if they understood. Obviously, I just need to explain ...* To be sure, these are never thoughts that should be followed. It's a mark of our culture that we can share our souls, give honest feedback, and keep returning with smiles. Perhaps an anecdote serves best. At a bad time for me personally, when I was feeling pretty raw, I had a chance encounter with a member's partner. He told me that the member in question, as a result of joining our group, has had their curiosity provoked, and life enriched. A burst of meaning hit me like warm sun. My spirits picked up. I don't think the partner's reflection is unique.

The Bunbury Writers Group has been functioning for a year and a half now. We have hosted open-mic nights, had a member publish a book, been awarded for plays and poetry, had short stories published and commended, including in state and national competitions. This anthology is our biggest milestone yet. I want to thank the other members for their passion and determination to storytelling. I'd like to thank them for our burgeoning friendship.

The ethos for this book, from day one, was to show that there are artists who write in Bunbury. Thus, there were no constraints on members to conform to a theme, or a genre, or linked stories. In some ways we are an eclectic bunch. Jackie has written a crime noir story; David provokes us with his flash fiction; Kim lets our imaginations flow with fantasy; Mark and Nina are our resident sickos (unputdownable); the surreal edges into Nat's work; Dan's fiction is just plain strange (and compelling); Louise has a touching story about our climate situation (crises!) ... I could go on ... But that gives some insight into the breadth this anthology covers. Our only guide was that we wanted to show what we are doing, and we wanted to put out our best possible versions.

Like any storyteller worth his salt, I will come full circle. I started this preface by complaining about art in the place that we live. Some honest feedback made me reflect on my own complicity in my perceived judgement. Putting myself out there, I have discovered an up-and-coming community of artists, who are increasingly starting to oscillate against each other. The lesson learnt is that the biggest difference between something happening and nothing happening is you. Bunbury has an exciting Arts scene, across its forms, and we are looking forward to playing our role in developing Arts in the region. For the community that has given us so much, this is our gift to you.

Ben Mason
Chairperson
Bunbury Writers Group

The Old Man and the Stars

Late at night was best to do laundry because the Laundromat was free, and he could get some decent work done. The old man was trying to look at molecular hydrogen from a different viewpoint in order to further the case for a Grand Unified Theory. The beat of the drier – badam-bum badam-bum – like a demented heartbeat, allowed him to find the meditative state required for such thinking.

Thuds slapped the pavement outside. A boy ran in, shrieking with laughter. The sleeves of his hoody flopped over his wrists. He asked the man for food.

'No.'

The boy walked along the row of driers with his outstretched arm flicking the machines. Black trackies frayed at his bare feet. The man had seen him before. He lived in one of the commission towers close to the man's apartment and university. With drugs and everything, these kinds of encounters were increasingly common. The man would vote for any party that vowed to tear the towers down.

'Wanna play a game?' The boy perched himself on a washing machine and swung his legs.

'No.'

The boy spied something beginning with c. The man didn't respond. Did he want to go first? Nothing.

'I spy with my little eye …' The boy started moshing in the middle of the laundromat, his little mullet flapping about, arms playing air guitar, while stupid sounds and saliva spilled from his mouth.

'Please. Please, be quiet.'

'I was being Metallica.'

The man lost his gaze into the clothes circling the drier, which he'd just put in. But he decided it wouldn't be worth leaving without drying them completely. 'Shouldn't you be in bed? Where're your parents?'

The boy grinned. You could park a truck through his buckteeth.

'I need to get some work done.'

'Oh yeah. Whacha working on?'

'Astrophysics.'

'What's that?'

'The universe. I study the stars.'

'Whoa, I love the stars. You should see the constellations I can name.'

'It's a little more compli–'

The boy was off, talking about saucepans, belts and crosses. The man cursed his own hubris; engaging in conversation.

'And you can see five planets with your naked eye.'

'Shut up. Shut. Up. For God's sake, can't you see you're not wanted?'

The boy dropped his head, pulled out a deck of Uno cards and started shuffling them.

The man sketched shapes with his grey lead in the hope of sparking focus. Except he couldn't. He remembered when he was a little boy, and his dad would wake him at absurd times when the night was darkest to look at stars through their telescope. He still recited those stories to students, explaining how he came to the profession.

It was dark now. And the telescope at the university would be free. He slapped his notebook closed.

'Hey, what's your name?'

'Deshawn.'

'Deshawn? What if I could show you all the planets?'

Ben Mason

Awake

'Coffee keeps you awake,' Mr. Perez said to Miss Carter in the hallway before class. Miss Carter replied that after the weekend she'd had, coffee was the only thing keeping her upright. They both grinned like they were sharing a joke. Kelly didn't know what the joke was. Adult stuff she assumed. But if coffee kept you awake – then coffee was what she needed.

Not from the foster house. They'd catch her. But teachers – teachers had the stuff in the staff room.

Stealing was bad. Kids who stole were bad kids. But coffee kept you awake. Kelly *needed* coffee. Guess that meant she was a bad kid.

It was dark in her room when she hefted the big jar out of her backpack and unscrewed the lid. The stuff inside looked like tiny brown rocks. It smelt awful and she knew it would taste even worse. But that wasn't the point – staying awake was.

She reached in a small hand and scooped out a palm-full. How much? She didn't know. More was probably better. She scrunched up her courage and smooshed the coffee into her mouth. It was worse than she'd expected. Disgustingness exploded behind her lips like a bomb. She gagged. Only the fear stopped her from spitting the horrible stuff out and vomiting on the carpet.

Coffee keeps you awake she told herself as she crunched up the bits with her baby teeth and swallowed. Tears dripped off her chin.

The taste didn't go away. It sat on her tongue like a bloated toad and made her want to retch.

*

On a normal night, Kelly would lie rigid under the blankets, waiting.

And she'd wait.

And wait.

For him to come.

Only he wouldn't. Not until her traitor eyes drooped closed and she fell – against her will – into a tense and unrestful doze.

He didn't come every night.

Sometimes he wouldn't come for days at a time.

But eventually, there he'd be.

Just when she'd fallen asleep.

There he'd be with his whispered promises that they would be playing another game. Games that weren't really games. With touches and movements that were always soft but somehow made deep cuts inside her where no one could see.

If she didn't fall asleep then maybe he'd stay away.

She waited.

Gritty eyed, she stared at the curtains – willing daylight to hurry.

There was creak from the hallway.

The coffee had kept her awake. But he was coming anyway.

Someone walked past her room. Someone small.

The sound wasn't big enough to be an adult.

It wasn't him.

Then who?

Still as a stone she waited, ears straining.

A muted clang. A child's yelp.

Something heavy hit the wall with a thud and there was a scuffling sound and panting.

Kelly was positive it was a kid.

But she was the only child in the house.

Who? Or what, was moving around in the dark?

She got out of bed.

On bare feet, she crossed to the door and listened. Quiet from the corridor. But there was definitely someone on the other side. Kelly turned the handle and slipped out.

A monster loomed by the bathroom. It was as tall as the doorframe, smelled of drains and rotten things. In one slimy limb, it pressed a small figure to the floor and seemed to be about to bring its other arm down on the person's head.

A year ago, Kelly might have shrunk back into her bedroom and tried to forget what she'd seen. Monsters happened. You dealt with them however you could. And you didn't bother telling an adult – they couldn't see them.

Adults were pretty useless when it came to monsters.

In her last foster home, there had been a thing that looked sort of like a cat – with six legs – which had crawled along the ceiling. If you hid under the blankets, it left you alone. Gary had only got eaten because he slept with his head outside the sheets.

Stupid Gary.

4

She dashed away a tear. She still had his Lego set. Playing on her own sucked.

That was a year ago.

This was now.

Monsters weren't half as scary as him. And she wasn't going to let another kid get eaten. Not if she could help it.

The hairy, dripping creature brought its limb down. Kelly growled low in her throat and ran at it.

She hit it with her shoulder, using all her weight. The impact was sticky and gross, but the thing staggered.

Partly covered in slime, Kelly pulled herself away from it and raised a threatening finger.

'Let. Them. Go!' She hissed in a fierce whisper. No point waking up the foster parents and getting into trouble.

It didn't have eyes, but the creature seemed to stare at her in confusion. Kelly stepped close and jabbed her finger higher. 'I'll get cross!' She snarled.

Her last foster Mum had said that a lot.

For a heart stopping moment it looked as though it would smash her to bits.

Kelly locked her trembling knees and gave it her most ferocious glare.

The monster shrank back.

It got smaller. All its hairy, gloopy bits pulled in and away from Kelly and the person on the floor. Kelly kept her finger raised and her face grumpy until it had sloshed back into the bathroom and gurgled down the plughole.

'Wow,' said an awed voice from the floor. 'How did you do that?'

Kelly stuck out a hand, the kid took it and levered themselves to their feet. 'I thought I was a goner,' they said.

Kelly shrugged. 'Monsters don't really bother me,' she said truthfully. *Not when you live with my foster dad.*

For the first time, by the dim light of the hallway, Kelly could make out the person she'd rescued. A girl, a bit taller than herself wearing some sort of black, Army clothes Kelly had only ever seen people in computer games wearing. And like the computer game characters, she carried a knife.

'I'm Amelia,' the girl said and handed Kelly a business card. Glowing gold letters read:

Amelia Oxley
Beast Slayer
Seven Seven

'Beast Slayer,' Kelly read. 'Seven Seven. Seven Seven what?'

'Seven-years-old for seven years,' Amelia said. 'It's a group that recruits and trains seven-year-olds to manage monsters.'

'Because seven-year-olds are the best at fighting them?' Kelly asked. All children knew that eight was when the *Change* happened. Eight-year-olds stopped being able to tell real monsters from imagined ones. They started to see stuff the way adults did.

'We are,' Amelia agreed. 'And Seven Seven has a way of stopping us from aging past seven. Well for seven years at least.'

'How long have you been seven?' Kelly asked.

'Four years,' Amelia said promptly. 'You could join us,' she said in a rush. 'You forced a level six beast to retreat! Without any training. That's …' She paused. 'Pretty amazing.'

Pretty amazing? No one had told Kelly she was amazing before. Annoying, yes. A waste of space, yes. Disobedient, disruptive, stupid, yes. But amazing? No.

Kelly felt a surge of something warm and new inside her. She swallowed it down. Who was she kidding? She couldn't go off with this girl and fight monsters. She'd get killed. And who wanted to stay seven for seven years?

You do, a small voice inside her said. *And what do you think will happen to you if you stay here?*

An image of him rose up in her mind.

Amelia waited.

'Ok,' Kelly said. 'Yes.'

At the other end of the house, the foster parents' bedroom door opened. The two girls froze.

'Wait in here,' Kelly said and pushed Amelia gently into the laundry. She snatched something from the girl's belt. On soundless feet, she fled back to her bed and bounded under the covers.

There wasn't any fear now. She held Amelia's dagger in her hand and waited. The door was pushed open. Big footsteps crossed the carpet to where she lay.

He stood over her.

Kelly smiled.

K. Dee

The Disappeared Eddy

It was a bleak and bleary Tuesday afternoon and Joseph Scotchman sat in his office, staring out of the grimy window. It was the dull, in-between part of the afternoon; too early for dinner and too late for lunch, but thanks to the inclement weather, just right for hiding indoors. Tucked away in his office, private dick for the slick, the shady and anyone else that had the dough, Joe sat. With a drink in one hand and a smoke in the other, it was his favourite thinking position – a comfortable spot to sit and listen to his gut, the smudged red and grey colours of a port city outside the window punctuating his thoughts. On this rainy Tuesday, with his feet propped up against the sill, staring at a spot on the window, he thought about his cleaner. His secretary would have him believe she had hired one, but the continued grubby state of the window left him perplexed as to what his cleaner actually cleaned.

'I'd be inclined to think I'm being taken for a ride,' he mused.

Joe's office, the place from which he ran his gumshoe operation, was on the first floor of a rundown building in the tired part of town. He liked it because the rent was cheap, and it was close to all the wrong places. There was a barber's shop downstairs that was always busy, yet never seemed to cut any hair, while the fumes from Yee's, the Chinese herbalist one floor above, did a fine job overpowering the smells of the street. Enveloping and ever-present, it was a sour and exotic, medicinal-type smell that surrounded the building like some kind of Asiatic cloud. Over time, it had tinged everything in his office a faint yellow-green, an olfactory patina of history and culture that coated every surface. The herbalist had occupied the upstairs space for longer than he could remember, and Joe had long since come to terms with the fact that he too probably smelt like something that belonged on the shelf at Yee's, but since he hadn't been sick in years, he had made his peace with it.

That Tuesday, he arrived at the office later than usual to find his secretary, Doris, sharing the small reception area with 'trouble in a tight dress'. He pretended not to notice the girl and greeted Doris.

'Say Doris, I thought we agreed you would find someone to clean the office?' he asked.

'Good morning Joe,' Doris replied.

'Good morning Doris,'

'As it happens you hired someone two weeks ago. Don't you remember boss?'

'Remember? Nothing looks different.'

'Leave it with me,' Doris said.

'You're a doll,' Joe said and strode through the door marked PRIVATE, into his office.

Inside the room, he busied himself with nothing in particular. It was Joe's policy to keep folks waiting. The reception area was far from inviting, and the hard chairs and lack of warmth in the room was considerately designed to allow visitors to stay nervous. That's where Doris came in. Joe didn't really need a secretary, most of what he knew about his clients stayed in his head, where it was safe. Doris was a spy, and a damn good one. Far from her secretarial skills, what Joe really paid Doris for was her uncanny ability to draw information from people and because she made a good cup of coffee. Her presence gave his business an air of legitimacy plus she did an excellent job keeping the liquor cabinet filled. In this respect she was worth every penny.

After a time, Joe had Doris buzz 'the dress' in. He offered her the chair across from his desk and watched as she sat smoothing her clothes and rear-ranged the chocolate-coloured fur on her shoulders. She was a looker, that was for sure and Joe knew the beautiful ones were not to be trusted. But he could overlook that – straight to her money. He had seen the baubles of ice at her throat and they were more than enough to hold his attention.

She introduced herself as Betty. Betty had a body built for lying, and Joe was willing to bet she knew how to use it to get what she wanted.

'Well now Miss Betty, how can I help you today?' Joe asked.

'It's my husband,' she said. 'He's missing. I don't know where he is.'

'Okay. How about we start with names? What is your husband's name Mrs?'

'Lowenstein. My name is Lowenstein. My husband is Eddy Lowenstein,' she said.

Eddy Lowenstein was the proprietor of Lowenstein's Laundromat on the other side of town. In some circles he was known as Low Eddy and this was either a play on his surname or a cruel reference to his height, Joe could never be sure. Short, rotund and far less good looking than his wife, Low Eddy was known for two things; his temper and the size of his bankroll. Joe had heard talk that clothing wasn't the only thing being laundered in Eddy's shop, and thought it made sense. How much money could there really be in other people's dirty smalls?

On that rainy Tuesday, Joe sat at his desk and looked at Betty. A picture was forming inside his head and it wasn't anywhere near as pretty as Low Eddy's wife. The fur, the diamonds, her incredible beauty and self-assuredness. If he didn't trust her before, Joseph Scotchman trusted her even less now.

'I know what you're thinking, Mr Scotchman, and you wouldn't be the first,'

'Oh, you do?' asked Joe.

'People might try to make you believe I don't love my husband, Mr Scotchman, but it's not true. I love Eddy very much; he takes care of me. He's the only man who ever took care of me.'

Joe only believed half of Betty's last statement. Any man punching above his weight, such as the disappeared Eddy, would be a fool to do anything less. But Betty's was a game two could play, and so he said;

'Well in that case, we'd better find Eddy and get him safely home to you. Hadn't we Mrs Lowenstein?'

As he listened to Mrs Lowenstein pour out her heart Joe tried his best to seem gullible, sympathetic and capable all at the same time. It wasn't so hard. Betty Lowenstein told a good story and she had plenty of fine features to enjoy – creamy white skin, dangerous curves and legs that went forever, but her most interesting feature was her eyes. And it wasn't so much what they looked like, but the way she used them that alerted Joe's suspicions. Big, brown and liquid, they looked deep into his own, when she pleaded with him for help, but avoided looking at him when he pressed her for details.

Through hooded eyes and with hands wringing, Mrs Lowenstein told Joe she had last seen her husband on Saturday morning when she left for church. After the service she visited her sister the next town over and did not return to the marital home until late Monday morning. When Mr Lowenstein did not come home for lunch with his bride, as was his custom, Mrs Lowenstein began to worry. A quick visit to the laundry revealed that Low Eddy had not been to work that day and the staff had not seen or heard from Mr Lowenstein either.

'And still, you never came to see me until today.'

'Well no, I … I didn't want you to think I was a hysterical woman.'

'What about the police, have you been to see the police?'

'Mr Scotchman, my husband is a good man. He works very hard, but he has a lot of bad habits. I worry that some of those habits finally caught up with him.'

'I see,' said Joe.

'And Mrs Lowenstein, tell me, what about a will, did your husband have a will?'

'But why does that matter? You don't think he's dead do you?'

'No, it's not time to worry about that just yet. But I do need to gather information for the investigation. You do want me to investigate don't you?'

'Please Mr Scotchman, you're the only one who can help me,' Betty insisted dramatically.

'That's a good girl. What can you tell me about the contents of that will? Who is the benefactor?'

'My husband does not have any family apart from me, Mr Scotchman.'

After Mrs Lowenstein left his office, Joe buzzed Doris, asked her to hold all his calls and sat in his chair thinking about the window, his cleaner and the disappeared Eddy. Betty Lowenstein was trouble and Joe knew well enough to believe only half of what she had told him. She wasn't the first person to lie to him, and she wouldn't be the last, but it had been a slow week and she had paid the way Joe liked – up front and in cash. The fat fold of hundred dollar bills sitting in his top pocket were all the reason he needed to take on her case.

Nothing good ever comes from Tuesday, he thought.

Mrs Lowenstein said her husband had bad habits; it was time to find out what they were.

*

The Thirsty Sailor was a dark, cramped bar that catered to a select clientele. Down a smelly alley and two streets back from the port, it was the type of place you went to if you were looking for trouble, or in Joe's case, information. Its basement location kept out the natural light, which made the atmosphere all the more suitable for the types of things that happened there. Joseph walked into the room and straight to the bar, where Derek O'Reilly was fixing him a Scotch – neat.

'O'Reilly.'

'Joe.'

'Low Eddy, what's he drinking these days?' Joe asked.

'Whatever the laundry man's drinking, he ain't drinking it here,' said the bar tender.

'You know that's funny. His bride hasn't been fixing his drinks either and she's wondering if someone's called in his tab,' said Joe, throwing one of Betty Lowenstein's bills on the bar.

'That is odd. Betty Lowenstein doesn't strike me as the type to worry about her husband, just his money.' O'Reilly replied, folding the paper into his pocket.

'You know her?' Joe asked.

'Everybody knows Betty-Lee Barker. She was one of the most sought after dames at The Loose Goose. How do you think she met Eddy?'

'She ever dance for you?' Joe drained his drink and waited for O'Reilly to refill it.

'Sadly no. Once she figured out how much Low Eddy was worth, she latched onto him like he was the last life jacket on the *Titanic*. O'Reilly said, pouring more Scotch.

'Mrs Lowenstein does not seem like the hard-working, laundry-lady type,' said Joe

'You noticed that too, huh?'

'She's smart though. Good with colours if you know what I mean,' the bar tender continued, wiping out a glass with a dirty rag.

'I'll tell you something else, there's a rumour going 'round that Mrs Lowenstein has started dancing for someone else.'

'Someone else?' Joe asked.

O'Reilly looked around the bar before he said:

'Bruce Malone.'

'Bruiser, King of the Tables? Mrs Lowenstein has been busy,' whistled Joe.

'Busy? You don't know from busy. My girl called in sick today,' O'Reilly complained as he walked to the other end of the counter where a drunk, being held up by the bar, was coughing and waving crumpled notes in his direction.

Joe finished his drink and left.

Outside it had started raining. It always rained this time of year. Grey and dreary on a good day, the poor weather made the streets even greyer and drearier. Accustomed to poor conditions, the people of the town simply put their heads down, turned their collars up and went about their business that little bit faster. Water rushed down pipes and through gutters, taking with it what scum it could and leaving the bigger pieces behind. Rain-smattered windows, like a filtered camera lens distorted stranger's faces, but not their intentions. In Little Italy, just on dark, Joseph Scotchman ran down a wet street, ducked under a dripping awning and entered a spaghetti restaurant. He walked between tables of families and single men bent over steaming bowls of food, through a curtain at the back and into a small room with a red door. He rapped loudly three times. A tall man in a shiny suit, with a long scar running down his face, opened the door and stared at Joe as though he had interrupted something important.

11

Joe said, 'Listen pal, I've got a box full of clams here and they're getting warm fast.'

The face looked him up and down, drew deeply on a cigar and blew the smoke in Joe's face before stepping aside.

'Don't spend it all at once,' warned the face.

Bruce Malone's gambling den was the biggest and the best in town. It was pretty classy for a betting shack and it attracted some high-flying clientele. While his competitors were routinely raided and busted up by the cops, Bruce's place remained untouched. This was because Malone knew exactly which hands to grease, and he did so liberally. Inside the large, smoke-filled room were several round tables, topped with green felt and manned by white-shirted croupiers with shifty eyes and fast fingers. Girls in tight dresses circulated, serving drinks and emptying ashtrays, and Bruce's bully boys strode about the room ejecting the drunks and gamblers who had run out of money and anyone who started winning too much.

Joe picked a table, threw some notes down and asked for a drink. A short time later, the stack of chips in front of him had dwindled considerably and he was looking for another drink when he saw a familiar figure. Wrapped in fur and balanced on high heels, she stood on the mezzanine floor in the doorway of the upstairs office talking to a gentleman in a sharp suit. Standing next to the meanest gambling boss in town, Betty Lowenstein did not look anywhere near as helpless as she had in his office.

Fancy that, Joe thought.

Malone and Lowenstein were standing very close together and seemed to be having a serious conversation. Joe was watching them intently when the bitter old gambler on the seat next to his began to accuse him of stealing his drink.

'A man can't even have a drink in peace without it being stolen right from under him. What kind of place is this?' yelled the drunkard, swaying dangerously.

'Quiet you,' Joe growled menacingly. 'Just shut up now and I'll buy you another.'

But the drunk was not going to be placated that easily.

'You got some nerve pal.' Getting louder, he stood up quickly, knocking down his chair, where it crashed to the floor. The noise was enough to make Malone and Betty Lowenstein stop talking and look over to where Joe sat.

Betty looked at Joe; Joe looked at Betty. Betty turned and whispered something in Malone's ear. Malone looked at Joe. In his peripheral vision Joe could see Malone's thugs sniffing the air.

Picking up the last of his chips, Joe put his head down and walked quietly out of the crowded room. He wondered if it had stopped raining. It didn't really matter; it was time for him to leave.

Outside the air was cold and the booze hit him hard. His office was close by, and he decided to walk there and sleep on the couch.

*

On Wednesday the sun hid meekly behind heavy dark clouds and Joe was woken from a boozy slumber by the sound of someone moving around his office. He opened one eye and saw a dark shape looming over his desk.

Joe's mysterious new employee hovered about his desk with some papers in his hand.

'I've got everything there just the way I like it,' he said.

'But be a pal and scrub that window good, you hear?'

The man straightened up slowly raised his head to look at his employer. Short and wiry and dressed entirely in black, Joe's cleaner looked him dead in the eye and said nothing for a very long time. Joe noticed a large black mole on the other man's face and that his right hand, the hand gripping Joe's papers, had an extra finger.

'Boss,' the man mumbled and let go of the paperwork.

Joe shrugged, rolled over and tried to get comfortable on the couch. Where the hell did Doris find these people, Goodwill?

From his desk came a loud buzzing sound.

'Joe, you're awake,' Doris stated.

He walked over to the desk and pressed a button down.

'I am now,' he said, squinting through bloodshot eyes to watch the cleaner move loudly around the room.

'Well, if you wanted to do any work today, you'd better get a move on. The city has started without you. They've found a floater down by Pier 5.'

Joe washed his face in cold water and pulled on one of the clean shirts he kept in the office. He walked through the door to the reception area where his secretary stood with a cup of warm coffee.

'Doris,' Joe said, handing the woman his dirty shirt and taking the coffee.

'Yes Joe.'

'Our cleaner has six fingers on his right hand.'

13

'Yes Joe,' Doris sighed as she balled up the shirt Joe had given her and put it in the bag for the cleaners.

'Do we pay extra for that?'

'Extra? Next to nothing is still nothing,' the woman said. 'You pay peanuts. This I know.'

'Now Doris, there's no need to be like that,' Joe said, drinking the coffee.

'Where'd you find him anyway?'

'Does it matter?' Doris sighed.

'Well, he's a little loud for a cleaner and he appears to be … aggravated. Doesn't that seem strange to you?' Joe enquired, handing back the empty cup and pulling on his hat and coat.

'There's plenty of strange around here,' Doris replied.

*

Joe ambled down towards Pier 5, where the wharf was crawling with police and rubberneckers out for a snoop. In another life he had worked the beat and he remembered how hard it was to recover a floater. It was harder still in the rain, and standing in the cold wind, a light drizzle hitting his face, Joe watched as dozens of policemen swarmed around the lifeless body of Low Eddy as it was fished out of the dirty sea. He noticed a familiar figure remove itself from the group of blue uniforms and head his way.

'Scotchman, what the hell are you doing at my crime scene?' asked City Detective Rayne.

'Picking up all the things you miss. Just like in the old days.' Joe said.

The wind changed direction and the smell of Low Eddy hit Joe in the face like a slap, as the detective led him away from the crowd.

'Let me guess, the widow Lowenstein came into your office, distraught and missing her beloved husband,' said Rayne, holding out a packet of cigarettes. Joe took one, lit up and inhaled deeply.

'Now you know I can't tell you anything about how Mrs Lowenstein claims to have not seen her husband since Saturday,' Joe replied, through a haze of blue smoke.

'That is *if* she was even a client.'

'Saturday. That fits,' said Rayne, gesturing towards the body.

'Mind you, Betty Lowenstein didn't seem that worried about her missing spouse last night, when I saw her with Bruce Malone,' Joe continued.

'Bruiser Malone, hey? Let me tell you a thing or two about lover boy Malone,' began Rayne.

According to the detective, Eddy Lowenstein had been racking up a lot of debt at Malone's tables. Meanwhile, Malone had grown tired of the gambling racket and was looking to expand his business. The King of the Tables, it seemed, was particularly interested in Low Eddy's laundering racket and, in Mrs Lowenstein.

'Good way to shift a lot of funny money, in a gambling den,' said Joe.

'It is,' agreed Rayne.

'What about Malone's friends? Does your boss know you're down here?' Joe asked.

'Police Chief Milton is a scourge on this city,' said Rayne.

'It would be my pleasure to weed him out like the poison he is. Him and his bully boys.'

A chaotic crowd of press arrived, asking a lot of loud questions and pointing their cameras in the direction of the lifeless shape lying on the pier. Rayne took off to control the scene, leaving Joe to finish his smoke alone.

*

Back in his office, the day had turned even more miserable and Joe spent the afternoon inside. As the sun went down, he sat with his feet on the sill watching the city cop a hiding from Mother Nature.

He noticed, with some displeasure, the pane of glass was still grimy.

'Well, I'll be damned.'

He poured himself another drink and sighed in defeat. It wasn't like there was anything that great outside his window anyway.

*

Joe had sent Doris home earlier and spent the rest of the day sitting at his desk drinking and brooding. Since Low Eddy had been fished out of the sea there was very little he could do. The heat would be coming down on Betty and Malone and Rayne would have to move fast if he wanted to make an example of Malone, before Milton stepped in. Milton; what an unpleasant excuse for a man. The fact that he was in charge of the city said a lot about the town Joe called home. Rayne sure had guts, thinking he could take Milton and Malone on at once.

'Either that, or he's just plain stupid,' thought Joe.

The telephone rang. In the silent gloom of Joe's dark office, the strong shrilling was ominous.

'Hello,' he said warily.

The other end was silent, save the sound of heavy breathing. He hung up.

After a minute, it rang again. In spite of himself, Joe shivered. He looked around the room and picked up the receiver again.

'Hello,' more forcefully this time.

'Shame about Rayne,' the voice said.

'What about him?' Joe asked.

'What about who?'

'Now you listen here,' Joe said.

'There's you and the detective,' the voice continued, ignoring Joe.

'No one else knows nothing. Except Low Eddy, and he ain't talking.'

'Hey pal, you sound kinda familiar. Have we met before?' Joe felt himself getting angry.

'Hey Scotchman, you all alone in there? Where'd your pretty little secretary go?'

The line went dead. Joe's caller hung up.

Doris! She would be home by now. Joe decided to call and warn her not go out or answer the door.

He picked up the phone and dialled her number, but there was no answer. He tried not to imagine the worst and dialled the police station looking for Rayne.

'First Precinct,' said a bored voice.

'Yeah, give me Detective Rayne,' Joe said.

'Hold please.'

Joe waited impatiently, fingers fumbling with a cigarette.

'Detective Rayne isn't here,' said the voice at the other end of the line.

'When will he be back?'

'Haven't a clue. You leaving a message?'

'No. Thank you.'

Joe's heart was racing now. He hung up the phone and tried Doris' number again.

Still no answer.

He looked out the dirty window. It had stopped raining. He grabbed his hat and coat and ran out the door. He would go to Doris' place, just walk past and make sure she was there. Just casual, wouldn't want to get the dame worked up over nothing. He knew women had a tendency towards hysteria.

Outside the night was cold and still. The streets were empty, and the smell of wet road and concrete hung in the air. The smell of a city after a storm;

industrial and organic at the same time. Joe pulled his coat tight and started a brisk walk. Somewhere behind him he thought he heard footsteps.

He stopped and listened.

Nothing.

You're getting old and paranoid Scotchman, he silently chastised himself.

He resumed walking, albeit a little faster and with one ear cocked. He rounded the corner behind the old metal works and heard the noise again, this time louder. He stopped and turned around. It was very dark; he couldn't see much without squinting, but Joe thought he saw a movement at the edge of the building in the shadows. He took a step towards it, reaching into his coat for his revolver.

BANG

There was a flash and the sound of gunfire rang out and bounced off the tin metal walls of the factory. Joe felt a sharp pain in his chest and fell to the ground with a thud. He could feel something warm and sticky spreading across his breast pocket.

It's wet down here, he thought idly.

Joseph Scotchman lay on the ground where he fell, his vision going fuzzy at the edges. He saw a shadow move away from the side of the building and walk towards him; a shiny metal glint reflected in the moonlight.

The shape looked at him, making sure he wasn't getting up.

He was growing cold. His head fell back onto the ground and as his eyes closed for the final time, Joe saw a six fingered hand slip a shiny revolver into a coat pocket.

The last thing he heard was the crunch of gravel as a pair of feet turned and walked away.

Jackie Coffin

I Am Australian

I am Australian.
These are my People.
This is my Home,
My Country,
My *Boodjar.*

Now ...
What do I see?
I see a great, white cloud
Rolling in across the sea
Bringing the white man.
He will change *everything.*
No fence.
No boundary.
No one's land.
Terra *Nullius*

Now ...
What do I see?
He raised a wooden stick to me!
He put me in chains
In that boab tree
He locked me up!
Far away
He threw that key.
A rope around my neck
Is all that is left for me

Now ...
What do I see?
Terror! *Australis*
He stole my *Moort*
My Family!

He stole our *Koolangka*
Our Babies!
They are *everything* to me
But to him
Who.
Are.
We?
Nothing.
Aborigine
That is everything to me.

Now ...
What do I see?
I am *Yongka*
Kangaroo
I jump
Fast and far
Away from you
I am useful to the few –
Blanket, coat, roo tail stew,
Food for your dog
Dwert ak meriny
But ...
I am
Just.
Like.
You.
My baby joey
Djoodiny
Grows within me
Only one
For many months
Suckling
Inside my pouch
And
Out.

He points his wooden stick at me
Bang!
He laughs at his trophy!
He ties a rope to me
For
Fun
He drives his machine
Recklessly
Bang!
More of us
Than blades of grass
In the sun
Bloated and rotting
With a live one.
Inside.
Useful to many
Not just a few
Our national emblem
With the Emu
Wejt
In full view of every man
Over the heads
Of our Ruling Gurus
We are your Boxing Kangaroos
One dollar's worth
We'll give to you.
Look out Skippy
It's the SUV!
Bang!
Less of us
Too many of you

Now …
What do I see?
I am Woman
Yorga
Born in Perth
Whadjuk Boodjar
The only one
To a single Kiwi Mum
And an absent Pommy Dad
With an Indigenous Godmother
From *Yawuru.*
Raised in the place
Of fat kangaroo
In a blended family,
In the urban fringe,
At the end of a bridge.
Second generation Aussie brood
In a multicultural neighbourhood
We are Australian.
These are our People,
This is our Home,
Our Country,
Our *Boodjar.*

Now …
What will we see?

Stephanie Fitz-Henry
Awarded Highly Commended at the 2016 Shorelines Writing For Performance Festival

Skidding in Sideways

The stench was overwhelming.

I gagged and longed for the scarf I had discarded due to the sticky heat and humidity. To get even close to describing the odour, you needed to add the smell of rotting meat and the sickly-sweet and metallic taste of blood to the pervading aroma of rotten onions, turpentine and raw sewerage.

We were two days into our visit; the initial excitement had become sensory overload and quite frankly, disgusting. Between me and the source of my next visual stimulus was a cement-lined furrow about thirty centimetres wide and thirty centimetres deep. Water flowed sluggishly towards the sea. I didn't dare look down and examine the contents of the furrow in case I saw what I did not wish to see.

So, I looked forward instead. The market – row upon orderly row of wooden structures serving as kiosks – was drowning in a sea of people; vendors with their colourful displays of wares and produce; locals dutifully attending to their daily purchases and tourists frenetically shopping. Dizzy with exhaustion – jetlag does that to you – I shook my head to clear my blurry vision and what I saw astonished me.

Right in front of me was a row of cows' noses, just their noses, taking pride of place along the length of the stall counter. They seemed fresh. Well, fresh enough to still be moist and some even had snot intact. There were about twenty of them. Behind them paraded an equal number of tongues from the poor beasts. These swollen, ghastly bluish-grey organs were neatly aligned behind their noses. Nailed to the crossbar above this display in ascending order of length were the tails, complete with the swishy end, sans the shit thankfully.

Now, who would buy a cow's nose? Cow's tongue is supposedly a delicacy but what on earth would you do with the tails? Swat or swish away flies, maybe. Give me my fly veil any day.

I turned away, my jetlag headache now pounding, seeking the source of the disgusting and pervading aroma. To my surprise, it came from the next stall where tiers of melons of all shapes and sizes and colours were precariously stacked. The cantaloupe mountain sloped off at one end of the kiosk worktop leaving room only for the stallholder's forearm on the counter. Her head rested on her arm. She was fast asleep, mouth wide open, drooling. I sneaked a camera shot. As I clicked the button, she opened one eye, smiled tolerantly and resumed her nap.

Up against her face, right next to her nose was a platter of brownish-reddish fruit squares. Ah! The horror of eating something that smells like pig-shit mixed with rotten onions. My guide, Amir, pointed out the small spiky-skinned watermelons stacked up next to the platter. He assured me that this was the king of fruits and despite the smell it would taste delicious. I, for one, have and never will, eat durian, ever. It made me feel better to learn later that durian is banned from certain hotels and public transport in Southeast Asia.

The camera flash alerted the stall owner on the other side of the bovine arrangement. Now to the perpetual surround-sound of hooting and revving tuk-tuks was added the urgent and insistent cry of 'Nego! Nego!' This stall held a forest of brightly coloured cloth. The stall keeper held up some glorious fabric for me to see and touch. 'Nego means to bargain,' said my guide.

That was Balikpapan.

I still on occasion wear that shawl, the *selendang* I bought that day. And I still feel guilty about my successful Nego attempt.

I who have so much and they who have so little.

*

Our daughter sent us a quote from the Hunter S. Thompson poem – a bit tongue in cheek. The one doing the rounds on social media about life not being a journey to arrive at your graveside all rosy and fresh but rather one that aims at skidding in sideways, all wrinkled and depleted, sipping martinis, clutching chocolates and wheezing about the cool ride that was your life.

She sent it just as we, at the end of our working lives and on the cusp of our retirement, were embarking on our travel era. Two days later we entered the local pub quiz under the name of *Skidding in Sideways*. We won and the name stuck.

We have been living the art of travel on that basis ever since. Our experiences in Indonesia; our encounter with a four-metre long zebra-striped sea serpent while meditating on a wooden jetty; and sharing a tuk-tuk, a tiny scooter-like taxi with two adults, a baby, a goat and three chooks are cases in point.

*

Travel has its defining moments. These moments can be inspirational, transformative or quite frankly terrifying. True, some of these experiences are yukkier than others. Travel also puts music in your heart.

I remember one magic day in Bruges when the music began to play – for me. Bruges, also known as the Venice of the North, is a charming medieval city crisscrossed by water canals, stone bridges and dotted with charming white and red windmills. I will spare you a rundown of what you would find in a travel guide, except of course to emphasise, when in Bruges you simply must do chocolates and don't skip the ride through the cobbled streets in a horse-drawn carriage. Oh, and if you haven't seen the movie *In Bruges*, you should watch it.

It was an exquisite spring morning when I set out for my morning run along the banks of the canal network in and around the city of Bruges. Bruges is the perfect place to run or cycle; through the many parks, along the tree-lined walkways, past quaint windmills, around the Lake of Love and over Lover's Bridge.

I wasn't in search of love. I just needed to loosen up from constant travelling, to recharge. To run until my endorphins kicked in and I could move just for the sheer joy of it. Tranquillity, that's what I found that day. Even now, years later when I reflect on it, I feel a sense of peace and have a surge of inspiration.

Here's what happened. After about an hour of running, on my way back to the hotel I became aware of people walking. These were no ordinary walkers. They walked with purpose and they walked in dead silence. They came from all directions. There was no interaction, yet I had the distinct impression that all had the same goal. They were heading to the same leafy tree-lined street where my hotel was.

I followed, conscious of not being on their level, wanting what they had and determined to discover their purpose. Each person carried what appeared to be a miniature wooden dog kennel; about the size of a large shoebox. Each also carried a 3-legged stool and a walking stick. I was consumed by curiosity. The language barrier held me back from making any inquiry, and my gut told me not to make a sound.

Two folks were without kennels, they carried clipboards and pens instead, whispering to each other. I latched on to them. The woman smiled at me and laid a finger on her lips. Breakfast forgotten and with no thought for the travelling companions waiting for me back in the hotel, I determined to get to the bottom of this secret society, even if I had to do it in dead silence.

We turned off into what I call a tree-tunnel street. A street where the trees are ancient giants and hold hands across the street high above. When you enter the tunnel, you know you are in the presence of history and its wisdom envelops you.

The clipboard lady, still smiling, gently laid a restraining hand on my arm. One by one the walkers lined up along the street verge, about thirty meters apart. Each one sat down on his stool facing the street, laid the walking stick on the ground in front of him, parallel to the kerbside and placed the kennel about twenty centimetres beyond it.

And then the music played. Literally. The clipboard couple paused in front of the first woman and nodded to her. She in turn leaned forward, picked up her stick and lightly tapped the top of the kennel. And the most heavenly music streamed from that box.

I was transported to a tranquil place where soothing streams of water bubbled, dripped and babbled, much like the sounds I heard as I ran alongside the waterways. My spirit soared and flitted down memory lanes; beyond the borders of Belgium to the heart of the *Schwarzwald*, the Black Forest, in Germany; as I touched down in the botanical gardens in Cape Town. Another light tap from the player cut off the flow of water as abruptly as it had started.

The judges moved on to the next competitor and canary-occupied kennel and the next. For over an hour I was entranced. *How do you teach a bird to start and to stop singing? How is it possible for such a tiny creature to have such a rich voice and cover such a wide range of notes?*

I later discovered that Harz Roller canaries, particularly the Waterslager, are especially bred in Belgium for bird competitions. They can hit higher and lower notes than any other type of bird. You can even teach these canaries to sing along with phone ringtones. Sometimes they sing quietly with their beaks closed and other times they open wide and let rip with sheer gusto. Think: Passionate opera singer.

*

It's easy to let rip or skid in sideways when you are travelling. After a few journeys you overcome natural and inherent reticence about stepping out of set patterns and routines and rules. There were several happenings during our trip to Venice that proved to be defining moments in shaping our future together for the next twenty, and counting, years.

In Venice we found our peculiar slant on the saying 'where ignorance is bliss'. We, of course, pronounce it ignore-rance. Let me explain.

Buzz pretended to hum and haw on the invitation to join me in running the Venice marathon. We weren't an official couple then, yet. He soon came back with a resounding yes and a suggestion. His plans included a three-week tour of Hungary prior to the marathon. No criticism, but big mistake that;

squeezing in a decadent tour of foreign climes before tackling a gruelling marathon. Nowadays, we get hefty physical stuff out of the way first.

We touched down at Marco Polo airport amidst great excitement. Here was where I could let go and match my exuberance to the Italian flavours. I fell far short as you will soon see. How exciting was this realisation of a childhood dream for me? Here we were at an airport named after a man famous for his travels seven centuries ago. I love history and had learned about this intrepid teenager not even seven decades ago when I was in my teens.

We loaded our gear into the back of our rented Kia Picanto. It spilled over into the rest of the car as well, it was that small. We crouched into the car and joked about hooking our feet over our ears to make more room. Swapping the car for a larger one was not an option.

We'd established that I would drive, and Buzz would navigate. A few years prior, I'd had practise driving a camper van around France and Switzerland in pursuit of Lance Armstrong and the rest of the Tour de France entourage. That made me the relative expert on being a left-hand driver driving on the right-hand side of the road. Besides if I were to be the navigator, I would have used the GPS rather than Buzz's paper Map.

My priority at that point was to understand the car, to accept sitting on the wrong side of the car, to cope with manual gears and the extra foot pedals that come with that and of course to get the car going. Buzz, as designated navigator had to establish where we were and where we were going. My private thoughts went something like this:

Hello! We're at Marco Polo airport, and hello again! It's early in the day and can't we just follow our noses in the general direction of Hungary via Austria – or not?

This man I had so rashly invited into my adventure space would miss out on life; would keep getting lost in more senses than one if he kept his head stuck in a map. Little did I know then, that our journey with maps, these direction showing thingies, was just beginning. He too resolved to teach me about maps so that I would not miss out or get lost.

But before getting wonderfully lost in Venice, we needed to get out of the airport carpark. Buzz unfolded and spread out the Map, then refolded it, optimising the use of the tiny leftover space once we and our baggage were stowed so we could still see where we were going directionally and literally.

'Okay, let's go, Babes!' That from my man.

'No wait, wait!' I cry, pointing to a flashing light on the dashboard. 'I've worked out all those whistles and blows, all that turns and indicates, but that light defies all logic. I want to sort it out before we get too far so that we can return the car if there is a serious problem.'

No problem to my engineer-man. He carefully folds, straightens and rear-ranges the Map and opens a pathway to the glove box. We look for the car manual in vain. I cross my arms, hold my chest very tight and bite my lip. So maybe we do have a problem.

Lucky us. The car next to us is also a Kia Picanto. Two Italian ladies make their way to the car, chatting animatedly and gesticulating wildly. I wait for them to stow their one modest bag. I hop out and approach them anxiously while enviously regarding their spacious seating arrangements.

'Yes, yes!' cries the most verbose of the ladies. 'I speeka de Ingleesh. Dees one heeja, she my seesta. No Ingleesh.'

She spreads her arms wide and emphatically and I duck and explain about the light.

The woman turns to her companion and they have an animated conversation that seems to go on longer than my question. I go and scrunch myself back into our car. The woman walks over to our car, Buzz's side of the car, she rests her arms on the window ledge, leans into the car, to peer across at the flashing light, brushing against Buzz's cheek with an ample bosom and announces:

'I speeka de Ingleesh. Dees one heeja, my seesta, she da mechanic. She sez, get out of car.'

Pronto! We untangle limbs, duck under and over luggage, mess up the Map and leap out of the car.

The mechanic leans into the car, fiddles here and there and turns a knob or two. Then she turns to her English-speaking sister and they have another intense and extended confab.

And then, we are provided with another skidding in sideways boosting phi-losophy. The linguist, not the mechanic, clears her throat and announces:

'I speeka de Ingleesh. Dees one heeja, my seesta, she da mechanic (just in case we forgot who is who) she sez, IGNORE!'

I've lost track of how many IGNORE announcements and reminders we have given each other over the years.

*

Travel and adventure are about getting away from it all, right? But not away from all things, apparently. It became clear that if our togetherness was going to last and our sanity to remain intact there was one travelling fundamental we couldn't ignore. Our mutual passion for travel could only be pursued meaning-fully if the essential accompaniments were in place. We knew. I'm a lawyer for heaven's sake and Buzz, an engineer. If you want things to work, you must follow the rules.

Buzz has a deep-seated mistrust of fang-dangled technology that is reliant on the stars, heaven forbid! Enter the Map – Buzz prefers a capital M, you'll understand later – as in atlas, as in one of those diagrammatic representations of a country showing roads and stuff. Totally reliable, of course, except the illegible crumpled parts and the bits that have been furrowed out from overuse, from folding and refolding or when the map is outdated.

Then add to that mix the global positioning system, GPS for short or Google Maps for ease of understanding. There is something so liberating about deliberately allowing yourself to get lost because you will always know where you are when you have one of these in your life. There's no memorising the way when you set out on a run from your hotel or when exploring a foreign city.

Mistakes do creep in and somewhere over the years and in the course of our travels, we dubbed our GPS *The Claptrap*. Our fond and indulgent relation-ship with her continues to share space with Buzz's folded and re-folded Map.

Did you know that when you are in a new relationship and you are armed with the Map and *The Claptrap*, Venice is the most wonderful place to get lost in without actually being lost? Not a single street continues in a straight line beyond a city block at a time, there's an angle change at every street corner and every turn means the street's name changes too.

But of course, *The Claptrap* is no misnomer and she gets it wrong, some-times. Her mistakes are random; every time there is thick cloud cover or upon entry to an underground tunnel and you really need her because the subterra-nean autobahn is so wide it even has traffic circles and direction changes to three different countries deep under the Swiss Alps. Once she insisted that the Department of Home Affairs office in Swellendam, South Africa was in a wheat field five kilometres out of town. We tested her there a few weeks later and she still insisted on that location. Our favourite getting-it-wrong episode happened when we were galloping along in *The Rattletrap* under the forest can-opies on the northeasern side of Tasmania. Our rental campervan was so-named for obvious reasons including the 465 000 km odometer reading when we collected her.

As the song goes *Every Man needs a Woman. The Claptrap* proved to Buzz that this woman needed a man and we reinstated Map. To elevate Map's status, we called him M-app, just to give him an IT flavour. But it wasn't one map. It was several, one for every region in Tassie and the rest of the world for that matter. The first place we visit in a new region is the information or tourist centre and our map collection expands.

M-app does not depend on satellite signals, nor does it get moody in inclement weather, but it does need space to spread out and space to be stored. M-app works the right way up for one person and upside down for the next, it's something to do with north and south. Stowing M-app defies all logic. There are a million folds and if you don't follow the folding procedure correctly you cause illegible furrows and it's somehow so bulky. So, when you need a new M-app, old M-app furrowed out and illegible gets saved because of all the sentimental marks and notations. M-app, of course, does not update automatically. We have a black box full of M-apps.

The Claptrap got it very wrong one day. Let's blame it on her. She found us the perfect spot for our morning cook-up brekky. A flat mown lawn area in the middle of a huge forest on the north-eastern side of Tassie. Our table and chairs were set up, we'd photographed some kangaroos and the sausages were sizzling on the gas cooker. We had encountered several fellow grey nomads like ourselves during the morning and were just commenting on the lack of them, making the most of this spot when we discovered the reason. A little distance away there was a similar grassy spot and a little further on, another and then another. People walking through the furthest spot looked suspiciously like golfers.

What the heck! Living the art of travel allows you to dance like nobody is watching. We ate our breakfast at a little less leisurely pace than usual and danced our way further around the Apple Isle.

*

Living the art of travel on a skidding-in-sideways basis makes it easier to live like someone left the gate open. There's another image that does the rounds on social media of a dog that has escaped from a paddock through a wide-open gate. He's flying, paws scrabbling above the ground, ears flapping in sheer exuberance and joy.

Our breakout of the paddock happened the day *The Claptrap* treated us to another lost situation. She left us on the doorstep of the Brauhaus in the middle of Jakarta. Yes, you read Brauhaus and yes, we were in Indonesia. Pleased with our lost position, we decided to take a break from Asian food and treat ourselves to some *eisbein*, that delectable German roast pork dish. What could go better with that than some good strong German beer? But it was not to be. It was the middle of Ramadan and we could not be that insensitive. But how can you enjoy red meat without the right beverage to wash it down?

Buzz has his ways and means and reeled our server in with chatty across-language-barrier signs and grunts. Half an hour later, just before the arrival of our food, we were served an elegant tea, complete with a silver teapot, milk jug and sugar bowl and Royal Dalton teacups. With a polite bow, Malik – we were now on first name terms - assured us that the full bottle of red wine had been poured into the teapot and Buzz would find his brew in the milk jug.

Cheers and prosperity to all! Or as they say in Indonesia,
'Makmur!'

Gogo Buzz

Five by Seven
A click to Haiku

You say hurry up
    I hurry to conditions
        We meet the deadlines

        Arriving on time
    Safe and sound be the journey
Destiny of hours

I dread the plodding
    Around in detours of risk
        Enter there with lust

        Characters surreal
    Alive and fantasy be
Reveal thy selves please

I think you are right
    You believe I am enough
        We know this of us

        You write justified
    Grammatically correct
I read it wrongly

I publish a scene
    With the hand of language
        Embodied in words

Apikara

Bottled Up

The court was heavy with tension and bated breath; I didn't blink for fear of the sound it might make. There was a dramatic pause before a loud, gravelly tone delivered the blow – GUILTY! – and I wondered what was next for me: images from tacky, made-for-TV prison movies flew through my head as if on fast forward; women in orange jumpsuits with swallows tattooed onto their faces forcing themselves on pretty doe-eyes barbie types – most likely in the shower – and that poor woman from then on labelled as the dyke's bitch.

The court room had erupted. Everyone was calling my name – 'Miss Johnston - Vivienne! Viv! How do you feel Viv? Do you intend to appeal the verdict? Vivienne why did you do it?' – ignoring the judge's pleas for order. Hands grabbed at me and pulled me from the dock, down a set of hidden stairs. I barely registered the movement – I was still wondering if orange would suit me.

*

As it turned out, I needn't have worried. It seems the garish orange colour is reserved for prisons in the US, and drab grey trackies were the best I could hope for in Her Majesty's Prison Bronzefield – mind you, they didn't suit me either. I was assured, upon handing over my own beautiful Phase 8 Merino knit and black tailored pants, that once I was placed in a wing after my sentencing, I'd be issued with the standard navy scrubs, like all the others. But the hearing wasn't for another four weeks, and in the meantime, the oversized grey jumper was doing nothing for my pale pallor and that spontaneous box of dye in Autumn Chestnut now proved a very bad idea.

'Johnston, Jennings, O'Mara, Holmes. All of you, come with me,' a voice rose above the cocky bravado and nervous small talk. We were the new intake, I guessed – the new kids on the block – herded like farm animals into a van and then into a holding cell large enough for the four of us and another six who looked considerably more dangerous and considerably less scared. I assumed they were off to Max.

We were cuffed, but thankfully not to each other. A guard led us down corridors where the strip lights blinked and cracked, and each door required a myriad of key locks, card taps and secret handshakes to open. The guard bringing up the rear would've been the same age as Amy – 19 going on 30. I forced Amy from my mind, refusing to give in to self-pity this early on.

'Johnston, Jennings – this is you,' the guard at the front said, stopping outside the first cell on an upper-level row. I didn't even remember climbing the stairs.

'Together?' I couldn't hide my horror.

Smirks all round.

'Unfortunately, the penthouse cell is already reserved, Your Majesty,' the second guard said sarcastically, loudly and directly into my ear, gripping my arm with glee and steering me towards the sterile 8 x 10 room. The woman behind me followed, not needing the prompt. Still in cuffs, the door slammed closed behind us and the hatch opened, allowing us to put our hands out to be freed.

By the time I turned around my cell mate had secured the bottom bunk and was furtively rolling a cigarette, her eyes wide open and twitchy.

'I'm Vivienne,' I offered, with my best *Sunrise at Six* smile. I didn't extend my hand – my lawyer had advised not to instigate physical contact.

'Yeah I know. Not that I give a shit.' None of the intended malice came across – she just sounded sad.

'Guess I'll take the top then,' I muttered to myself, picking up the rough blanket that was labelled with my name and throwing it on the upper bunk. The mattress was barely thicker than a pre-packaged sandwich and from within a foot of it I could smell that there would be a bloody stain hidden somewhere.

I wasn't expecting the Shangri-La but this … it was a soap opera come true. The walls were completely bare and probably had been white at some stage, although now they were dirty grey and chipped. The lights on the ceiling were the same almost-blue crackling strip lights that the rest of the prison was lit with, and the bunks were plain solid metal in hospital green, with tough grey blankets and starchy white sheets. There was a window – no bars – but a lattice grate on the outside, to stop us attempting to hurl ourselves out, I supposed.

A small corner was sectioned off with white tiles – a toilet, a sink and a mirror, albeit misty tin rather than actual glass. Placing my standard-issue toothbrush into the blue plastic tumbler, I gave my reflection a cursory glance; I supposed I would become used to the slightly warped, matte reflection that it offered.

My gaze flicked behind me to my cell mate, lying down now, silent and rigid, staring at the bottom of my mattress. I wondered which of us would snap first.

'I used to watch you on the telly – every morning when my son was born.' I turned towards the voice; her tone had lost its pseudo-aggressive edge and I was surprised to hear a softened Northern lilt to her accent – I picked it as Liverpool-born, West Country-raised, a little like my dad. I forced away a flood of memories and focused back on my cell-mate. I didn't know what the appropriate response was; everyone knew me and therefore they knew what I'd done. I listened to her shift on her bunk. 'I never thought you'd did it.'

Done it, I thought. 'Yeah, well. I did do it.'

'I did too. Run over the guy that raped me,' she said, her voice low. She wasn't proud of herself; her tone was resigned and conversational. 'He said he never did, but I ended up with his kid. He's in a wheelchair now, so at least I know he won't do it to anyone else.' Her openness was jarring. I searched for the right thing to say.

'I'd do it again,' I whispered.

'Me too,' she whispered back.

*

'I'm not asking you not to sell her anything, just not alcohol!' My tone was more pleading and desperate than 'I'm in charge here', but it seemed neither angle was working.

'I'm runnin' a business here and your mum is keeping me afloat,' the bloke behind the counter shrugged. I think he was aiming for a rueful look, but he just came off looking like a greedy prick.

'She's unwell. She has an addiction!' I could hear the shrillness creeping into my voice. I looked around to check there were no witnesses to my little scene.

'And that's sad. But I aint' a pub and I don't cut people off. The woman comes in sober and asks for wine, I'm sellin' it to her.'

'Sober my arse – she hasn't been sober for twelve years!' I suddenly realised I was oversharing. I took a deep breath, slammed the counter dramatically and turned to leave.

'Oi just before you go … I couldn't get your autograph? My missus won't believe this!'

I bit my tongue hard as I left, the taste of blood souring my mouth.

*

When I return to the house she's got The Beatles on in the kitchen and is tunelessly singing along to a song I don't recognise. A bottle of wine stands open on the counter and she's picking through a bag of Bombay Mix like a bird picking the best worm from the bunch. She doesn't eat properly these days; I thought it was because she preferred the wine, but her doctor says that a suspected onset of Korsakoff syndrome could be making her forget.

'Where did you come from?' She asked, delighted by my return.

'I just nipped to the shop, remember? I got you some pre-cooked chicken for dinner.'

'Oh, you're such a good girl. I was telling Ellen from next door what a good daughter you are.' The pride in her unfocused eyes made my heart hurt.

'Shall I make some tea?' I asked, always trying.

'No, that's OK love I'll have a coffee in a while,' she lied.

'I've got to be going soon, I have to drop Amy's hockey stuff off before her game this afternoon.'

'Is that Violet's girl?'

I close my eyes and inhale hard, knowing that getting angry at her won't make any difference, won't change her. I've had the same internal argument a hundred times before; correct her, get mad, tell her to sort herself out … or let it go over my head, go along with it. Accept that you can't help someone who is so intent on not being helped.

'Right, well, I'll pop to the loo, then I'm off,' I put the chicken in the fridge – knowing it will go uneaten thanks to the three bottles of Chardonnay standing in the door – and head for the stairs.

'I saw Ellen yesterday,' she calls through the door. I roll my eyes. 'I was telling her what a good daughter you are,' she added, her tone a little more uneven than before.

When I open the door she's not there. I enter the kitchen in time to see her put the bottle to her parched lips and take a long draw on the room temperature wine. It doesn't even surprise me, I realised with a sadness that ran deeper than the relationship we'd already lost.

I snatch the bottle. 'Pretty sure the doctors didn't remove those tumours to free up room for some more,' I hiss, pouring the remaining mouthful into the sink and throwing the bottle into the full recycling bin with a crash.

'You owe me a bottle of wine,' she spits. Like a child flaunting its insolence she opens the breadbin where a half-drunk glass of wine has been hidden.

I shake my head and with as much calmness as possible I pick up my beautiful soft leather bag and make for the door.

'Off you go then, off to your fancy house. I expect I won't see you for a month now,' she called. There wasn't really any venom; by this point in her drunkenness she dipped and dived between maudlin and ecstatic with startling frequency. 'I was a good mum you know!'

I do know; that makes it worse.

'I'll call in the week,' I say turning, my hand already on the latch.

'I see you more on the telly.' She's muttering to herself.

'Mum ...'

'DON'T MUM ME! Just go. You're going to anyway. And there's me the other day just telling Ellen what a good girl you are ...'

*

'... and then I just couldn't take it anymore.'

'So, you killed her?' Jennings asked, although she already knew the answer.

'It wasn't like that. You know people talk about a red mist, that sort of thing? Nothing like that happened to me. One minute I was by the door – I was fifteen goddamned steps from my car. And then I couldn't stop all these memories coming at me. It was the weirdest thing ... mum dropping me off at school with me in my shiny new shoes ... picking me up with a bar of chocolate because it was Friday. And on this one occasion she picked me up early from school and took me to Butlins for the weekend – the whole weekend, just the two of us. And you know right up to the end she watched every show I was in. Recorded *Sunrise* every day.'

'Sounds like super-mum.'

'She was. And then it all changed.' It wasn't the first time I was telling the story, but it was the first time I cried doing so. 'She lost her job. My dad died. She managed to alienate all her friends. I think she must've just been very sad and lonely.'

'Didn't you try to help?'

'Everyone did.' *I could've tried harder.*

'... so then you killed her?'

'It wasn't what I set out to do. I was frustrated and so sad. But I'd already lost my mum a long time ago – she'd been a different person for most of my adult life, and I didn't like her anymore.'

'You didn't like her?'

'I didn't know her.'

36

Outside, the wing was silent; the white plastic clock was coming around to midnight. The catcalls and threats that were bandied around earlier in the evening had died down.

'Then you killed her?'

'Then I killed her.'

Nina Peck

Gilda

We didn't find her in my bed. My parents and I were watching a program about the species integration vote when we heard a noise. We went to the kitchen and found her eating my porridge – so that part was true. She jumped up when she saw us and was halfway out the back door when Mum said, 'It's okay, you can stay.'

To my surprise, she hesitated.

Dad added, 'You must be hungry, sit down and finish.'

She turned around. She was a pretty teenage girl with long blonde hair, but she looked thin and like she hadn't washed in days. Mum told Dad, 'Go run her a bath while we eat.' Dad left, and Mum and I sat down and ate our porridge with her. I had Dad's.

When her bowl was empty, she looked up. 'I'm Gilda,' she said in a quiet voice. 'My father calls me Goldilocks.'

'Hello, Gilda,' Mum said. 'I'm Bruna, this is Thoms, and my husband's name is Danesh. You are very welcome in our home.'

'I didn't know you were ursine when I came in,' Gilda said. 'I'm sorry to intrude.'

'That's okay,' Mum said. 'No harm done.'

My curiosity got the better of me. 'But why are you here?'

'I ran away from home. I couldn't go to my friends because Father would find me. I thought I'd be safe this side of the woods.'

'Safe?' asked Dad, from the doorway. 'Weren't you safe at home?'

'Well,' she said, and hesitated, 'I've looked after Father since Mother died. But when I don't please him, he punishes me.'

'Oh,' said Mum and Dad together. They looked at each other. I was a bit lost.

Mum stood up. 'First it's a bath and upstairs for some rest in Thoms' room. That's okay, isn't it Thoms?'

'I guess,' I mumbled. Mum, with a firm but gentle hand, steered Gilda out of the kitchen.

'Dad,' I said, 'she can't stay here, can she?'

'Thoms, she needs some sleep. Then we'll see. It's unusual, but I hope if you ever needed it, someone would help you.'

Dad and I were still in the kitchen when Mum returned.

'Gilda had me cut off all her hair,' Mum said. 'She said it wasn't real. But she's sleeping now.'

All that day Mum and Dad called lots of people: ursine and human. Later, Gilda came down in her freshly laundered clothes and one of my caps.

'Would you like to stay with us for a while,' Mum asked, 'until things are sorted out?'

Gilda nodded.

When the media found out there were silly headlines and far-fetched stories. Emotions were high and opinions were divided over whether Gilda should be allowed to stay with us. In the end, though, she did.

She got my bedroom and I moved into the attic. Plus, she spends ages in the bathroom. It's totally like having an older sister. And when her hair grew back, it was black. Just like my fur.

David Rawet

Boy Can I Run

I'd always been that typical allrounder, especially when I was a teenager. Good at almost anything I put my mind to. Back then I could sing, hold a tune, play a range of instruments, I was smart and athletic, boy could I run. I might have been anything, except Mum's poor single parent income, my low self-esteem, and stifling anxiety made sure I did close to nothing.

In my late teens when my husband, now my ex-shining knight on noble steed swooped me off my feet, I thought I was saved. He was tall, dark, and handsome. I should have known better though considering his noble steed was a white Holden V8 Monaro. Over time, the colourful fairy-tale life I had lovingly painted in my mind began to run. Love did not stand a chance of conquering all. His early mid-life crisis and eventual abandonment of me and our girls in chasing that younger bit of fluff made damn sure of it. That perfectly painted picture changed over the last couple of years into a skewed smudge of my new single parent life.

I'm sitting on the front step and just waved the trio goodbye as they've driven off down the road, in his new four-wheel drive. It's the girls' weekend with him and a small part of my heart has left with them. The concrete's coolness against the back of my legs balances out nicely the sting of morning sunlight streaming across my face. I'm waiting and hoping for some energy to kick back into my tired, dying body. When it does, I know exactly where I'm going, to the backyard and swing chair underneath the large Peppermint tree. Ex-shining knight lives one miserly block away and I've heard that distant delightful sound before on quiet days, the girls' infectious laughter. Their innocent giggles floating with the breeze, feeling as though they're right next to me, touching my skin with each leaf that drops onto my lap and gets caught in my short hair. Molly's eight, Hannah's ten, both too young to be losing their mum. Considering the circumstances, you'd think he'd let me spend more time with them.

I sigh, my mind is full of thoughts with life and I'm just not sure what my take on it is at the moment. Luck of the draw, God works in mysterious ways, we all know that we're born to die. None of them give me any sense of peace or make things easier when I know that my death is only a handful of weeks away.

My eyes follow the line of rose bushes that run the length of the driveway, they're in dire need of a prune. I tilt my head and lean forward a fraction to see past the large for sale sign with the Under Offer sticker plastered across it, pegged into my front lawn. From here I can glimpse the recent new neighbour across the road. The peculiar, elderly man often sits out the front on his white wicker chair and can be deceptively hard to spot. He camouflages into the big padded chair with his usual white shirt, baggy white pants and long silver hair sleeked back into a ponytail. In the couple of months since he'd moved in, I've seen four different cats coming and going from his house, then they disappeared, except for one. That one, his youngest looking creature is gloriously sunning itself in the garden bed closest to my feet. Its long grey fur is collecting granules of sand as it playfully rolls on its back, paddling the air momentarily with its petite white paws as it turns from one side to the other. Cute, but definitely not my fancy, they're more my ex-shining knight's thing. He's always had a soft spot for cats, even promised the girls that when things get too sad, with me, he'll get them one.

'Hard life,' I say to the little green-eyed feline.

It flops onto one side then sits up quickly and curls its tail neatly around its front paws to look back at me. I rest my elbows on my knees, cupping my face in my hands then remember with another sigh that Mum said she'd come over this morning. She'll be painful in trying to encourage me to keep my chin up and make the most of the time I have left. Apart from spending more time with my girls I'm not sure what for, I don't have anything on a bucket list, I can't even plan and think of a future too far away. Right now, my mind is, and has been, caught in a cyclic pattern of thinking and living in the yesterday *what if*, and the what if yesterdays of a backwards future.

What if I'd had some help when I was young? What if I never met him? What if I'd never had kids? What if I'd found that bloody lump in my breast sooner? The what ifs were rampaging through my mind as viciously as the cancer racing through my body.

Frustrated, I stand up and shake my head, hoping the motion will somehow make the questions magically drop out from my ears as I turn and take a step towards the front door. Something doesn't feel right. White spots begin flashing in my vision and I feel faint, the world is spinning, then I'm falling, dropping as if in slow motion with the concrete nearing my face, then there's blackness.

When I open my eyes I'm right where I had been, sitting on the step and the grey cat is now standing in front of me. There's no sound, no warbling magpies or distant hum of traffic. Around the front porch and steps the air is still and clear. The front yard and driveway are partially hidden in a haze of white mist that thickens as it wisps down towards the road, blocking the rest of the neighbourhood. An aura of calmness surrounds me, I'm not frightened, not even when I hear a female voice.

'Nine,' it says.

I look around and gasp when I see my limp physical body lying on the ground next to me.

'Nine,' the voice says again.

I'm startled and turn quickly to the only other being visible, the grey cat, 'Are you talking to me?' I ask.

'Do you see anyone else?' she replies and sits down.

'Oh, I see, I'm dead right? Or dreaming, because you're a moggy and moggies can't talk,' I say.

'Let's move this along,' Moggy says with a flick of her tail, 'Nine.'

'Nine what? Wishes?' I ask hopefully.

'You have nine what if opportunities to see how your life may have been. Oh no, sorry, got that wrong, it's eight, you're living one now,' Moggy says, and her green eyes have a twinkle to them.

If a cat could smile, I think I've just witnessed it.

'Is this Heaven? Are you an angel?' I ask.

Moggy turns and looks in the direction of the old man's house across the street, 'At the moment you're nowhere, and I'm that angel's helper,' she says.

'Oh … so,' I begin with my next question, I want to ask a thousand.

'We have limited time, you have eight,' Moggy says firmly and her whiskers twitch.

I'm grappling with the reality that I'm conversing with a cat and smirk, 'Eight opportunities to see what life could have been like if I'd chosen different paths? Well what if I don't want to know? Or what if I like one of those lives better?' I ask.

'The choice will be yours,' Moggy replies.

What's the harm, I think. 'Why not,' I say, with a dismissive wave of my hand.

*

A whirling mass of images like a kaleidoscope appears behind Moggy. It moves forward, turning, engulfing us as scenes from another life flash around like a movie preview. University, study, drinking, wild nights with friends, backpacking, my nurse's uniform, marriage, childbirth, mothers' groups, childbirth, parenthood. The spinning stops with a grounding thud leaving a heaviness in the souls of my feet. My long black slinky gown is swishing around my legs and I can't wipe the smile off my face. My husband Mark, an orthopaedic surgeon, and I are leaving a charity gala ball, his arm is wrapped around my waist as we walk over to our silver Mercedes waiting out the front. This life and memories seem perfect, and the discussion on the way home moves from the evening's events to our son and daughter. The brightness of headlights coming towards us didn't seem unusual until I recalled we've got the green traffic signal. The oncoming car has run the red one and ploughs into us. The shards of glass splintering around us, glistening in the streetlights stop in mid motion as if put on pause.

With a blinding flash of white I'm back on the step with Moggy.

'Do I die? Do we both die?' I ask, wrapping an arm tight around my waist where Mark's had been, 'What was the point of showing me that life? I die, don't I?' I ask again.

'Hmm, maybe — try number seven,' Moggy says, and the kaleidoscope begins.

*

In this life I'm a singer, made it big. Everything was over the top, grandiose, from the parties, houses, drugs and the loneliness. I'd fixed that with the big, white powdery overdose.

Then I'm back on the porch with Moggy.

'Are you kidding me, come on, I'm a popstar druggy, I die from an overdose!'

'Do you? Here's six,' Moggy responds.

*

Life six, I'm a teacher happily living on my own. I was on bus duty when I stepped out in front of the school bus to push my least favourite student Jeremy out of its path.

Life five, I'm married and a content part-time office worker and stay-at-home mum. Life's great until I get the news that my son has been hit by a school bus.

This time when I find myself back on the porch with Moggy casually licking her shoulder, I'm over it all.

'Okay I see what you're doing, I've had enough,' I said putting my hands up in a sign of resignation.

Moggy's eyes widened, 'But what if?'

43

'I get it, no matter which, what, if, or life, I would have chosen I'm still meant to feel some pain or die at this time in my life. I get it, okay. So, what was the point anyway?'

'To maybe take that risk, choose another life, live longer, who knows,' she replies arrogantly.

My brain is swimming in thoughts, would I be able to start over and change something, anything to make it last longer? There was always pain in the other lives, all around the same point in time, and my girls, I wouldn't even know of their existence. What I wanted reconciled, it was so simple, I just needed more time with them. To be there, watch them grow into the beautiful young women I hoped they'd be. The common link of pain was now in the forefront of my thoughts.

'Can I really choose any life?' I ask shuffling closer to Moggy.

'Any that you have seen and are before you,' she replies and looks at my body lying next to us.

Swiftly I lunge forward and grab her, 'Then I choose yours,' I blurt and scrape her claws across my arm.

'Wait! What! Can she do that?' Moggy calls out in confusion.

*

I open my eyes and blink a couple of times; from my low viewpoint I guess I'm lying where I had fallen. Mum's car is in the driveway, she's left the door open and is running towards me screaming my name.

'I'm fine,' I call out, but she doesn't react.

I try to push myself up, instead my body moves backwards, and Mum rushes past me, to my body lying on the hard concrete. Baffled I look down at my arms, they're furry and grey.

'Mum!' I yell, her face is streaming with tears, she's cradling my human head in her lap and fumbling with her mobile phone trying to make a call.

Uncoordinated I gingerly step around them, concentrating on my gait as I start making my way down the driveway. The old man is out of his chair and walking briskly towards me. By the time I reach the footpath there is rhythm in my stride, he's crossed the road and is only a couple of steps away then pauses and looks down at me. His eyes are filled with a knowing that's replicated in the gentle smile he bestows upon me, then he continues in a shuffling jog towards my mum offering help.

It takes all my effort not to race back and somehow let her know that everything is fine, I'll find a way with time. My heart is filled with a mixture of sadness and joy, I know what I need to do. I look down at my little white feet and start to run. Faster and faster, they skip over the footpath, my ears fold back with determination. I only have one miserly block to go, and boy can I run.

Laura Ferretti

A Bus Stop Gutter

I never realised how sublime it would be watching one's life trickle into the gutter. I hadn't meant to get involved, just standing there watching the drunks fall out of the pub. She had walked into a sweet left hook meant for him. The lads continued unaware and I ran from the bus stop to kneel next to her. She was out cold, so I started to turn her over. Thought I could put her into the recovery position. Thought I would help.

'What the fuck are you doing mate?'

'I'm just making sure she can breathe.'

'Like fuck, you bastard, get off my bird.'

I stood up, 'I wasn't the one that punched her, you did.'

Surprisingly he never said another word. He just reached forward and patted me with his clenched hand. Or so I thought until I looked down and saw the metal blade coming out of me. His hand held the knife tightly. I'd felt nothing, but when I looked into his eyes I saw his fear.

He ran and I fell.

Now I'm lying here. My hands pressing hard onto my chest. The blood is turning my blue jumper a deep red. No one seems to have noticed and I can't seem to be heard. A gutter at the side of a road, next to a bus stop. Not what I had envisaged.

Ian Andrew

Amuse Bouche

Em's invitation to dine at the Amuse Bouche club, arrived with no pomp or ceremony, it was simply couriered to her door. She heard the 'ping' of an incoming message as she finished signing the receipt device.

'That'll be your phone,' said the driver as he turned to leave.

She was surprised to get a delivery at this time of the day. It was about 5.30 pm and she was unwinding from her day at work as a journalist at OW: Our Writes, a civil watchdog organisation of humanitarian and environmental groups.

Em opened the envelope first, *I'll get my message later*, she thought.

Speed reading, daa daa daa da **Amuse Bouche** dum dee doo **attendance required,** she did pause here for a moment at this detail, but stopped being so blasé when she read:

'**1 July 2020 at 7 o'clock!**' Em yelled at the invitation as if it could respond, 'Shitty, shit, shit! Are you kidding me?'

Em frequently talked to herself when she was on her own and at times like this she liked to roar out the detail in sound. A lot. After a few more panic moments in stereo, Em continued reading and saw the part that said:

*the location has been sent to your mobile.

Em grabbed her phone and retrieved the message. By now, sense had gone with the courier driver and mayhem overtook her rational thinking. She resorted to her 'shit and shitting'. Her space was occupied with crazy and she needed to come back to her sanity spectrum. A few deep breaths, in through the nose and out through the mouth, Em slumped into a chair, ready to succumb to its nightly comfort. It was on the last body flump, that she saw her reflection in the tv. Her face said it all, another night at home, same ol' same ol'. The thought of comfy vs confit was enough for Em to get her arse into gear.

Amuse Bouche club had come into Em's radar through investigating alternative food and sustainable processes. Its closed group and mythical reputation had triggered Em's interest several times, but it soon got put on the back burner with other interest stories. Her invite couldn't be ignored really, she had to give

47

it a crack. Em was transitioning from organic eating to becoming vegan, so with one more 'shit' for good measure, she got ready to go.

Showered and dressed for the night. Black as usual, her urban activist look came in handy when she didn't know what to wear. This look usually scared the wannabes off, attracted the academics with curiosity and was her attire of safety when she was going somewhere new. She was hoping that there would be urban chic there too, so she wanted to be armed with clothing that gave her self-confidence.

With Google Maps engaged, she set of in Teens, her little Go-get-Em car.

'At 200 metres on the left, you will arrive at your destination.' She turned into the next gap in the trees, hoping to see the Amuse Bouche sign. The only sign of life was a forbidding Private Property sign swinging from a wrought iron gate.

Fuck, this time. 'Shit' was lower case swearing. Em was lost.

She grabbed her invite to check that she'd typed in the right address; as she was bringing it up, her phone pinged.

'Not now Marianne,' she yelled, 'I'm fucking lost! I'll ring you later.'

Fuck!' Another mind bomb exploded. 'It must be 7 o'clock.' Marianne always messaged around 7 pm for a catch up – 'Friggin' heck, I'm late as well as lost!'

In a vain attempt to recover some sanity, Em looked at her invitation again, hoping that she'd read 7.30 pm as 7 pm. Nope, she'd read right.

Dejected, she decided to go home.

She reversed Teens onto the main road.

Suddenly, a silvery cocoon snapped around her, encasing her within its intestinal tract. Sharp, cutting lines of metal pressed into Em's skin from all sides and the smell of metal bile invaded her nostrils. Panic squeezed her eyes shut. Hell was consuming her.

Silence made Em open her eyes to see that the evening light had been restored. Teens was immobile on the bitumen, but the road ahead wasn't what she'd left a few moments ago.

Please, for Christ's sake say this was here all the time
Please say I haven't been abducted by food aliens
Please say I'm still in this universe and I'm still Em.

Madness had returned like incontinence for Em, and she questioned her capacity to deal with all of this, whatever This was?

'Please God help me!' Em's atheist beliefs flew out the window in crisis, fear or lost items. 'Fuck You, Amuse Bouche!'

A tunnel in the shape of a mouth with braced teeth filled the space in front of the car.

For a moment nothing moved. Then the ground lurched below them, like an undulating tongue. The road was dragging the car towards the tunnel.

She had to get out! The car was careering into the jaws of death, to be chewed up like a tasty morsel.

Teens wasn't Teens anymore, she'd abandoned her relationship with her car, it had become a death trap.

Em grabbed the door handle, it didn't move! Em tried to free herself from her seatbelt. Her thrashing merely locked it in place, and it refused to release.

Em slammed both feet on the brake. The car kept moving forward. The tunnel was looming closer with each action.

Shrills of fear gushed from her now as she tried in rage to pull the keys from the ignition, slam it into reverse or derail the car off the conveyor belt of doom. Each action offsetting a vice grip to her body.

'Fuck you!' She screamed. 'Whatever you are? Take this, you piece of Fucked up shit! One, smoked carbon monoxide roadkill coming up!' And she slammed her feet on the accelerator and brake at the same time and braced for impact by grabbing the steering wheel.

Exhaust fumes and acrid smoke filled the air and her car squealed at the impaling pressure to her system, combustion was imminent.

Em blacked out first.

Em woke, feeling sweat from her experience all over her body, and her clothes stuck to her like skin, waiting to peel off from heat. She looked up to see that she was in front of the Private Property sign again and she retched, gagging at what had happened and that she was immobilised in this surreal, not real, she-didn't-know-what-place.

Em was still lost.

Teens was labouring in neutral awaiting Em's next move. Em just wanted to get the hell outta there, but she turned the car off to compose herself. Fear was still hovering over her and she pinched herself to feel. Once again, she embraced the steering wheel for comfort and closed her eyes for a sec.

Through the gap in the steering wheel, she saw that her phone was on the floor and the red circled 1 in her Messenger icon. She tapped it open to see that it wasn't Marianne, it was **Amuse fucking Bouche** …

You have arrived at the Entrance, please look up to the right and state your name to proceed.

Do not Reverse your vehicle

Em looked up into the trees and a security camera appeared.
'Mary fucking Poppins you Fuckers!'
The gate opened.

Apikara

A Break with Tradition
(Something I wrote that is not about love)

The absence of the rug is jarring,
but not unexpected.
Bare floors bring no distraction,
and empty rooms welcome solitude; your bedfellow.

    Enticing. Encouraging.
    Creating space for,
    allowing the arrival of,
    things that are good and quiet.

She who seeks to misplace herself,
finds bravado in the seeking.
                 (Even if sometimes,
                     it plays truant
                         with the doing.)
                           Lord, I asked for courage,
                             and you sent me danger.

The closest I ever came to Heaven was through a spike in my vein.
And true danger is blind faith.
I stopped believing in You the day I left my father's house.
Escaped his authority,
and gave up paying lip service to Yours.
                 (Although I suspect,
                     his faith was an act,
                         designed to comfort his mother,
                                 or mine.)

This is where our faith paths crossed.

Father please tell me;
whose face did you see the morning of your final sunrise?

A strong moral compass
A sense of right and wrong
The burden of the eldest child.

Jackie Coffin

Decomposure

This story is all in my head. No one will ever hear it. No one will ever know the terrible truth. Believe me, that's a good thing – nobody would sleep again if they knew what I knew.

I'm dead. I don't mean brain dead, or emotionally dead. I'm dead as in not breathing, no heartbeat. I am deceased, passed away. The bucket has been well and truly kicked! Have I made that clear enough? Sounds crazy doesn't it? Wait till you hear the rest – being dead is only the half of it.

My name is – sorry – *was* Brian Turpin. Quite a dull name I know, but that just about sums me up. I live – oops – *lived* in a little one-bedroomed flat on a stinking, filthy estate in North London. It was the sort of place that the local council – in their wisdom – stick all of life's bottom feeders. All the prostitutes, paedophiles, drug addicts and just about every other low life you can think of. What was I doing on such an estate you are no doubt wondering? Well, I've often asked myself the same question. In fact, I asked the council the same question. I never got an answer, just a load of *we are looking in to it*, from a teenager.

I was born in 1957 in Epsom, Surrey. My father was also Brian Turpin. I cursed him all my life for giving me the same name. Why couldn't I have been named Vince, or Brad? Anything would have been less dull than Brian! Except for Dick. Dick Turpin wouldn't have been good. My father was a pillar of the community – a pharmacist, as was his father. I guess that's what he wanted for me. Boy was he disappointed.

My mother, Rose Turpin, lived in his constant shadow. She was a timid woman. I can't remember her ever raising her voice, let alone her hand, to me. Discipline was definitely my father's speciality. Whether it was Mum or me at the receiving end, you could guarantee at best bruises, at worst a broken bone or two. Luckily for Mum it was usually me at the end of the bastard's fist. Of course, Mum would have gladly taken my place. That was Mum all over. She would have willingly taken the lost teeth or a busted rib instead of me. All she could do to comfort me was to do what she knew best. Feed me. I suppose it was her way of saying sorry. A way of making up for what he was doing to me. If only she knew that she was leaving me wide open for even more abuse. I mean, at the end of the day, who likes a fat kid?

By the time I was twelve I weighed sixteen stone, or as my French teacher insisted, one hundred and two kilograms. I sat on my own at the back of the class. If I wasn't getting a beating at home, you can bet I was getting one at school. I still remember the times I came home with a bloodied nose or blackened eye. The first thing Mum would do was to stuff a pork pie or chip butty in my face. Dad would often make a snide remark.

'You'll be able to roll home from school soon, lard arse.'

Or some really useful medical advice like: 'I'll have to bring you some laxatives from the shop – if you can't stop eating shit we might as well give it a fucking quick way out.'

Mum would always defend me.

'He's a growing lad, just needs to grow into his skin, that's all.'

I left school at sixteen. No qualifications. No trade, (of course, I got a few beatings for that), Dad would sit in his armchair scowling at me as though I was something he had trod in.

I left home at eighteen. I felt guilty at leaving Mum with that bastard, but he was getting slower in his old age and Mum had her ways to pacify him. I moved in with my Auntie Gloria. She was my mum's older sister. To say she was a polar opposite of Mum would be an understatement! She was a huge woman, I should have fitted right in, but we clashed from day one. For all the physical abuse I received from dad, Gloria matched it with emotional beatings. She knew just what to say, her tongue was as vicious as any punch I received at home.

Mum was sending Gloria money to cover my keep, a fact that she had great pleasure in telling me every time she opened the little white envelope with cash in it.

'Eighteen and still sucking at ya mum's tits – useless, and you'll always be useless. Jeez, what did she do to deserve that self-righteous prick of a husband, and then Fatty Arbuckle for a son?'

I tried to find work, I really did. Sometimes even got an interview, but it was always the same story. I could see the look of disgust as soon as I walked into the interview room. I guess if I was in their shoes, I'd be the same. Who wants to employ a sweaty, twenty-stone teenager?

Food was my only comfort and boy did I like comforting myself! It became an obsession. If I was eating, I was happy, that's all there was to it.

1980 was a bad year. Very bad! It was the later part of September. I had just attended another pointless job interview and had come home and crashed on the sofa with a bowl of crisps. The telephone rang. It was always like a game between Gloria and me. Who would get off their fat backside and answer it? Today I was in a stubborn mood – the phone continued to ring.

'Are you going to get that Fatso?' Gloria shouted from the kitchen.

I turned the telly up. *Take that bitch!*

'You lazy fuckin' git.'

I heard a pan being thrown, followed by her heavy footsteps coming up the hallway. I was hoping the phone would ring off, that would have really pissed her off! It didn't. She answered the phone, the irritation clear on her face. I turned the volume down so I could hear the conversation. If it was Mum, I wanted to see how she was. Gloria had this nasty habit of talking to Mum on the phone then ending the call knowing full well that I wanted to speak to her. It wasn't Mum on the phone. Whoever it was, was giving Gloria some bad news. Her voice had reduced from a boom to a faltering whisper.

'When did this happen? Are you sure? Yes, yes, I'll come right away. Brian? Yes … yes he's here, I'll bring him.' I didn't like the sound of this at all.

*

Mum had died instantly in the crash. Dad held on for three days – actually regained consciousness briefly – but then a blood vessel in his brain burst and that was that. I was comforted that Mum didn't suffer. I didn't give a toss about him. If he died in pain, then that was rough justice! We reap what we sow, those who live by the sword … blah, blah, blah. They were buried together. Poor Mum, even in death she wasn't free of him.

You think I would have done ok financially out of my parents' deaths. Huh! Think again. As a last act of nastiness, my father left his pharmacy business to his brother Sidney. I guess I could have contested, but to be honest, I couldn't be arsed, that's the truth of it.

I stayed at Gloria's for about four months after they died. We had one last blazing row, and that was that, I got the hell outta Dodge.

So, there you have it. A twenty-six stone, tub of lard. Homeless. No job and little prospect of getting one. This is where the Great British National Health Service came into its own. My doctor, a legend, decided in his infinite wisdom to get me registered as disabled. At first I wasn't too happy about it, after all, who wants to be labelled a cripple? After my initial reservations, it was clear that it was in my best interests. I was given a respectable amount of money every fortnight. I was given a 'lovely' council flat. They even offered me a car, which I had to decline because I couldn't fit behind the wheel, let alone drive the bloody thing.

I lived in my 'lovely' flat for about twenty years. My eating habits never changed. You have seen guys like me on reality TV shows. You know the ones, where eventually they are lifted out of their homes with a crane to get them to a hospital for help. I didn't leave the flat in eight years. I didn't need to. I could get any cuisine that took my fancy brought right up to the front door: Chinese, Indian, Mexican, Thai. I even had a Vietnamese takeaway that delivered! Viva the 21st century.

Food. The death of me. The night I died was Indian night. I had ordered all the usual suspects. Chicken Tikka Masala, Lamb Bhuna, Prawn Biryani, Onion Bhaji, Bombay potatoes, Naan bread stuffed with mincemeat, I think they call it Keema, and a heap of pappadums to add a bit of texture. I was going easy as I had been suffering a bit of heartburn lately.

Sitting in front of the telly, in my boxers, tray on lap. Gorging. *Home and Away* was on. I loved that show. So much less depressing than English shows like *East Enders* and *Coronation Street*. I always wanted to go to Australia. Yeah, like I could have fitted into the fucking plane seat. I had just finished my fourth can of lager – curry always gave me a thirst. I put my tray to one side and rocked back and forward in my chair to get the momentum going to be able to get up and get some more beer. As I got to my feet I started to get a sort of dull ache down my left arm, didn't give it a passing thought. However, the pain, like a thousand red hot knives stabbing my chest, did grab my attention. It was at that point that I accepted it was not heartburn. My heart was doing the death march in my chest. I could feel my legs starting to buckle underneath me. I grasped for the nearest solid thing to try and steady myself. This happened to be a pine, freestanding mirror that I had bought from a charity shop years ago. I might just as well have used a house of cards. The mirror and I went crashing to the ground. I landed on my belly, my head tilted to the side. The mirror lay on its side. The dying guy in the mirror staring at me was … Me. I think I heard a couple of bones snap as I fell, but any pain from that was masked by the incredible agony radiating from my chest. I wasn't stupid – fat yes – but not stupid. I knew I was having a heart attack. I had white foam around my mouth, and I was aware of a gurgling sound coming deep from the back of my throat.

My bowels and bladder both let go. I felt my hand twitching wildly for a few seconds. Then everything stopped, including my heart.

So, what happened next? Did I leave my mortal body and rise up with a choir of angels singing me along? Did I become a ghost, and this becomes the story of Brian and his ghostly antics? Nope. I lay there. I knew I was dead. I had no doubt about that. I was half expecting a white light to appear, I'd read about that in a book. What a load of crap. Unless I am different, or this is my own personal hell, then this is it. Sorry if I am shattering any illusions or religious beliefs, but this is it folks!

To paint a perfectly clear picture for you. I was lying on the floor facing an upended mirror staring at my own lifeless eyes. Surprisingly I still had all my senses. I could see, I could hear, and I could smell. I think that was the worst thing. I could smell the acrid stench of my emptied bowel. My thighs were stinging, must have been the acid from my urine. I had a pretty good view of myself in the mirror. I could see most of my body to just above my knees.

The deep purple colour of my face as I was dying had paled. I looked like one of those French noblemen, the ones who used to put powder on their faces and wear ridiculously large wigs. The telly was still on, I could hear Alf Stewart complaining about some Yahoo – whatever that was.

My whole body felt strange. It's like when you cut yourself real deep and you have it stitched up. The wound starts to heal but then you get that itch. Not just on the surface but deep down, right under the skin. It felt like that all over.

I had some strange brown liquid coming out of my left eye, making my sight a bit blurred. I started to get used to the smell. I always thought it was an old wives' tale that you shit yourself when you die. Turns out I was wrong about that.

To be honest, I reckon I was quite lucky. I know I was lying here in my own filth – dead – but it really could have been worse. If this was the same deal for everyone, just imagine the other scenarios. I could have been in a funeral parlour. Fully aware whilst some guy or girl rammed tubes in every orifice and pumped unpronounceable liquids into me in the name of preservation! Then I could have been put into a thousand-degree oven – which would have been the better alternative, the other option was to be put in a coffin and buried. Nothing but silence and darkness for, well, who knows? I, on the other hand, was in my warm flat, the telly was on and the chances of someone finding me in the near future were unlikely to say the least.

I had no concept of time. How long had I been dead? My body started to show some clues. My skin was turning a strange yellowy grey, almost like storm clouds. I saw dots in front of my eyes. I thought it was just another symptom of death.

Then I heard the buzzing.

I guess it was my rancid faeces or possibly my rotting flesh that attracted the flies, I don't know which. At first it was just a few, then a swarm! *Is that what a lot of flies are called?* I could feel their bristled bodies all over me. I could see them partying on me. The grossest thing was I could see and feel them in my mouth. *Maybe a good thing I didn't visit Australia!* I was alive with them. *Alive* – Oh the irony!

How wrong can a person be? I thought the flies would slowly devour me, but no. It would seem that I was to become a crèche, a living nursery. I was quite disgusted when I first saw the maggots writhing in the open sores where my flesh was starting to recede, but it's surprising how quickly you get used to the little buggers! The feeling – if I'm honest – was quite pleasurable. It felt like getting a massage from thousands of tiny fingers. Some seemed to be feasting on the dried pus that had secreted from my eye. I was seeing them in stereo – both in the mirror and when they squirmed across my eye. Bizarre.

*

And so, the days – maybe weeks – have passed. But guess what? I'm still here and I am still dead – of course I am, no cure for that is there? My skin is starting to get hues of green, maybe some sort of post-death mould? I can't see out of my left eye now. I watched the maggots slowly eat it away. I can't work out why they didn't eat my right one. I wish they had really – I would be spared the trauma of watching myself rot away. Everything is a bit blurry. Eyes. Mind. Mind's eye.

Well, things just keep getting better at Hotel Brian! I have gone blind in one eye; did I already tell you that? Large clumps of flesh are just sliding off me now, every time it happens the maggots go into some sort of feeding frenzy. For the first time in my life I can see my cheekbones. My face looks like it has cling film pulled over it. My gums have receded making me look like I have a stupid grin on my face – like I've got lots to smile about!

OK. It's all getting a bit sketchy now. I think I said, I had gone blind in one eye? Did I? Had I? I think I did? Well the other has just about had it now too. Everything is itching! Feels like maggots are crawling all over me, oh hang on, they are, aren't they? I think I am blacking out. One minute I can hear

Inspector Morse on the telly, and then all of a sudden, it's a *Touch of Frost*! Its *Breakfast TV* now, I've lost about eight hours somewhere! Something is sliding down my face, oh it's OK, it's just my forehead. Where's my mum? Oh yeah, she died.

It's all gone dark, and quiet. Not completely quiet though, I can hear voices, muffled voices. It's warm, quite cosy in fact. I feel like I'm floating, yeah, floating in a warm salty ocean. I always wanted to go to the Dead Sea. Is that in Australia?

Pressure, I can feel pressure …

Light, oh God, bright light, too bright. Voices. Loud voices. Booming!

'Congratulations Helen, you have a healthy baby boy, he's a whopper – an eleven pounder for sure.'

Shit, it's cold … And hungry … I'm so fucking hungry.

'Wow he has a good set of lungs on him, doesn't he?'

Mark Townsend

Drowning

I didn't know it was possible to drown on dry land. Until it happened to me. I didn't know you could feel like sinking even though your feet stood on solid ground. I had watched my children walk away from me, my mouth a silent O as I fought for air. They both turned to look at me, their faces a flash of light, which contrasted with my despair. I fixed a smile on my face and waved at them. I blew them a kiss and pretended to catch theirs when they blew one back. I watched as Renee buckled them into the car, and I saw the way she kept her lips tight as she drove away without looking back. It was in that moment that I felt myself start to crumble. Like a ship plummeting to the depths of the ocean, no one had heard my distress call and so deeper and deeper I went, until all that was left of me was my shell.

*

'I'll have another,' I said to the bloke behind the bar as I pushed my empty glass across the counter. One turned into four, and then another again. I began to lose count of how many times the bartender had taken away my glass and replaced it. My vision was blurred, and my brain was foggy, but I hadn't forgotten, which meant I wasn't done. The alcohol burned my gut, but it hadn't dissolved the fury that sat in the pit of my stomach.

'Might be time to start going easy, mate.'

I glared at the man who had poured the fuel on my fire. I curled my fingers tight around my drink, guarding it like a wild animal guards its catch.

'I'll be done when I say I'm done … mate. C'mon, I'm a paying customer.'

The bartender looked at me, doubt and pity in his eyes. Could he see that I had drowned? 'Rough day, hey?' he asked. As if he cared.

I stared at the clock – 7.30, the kids' bedtime. Instead of tucking them in, I was sitting alone in a bar, pissed at the world.

'Rough doesn't begin to describe it …' I swallowed, tried to hold it in, keep it contained. But it spilled out; the booze loosened my tongue and released some rage. 'The bitch, the woman who I … who I thought I loved … she's taken my kids away from me. She's gone and outright LIED to the judges, and those pricks believed every word.' I spat the words out, the saliva in my mouth like venom. 'She said I'm violent and can't be trusted! But they're my kids, man,

I'd never do anything to hurt them. She's the one who can't be trusted! I couldn't even explain it all to them, and now she's gonna go and turn them against me.'

The room was spinning; I clenched my fists and banged them on the counter. Some heads turned in my direction and the man gave them an apologetic smile.

'Mate, that's terrible. I couldn't imagine what that'd be like.'

I looked him in the eyes, searched for the sincerity in his words. One of his eyes twitched, and he looked back towards the kitchen.

'You don't wanna imagine it. She's taken everything. She's sleeping under my roof; she's taken the car. She's tucking MY kids into bed at night and she's turned everyone against me. SHE'S gone psycho and I'm the one losing my mind.' I was breathing like a wild man, my hands trembled.

He shook his head, offering feigned sympathy. 'Fathers don't get equal rights; the justice system is a joke.' He paused, looked at me. Tentatively said, 'I'm looking out for you, mate. Think you need to take a break from the drink.'

He reached under the bar and put a water bottle in front of me. 'Sober up, buddy. You won't find the answers to your problems here.'

I scowled at him, hoped he could see the truth in my gaze. But I guess he saw what I have been painted as: a dangerous, untrustworthy man, incapable of looking after his children. People believe what they want to believe. They get snippets and fill in the rest of the story with their own details. Nobody bothers to look deeper.

The stool toppled over as I staggered away. Nobody had bothered to hear my side of the story. If they did, they'd see an innocent man, a puppet to his vindictive wife, who used their children as a way to get back at him.

I made my way out onto the street, steadied myself on a light post. I looked left, then right, up and down the road. Disorientated, I didn't know which way to go. I sunk to the floor, despair dragging me down. I put my head on my knees, surrendered to the feeling. I rolled the names of my children around my tongue – *Ava, Max, Ava, Max, Ava, Max.* Over and over I whispered their names, until my heart rate slowed. I clung to the thought of them; they were what would stop me from sinking too far. I pictured their sleeping faces, cocooned in their blankets and I hoped they dreamed of me.

Suzanne M. Faed

The Big Blue

Maia sat suspended and weightless. The cold seawater sculpted her body, holding her delicately still in its midst. She stared into the great vastness of a world that refused to be understood by some at the surface. Acutely aware of her humble position in the Universe, Maia gazed with zeal at the silent spectrum of blue unfolding before her. Pale turquoise gradually transforming to rich violet hues before drifting into the perpetual obscurity of ancient wisdom. The place where the secrets to the origin of life resides. The hammerhead sharks moved as one on their migratory passage. Unfettered by her meagre presence, the dark silhouettes of their distinctive shape crossed overhead. *There must be close to a hundred of them*, she thought. The ones she could see anyway.

Maia's first close encounter with a shark happened soon after she started diving. Her dad had just begun taking the underwater camera with him to capture their encounters. On one occasion, a couple of tiger sharks appeared in the distance. Maia observed their graceful movements and behaviour. They swam peacefully, circling around her at a safe distance. When they were close enough to them, Maia reached out. Applying no pressure, she momentarily touched the flank of the closest one. Its skin, coarse like sandpaper, surprised and intrigued her. Looking back through the camera lens, one turned and moved swiftly towards her. Plunging into the camera, Maia was forced backwards until she was lying parallel to the shark. He continued to circle back, pushing at the camera with his nose. Maia landed against the bed of the reef, her body arriving at a jarring stop between the camera and her oxygen tank. The overly curious creature returned to take hold of the camera in his mouth. After a moment of showing no further interest in the object, he retreated, leaving Maia to return to the surface with everything intact and wondering how soon she could be back down there again.

*

Adam sat transfixed, watching the dark crimson petals flirting with the breeze. The flowers appeared to transform strangely into large droplets before splashing onto the beach like pebbles dropping through the surface of a lake. The sand began bleeding profusely, seeping down to the ravenous water's edge that cleansed the stain as it lapped at the blood. Adam's hand was an empty cup. He stooped down to fill it then brought the salty, viscous liquid to his mouth and swallowed the contents. He heard the faint sound of a woman's voice calling out to him.

'Adam … Adam … Beep …Beep …Beep …'

Adam sucked the cold air into his lungs with a jolt and opened his eyes. Relieved to be awake, he checked the time. 5.45 am. He had slept through his alarm. Again. He was due to start work in fifteen minutes. Better get a wriggle on. Everywhere Adam ventured in this town was a piercing and unwelcome link to his past. It was still too raw. He refused to call it a memory. Surely something can't be called a memory if it could still be felt?

Adam's hands clenched into fists and his throat constricted. He couldn't swallow. He could barely even breathe anymore. His chest was crushed under the weight of guilt, and the spasmodic pain in his shoulder reminded him he was still here. More and more he wished he wasn't, and that it was him who was taken by the shark instead of his wife and unborn child. His thoughts were of little comfort as they circled around his mental turntable on replay, slightly altering something each time in an attempt to change the outcome. Adam still walked hand-in-hand with the illusion that he could have done something to change the situation. He should have been able to control it. Adam was paid to take risks in dangerous scenarios every day. It was his job to protect everyone else and he was good at it. What was the use of all this police training when he had failed to protect his own family?

Kelly loved the ocean and was mad about getting on the waves. She used to say that out there we are all equal. The sea that claimed Kelly's life is the same sea that runs through Adam's veins, connecting him to the Saltwater people and to the Spirit place of the hammerhead shark. Adam wondered if he still carried it within him now and if he still belonged to that place. These days, Adam struggled to find a connection. He wasn't sure he ever would. *That shark picked a fight with the wrong bloke.* It failed to make any sense to Adam why he was still here, and Kelly was gone.

'Is,' whispered Adam to himself. 'Kelly is gone.'

And she won't be coming back.

*

The regional shark conservation and anti-cull rally is today. Adam rocked up late to work and as a result, drew the short straw. His Sergeant said it would do him good. Adam had to be there early to make sure there were no potential troublemakers around. He always copped it from the few loud and obnoxious in the crowd. There was always one who tried to take the piss out of the Indigenous officer with his racist comments and pathetic imitations, right before taking a swing. That was bad enough until it came time to make an arrest and throw them in the back of the patrol car. Adam's pulse was pounding in his temples. He couldn't wait for this day to be over.

'Welcome everyone and thank you for taking the time to be here today to show your support for shark conservation. Please take a moment to voice your protest against the Government's decision to cull sharks by signing the petition addressed to the State Premier. Today we have a special guest. I'd like to introduce Maia. Most of you would recognise her from the work she has done with sharks and from her recent publicity. Please make her welcome.'

An elegantly confident young woman stepped up to the podium.

'I've been on this planet for nineteen years. I don't have a trade or a degree. I don't even have a drivers licence for that matter!' A hint of amusement circulated. Adam stood inconspicuously at the back and scanned the crowd. Maia continued but Adam had already tuned out.

'Sharks are apex predators and they determine what lives and what dies. They are necessary for a thriving ecosystem. If you start taking out the apex predators, especially when numbers are low, you upset the balance. We don't know why we are seeing a recent spike of shark attacks in the area.'

A rush of adrenalin burnt Adam's gut and flooded his limbs like wet concrete. He shivered in the hot sun, sweat flooding his palms

'We don't know very much about them at all, but it's time we found out. There are alternatives to culling. Education is one way. The Government and the media use fear tactics to create a void between our world and the world that exists in nature. In that darkness, they take what they want.'

Adam wished he could leave without anyone noticing.

'Humans are not on the menu but occasionally we do get in the way. We have the power to make choices. When we choose to step into the ocean, we choose to enter their home. Many of us make this choice every day but we do so in a way that proves that we can exist together and without fear. Please ask the Government to find another way. Thank you.'

Her supporters vigorously applauded as Maia stepped down from the podium and made her way to the information table. Adam figured this was a futile exercise but admired their enthusiasm. He apprehensively approached the table and waited for his turn to speak. His uniform sometimes helped in these matters. Often it didn't. When he was close enough, Adam asked, 'You do realise that the people here don't need converting? They've already made up their minds.'

'Really?' Maia replied without hesitation, before looking up at him.

'What about you?' Maia reached across and grabbed the nearest clipboard and pen.

'What's your name? Is it on our petition?'

Adam glanced down and shook his head. 'Adam. I'm here on duty.'

'Okay. So how often do things get out of control?'

'Not often. Our presence is usually enough.'

Maia nodded and paused thoughtfully for a moment.

'Just like sharks, I suppose.'

Adam lifted his head and looked at her questioningly. 'What do you mean?'

'They both keep things in order, making sure nothing gets out of control. Everything slows down around them. Other fish meet their cruising speed just like we do when we see a patrol car on the highway. When a shark is present in the water, there's a distinct change in the energy and in everything around it. There's a definite air of authority. They have a necessary role to play to keep the order balanced and maintained.'

Adam suddenly felt way out of his depth and thought some humour would deflect the situation. 'Is this your way of getting me to sign your petition?'

'You stand up for justice in your job. That's all I'm doing. I'm standing up for those who can't speak for themselves.'

Adam shuffled awkwardly while staring at the underwater photos of Maia surrounded by sharks.

'Tell you what, why don't you come diving sometime? I take off most mornings from the main jetty at around seven.'

Adam looked over his shoulder for a few moments before turning back.

'One took my wife. Last summer. She didn't make it.'

Maia's diminutive stature stood squarely in front of Adam. Her blue-grey eyes looked right into his troubled dark ones. It was only a matter of seconds but to Adam it felt as though a lifeline had just hoisted him up to safety after months adrift at sea.

By the time Adam got home, he was irritated. Something about that girl had really triggered something in him, and it was rapidly rising to the surface like rotten driftwood.

*

A number of weeks had passed since the rally. Adam buried himself in work to avoid seeing or talking to anyone he knew. He was told to take a few days off. He hadn't been sleeping well and was up early each day for his morning run. He liked to stop at Goldilocks Café on his way home, sit in the corner with a black coffee and the paper, and catch up on the latest news. He opened the front page to find an article on Maia. She had just released a short shark documentary. Adam thought back to the day at the rally and remembered their conversation. He quickly finished his coffee and ran in the direction of the jetty.

*

Maia was squatting down port side of her vessel, checking the apparatus before her next dive. She was talking to a mature-aged man in a black wetsuit, when Adam approached the boat.

'You came,' her voice showing surprise.

'Actually, I have something to show you.'

Adam reached into the pocket of his shorts and produced a photograph.

'Her name was Kelly. She was pregnant when she died. I haven't been able to go back home since it happened.'

Maia reached out and touched Adam's hand.

Something from inside Adam lifted.

A man's voice boomed from the bow of the boat. 'Maia! You ready to head out?'

'Yeah Dad. Let's go.'

Maia turned back to Adam. 'Why don't you come out with us?'

Adam boarded the boat and they took off for the edge of the reef. Eventually, they pulled up and lowered anchor. Maia and Adam sat peacefully on the side of the boat, their feet dangling over the edge. Maia beamed at Adam through her diving mask.

'Ready to go home?'

Stephanie Fitz-Henry

Distance

I see you through technology,
the distance closed by light.
From over half a world away
I hold you in my sight.
I watch you as you talk to me
my mother, always there.
Yet the heartache that I feel tonight
is difficult to bear.

For you look like her,
you speak like her,
your eyes are full of life.
Your spirit so unbroken,
your wit, the sharpest knife.

The memories of your girlhood days,
those years left far behind
are fresh and sharp and focused;
vibrant colours in your mind.

I know I'm blessed to have you,
when so many are forlorn.
Those adults who are orphans,
no parents, save to mourn.

While I can still hold on to you
like the child I'll always be.
For the years have made no impact,
on that bond twixt you and me.

Yet now my heart is breaking
though my tears are kept at bay,
as you recall your history
yet know little of today.
The simple tasks confuse you,
in a fog that seems to bind
and I dread the time that's coming,
when I'm a stranger to your mind.
Shall you ask me who I am
And why I visit here?
Will I lie, conceal the hurt
and wipe away a tear?

But that day; it hasn't come yet.
For now I'm still your child
and the fact a God so loving
causes heartache makes me wild
with an anger that consumes me
and a rage that hurts my soul
and a knowledge of futility
that takes a heavy toll.

Yet if I let that anger
pull the focus from my love,
I will never truly see you
as the angel from above
that you are surely meant to be
when you have slipped away,
from the sadness and the loss of you
… that the mind brings with decay.

Ian Andrew

Failure to Thrive

She has cleaned this same spot over and over until the blue patterned surface has faded to grey. Her eyes glaze as she moves along the countertop from sink to bench and back. Wringing out the cloth in the bucket of water, conserved for this very purpose.

AJ, with an ape-like teenage gait, waves a piece of paper under her nose. She swats it away like she does with the flies that always manage to find their way through the fly screen.

"You've got to sign it,' AJ grunts, 'I need your permission to play in the game on Friday.'

He's getting annoyed with her, copying his father. She can smell the testosterone. Pushing for a fight, wanting her to bite back. Instead, she snatches the paper from his hand, and, walking to the old oak dresser clawed at the front where the cat has sharpened her nails, she signs her name with the fine liner that isn't quite a pen but will do the job. Handing it back she's met with silence and the swish of his backpack as he throws it onto his back, narrowly missing her. He's too young yet to realise the weight of responsibility it takes to keep control in this overheated world.

'Will you come home straight after school?'

She asks, her soft tone beckoning reconciliation.

'I don't fucking know. I suppose so!'

And AJ is out of the door; she would never have spoken to her mother like that! But then her mother had been fierce, strong, a woman you didn't mess with. She tries to recall her mother's face, but she can't dredge up the image in her mind's eye. Instead, she remembers a version of her, an older, tired version in the blue housecoat with the small daisy pattern, hands lumpy with arthritis wrapped around knitting needles. Her mother's hands were never idle, even when her mind was absent. And although she can remember the small grey-white curls at the nape of her neck, somehow the face won't come. She thinks about going to the dresser and pulling out a photo, but her body moves to the cupboard and pulls out the broom instead. She'll sweep the patio first, clear up from the party that didn't notice her absence, pick up the bottles and discarded cigarette butts. She will spot the ones with orange lipstick crowning the end, knowing that the stain matches her rival's lips.

Brad will stir soon; his head will hurt from too much beer and barracking at the football game and from the guilt that he still has the decency to feel from pashing with the woman who wears Burnt Sienna. The anger she feels towards him is volcanic and, like Pele, she wants to tear him asunder, reduce him to ash. Whenever he speaks to her, his stilted words that lack any emotion just stir her agitation further. She notices how he speaks carefully, choosing each word like a connoisseur, sensing the simmering anger, knowing that she is a volcano, unstable, practising caution, not knowing when or if she will blow. If only he knew that containment is her medium, her art, her canvas coloured with passive aggressive pauses and deep sighs. She manages their encounters to small ash clouds or the occasional basalt rock, thrown out casually in conversation. She too is terrified to let the explosion happen. To lose control and watch another unnatural disaster unfold.

Finishing the sweeping she deliberately rattles the broom into the cupboard making as much noise as possible having already slammed the patio door shut. If power didn't cost so much, she would have vacuumed outside the bedroom, and maybe sang one of his stupid football songs. She hopes his head is banging.

It's always the same the night before he goes back to work, his foul temper takes over from his usual caution, and when he wakes, he'll make a scene that she hasn't made him breakfast on his last day. He'll tempt her rage, climb the summit and look into the abyss. But even if she makes the breakfast, practises polite conversation, it won't change their reality. She just has to make it until tomorrow when he'll be gone, and the risk that their lives will be torn apart will remain dormant for a while longer.

So instead of cooking breakfast, she puts on her old musty trainers and heads out the gate. There is a small piece of common land that leads to a park a few minutes away, and she determines to head there. The air is sticky, and she feels grimy after her exertion in the yard, but the act of putting one foot in front of the other soothes her like a mother rocking a child. Her mother wasn't some-one you ran to for a hug. She wouldn't pick you up and cover you with kisses. Her mother had an invisible boundary and even as a child, you didn't dare cross it, but at night she would always come into her room and fuss with the bed covers, hovering at the door before turning out the light.

Parrots screech and swoop from the now sparse trees lining the path down to the small lake. Their green feathers offer a flash of colour on this grey day. The air is thick with moisture. She only sees parrots on her walk now, they seem to thrive where the smaller birds have failed. Failure to thrive. It had become a catch-all term in a poisoned world where everyone and everything was failing to thrive at one level or another. Her mind stretches back to that day, the ride home from the hospital. The tears that wouldn't flow. She wishes that the sun would break through the dense cloud. This constant grey makes her thoughts maudlin. It makes her think about all that has gone, all that has been lost, rather than what remains. And surely, it's what remains that needs attention?

Lazily she allows her mind to float back to her childhood. Time spent close to the sea, bright sunny days swimming in the fresh ocean. A day in December where her mother packed them a picnic and set up a brolly on the beach. Zinc cream on their noses, rashies covering their pale bodies and big wide-brimmed hats that had allowed them to play out for hours building their imagination and dreams for the future in the sand. They stayed until the sun went down.

In another hour, it will be too hot to stay outside, already the humidity is rising uncomfortably. The air thick and cloying. It feels like the world wants to smother her, and the exertion of walking is taking its toll. Lately, everything feels like an effort. She is alone in the park; the straggling dog walkers having already gone. Small beads of sweat run down her forehead and she catches them with her tongue, revisiting a time when she was sixteen and had travelled to Singapore.

It had been a special trip for her birthday and her first time on a plane. Her mother hadn't wanted them to go, having recently joined the 'No to Air' campaign, and had fought with her father about him buying the tickets. She remembered them arguing and praying that this time, her father would win. He did, but her mother refused to go, and didn't hide her disgust that her two daughters had sided with their father. It was a dream fulfilled to be part of a world where you could fly to exotic lands and have new clothes rather than hand-me-downs. Her mother had told them that she was trying to keep them on the 'right side of history', and that her grandchildren would thank her. But being on the right side of history only counts if you win. The cries from people like her mother for a war time effort after the IPCC released papers in 2018, pointing out that two degrees warming would be catastrophic, had landed on deaf ears. By the time any real action happened too many tipping points had been passed, and the war was already lost. Singapore had felt like being wrapped in a warm wet blanket, exotically different from the dry air and vast skies of home that had been her reality then. Her father had given her $500 spending money, and she had 'shopped till she dropped'. They had gone out to dinner and drank 'mocktail' Singapore Slings. She had felt like a princess, like one of the girls she followed on Instagram. With her sister Bindy, they had posed for one photo after another, while her father watched. She had pored over those photos for months afterwards, deciding which ones she liked best, which ones she would post on her feed. Her father left the family home shortly after their return.

She hadn't seen Bindy since the funeral. Getting about isn't easy these days and a plane flight impossibly expensive. She wonders how Bindy is coping as the fires in Victoria burn out of control. She pushes her mind away from the nagging thought, which creeps up on her each night, that Bindy is one of the many casualties. It's stupid that they haven't kept in touch. Either one of them only needs to pick up the phone. But even as she thinks it, she knows she won't. What is there to say?

Some people are like glue. They hold everything together. Without them, the individuals that make up our worlds drift apart. They are keystones, integral to the system functioning, but you don't realise this until they are gone. Nature works in the same way, and certain species are crucial to an ecosystem's survival. Their family system had begun to collapse as her mother's mind began to break down. Mimicking the collapse that was happening around them in so many different ways. An epidemic in elderly dementia had claimed, and continued to lay waste to, so many and her mother was just another victim. She wasn't special. Her case wasn't out of the ordinary. Yet for their system, it had meant the end. When a hive loses its Queen, the colony collapses. Her mother was their Queen.

She had inherited the house, though in these times it wasn't much of a boon, but it had meant that they could keep food on the table, which with skyrocketing prices was no easy task, even with Brad working three weeks on. And then there was the back yard for growing a few things, resistant varieties. When she was a child, her mother had always kept the garden fully stocked, fresh veggies and the chooks of course. She remembered when they had planted the avocado tree, and her father had joked that they should plant more and sell them and become avocado millionaires – avos being three dollars each at the time. That tree had survived unlike many of the others that had withered and died, but like her father, it too was now gone. And she couldn't remember the last time she'd eaten avocado?

*

There used to be eucalypt trees lining her street, now as she walks home, she only vaguely, notices their absence. She wonders too how she can only keep her mind on the past, not the present. Whenever she tries to bring herself into the moment, her mind wanders, but instead of the past lying behind her, it stretches ahead and it is the future that is lost, a memory of what might have been. She can taste the heat on her tongue, and the moisture build up on her face makes it feel like she is crying. They are fake tears. Once upon a time, she had shouted, was angry, campaigned and waved banners, signed petitions. What is there to do now on the way to your own extinction? Except perhaps remember what was?

Memories flood her mind, one in particular of her mother kneeling, head down, weeding around the brassicas that grew tall and strong in the raised beds fed by the chicken shit. She's standing in the garden of the house, maybe she's 5-year-old, those details are vague. But as she watches her mother garden, a bee lands on her finger, and she stares intently at it, seeing the small hairs it wears around its neck like a woman wearing a fur stole; she counts the stripes on its back. Then for no reason, it stings her small finger and screaming she knocks it off and stamps on it as it hits the ground. Now she remembers her mother's face with intense clarity, a younger angry face. Full of pain, green eyes flashing with shock that her daughter could do such a thing. It is an unforgiving face, and it launches at her, mouth screwed up as if she will spit her out. A hand raised slapping her small face so hard that it had almost lifted her off her feet. The pain in her finger dulls compared to the sting on her face that reddens and begins to bruise her young cheek. Then her mother is on the ground, crouched and wailing, staring at the small bee. The sound she makes is intense, primal. She touches her face at the remembering, it is damp still, and the handprint of her mother still resonates after all these years. She recalls how she went to her mother's side that day and held her leg rocking with her on the ground. Her own tears and sobs joining the cacophony of pain.

One foot in front of the other, her awareness shifts back to the present as she unhooks the gate and walks up the path. She hears Brad who has the TV on loud while bellowing into his phone. As she opens the door, he doesn't acknowledge her presence, so she begins to shut the house up. Moving diligently from room to room. Bringing down the shutters. Drawing the curtains. In a moment, the TV will cease as the power allowance will be entirely utilised by the air conditioners. She flicks a switch, and the fans began to whirl, knocking out power to the TV, and she hears his voice quieten as he realises he no longer needs to shout. The air conditioners just about keep the house bearable.

Heat stroke can come on quickly, she has seen the effects, sweating, nausea, headaches, till eventually you stop sweating, become agitated, and finally, your heart succumbs. She heads to the bedroom, removes her trainers and lies on the bed fully clothed wondering what time AJ will get home.

Louise Tarrier

The Man Outside

Soundlessly, Holly opened the curtains of the little window next to the bed and allowed the silver shard of moonlight to illuminate the tiny room. Next to her, the six-foot-something stranger continued to snore quietly, his alcohol-stale breath pungent in the sticky post-coital air.

Sliding from the bed, Holly curled beneath the window and lit a cigarette, drawing hard on the filter, watching the little orange tip glow with a satisfying crackle.

Outside the window the traffic was virtually non-existent; the occasional Uber delivery bike, a few black cabs. Her eyes were focused on a small bar across the road, and the man sitting outside it, sipping a glass of red. Even though it was hidden from her eye-line, she knew there was a book open on the table in front of him: *The Tell-Tale Heart*. She was reading it too.

The man turned his head slightly, his nose – once broken in a bar fight – was slightly crooked. Holly admired his profile, the high forehead and a devastatingly sharp jaw line. She could sense him smile, and she smiled back.

Drawing on her cigarette, she looked across at the stranger in her bed. His parted lips were dry, but a string of saliva hung between them. Unlike her friend across the road, this man had jowls which hung loose and round, aging him. *Not that I know how old he is*, she thought to herself, *in fact, what's his name, again?*

On the bedside table, Holly's phone buzzed to life. Before she had a chance to reach out for it, it buzzed a second time, and then a third. The glow of the screen and the insistent sound wasn't enough to stir her guest, he was in too deep a sleep.

She read the messages with a smile, her heart full for the first time that night.

Another one?

Are you OK – was it worth it?

I'm halfway through Poe. Join me?

He always asked, but she never went.

She pondered his questions; his concern. She saw him across the road, his phone on the table, the screen dark, but he was waiting for her response. She hoped he could sense her looking, her appreciation.

Standing, Holly tiptoed across the room and pulled on the jeans she'd so readily discarded a couple of hours ago. The moonlight didn't allow her to pick her underwear out amongst the pile of clothes that lay strewn around the bed, so she pulled on her over-sized University sweater and felt the familiar tingle of arousal she got when she was *sans underwear*. Except this time, she wasn't on the hunt – not in the usual way.

Would she make it across the road this time? She was unsure. She slipped the house key into her pocket. Behind her, through the little window, she could hear the gradual fall of rain. Full of good intentions, she slipped from the room, towards the front door.

She wanted to be different. Maybe he was the answer. She had to see.

Nina Peck

El Trabajo, the Job

A feather fluttered into her sight as she walked along the side street towards the town centre. She knew instantly what it meant for a feather to land in her path and she grimaced in annoyance. 'Dang! Not today,' said El.

El was still reconciling what her 'el Trabajo' was, or what her accountability to be a Feather Responder, Crisis Interventionist, Accidental Angel meant. No matter what she called herself, she wasn't up for any Feather call outs today. She wanted to be making merry with her girl pack at the local pub, shops, café; gossip and just abandon the responsibilities of her calling, so she crossed the street.

As she raised her foot onto the footpath, there was the feather, in fact two feathers. In believing she had dodged a job, an el Trabajo, she had been given a combo or possibly two jobs, dos Trabajos. Being on call was another part of her calling that El struggled with, and feeling dismayed, she bent down and picked up the feathers and proceeded on her way.

El's steps were leaden with dread, and dreadfulness encompassed her outlook of faceless victims, writhing in pain and yet she still went forward to the meet-up venue. Her attitude didn't improve on seeing her girlfriends either.

The café was ground zero for their day's outing and El was on tender hooks waiting for her job to appear, and she didn't really contribute to the excited chatter about the day's activities, she just kept saying, 'I might be called away for work,' to a response of: 'rubbish, work is not on our agenda today.'

The problem was, that the girls thought El was primarily a Victim Support Officer, with First Response Paramedics. It was easier for them to understand the functions of her job that way, than to question why she was present at the scene of so many accidents. She wasn't prepared to divulge the mechanics of what she did or that she received her work alerts via a feather, and that her destiny was to intercept a crisis, usually accidental, and pending death.

Her reality, and that of her friends, were sliding door moments of calling. She was often asked to speak about el Trabajos, and how her accidental presence, somehow altered the course of events and saved lives without any supernatural rescue methods. Her online blogging had gathered enough of a following to attract financial investment to enable her to venture out as a writer of misadventure and intrigue stories.

The coffee and cake wasn't strong enough to spur El into a caffeinated high, but she went along with the others, engaging when asked and hoping like heck it wasn't going to be one of her girlfriends that needed her help. A constant fear to El was the thought of having to respond to a job that involved a loved one or someone that she knew. She had no control on choosing el Trabajos, each Job was called to respond, without volition. Apart from her relentless unease, she stayed present.

First on the itinerary was the leather or lace challenge. Everyone had to buy a leather or lace item from the op shop within a 30-minute timeframe. The purchased item, then had to be worn throughout the day. El had drawn leather from the lucky dip and the other four women went about the musty op shop squealing and giggling at what was on offer. An eighties styled red leather belt with a huge buckle was El's choice and she pulled her blouse out from her trousers and put the belt on, to appease her fashion sensibilities. It kinda looked cool she thought, even though her tummy griped as she tightened the belt. She put that feeling down to feathery nerves. A group photo of five women with random bits of leather and lace accessorising their clothing and off to test the retail market.

Second on the itinerary, they each drew a number, from 1 to 5. The number corresponded to five retail neighbouring outlets and again, 30 minutes to purchase something. The industrial area proved to be an unknown for most of the women, so that was the chosen location of their next challenge. El had drawn 3, it was an industrial chain store, displaying huge metal chains and pulley things. What the heck was she going to get from here, she thought as she entered the store. The coldness of the steel outweighed the size of some of this store's products and she felt the chill in her chest of being in an uncomfortable place.

The 'Can I help you, madam?' was generous but definitely without intent of assistance, he was just having a laugh at her expense. El responded with 'You certainly may, I'd like to see what I can get for five dollars?' The assistant laughed, a 'do you know where you are lady?' to El's 'of course, I do,' and though she'd now gone from being a madam to a lady, whether this conversation was spiralling downward or not, she again asked to see any products for five dollars. El could sense time being wasted with this backwards and forwards dialogue and pulled out her phone to google the shop and price range of products. This action must have frightened the assistant and he quickly advised that a pack of industrial ball bearings had been opened and that she could buy one for five dollars eighty-five. He showed El the item, she liked it, paid for it and left a bewildered assistant to query 'what just happened?'

Another group photo, with products and purchases ranging from five dollars eighty-five to $585 plus. El's ball bearing and her friend that bought the tek screws were the only ones able to take their items. The party supplies, forklift licence training, a banner from the sign shop were purchases yet to be supplied. El attached her ball bearing to her buckle and her tummy lurched, a little steely this time. Still no Job.

It was lunch time and the girl pack always chose to dine at the latest eatery on these outings. A new 'share plate' place had opened, and they were lucky that this day was one of the days that was open for lunch. It was licenced as well, which added to its attraction. The only possible drawback was they randomly selected their venues and with no booking, this could cause a rethink.

Off the Market, a foodie pun-named restaurant, that sourced its food from local producers: fresh, homegrown and all that organic, good-for-you marketing was close to the industrial area and they did consider walking there but didn't.

Food was the only thing that was free choice, sometimes they had crazy challenges with food, not today. Everyone easily settled into the industrial meets farm barn restaurant when one of the girls, said 'no knickers' challenge.

El ewwwed at the thought. Her unsolicited visions were enough to make her want to pay the penalty for not participating, however, an unknown penance could be a problem too. El was still out of the vibe of this meetup, but she was trying her darndest to join in. They decided to wait until after lunch for the start of this challenge, as no one wanted to be put off their food with fanny talk and images, although it was probably flashing across everyone's mind.

Salads and Sauvignon, veggies and more Sauvignon, seafood pasta with Sauvignon and water, was the share menu. El held back from the wine, awaiting el Trabajos and she still wasn't feeling that great. Her tummy kept spiking signs of disturbance that she put down to nerves brought on by her reluctance to do this job; or it could be indigestion. As the last toast to the day was glass-clinked, they all proceeded to the rest rooms to de-knicker.

El had just got into a toilet cubicle, when she heaved and buckled in pain. She fell forward over the toilet, the pain and accompanying screams slammed her upright into the door. The girls were busy pulling up knickers, banging on the door, screaming out to her, 'What's wrong? Open the door El.' The pain was excruciating for El and as she turned to open the door, the feathers fell from her purse and she felt a trickle down the inside of her leg. She collapsed.

The Job had arrived ...

Apikara

Behind the Smile

The smell of coffee brewing filled Sarah's nostrils. She tapped her manicured nails on the bench as she waited. It had been a busy week. An even busier weekend. Her muscles still ached from the workout she did yesterday.

Her phone lit up, alerting her to a comment on Facebook. She smiled as she went to the notification. Her friend had commented on a photo they had taken the night before. Their smiling faces beamed at the camera. Cheeks flushed from dancing; eyes slightly glazed from the one-too-many cocktails.

'Best night in ages, Sarah! Let's do it again soon! xo'

Sarah paused as she thought of a response and then typed a reply: 'Had so much fun, Belz. Love you! Don't you forget it!'

Sarah suddenly remembered she hadn't checked the mailbox that week. Coffee forgotten she went outside. She was peering into the mailbox when she heard a familiar voice.

'Hi, Sarah. How are you?' Next door, Julie was watering the lawn.

'Hi,' Sarah smiled. 'I'm great thanks. Just enjoying a quiet Sunday.'

They chatted briefly until Sarah looked towards her front door.

'Have a good week, Sarah. Let's try and catch up for coffee some time.'

'Uh, yeah, maybe.' Sarah smiled again. 'Hey, thanks for being a great neighbour.'

They waved and Sarah went back inside. She prepared her coffee. With her steaming cup in hand, she went around and closed the curtains.

She took her photo album from the shelf and sat in her favourite chair. As she turned each page, Sarah smiled as she remembered the captured moments. Graduating from university with a nursing degree. Holidays by the beach. Family. Friends. She examined the features of her face. Bright eyes, smooth skin. A wide smile. That girl looked free and happy.

She had everyone fooled, even herself. Those photos, they hadn't caught the moments in between.

She savoured the taste of her coffee while she flicked through the album. When she was done with both, she put them aside.

Taking a deep breath, she reached under the couch and slid her hand around, searching. She found what she was after. The anti-depressants rattled as she pulled it out. Sarah read the unopened container. Her name stood out in bold, black letters.

It's going to be okay, she told herself. Twisting the cap, she broke the seal.

Then she took the whiskey from the table. One by one, she put the tablets in her mouth and each time took a sip of whiskey to wash them down. She grimaced, each mouthful getting harder and harder to swallow.

And then she was done. Gagging, choking, dizzy, confused. This is what life had been like for her, in between the 'happy' moments. What she kept hidden. The brightness of her smile hid the darkness within.

*

Her home swirled as her vision clouded. As her grip loosened and the whiskey bottle fell to the floor, the home phone rang.

Then it beeped as the answering machine clicked on. A voice filled the room.

'Hello, Sarah. It's Nicole. Just checking on you because you missed your therapy session on Friday. I wanted to see if you had started taking the medication yet. Hope you are doing okay. Call me when you get this ... hope to hear from you soon. Bye.'

There was one last beep. Then nothing.

Suzanne M. Faed

He Wore Yellow

You know, lying here, looking up at all this blackness, I sometimes wonder what's really out there. When I was little, I thought the sky was like a floor, not a roof, like it was the floor of heaven and that on the other side of the stars was where God and the angels lived. I thought that's where you went when you died. Did you ever get told that? That heaven was 'out there' somewhere?

I wonder, how did the explorers even know where to go just by using the stars? And the sailors, how did they know how to get to point A to point B just using the stars? Who taught them?

I imagine sometimes, when I lie here, what it was like. Especially for the ones who discovered things no one had before; putting their faith in the stars and the boats and the wind, and just sailing into the unknown. It's pretty fucken brave, right? Ballsy and a bit crazy.

People used to tell me I was crazy and ballsy once too. Not anymore though.

They also said I talked too much, but I don't really think that was true, and it certainly isn't anymore … but it's been so long since I had someone to natter on to, so … sorry if I go on a bit then.

*

Oh! Don't be frightened, that's just a kangaroo – a Yongar. They come by here sometimes. I think this place is sort of like a bit of a, not a road, but like a pathway for them; they use it to try to get to that bit of bush across the road – they said there's some good tucker across there, but then, the water is on this side, so they have to come back again. It's sad to see them cross the road. A lot of them get caught on this bend. I mean, they're sweet creatures and all, but they have no road sense. They're a bit daft. The headlights is what does them in. I think they get spazzed out by them – like the deer back home. I've counted fifteen dead ones so far just in this area.

*

People say that Australia is a dangerous place because it contains some of the deadliest animals on the planet.

Did you know that? No?

Ask me about them.

Go on …

Really … just ask away.

Well, for starters, there are around 140 species of land snakes and about thirty-two species of sea snakes identified – mad, hey? And, of these 100 are venomous; although only twelve of these would kill you. Spiders? Everyone hates them, but really, they're not as bad as people make out – more people die from bee stings, and people think bees are cute. You just can't tell with killers, right? Then there's deadly jellyfish, man-eating sharks, crocodiles, stonefish, cone shells, stingrays, cassowaries … all up, it's a dangerous, but beautiful country.

I know so much about Australia – well for a Pommy girl any way. I'm like a walking, talking encyclopaedia.

I always dreamed about Australia. I couldn't read enough about it when I was young. Poured over the encyclopaedias and watched everything I could about it on telly. My Aunt Laura came here once, travelled around and sent me postcards from just about everywhere; Uluru, and Mission Beach, Sydney, heaps from Tasmania and one from Coober Pedy up on my wall, and once she sent me a long fold out postcard thing from WA and it was all I could dream of. I always wanted to be a gypsy woman like her. Wanted to see this place for myself, you know? So mysterious and old and beautiful – I didn't think of the dangers, because all I saw was the beauty. And the possibilities.

I saw beaches with the whitest sand, and the most stunning blue waters – blues like the colours in the fine Turkish glass beads I picked up going through Istanbul, blues like the Aegean Sea. I saw wide open skies, days filled with sunshine and nights filled with endless stars spinning above me. I saw the friendliest of people who, despite living in a caravan park full of drama and using funny phrases like 'stone the crows' and 'flaming heck', enjoyed the life that I dreamt of and I wanted to run right into it – just like they run right into the waves. Even if it was just telly – well the last bit anyway; I'd heard the stories from Aunt Laura and some of her friends and I was hooked.

When I was a bit older, she told me about the Aussie blokes, and that kind of settled it for me, I mean, hello – tanned and buff, down to earth and so goddamn sexy. I was completely sold when she gave me a calendar of the smoking-hot firefighters in not much, not even their yellow pants. I mean, yes please, and thank you very much – I'll take two.

Have you travelled much?

No? That's sad.

I have.

I was nineteen when I backpacked France solo so that was a good starting point – not too far from home – I mean, catching two or three trains from anywhere could have me back home-side in no time really. I can speak French quite well. I just *loved* the South. And Paris. *Loved* Paris – my Aunt Laura was shacked up with a poet named Cesar in the Latin Quarter then, so I never felt really alone. It wasn't like disappearing on the other side of the world.

After France, well, I went home, and I worked a lot, and saved a bit and then tried Eastern Europe. This time I went with Cassie – she's a bloody nutter that one – and we worked the standard backpacking jobs that you only find out about when you're in the questionably clean hostels, or couch-surfing in other traveller's divey, too-many-peopled apartments, or the jobs you found out about because you were a pretty, white, big-boobed blonde who liked to have a laugh and could hold her own when drinking with the lads. But we had heaps of fun; worked loads of different jobs, met some nice people. I felt like I was living my best life. I feel bad for people who don't get to travel. I always took it for granted that I'd be able to move around and explore the world – so I'm glad I got to while I could.

Cassie and I went over to Turkey too. Turkey was amazing. It's a shame you never saw that place. Oh my God! The food! It's to die for – not like the shite kebabs they sell back home, and the local brew, Efes, is really yummy – you don't have to worry about not being able to drink there, for a Muslim country, they're pretty cool as long as you're respectful. And, oh man, in Cappadocia you should see the hot air balloon-filled skies; it's a bit touristy, but so worth it. I went up in one at dawn, rising above the landscape, the gas roaring overhead. I felt like an angel going up to heaven, but, ha! I don't think angels drink champagne as they ascend. It was truly beautiful. We watched the sun rise and creep over the land, its changing colours shut me up for a bit and the air was so fresh, I felt like I was breathing for the first time. I pretended that I was a bird. I still remember how that felt, to feel so free, like I could go anywhere, fly anywhere I wanted just by looking and deciding to go.

Of course, traveling wasn't all great. You must trust people and, you know, there were typical red flags you found, the blokes that were too nice, too accommodating, and took payment however they wanted. It happened to me once.

I haven't had anyone to chat with for so long.

It's not so bad though, you get used to it after a bit.

I've decided that trees have their own language and I tried to crack their code. I don't think they so much as use words, but they seem to talk with intent. Funny isn't it, thinking of talking without words? At first, I think they were curious about me, they didn't say much, but after a while, I guess, when they knew I wasn't going to hurt them and I wasn't going anywhere, they chilled out a bit. Now they bring me little whispers, usually if a 'roo has been hit nearby, or sometimes if there's been an accident or something. I don't know how they know things, it's not like they have eyes like us, but they see *everything*. And they talk. So much. It's all in the way they move their leaves and the way the feelings of the bush change. I can teach you to understand them, if you like.

Sometimes I don't hear the sirens. Maybe I'm asleep, or just … away? The days kinda just roll into each other really. Oh, I mean, I can tell when the seasons are changing, for sure. I love the wildflowers. Remind me to show you this beautiful orchid that comes out in Djilba. I think it's around August, the nights don't seem as long then and the wattles blaze yellow through the greens and browny-greys of the bush. It's like a tell-tale sign, all that yellow. Like a beacon, or maybe like a warning that change is coming. And, yes! you'll love this … just down the hill a bit is a patch of Boronia. Have you ever smelt Boronia before? Oh my God. It's heavenly. I sleep there sometimes when it's flowering. Sometimes when I wake up, it's gone and I'm sad and I think, *for fucks sake Jilly, now you have to wait until next year!* Grrr … but it never seems I have to wait too long though. Swings and roundabouts, summer to winter, spring to autumn blah, blah, blah, on and on it goes.

It was the trees that told me he was here again.

Fuck him! I wish I could push him out in front of a truck or something.

He's been here before, you know. He came here once, pulled up near the bin over there at the rest stop, got out of his car and wandered right over and pissed on me. Can you believe that! Fuck me! What a tosser. And then do you know what he said? He said;

'How's the ground feeling, girl? Are you just bones yet?'

And then do you know what he did? While his knob was still in his hands, he started talking about how he dreams of me, how he remembers how I taste and what my cunt felt like. He said he still has my knickers that he saves for his special times and he can still smell me if he breathes 'real deep'. It was disgusting, right? He asked if it was me causing all the trouble on the road, and that I was doing a good job of keeping people away because now people are saying that this stretch of road is cursed. He reckons that people say they've seen a woman standing on the verge. They say the ghost lady is causing the trouble. I mean, it could have been me, I do watch the traffic sometimes … I don't know anyone else who's hung around for that long here.

Oh, I see some of the *old ones* every now and again. Sometimes I hear them playing didgeridoos and then they wander through singing the boodja – that's what they call the land – and chatting away in their language … but we can always still understand each other. Funny buggers, they always have a joke with me. They say, 'hello,' and that one day I can join them and move on from the space between 'this' and into the dreaming. They're very kind. Their teeth are so white against their dark skin when they smile. They said they'll be here when I need them. I just need to sing.

With the others, I only get to have a little chat and then next time I wake up they're gone. Sometimes I go and sit next to their crosses, or their spray-painted trees. Sometimes I hug the teddy bears, but they never really come back. And then it's just the bush for conversation.

That's why I was just a bit excited when the trees whispered, he was here again, and he wasn't alone.

I remember arriving here. It was all a bit of bloody shock let me tell you! I don't know how I came to be next to him, out here, but here I was, and there he was, and I felt so scared, not knowing where I was, why I was out here, why everything was so quiet, why I felt like we were being watched. So, I tried to hide, right there, behind that tree. I wanted to run away, but I couldn't go. So, I stayed. He didn't see me anyway.

I don't remember much about the before bit, I mean, how it all happened, although sometimes I dream of things, but I don't know if they're just dreams of *it* or if they are memories …

I remember meeting him; it was my last night at work. I was heading up North next. But he was so handsome – in that rugged Aussie way; I thought, *here we go Jilly, chuck another shrimp on that barbie,* he was bloody fit as. He was charming and funny. Was he like that with you?

Yeah, figures. Wolves in sheeps clothing …

He wasn't what I thought he would be. He ticked all my boxes; he was calendar worthy; and when he showed me pictures of him at work – action shots – whoa. I must admit that I wanted to let him check my other box. I know. I sound like such a slut, but honest, I'm not. I appreciate a fine male specimen, true, but I have standards. He had a way of teasing me just a bit, you know? Flirted with me straight off, said how I talked was cute. He had me say things like: 'G'day mate,' 'bonza day,' and 'Dazza's a dardy drongo divvying up the durries in the dunny,' well, that last one we used to play shots with … after.

He'd had a late shift, come in to relax, have some coldies and have a bit of a chat and then I met him for staffies after the pub closed. He was so nice to start with, and then stupidly I went back to his for more drinks.

Did you work in a pub too?

Oh, a café …

It was all going well, shaping up to be a nice night, he asked me heaps of questions about home and my family and how much I'd travelled. I thought he thought I was interesting. I thought *maybe Jilly, maybe this is your ticket to the colonies*, you know, snag an Aussie and get citizenship. I never wanted to go home, back to grey skies and the bloody cold, all I wanted to do was stay here forever. And then the shots turned into stripping dares, and then, well, I was feeling so good and relaxed – probably *too* relaxed now I think of it, and I just didn't care about anything except shagging him. Terrible. I know how it sounds …

And then he … well … he said he was used to rescuing people and asked me if I wanted to be saved from a bad man, and I thought, ok, well obviously he's a bit of a kinky bastard, and it turned me on, I got a flutter in my fanny, so I said yes … Then he tied me up, you know, wrists together above my head, tethered to his bed, prisoner like, and told me that he was going to be the bad man first and then he would come and rescue me, and he'd even wear his uniform. I just went along, I mean, nothing else I could do right, when trussed up like a roast goose?

I don't think I was really concerned until the dirty talking got too serious.

'You're not going anywhere are you, you dirty little whore?' he licked his lips. 'Tell me, girl.' he whispered that bit so close to my ear that I felt his sharp stubble scratch my cheek. His eyes were fixed on me, pupils blown in excitement.

'I'm not going anywhere.'

'Nup. Got you right where I want you. Right under me. Haven't I? Haven't I?' he demanded. The look in his eye changed then. Gone was the look of sinful encouragement and false promises, in its place was a darkness, cold and cruel. His breath hit me first, the putridness of it, stale with alcohol and cigarettes and malice.

I shivered, goose bumps covering my body. He wasn't playing now; was he ever?

'Yes,' my voice was barely above a whisper.

'Are you scared, bitch?' he was calm, his voice was low.

I couldn't talk. My mouth had gone dry. My muscles could hardly move from fear so I could only nod my head.

'I'm going to be it for you, girl. No more after me.' The monster in him growled this out in a slow, gravelly voice.

I remember him straddling me, heavy over my hips, weighing me down and smoking a ciggie; I remember ash falling off the end and into my eye … and then I felt the burn of it when he put it out on me arm, right on the soft bit. That bloody hurt.

Well, I wasn't very happy about that as you can imagine. I tried to get him off me then, I tried to fight him, but he had me pinned down, just like one of those collectors who pin bugs to boards and labels them. I couldn't move, and then of course, I was tied up, and my body felt so heavy, like I was trying to move through sand. I think I tried to buck him off, but he was too heavy and then he hit me right in the mouth … with a bloody closed fist too! What a fucker!

After that, I don't remember very much at all, it's still hazy, even after all this time. I do remember him touching me. I didn't want him to; I wanted him to stop; I didn't like the feel of him …

I do remember seeing him a while later, being right next to him, smelling his stank-ass breath and his body sweat tinged with excitement, and cigarette smoke on his clothes and on his hands. He was carrying something wrapped in an old bedspread. And then, I was next to *me*. I was looking down at my face.

It's strange; even though it looked like me, it really wasn't me.

My hair was matted and stained for starters. Lots of blood, turned from 'blood red' to 'russet red', spots of rust flaking on my cheeks … even the colours didn't want to stay here anymore; and I was … kind of greyish, like old tofu grey. Not even my lips were red anymore. Gross. Even though it was night, it wasn't dark. Not at all. I could see everything. Everything in super detail.

Don't you think it's amazing how much we can see now? Like, before, it was though we were looking through muddy water or smokey air all the time – but now! Wow. So. Clear.

Also, I remember that he had dug the hole first, like he did with you.

I tried to push him in this time. I *was* brave and I tried to fight him. More than I did before. But it didn't work of course – straight through him. I really yelled at him, gave him a proper serve. Screamed even. Asking him what did I do? Why me? but just empty words. No one hears them.

Did you hear me yelling at him before? I'm sorry if I scared you. I was pretty wild about things. The fucking nerve of him to come back here. I want to fucking kill him. Decimate him.

The trees heard. They don't like him either.

Did you see how it all went?

Oh … don't feel bad … that probably means that you weren't, you know, here just yet. Maybe you were still hanging on.

Do you want to know?

Ok then.

So, he had you wrapped up in a blanket, I couldn't even tell who you were at that time, and he carried you like he was a groom carrying his fucking bride over the threshold, like a fucking hero carrying a damsel in distress – I mean, he was, well, tender I guess. And then he came to your bed – I'm calling it a bed, not a hole – and he place you down, really gently. He uncovered your face then, said to you:

'I'll never forget you, Celeste, thanks for the memories.'

Are you ok? Don't cry … shhh, it's ok. It's ok. I'm here now, Jilly will look after you. It's all going to be ok. Oh, you have really lovely hair, it's such a pretty colour and the way it curls …

Are you sure you want me to go on? Ok then. Where was I?

And then he went back to his car and he … are you sure you want to hear this bit?

Ok.

Well, he bought back a long gun – a rifle maybe? And, this is so gross, he, ugh, he reached into his pocket and pulled out your knickers and he, well, he sniffed them and held them to his nose. Well, he, oh gawd, he wanked all over you like the depraved psycho that he is. Said something about sowing his seeds and when he was done, he, well, I turned away so I didn't have to see it, he shot you in the head. To make sure, I guess. Then he covered you over. He said that they were burning this area tomorrow, and no one would ever find you just like they never found me, and that hiding us in plain sight was 'bloody genius' and that if you see me, to say hi.

He laughed. He actually laughed when he shovelled the sand and gravel on top of you. What a sick prick! I think he got a splinter though from the logs he dragged over you. I hope it gets infected.

And, then he packed up his shit and drove off.

They did burn this area the next day. He was right. They do that every few years here, to stop bushfires, I think.

It's a bit weird now. The land. The trees talk is different, sad almost. Like they go into themselves for a bit. Things are … quiet.

I was waiting to see if you were going to stop on by.

The fire did a great job of hiding you. At hiding us.

He came back when the ground was still smoking. He was wearing yellow. He came back, kicked the embers around with his big black boots, and he smiled.

He blew us a kiss.

Lee Harsen

Mary the Scary Fairy

Before I start
Here's the deal
I know for a fact
That fairies are real!
They live far away
In fairy locations
They have fairy towns
With fairy train stations

My story today
Tells of Mary the fairy
She's a little bit different
Our Mary is scary
Other fairies wear glitter
From their heads to their toes
Mary wears makeup
With a ring through her nose

Her friends wear pink dresses
Mary dons an old sack
They have silver wings
But Mary's are black
Fairies love to dance ballet
Doing pliés at the bar
But Mary loves head banging
And riffing guitar

At school they all whisper
'She's not a normal fairy'
When she flies into class
They shout out 'Scary Mary'

At lunch she's alone
She doesn't know why
Everybody's eating fairy bread
Mary's eating snail pie

Music lessons are funny
The class is learning to sing
Except for Scary Mary
Smashing drums is Mary's thing
And fairies love Christmas
But that's not Mary's scene
She can't wait till October
Her favourite holiday Halloween

Now I know what you're thinking
That Mary's lonely and sad
That she has no friends
And the fairies think that she's bad
But my friends that's not quite true
Although she is quite scary
Every fairy in town
Really, really loves Mary

At weekends you will find her
At the fairy nursing home
Caring for old fairies
And sometimes garden gnomes
After school she's cooking dinners
For the fairies with no money
She bakes them toadstool cakes
All covered in honey

The reason she loves Halloween so much
Is to play trick or treat
And give her candy to Goblins
In the hope they'll be sweet
Mary's mum is so proud of her
And her dad just beams with pride
'Yes, she is different,' he says
But her beauty is inside

And of all the fairies everywhere
Mary always wins by a mile
The Annual Competition
'The Fairy with the biggest smile'
So though Mary looks quite scary
She is a shining star
Like Mary be happy
Be proud of who you are!

Mark Townsend

Hook, Line and Sinker

'Ever had a crush on a girl that made you do something you regretted, Felix?' Sick of more footy talk, Tom threw something personal in the mix. Footy seemed so trivial right now, he had something more consuming on his mind.

'Well, yeah, probably, I'd find it hard to pick one though. I mean with regrets, I've had a few.'

'Care to try?' His head tilted in invitation, 'I've seen you run from a few girls, but hasn't one of them stuck with you a bit?'

'Not really. Want another beer mate?' A sledgehammer deflection, Tom conceded with a nod. Felix would share beers, but rarely heartfelts. He was ten years younger, but all the talk about the younger generation being more emotionally in touch didn't show with Felix. Tom could see the risk of a whole night of sport and work talk was laid out ahead of him.

'So, here is the thing. In my life Felix, I've had a crush on three different girls, with one thing in common, you know what it is?'

'Are we talking about physical attributes here?'

'No. Surprisingly, I'm not.'

'Ok.' Felix paused then continued deadpan, 'because I was going to say each had two arms. So that's not it?' He was smirking now.

'Smart arse, I set the bar higher than Prickles, mate,' they both looked across the room and sure enough Prickles was there, cornering a girl with a cigarette pack stuffed down her top, his beer goggles firmly focused on her arse as she abruptly walked away sneering. Hilarious in its timeliness, they laughed as one. 'All three were rather easy on the eye actually, high cheekbones, sexy eyes.'

'So, they all turned you down then, perhaps gently with a story of a boyfriend I'm guessing; that it?'

'You're quick tonight mate, but since you're such an idiot, I'll tell you the answer myself. They all worked in a bakery, serving hot buns.'

Felix pushed out a disbelieving laugh, throwing his hands outward and up. 'How was I s'posed to guess that?' Then, breathing the words lasciviously, 'Hey Tom, you like some hot, butt-er-y bread?'

'That was quite good Felix, but here's the thing. One of them exists now, I saw her just this morning.'

'Whoaaa married man, what you saying, brother?' Felix leant back on the bar stool as he flowed theatrically through the performative line.

'Look stay cool, nothing much has happened, I felt like telling someone, that's all. You may have noticed I was a bit edgy and distracted at work today. I'm curious about this girl, it's a kind of research thing.'

'What kind of research?' Felix did the air quotes in the air with his stumpy fingers.

'Well, I know you don't get this writing thing that I do. But in the group, we're set writing challenges. The current one is to write a little sex action into a story.'

'And?'

'I told the cute young blonde girl at my local bakery all about it. How I was finding it tricky, was feeling blocked.'

'Maaaate, you serious, and you used the words *sex action* with her?

'I did. It began with a bit of a playful conversation, I dropped it in harmlessly, that was all really. I may have twisted the truth a little. Said I was a published writer – which is partly true – if anthologies count. I sensed she was a bit more into me after that.'

'Makes sense, I'd be impressed.' Then the kicker, 'if someone my Dad's age said that!'

'Settle down, you're just jealous mate. Next thing it got a bit flirty between us, well that was my read into it, her eyes were locked in and lively. It felt damn good. As we were chatting, I was telling myself *shut up old man* but then at the same time I was thinking what she'd be like, you know so young and full of eagerness. I was impressed at my composure actually, given that I was undressing her in my mind at the time.'

'Alright, stop. This is all very fanciful, but your missus, what about her?'

'Trish? I'm sure she fantasises too.' Tom's mirth was quickly slapped down by Felix.

'I mean, what about her Tom!?'

Tom responded calmly, in control. 'She's away on business, not back until Tuesday, I think, and Carmel – that's her name – she said we could catch up tomorrow after her lunch shift. Brainstorm some plot ideas, she likes to write too, poetry and song lyrics mostly, but she might be able to help. She'll come over once she's finished selling *hot, butt-er-y croissants.*' Tom mimicked Felix's earlier effort. Felix just looked at him, mouth ajar, disbelieving. Tom steadied, 'Look, I'm not saying where this will go, nothing has happened yet. Breathe mate.'

'Tom I can see it in your eyes. You saw what Sheps went through last year, all over a *harmless, getting lucky fling* on a footy trip. Madness.' Felix was almost whispering now, with some urgency coursing through him, 'You're not like the other guys here mate, for one thing, you write stuff! And I see you step back when the guys get that blokey bravado kicking in; overriding their brain cells. If I had troubles, shit mate, I'd be asking you what to do.' Felix went to take a swig of beer, but paused his forearm at the forty-five, 'I think Trish is pretty hot too by the way.'

Tom went from the glued, unshifting listener to one slightly pleased, 'Yeah, she is, I'm lucky in some ways hey?'

'That's why I'm telling you, I think this is a mistake, it can't end well. I think you should write that story tonight, have a beat if you must and move on, put this Carmel crush behind you.' Felix suddenly grabbed Tom's arm, leant closer and erupted into a wheezing laugh, 'Car-a-mel Crush, Hah Hah Hah, Car-a-mel Crush ... oh, that's too good!' More uncontrollable laughter and Tom once again looked amused and broke into a laugh or two himself. Felix was one of the younger players that Tom hung out with. In moments like this, he was a funny bugger and it was interesting to hear his take on things. But on receiving advice; he wasn't so sure.

Tom saw a chance for a laugh himself. He leaned in and whispered to Felix's ear as he was still recovering from his fit, 'Inspiration is coming Felix, I'm going to unwrap the baker's daughter, I am. Peel off her body hugging cotton tee, slide my hands over her hot, butt-er-y butt as I work her pants down. I'll lay her down on a plump bed of hessian flour sacks and decorate her pert young breasts in raw sugar crystals for my tongue to garnish. Oh, my hot Car-a-mel crush, I'll cry out above the beeping oven timer, as I work her into a writhing blissful state of sliding fondue ecstasy before I pene ...'

'Shut it Tom!' Felix wasn't laughing anymore. 'You're a seedy bugger, making yourself out to be a writer and all, get a grip, how old is this Carmel?'

'Old enough to drive. She's driving to mine tomorrow. Hey, it could have been worse, she could have been called Candy,' Felix looked quizzically at Tom, not seeming to get the joke, staying serious.

'I can't talk you out of this can I? I mean truth be told, you really want to shag her, don't you?

'I never said that.'

'Not everything needs to be said, though, does it?'

'I'm doing research, that is all. I'll see what I can write without her, but chances are by the time she gets to mine tomorrow, I'll not have it nailed. A brainstorm session could be just a little fun that gives me the piece I'm after.'

'You getting the piece you're after is what I'm concerned about. Here's a coaster, start writing, show me what you've got.'

'Really, you suddenly a Writing Coach?'

'Call it a Life Coach, I'm saving you from making a big fuckin' mistake.'

'It's got beer stains on it.'

'Lots of things we do leave a stain, Tom. Start writing.'

*

Tom looked a little grudgingly at his phone as it vibrated on the kitchen countertop. It was Felix, checking in on him. The typical kind of morning after conversation followed, centred around how's your head reports and various humorous recollections.

These conversations rarely centred on Tom. But not this time. For starters Felix was asking about Tom's progress beyond his opening line. 'You mean the first lame line on the beer coaster I wrote to shut you up last night? It's no good Felix.' Then onto the Carmel situation. As Tom laid the situation out more clearly for Felix, he wondered whether it was for his benefit too. This was new ground after all, he was trying to understand his own motives.

'Inspiration is the key here, nothing else matters; and I may just have found a little of that with Carmel. I'll catch you tonight at the pub, OK?' Tom added teasingly, 'if I'm not otherwise entertained that is, it's awfully quiet here with Trish being away.'

'You're a tosser Tom. Behave. And yes, see you later, should be your buy though, you're causing me to worry and when I worry, I need a beer.' The green button on the display switched to red as Tom considered whether he should have said anything to Felix at all last night; perhaps he would have preferred the longer tenure a secret entwined between two can bring.

Felix was in a different life phase, at that age there were plenty of opportunities for him. Tom smiled at the thought of Felix as *The Very Hungry Caterpillar*, with so many treats parading before him, working across the dancefloor, concertinaed; chomping watermelon, ice cream and butter cake. The thought that Felix might understand his longing now, his ache; how ridiculous it was!

Tom stood still looking down, his phone now hushed, he watched the screen return to the wallpaper picture of Trish. That took him back to the Central Coast weekend away, her laughing eyes. He recalled how much fun it was, how much sex they'd had; and how they'd agreed at the time they should get away together more often. If only they did, before she started working away so much and being home became all too boringly special for her. At least he could write while she was ignoring him.

Picking up his phone he went to the settings and changed the wallpaper pic to an emergent butterfly easing out of its sleepy-eyes cocoon. He was chuffed when he got that picture but hadn't thought of it holding too much meaning for him; until now. Tom looked across to his office, he needed to make that coffee and write something to escape again. It was his way to wander, always just on paper, but today, the idea felt claustrophobic, like he wanted more.

What if Carmel didn't come?

*

'You're here to buy me a beer mate? I thought you weren't coming.'

'You know I look forward to our weekend catch-ups Felix, I was always going to make it, what could possibly keep me away?' Tom smiled too brightly. 'You had a good Sunday Felix?'

Tom beckoned the bartender to bring Felix another pint and him his first. The beer of the week was called Hook, Line and Sinker; a great name.

'Yeaahhhh.' it was a drawn out yeah, the kind rolled out with a mind ticking over, 'I had an active day. After I called you, I worked up a thirst on that new mountain biking track up Sandy Split way. Took Jack Hanbury along.'

'Jack Hanbury? You mean The Cleaner?' Tom looked surprised, especially because when Felix last asked him, he'd declined partly out of a fear of falling.

'The very one, I was impressed how well he kept up, it was his first run up there too, but we both nearly wiped out on a switch back where a tree was down. Could have been ugly, he's older, would scar up bad I'd guess.' Felix switched gear, 'But enough about that, how was your day? Did young Carmel show up?'

'Well, actually, I was thinking about closing the vault on that matter.'

'Hey?'

'Well after you hung up this morning, I began wondering why I'd told you anything at all about Carmel last night. It dawned on me, you're only twenty-five, unattached and free of real responsibilities, so how could you begin to understand what I'm going through right now?'

'We're mates, that means we listen to each other when it's needed.' Felix was so matter of fact.

'Hmmm, that is true. But rather than burden you with details, I realised I could use you instead as a plot device to develop my story.'

'Nahhhh …' Felix was shaking his head as he uttered the words, 'That's not cool Tom. I don't actually know what a plot device is, but I know I'm your mate and more recently your life coach; by necessity as of twenty-four hours ago if you recall. You have to tell me what happened, at least tell me if she even showed up?'

'Try and understand this, and take it the right way, you're the perfect plot device for me, you help me shape my story, because we're not the same. If I just blurt it all out that's kind of boring, and you learn nothing while thinking you know it all. Instead if I create a little tension between us …'

'Well that's working Tom!'

'… a little tension that makes you desperate to know more, yes? It makes you ask better questions. You're someone for me to butt up against, as I try and understand things better for myself.'

'You admit you're mixed up then?'

'Look, I already know you disagree with me messing with Carmel – not saying it's happening by the way – so what's the point going there with you, when I know what you'll say? Plus, you know Trish, so if I was doing anything on the side, and you knew, I'd have to kill you.' Tom delivered the threat with a smile. He'd never said that set of five words to someone directly. What a thrill it was, even in jest.

'So that's it then, you're keeping your secret from me? Why'd you even buy me this beer?' Felix looked hurt, put out and pissed off.

'Hang on mate, I've more to explain.' Tom took a theatrical swig from his beer and leaned in closer, conspiratorial-like, 'As I said, that's what I decided this morning.' Tom had his left hand perched a little in front of his mouth, the thumb and forefinger also speaking the words carefully, 'But I can tell you more now, because everything has changed since then; after Carmel's visit.'

'So, she did show. And you're prepared to tell me what you got up to?'

'Yes, but not all of it. I'm only telling you the things I need you to know, about Carmel.'

'Go on then.'

'Well look, she is amazing mate; I can't believe she is just nineteen, she's so strong.'

'C'mon mate, did you do her or not?'

'That's not a great question Felix. Like I said, we were going to brainstorm some ideas, but we straight away connected, got to talking, and she opened me right up. I told her about Trish, the disconnect I was feeling.'

'Are you?' Felix looked surprised. Tom didn't notice and careered on.

'She spoke on love and the peculiarities of the emotion, how it works differently for different people. She's a Scorpio and she is right up there for thinking outside the box. She told me she'd never settle down with anyone, why would she do that she said? She shared this concept with me, have you heard of Switch Love Theory?'

'No. Had you?'

'No, I hadn't either. I've looked it up since though, just to check and it's definitely a thing. But Carmel explains it best. She says it's the way we can intently choose to turn love on and off. That as long as our love has a new place to go to, to switch back on, no one gets hurt by the shifting of devotion.

'That's her explaining it clearly?'

'You not following?'

'Not really.'

'Basically, love is split into tastier, bite-size portions, it's always fresh, a pre-arranged flowing exchange on a continuum, love and passion is always there but never needy, there is no scarcity to fear. You see, love can get stale, but not this way. For a while I might be Carmel's lover, then for a while it will be Trish, but always, there is love. What's incredible is they have a whole switchboard system – if you pardon the pun – to help them find their next lover, or 'spark' as they call them. But the key to it all is being able to switch love on and off, and that's the amazing bit, apparently it's quite easy to do it.'

Tom had got carried away and Felix now looked around the room like someone does in a moment of 'are any of you hearing this guy?' He reached across to Tom and began tapping his forehead with his pointer finger while singing softly: 'Ground control to Mixed-up Tom; you have to tell us where you're from; and what the fuck is going on?!'

Tom whacked his arm away, 'This is for real mate!' It was Tom's turn to look put out, he wanted, needed, Felix to understand and be onboard with Switch Love Theory, but at the same time he knew he was acting over excited and slightly crazed.

'Yeah, but c'mon, isn't this sounding a bit woo woo to you as well? Did she explain how Trish fits into this?'

'Well of course she did, that bit's obvious. I've been doing the switch off part already with Trish, turning her off when she goes away, but the switch has jammed for me, and for Trish. That's been hurting me for ages. I did tell Carmel about my crush on her, how it's made me feel suddenly alive.'

'No way! What did she say to that?'

'She said that it's a pure and natural thing, not to run from it, and that it could help bring things back to life with Trish too.'

'Mate you sure, you trust her on that?'

'I do, she also said she could see me being a spark for her, that it could be a lot of fun, I reckon her nipples stood firmer as she said it. She even said my age profile was in her interests list, that I'd be her first thirty-something.' Tom winked at Felix who just offered up a sucking in of air with a *you for real?* look.

Felix spoke across his beer flatly. 'For years you see someone one way, and then they look back at you as another.' Felix gathered himself together some more, tugging his bottom lip. 'What I said last night, about you being different from the rest, it appears you certainly are Tom. One of a kind. But you're not being gullible are you mate? This is big, how could you tell Trish about this? If she sees you with a hot 19-year-old, while telling her about this amazing new theory ... I'm thinking you might get a switch hit rather than a love switch mate.'

'Perhaps, but I think she might listen to me. I'll tell her everything when the time is right. But first I want her to see the change in me.'

'Sounds dangerous Tom.'

'Maybe, but nothing has happened yet, though with an attractive, young blonde a wonderful package of distraction, I completely get how it looks.'

'Good to hear, I was wondering if you did.'

Tom sat up taller, he needed to deliver this right. 'There is something standing in my way though, I got a kick in the guts today and I'm reeling from it actually.'

Felix gave back dryly, 'I'm out of guesses mate, what happened?'

'I found out that on Tuesday, Carmel leaves to go interstate to meet her next spark. The way she put it, one spark leads to another and she can't say when she'll get back to this place.' Tom went quiet.

'It could be for the best mate.'

'I don't agree; Carmel would love me to sort something out and I would too, I've never felt quite like this about a girl before, Felix. It's just two more weeks until Trish leaves again for another three-week stretch. You should have seen the look on Carmel's face when I told her that. That's when she told me, there is another way to make this work.' The answer hung there, silent and hidden from all sides.

'So, what is it?'

'Before I tell you, do you see how this can help things between me and Trish. I know that it might, but can you see that it might help?'

'Not really. Then again, if it would make you happier when she's around, that's a good thing. But I don't want to see you hurt her at all. I didn't know things were so rough for you guys. Is there any way I can help?'

'Well it turns out there is. You might enjoy it too. I haven't just told you all this because I'm excited and full of energy for the first time in a long time. It's because Carmel needs your help, she told me to share this only with you, to trust you, it's a secretive group that she's in.'

Tom continued with care; Felix looked unsure.

'Promise me, this idea I have, you'll let it sink in first. I have to run in a minute, so I'll leave it with you, but Felix, don't discount this straight away. Alright mate?'

'Toommm, you're worrying me, what you getting at?' Felix was immediately on retreat, he knew being asked to keep a promise, was often loaded up in some way.

'Carmel needs a reason to be here for two more weeks, so I need to find her a two-week *spark*. Someone who appreciates her near-perfect female form – she is gorgeous, trust me, perfectly proportioned – but who won't become too obsessed. You told me last night, you don't do crushes, so we're hoping you can be, her spark.'

Felix sat with his mouth hanging open as Tom stood up to walk out. He found some words just in time.

'You want WHAT? Are you making this love switch shit up Tom?'

'I have to go mate, call me later, you'll be doing me and Trish a huge favour!'

The door swung firmly shut behind him.

Dan Depiazzi

103

Even Mummy Farts

My Mummy doesn't fart. She wouldn't do such a thing. Whenever Daddy drops a stink bomb, she shakes her finger at him. 'Peter, that is disgusting! Take your smelly bottom outside.'

Most of the time she needs to open a window. Daddy just laughs. That makes Mummy even grumpier. We like to stir Mummy up, so when my tummy is grumbling, I'll give Daddy my secret signal.

Daddy will say to me, with a twinkle in his eye, 'Toot your horn, Evie.'

I smile and squeeze.

TOOT, TOOT!

We laugh but Mummy shakes her finger at us. 'Honestly, you two are as stinky as each other.'

She waves us outside, shuts the door and opens a window. I wonder if Mummy farts? I find it hard to believe that she could eat baked beans and not squeak out one or two. But my Mummy, she is a *lady*.

One afternoon, Mummy was cooking in the kitchen. I sniffed the air. My eyes watered. It smelt like mouldy banana mixed with wet dog and a dash of sweaty feet.

'Mummy, what's that smell?'

'Must be the rotten eggs in the bin.'

And she kept on making her brownies.

The next day, Mummy was doing exercise. She was on all fours, stretching like a cat that had just woken up. That's when I heard it.

BA-BRAAAAAAAPPPPPPPPPPP!

The noise made me jump. Even our sleeping dog opened his eyes and tilted his head. His nose twitched. He whimpered and covered his snout with his paws.

'Mummy, what was that noise?'

'Must have been some thunder outside.'

And she kept on stretching, her bottom up in the air.

I looked outside but the sky was clear. I watched her suspiciously. Why was she smiling?

The day after, Mummy took me to the swimming pool. I was pretending to be a mermaid when I saw bubbles floating up around Mummy.

'Mummy, where did those bubbles come from?'

'Must be a frog in here.'

And she kept on swimming, even though she doesn't like frogs.

I know that Mummy is a lady but I'm starting to think that even *Mummy* farts.

I begin to watch her closely. I become a fart detective. I follow Mummy around the house, sniffing the air and listening for noises. She goes about her business, as ladylike as can be. I sneak up on her, put my ear to the bathroom door. Nothing. No rotten eggs. No claps of thunder. Not even a frog.

Maybe Mummy really is a lady. But maybe I'll try one last tactic. I'll be bold and just ask her. Then I will know, once and for all.

'Mummy, do you ever … you know … toot your horn?'

'Sometimes I toot the horn in the car,' Mummy says with a smirk. 'But not too much because it's frowned upon.'

I shake my head. 'No, not like that. I mean, do you … *fart?*'

Mummy laughs and flutters her eyelashes. 'Oh no. I'm too much of a lady for that.'

My head drops.

'Evie, can I show you something?' Mummy whispers.

My eyes widen. 'Yes,' I whisper back.

Her eyes twinkle. 'Pull my finger.'

So I do.

BA-BRAAAAAAAPPPPPPPPPPP!

We burst into laughter.

'See. Sometimes, even Mummy farts,' she says.

I giggle then gasp. A window needs to be opened.

Suzanne M. Faed

I Study Shame, Actually

April 2019
Dear Diary
(and you who will be taking a sneaky peek at this when I am gone. Annie, you
might even get to read this, but by then you will know it all anyway)

Before the worm arrived last Saturday, I was close to eating worms in sheer
misery. At that stage I had very little hope of experiencing clouds in my life that
are all light and airy and feathery.

But now, it's the next Saturday and I am still riding the wave of my sobriety.
If all this seems nonsensical, it will make sense – eventually, like everything else.

It was different last Saturday, the being sober bit. I was hungover then. It
was the morning after the night before and about that time where I sink down
into that most primitive of human emotions. Believe me, no one does shame
spirals quite like I do.

It's not the guilt so much. I can do guilt. There is forgiveness in this world.
When the grief of my drunkenness strikes, it sometimes feels like that is
enough. I wail and I cry, and I say I am sorry. And I mean the sorry part. Somehow my sorry state seems to be enough to wipe out what I did or didn't do and
start again. I make promises I really mean, and everything will be okay again –
until next time.

But shame is a different kettle of fish altogether. Shame only hits you later
and then it sticks to you. It's a bit like throwing a Velcro-covered ball at a wall.
When a ball hits you, it hurts. It sticks. When you're in pain, you bend double
and you don't have to – you can't – stand tall and look the world in the eye.
You stay curled up real small and let it wrap you up like it always did when they
did that thing to you. And you hate – yourself.

There comes a time when you need to peel off the shame; but you can't
simply unstick it or even wash it off. Bloody Marys and paracetamols don't go
into the blackened greasy cracks of your soul. It takes a hell of a detergent and
specific scrubbing brush to clean the black oil from a grease monkey's hands.
Yes, I do have that kind of grit in my soul. How does one handle or step away
from shame when you can't look yourself in the eye when you're brushing your
teeth and scrubbing your tongue on the morning after?

When your measure of life is a cumulonimbus cloud it is time to take stock. When a dark and angry vertical mass of your own doing towers over you and diminishes the beauty and tranquillity of a glorious cloudless morning, that is shame catching up with you. Just as humidity precedes a storm, shame creeps up on you, sluggishly at first. Then as the clouds build and whip up a fury it isn't long before you are hurtling full-throttle into a familiar downward spiral – of shame.

So, what's with the cloud thing I hear you ask.

At our last session, Annie, my life coach, therapist-thingy told me to think of my emotions as drifting clouds. We thrashed out the futility and transience of clinging to clouds, especially a single cloud. But not enough apparently. Judging by last Friday night and Saturday, that is, until the worm arrived.

All week on my daily commute I looked at the sky and mentally matched thin wispy cirrus clouds to fleeting snatches of annoyance or to feathery streamers of humour. When that cold front hit town on Wednesday I matched the hazy grey veil in the skies to the ever-increasing boredom and concomitant depression shrouding my dead-end job. I watched the clouds build up until there was that Friday evening syncing with my leisure time shame. I didn't realise the connection until it happened, and I had slipped – again.

On Saturday morning, awake early, I laid my burning, aching head on the cool windowsill overlooking the park below and the ocean beyond and groaned, reflecting. It was a beautiful morning; its beauty penetrating a fuzzy, hopefully misremembered memory of what happened on the dance floor and in the dark recesses of the club; piercing a haze of self-loathing and unworthiness.

Poets use words like azure sky, emerald landscapes and turquoise ocean. It was all there in front of me and perhaps the fact that I could, for once, look at this and see it, might just mean that I'm on a winning wicket – improving. And could lessen my search for clouds to cover and explain my shame.

'What have I done this time?' I must have thought that one aloud. The answer was most unexpected.

'*Drunk? and speak parrot? and squabble? swagger? swear?*' The voice was pompous and had a definite hot potato ring to it.

'What?' I was startled.

I squinted through the branches of the weeping bottle brush to the park beyond to find whoever was talking to me. A movement in the closest branch caught my eye. A green worm wearing a bottle brush-red scarf and a black top hat was parading up and down on the branch. He stopped marching and looked me in the eye.

The worm cleared his throat.

'It's always something like that isn't it?' he said.

He continued, 'Drink, sir, is a great provoker of three things … nose-painting, sleep, and urine. You were lucky, Sir … it provokes the desire, but it takes away the performance.'

I was confused, astonished.

'But that's Macbeth. Who are …?' I was interrupted:

'Oh! So, you **do** know Shakespeare? Yes, and the speaking parrot part comes from Othello. My name is Billy.'

I reached for my sunnies. The day was far too bright and was this worm for real?

The worm explained, 'Billy the 87th actually.' He cleared his throat importantly. 'I study shame, actually. I'm doing a doctorate.'

I did not say anything. What do you say to something like that? Do you even engage with a worm?

Billy the 87th did not seem to be expecting a response. He went on, 'We Waggle-Swords are known for our longevity and live longer than most worms. That is why we are only on 87 since Shakespeare was buried. My ancestor Billy the First was the first worm assigned to William Shakespeare's grave.'

Headache; heart ache; soul anguish forgotten; I stared at this weird and wonderful descendant. I remembered Othello again.

Good wine is a good familiar creature, if it be well used.

I carefully did not think this one aloud though. Was this situation for real or had I abused so badly?

Oblivious to or ignoring my dilemma, Billy the 87th continued his narrative.

'My ancestors have always hung around Up-Top, but my children will be the first Down-Under generation of Waggle-Swords.

'On 23 April 2014 the world celebrated Shakespeare's 450th birthday. We decided to investigate whether, and how well, our friend is known Down-Under. His name and his fame live on, on our island Up-Top but what is the situation on the island continent Down-Under?

'Did you know that Shakespeare is somewhat of an expert on liquor-ish literature? He soaked forty plays and over 150 poems in wine and ale and other distillates?'

He looked at me searchingly, peering over the top of his green rimmed spectacles. I hadn't noticed them before – the spectacles. I ignored the question.

All this was too fantastical for any word on my part. Who was even going to believe me when I told them about this conversation? I didn't want to block the flow of the narrative and was curious to see where it led. I did some fact-checking later. Shakespeare's age is anybody's guess but he really did write that many plays and poems. I'm not convinced all his writings were saturated with alcohol.

'At the annual general meeting of MOFT Inc. (Management of Famous Tombs Incorporated) it was accordingly decided that the 87th contingent of Waggle-Swords would be delegated to burrow Down-Under to uphold the Shakespearean name. The sponsor and funding for my PhD were also confirmed.

It took five years of burrowing. But here we are.'

Billy the 87th paused.

Was I supposed to congratulate him? Would the we-part of his family now descend on me? Heaven forbid!

He rearranged his scarf, tilted his top hat and adjusted his pair of spectacles, balancing them on the front tip of his body.

Irrelevantly I wondered whether a worm has a nose to rest his reading glasses upon.

'I've got something to say to you,' he said, clearing his throat. 'I've noticed you don't do worms much. That's okay. I'm not offended. But you've got to start doing you.'

He went on where Annie had left off. About clouds and stuff. But he made it real. He spoke so much sense. I remember bits and pieces.

'That black angry pile of storm cloud messing with you will go away as soon as you start talking to yourself with compassion. You're focussing on the wrong clouds. Talk to yourself like you would to someone who doesn't love himself, but you love and care for him anyway. Reach out to trust and accept love and kindness from others. You've got some forgiving to do too. That's yourself too. And don't be scared to tell your story. Others need to hear it.'

What can I say?

Annie and I had a different kind of week. I'm learning things. It might surprise you to know that all clouds are white. Those dark clouds, their shades of grey depend on the depth of the clouds and the intensity of the shade cast by higher clouds.

We're getting somewhere, Annie and I – at last. I won't be going to the club tonight. There is cloud work to be done. I'll update you later, dear diary.

Gogo Buzz

Jazz Hands

The iron sights from the gunner's position fell squarely over the conning tower of the submarine. Johnny Markam's training told him to squeeze the double-handed triggers and send searing cannon shells into the mass of men crowded atop the stricken vessel. Yet he hesitated. The intercom, its static hiss a constant companion to his freezing backside and numb hands, crackled with the voice of his aircraft captain.

'Gunner, what are you waiting for?'

Johnny didn't answer. The aircraft banked around, maintaining his direct line of sight to those below. Still he held his hands steady, triggers unused.

There was no fire coming up at him. The deck-mounted anti-aircraft gun was a mass of twisted steel from where a depth charge had hit. That had been a good drop, Johnny reflected. They had seen a periscope, estimated a position and loosed a stick of five. Right on target. Pretty good considering they hadn't really practised much with the new dispenser. First mission using it, first U-boat sunk. Only it wasn't sunk was it? It had come to the surface and wasn't fit to submerge, but she could still limp home. Back to the French pens, repaired, refitted. Able to renew her assault on Allied shipping.

'Gunner! What the bloody hell are you playing at? Are your guns jammed? Are you alright?'

Johnny wondered how many ships she'd sunk before they'd caught her. Was her Kapitän a Wolfpack ace? Was he one of their famed warriors of the deep? Was he a fanatical Nazi just baying for the blood of the Englanders?

Who knew? Who would ever know? Some on board might be fascists, but some might be just kids, drafted in to do the bidding of their masters. Of their master race. Sent out on her to sink the light of the world.

'Gunner!'

'Johnny!'

'Markam! Are you injured? Talk to me you bastard.'

But it might not be a her. They didn't call all their ships by a feminine descriptor like the Royal Navy did. It depended on the name. The Bismarck had been a he. What on earth would you do that for? They really were a weird and mixed up bunch.

'For fuck's sake Johnny, speak to me.'

They'd even banned jazz. How screwed up was that? His sister had told him when she came back from Berlin, before all this madness kicked off. Who in their right mind would ban jazz? Seriously, what moron would do that? The aircraft banked again. Johnny had played trumpet before he played machine guns. He felt the tightness in his jaw, the stiffness in his shoulders. Why would anyone ban music? Who would do that? What type of savage? What complete bastards? How dare they!

'Johnn–'

He played the guns and the staccato clattering of a thousand shells echoed like a jazz drum solo. The rhythm vibrated his hands and arms and he hammered death into a hundred lives.

'Sorry Captain. Bit of intercom trouble. I think that's finished them. Shall we go home now?'

Ian Andrew

If Your Sponge Fails, Make Trifle

It is often said home is where the heart is, and the kitchen is the heart of your home. It is the place where traditionally a big serve of love comes with every meal. Yes, this kitchen is the heart of my home, and when I look around, I am assaulted by a lifetime of memories. I drink them in.

This big old room isn't flash, but it is mine. Looking down on me is the high and age-worn ceilings peppered with fly poo and flaking ceiling paint. In places it looks quite like the white chocolate curls I once tried to master for my husband's birthday cake. In the end, I grated the chocolate instead. My sun-bleached curtains are worn out and pinpricked now with the tiniest of holes, but if you don't pay attention and look too closely, if you are looking out onto the rose garden, you don't even notice them. I never noticed them in the end.

But it really is the bench top, this chipped and life-stained piece of laminate that holds the memories. I believe it is big by modern standards. Wide enough to accommodate years of chatter, kids and friends on one side – me on the other – and long enough to allow the tidal flow of cooking ingredients to over-run the countertop. I am an ordinary woman, who did ordinary things, and I accepted life as it came my way. I'm not a chef, merely a home cook, and my kitchen reflected this. Ah! But don't they say a messy kitchen is a happy kitchen?

I learnt from my mistakes, made do with what I had. Did what I had to do. The memories made here are trapped here. Some, the good ones, I will forever cherish and savour as my sweet rewards of this life. Others are as bad as rotten eggs. Some of those eggs could have ruined me; but as much as I thought they fouled my life at that moment, I remembered that the chooks would lay fresh ones tomorrow. After all, when your sponge cake falls on the floor, pick it up and make a trifle.

It was here that Mum tried to teach me to make her coveted sponge cake. The blue-ribbon envy of the local show for many years, Mum was determined to pass on the 'Sponge Legacy'. I am sure she thought that it would be encoded in my pastoral genes, but for some strange and unknown reason, my sponges never lived up to her (or my) expectations. 'Don't worry love,' she said, 'just soak it in brandy and cover it with custard and it will make a fine trifle.' In the crusades for sponge perfection, we ate a lot of trifle, and I used a lot of brandy. Most of it even went in the dessert.

It was here that I sat alone, under the flickering fluoro, with a glass of Napoleon and made the decision to put Mum in the nursing home. I knew it was the only option. A grey-handed wraith had stolen my mother and left a vacant, broken shell behind. I couldn't care for her anymore. I had failed the one person who had loved me unconditionally since I was a flutter in her belly. A little part of me curled up and died then, an end to our story … the rest, just motions through time really.

It was *here*, just as I was walking to the door to go and see Mum, that I took the call from the nursing home. Mum was gone. A stroke they said. In her sleep – apparently she didn't feel a thing. I didn't either at the beginning. I don't want to think of the rest now. Let's move on shall we?

Where was I? That's right, the kitchen bench, the silent witness and marker of lifetimes. We once seriously considered renovating the old place, right after Mum died, with the modest amount she left to me. I had dreamt of a brand-new kitchen for so long that I was giddy with excitement. Imagine! A new kitchen just like the ones in the Women's Weekly. I had grand plans of a new oven; you know the ones that you could cook casseroles and cakes in all at once? The ones with fandangle features that helped you cook better. I thought, perhaps, that a new oven would help me in my elusive dream of sponge per-fection. My husband said that only poor workmen blamed their tools. I told him … well, it's not really the place to repeat that here. It did have something to do with eating elsewhere though. He muttered that that's why he enjoyed the pub so much. If only I had known then how much he enjoyed eating else-where.

Needless to say, the renovations never happened. A few bad years of drought, then floods, and then, when it was finally looking good, the deluge of mice which came and nearly ate the house off its foundations. Stinking little bastards. My skin crawls now even thinking of them. Our savings dwindled and any renovation funds went into covering our losses and stemming the unending musty tide of brown fur.

Hubby, being a proud son of a son of a son of the land, had an arsenal of chemical weaponry at his disposal. The paranoia of losing 'our' living from the land passed from father to son, and the evil scourge of rodent warfare was a battle that he did not consider losing. He did not like things that didn't go his way. Planning for the Armageddon had resulted in three generations of stock-piling this arsenal, a locked shed full to the roof with poisons. It was most fortunate that we had this accumulation of weapons for mouse destruction.

The poisons proved very handy, the Thallium especially. With no taste or smell, the rodents were none the wiser – for a few days at least.

Anyways, side-tracked again! Back to that bench.

It was *here*, at this very bench that I found a scrawled note on the back of the shopping list. It was a simple note, writing I knew by heart, and the words that broke it. He had decided we were not to be married any longer. He decided? So, I was to be replaced, was I? I know that times had been hard, but the insult of being updated by that … woman at the pub? That bottle-blond bitch with blue eye shadow applied with a paint roller, the 'friendly' one with the big 'personality'? I was beyond stunned. I was bloody furious. That mongrel-bastard-son-of-a-whore. Oh! and he wasn't leaving his land. No, of course not!

I sat at that bench most of the evening, staring past the faded curtains and past the roses into the nothingness that was in front of me. I felt utterly devastated. I grieved for the death of my marriage, the loss of everything I had known for most of my life. Where had the love gone? I looked around the big old room and felt as worn and wretched as the cracked forties lino. Was I to be just another stain on this bench top? I was alone. Then I realised all the years of happy memories that this room held, the memories of sadness and woe. Everything; I would lose it all. Everything I had done for this man, for this family, sacrifices I had made, the years of anguish and uncertainty that goes with being a wife on the land, I'd be damned if I would be cast aside like old out-dated rubbish. No way José. Not on your life. Over my dead body.

It was on this bench top that I watched my last sponge flop in the centre, a testament to my unfulfilled ambitions. I resigned myself to the fact that I would be making a trifle again. I didn't mind. Not really now. Well, this would be the best bloody trifle I would ever make, and it would be the last one hubby would get. As much as he ridiculed me, especially on my sponge making abilities, he adored my trifle. I set to work mixing my special ingredients for the ultimate farewell gift. Made with love, of course.

I placed the trifle in the fridge for the next day. It was going to be a warm day, and as every good wife knows; this dish is best served cold.

He stayed out that night, but on his arrival home the next morning, I presented him with a glass of brandy and a large serving of trifle. He was surprised I guess by the congeniality of it all, being rewarded with a stiff drink and a sweet delight. Not so surprised though to dampen his appetite as he gulped down the Napoleon and shovelled in the trifle. He looked at me with a detached indifference; I looked at him and smiled as I gave him another helping of trifle. He always did think I was a simple woman. When he left, he took the leftovers for smoko. He was going out to the back paddocks, and then on to check the fence lines for the next day or two. Good to give us some time apart, he said. Good to put some space between us, he said.

It was here; at this bench, I sat and watched his red taillights disappear in the driveway dust cloud. Mum was always right. If your sponge fails, make a trifle.

Lee Harsen

Paying in Pain

My heart renders the pain
Accordance of trying to sustain

The beat of coping
Delirium of hoping
Without a complaint

    Futile is my restraint

The parent wishing in fear
Of the despair, from the unclear

The child of the adult
The adult holds the fault
My child wallows alone

    Drifting away from home

My adult not wanting to infest
The scourge of his invest

My adult not wanting to infest
The scourge of his invest

It's his to own,
Unbeknown, his cover is blown
All is not lost

    Without, is the being of
cost

A price may be tendered
Possessions surrendered

Loving is forgiving
Forgiving is forgetting
There simply is no gain

    By paying in pain

Apikara

117

Immolation

'He got fired?'

'He asked us what we wanted to do with our lives! He deserved to get fired!'

The scandalised voices of Megan's classmates echoed around the locker-bay.

'Insensitive bastard!'

Megan stayed silent. Half of her agreed with them, the other half thought, *in any other town, a teacher wouldn't get sacked for asking a group of sixteen-year-old girls to think about the direction of their lives.*

Only it wasn't any other town.

When Megan and the girls around her thought about their future, two paths stared back at them. A bright place full of opportunity … and the other. Which was, Megan thought, considerably shorter and if it was bright, that was only because of the flames.

The bell rang and the students headed to their classes, bemoaning the poor quality of their educators in general.

*

In chemistry Luke copied her homework in his unreadable handwriting.

'Would you have fired him?' He asked.

'No,' Megan said. 'Wasn't his fault. How could he have known?'

'Pretty much,' Luke said. 'Imagine if someone had simply been honest?'

Wordlessly, Megan handed him her essay. Luke read the first sentence and choked.

'Something amusing, Mr Dwyer?' Ms Hutchinson asked.

'No, sorry,' Luke said and waited for the teacher to turn away before mouthing 'are you serious?' to Megan. Megan shrugged.

The Concede was on Friday.

*

By the end of the week, Megan was dizzy from rolling her eyes. *Sure, it's the end of the world for one of us.* She told herself, as yet another of her hysterical classmates – this time, Brenda – was led away in tears, *but they could show a little grit!*

Thing was, Megan knew it would be her. One girl every six years! With her luck? Please! No competition. It had to be her. Hundred per cent.

And because she was certain, she'd made plans.

She hadn't told anyone, not even Luke.

Luke was a good best friend. Loyal, a bit of an idiot in all the right ways. But she couldn't lay this on him. He already felt guilty about being excluded from the lottery. Which was stupid, she thought, though she knew she'd feel the same in his position.

On Friday afternoon they stood on the footpath outside school.

'See you Monday,' Luke said in a voice as rough as dragon scales. He didn't cry, but only because Megan had spent the whole week telling him he couldn't. Part of her felt suddenly cruel for doing so.

To her own surprise she found herself seizing him in a desperate hug. 'Monday,' she whispered. 'One way or another.'

*

At 5 pm the mayor would announce the name.

Megan had a few last-minute adjustments to make to her plan.

So, while the people she'd know all her life gripped their phones, or stared at televisions, or clutched hands and twisted fingers and toes into crosses, Megan built her model. She pulled the saw through the wood and let the blade bite. It was sharp and she knew the rhythm of the work. Back and forth, the teeth cut a line as straight as a ruler. It was an old project, deserted and returned to multiple times over a span of years, but now the model was almost finished.

Tiny versions of streets and buildings, parks and bridges – every detail a replica of the landscape that started at the end of her bench and wandered out of the window into the sky. The only difference between her replica and the real town was the miniature dragon wrapped around the spire of the cathedral.

Her Mum entered and found Megan sanding the roof of the cinema. Megan read her fate in the white mess of a tissue in her Mum's hand.

'It's you,' her Mum said. *Unnecessarily*, Megan thought.

She put down the sandpaper and nodded. 'Let me finish up.'

Her Mum retreated and took the sound of stifled sobs with her.

Megan sketched a symbol on the edge of the model cathedral – next she raised her shirt and carefully drew the same symbol on her stomach.

'As above,' Megan said. 'So below.'

The mark turned ice-cold. A single staccato burst of *Otherness* flared across her skin, coiled inside her, then lashed outwards in a concentrated whip. An echoing *otherness,* much smaller than her own, unfurled from the model and latched onto it. The connection rippled through her and she felt herself *click* into unison with the little replica. Synchronised.

So far so good.

What did she want to do with her life? *Be prepared to have one*, she thought.

*

They told her she could have any meal she wanted. Megan thought the concept of a last meal odd. Who felt hungry when told they have to die the following day? But they said she could have anything, so Megan requested lobster thermidor. It was the dish she'd read about several years ago and had always been curious to try. It also wasn't a recipe on her Dad's short repertoire of meals. If she'd chosen spaghetti bolognaise, for example, the memory association might have ruined a perfectly good family staple. No risk of that with lobster thermidor.

Mild panic met her request. Lobsters weren't easy to get a hold of. It took the apologetic town officials a few hours to get it sorted. But they were as good as their word and before the end of the day Megan, along with her parents and younger brothers, were all seated before a cooked crustacean.

'This is gross,' Ian told her after a mouthful. 'Couldn't you have asked for pizza?'

'Next time,' her Dad said, 'we can have pizza.' And then he realised what he'd said.

The rest of meal was full of started sentences, unfinished like Ian's lobster and accompanied by the soft percussion of cutlery on china.

Then it was over and shortly after, there was a tentative knock on the door. A solemn woman with a long thin face and pianist's hands stood on the step. 'It's time,' she said.

Megan followed the woman out of the house and took her first deep breath in hours. The confusion of her brothers and the raw pain of her parents had been an impossible weight, heavier than she'd expected. The plans she'd made had not included the lost expression on Mum's face, or her youngest brother's innocent question about where she was going and why everyone was acting so weird. She'd said goodbye quickly and had not lingered.

It had been raining. Wet bitumen made watery reflections with the streetlights. Megan climbed into the woman's four-wheel drive, which smelled of dog and there were white, wiry hairs on the seat covers. An attempt had been made to clean the car, the mats were vacuumed, the dash was wiped, only a few stray straws and chocolate wrappers remained in the drink holders. Megan sat in the passenger seat and immediately got up again to remove what turned out to be a Lego man from under the seat cover.

The solemn woman smiled when Megan placed the toy on the dash. The blank-faced banality of the little plastic man stared down the road, oblivious to the coming storm.

Megan didn't put her seatbelt on. She saw the woman in the driver's seat notice, consider commenting and then decide not to.

It was the first time she'd ever been in a car without wearing her seatbelt. Megan decided it had been a waste, all those things her Mum and Dad had put time and energy into making her do. Cleaning her teeth – ultimately pointless. Putting on her bike helmet, eating cabbage, coming home before dark, not smoking or doing drugs. She wondered if she ought to have tried a few more dangerous things. But too late now. And no point regretting any of it.

Out of her side window, up in the cold, cloudy heavens, she glimpsed a knife-edge of moon.

Watch out, she told the sky, *I'm coming for you.*

The solemn woman said nothing. A few times she opened her mouth as if she might, but she shut it every time. Megan didn't blame her. What do you say to a nearly dead sixteen-year-old?

'Thank you for driving me,' Megan said into the silence. It occurred to her that the woman's job was not an enviable one.

The woman nodded and Megan saw a tear trail down her face.

'You're welcome,' she said in a voice as tight as a bear hug.

Words evaporated. The car was warm. The rain started and then a squall engulfed them. The road shrank to a single lane, then the blacktop ended. They jutted along on sodden, graded gravel.

It was hard to see. Water gushed down the windshield and the wipers couldn't keep up. They slowed to a crawl. The track got rougher.

Megan wasn't sure how long it was before they stopped.

The rain had eased. The solemn woman opened her door and grabbed a raincoat from the back seat. Megan got out and landed in a puddle that swallowed her sneakers.

I'm going to die with wet feet, Megan thought, as the water settled in around her toes. *I wish I'd brought my boots.*

Megan's guide led her up the steep and overgrown trail on the side of the mountain. They scrabbled and stumbled up the path with head torches to guide the way. Megan wondered why it wasn't better maintained. Between panted breaths she decided it was probably that no one wanted to go anywhere near the place. She slipped on a wet tree root and her feet skidded out from under her, one hand snatched out and grabbed a branch to save herself. The wood tore her hands and she sprawled over backwards on to her side, most of the small shrub followed. The woman came back and helped disentangle her.

'Be stupid to die in the wrong part of the hill,' Megan said as she pulled herself free. She hadn't meant to say it out loud. The woman didn't speak, and Megan couldn't see her face under the head-torches brilliance, but somehow, she felt her pity anyway.

They kept climbing. On and up. The track sometimes widened where it crossed stony ground. In other places it slimmed so that they could scarcely squeeze between the undergrowth.

Former sacrifices were dragged up here, Megan thought when they stopped to rest against a giant tree stump. She imagined trying to fight back as people—pitiless and strong hauled her up this same path. *They could have done that to me,* she knew. *But they know I'll keep my promise. For my family and my town.* Megan got to her feet and the solemn woman followed.

For a long time, Megan's mind lost itself in the journey. Stepping one careful footstep after another, darkness kept at bay by the sphere of her torches' light. Water from the wet foliage drenched her and while her legs and arms were heated by the climb, her back and face grew cold.

They climbed all night.

*

Her feet ached. The muscles in her legs were hot knots and Megan was sagging from tiredness when they finally broke out of the trees.

Chain Rock: a triangle of granite the size of a school bus, loomed before them, a deeper slab of darkness against the faintly brighter sky.

My exit, Megan thought, but her weariness made it difficult to feel anything but relief that she didn't have to walk any further. On protesting legs, she climbed the stairs hewn into the rock's side, reached the top and allowed her body to fold down into a sitting position. *Could have done with a big muscly person to carry me up the mountain,* she decided. *Next time I'll insist on one.* She grinned to herself.

The town below was vanished in mist. Megan could see points of warm light scattered across the valley, like a candle in the window, guiding people home. Only she wasn't going home. Her fate was in the dark and heavy, clouds above.

Dawn was a pale curve of silver on the rim of the Eastern sky.

Megan wiped her sweaty forehead and stared at the spot where the sun would rise.

It's time.

'As above, so below,' she said and felt the tiniest tingle crawl across the symbol on her stomach.

Sunlight pierced the horizon. Splashed over the stone where Megan stood.

A tiny speck darkened the new day.

It could have been a bird, but Megan knew it wasn't. It grew from a speck to a smudge and from a smudge to a threat.

The dragon was coming.

With a wingspan as wide as a jet, it ghosted over the town. Four clawed feet, bright leathery wings, great orange eyes and a maw of fire.

Megan heard herself whimper.

*

Of course, they had tried to kill it. Four years before she'd been born the Airforce had flown into town at the appointed hour, intent on bringing the mythical protection racket to an end. Modern technology would defeat the dragon! The town would be safe. What could a big flying lizard do against the might of modern weapons?

A lot, as it turned out. For they had managed to injure the creature, but they had suffered gruesomely in return. Wounded, the dragon had retreated to the lip of the horizon and was gone. The celebration lasted a day. Then the beast returned. In the company of its kind.

Dragons had darkened the sky. The modern weapons could not match them and the town was drenched in flame.

Neither side could shift the other. The dragons did not seem able to fly beyond the border of the valley. Whatever strangeness allowed them into the world did not extend beyond the town limits. However, they would not relinquish their small hold. And the people would cede nothing.

Many died. Too many died.

It was deemed inconvenient to continue.

So, they reverted to the old treaty. It had worked for centuries.

One girl. Every six years and the town would stay safe from the dragon's wrath.

They told the world they had won.

Another species might have simply moved on.

But that was humans for you, Megan thought. *Why move out today, when you can sacrifice a random stranger to appease an angry lizard tomorrow?*

*

Then the beast was in front of her. A roar of air pressure and scaled power threw her backwards. Her palm jarred against the stone and her hip cracked painfully after it. A scorching gust burned her face and she scrambled to get out of its path. Under her body the ground vibrated with a deep bass purr akin to a hundred idling engines. A clawed foot the size of a hatchback touched down with airy lightness a few centimetres from her shoulder. Megan trembled.

Heat poured down on her and an involuntary glance up revealed a hot maw. All inferno, red gullet and wicked fangs.

No more time, she realised, and rolled out of the way of the gaping jaws towards the foot. With one hand she pulled out her permanent marker. Ripped the lid off with her teeth and flickered a messy symbol on the nearest bit of the dragon she could reach. Then she pulled up her shirt and pressed her marked skin to the marked scales.

'As above,' she cried, 'so below.'

Otherness, staccato sharp, rolled out of her and snatched the tendril that flickered from the symbol on the dragon. *Click* went the *otherness* and Megan felt a wrenching in her mind, her consciousness stretched out to reconnect with the model town far below and spiralled out of her belly and into the consciousness of the dragon. For a second she was a bead on an elastic band vibrating between the two points.

It wasn't *real* magic. This was merely the binding of unrelated objects. Binding one item to another by means of symbols. Easy enough. The tricky part, came next, the Convincing. A binding of one thing to another meant nothing if she couldn't convince the objects to take on aspects of each other. To persuade dissimilar shapes that they had a relationship, when they knew, and she knew, that they didn't. Once done, to Convince the object that what they wanted to be, was other than what they actually were.

Megan had always thought it simple. When she tried to explain it to people, they hadn't found it so.

In this instance the symbol on the dragon and the symbol on the girl was the same as the symbol on the model of the town. And the model of the town was a symbol of the town. And a symbol fashioned with delusions of grandeur might fancy that it *is* the town in fact and not in fancy. All things being linked: girl, dragon, model, town. Might have a difficult time convincing themselves at that exact moment that they weren't what Megan told them to be.

Megan sent her awareness thrumming down the connection like a message from a satellite. Quick as thought, her mind entered the replica town. She was the glue and paint and chipped edges of the Bunnings building. She was everything in the model and nowhere specific.

The mark.

She had to get to the Cathedral. And so was there. Without form she hit the mark that she had carefully tattooed to the side of Cathedral. Again, her consciousness stretched with almost painful elasticity between the symbol's anchor points. She could feel her body attached to this fragment of her mind by the drawing on her skin, far away, clinging to the dragon's leg, another anchor point. She could feel herself pinned to the same symbol in the model and now the pinched detour of her spirit tearing out into the physical town through the symbol drawn on the actual Cathedral brickwork two weeks ago. It hurt to be in so many places, her mind thinned by over-extension, but this was the plan. And it was working!

Her spirit stood in the town below, misty daylight met her unreal eyes. The church grounds were empty.

And there it was, curled around the cross just like her model, the wooden dragon. There and not there. Real and not real. But all things being linked: girl, dragon, model, town, the dragon on the spire and the dragon in the flesh were having trouble telling themselves apart. So much trouble in fact that the wooden dragon was bellowing rage to the fog-smothered streets.

The bit of Megan that was staring at the wooden dragon took herself up the side of the church. Gravity being meaningless to a bodiless thought.

High above the ground she floated. Up to the carved dragon and its fierce orange eyes. In the unreal world between what was and what wasn't, Megan saw the dragon fighting to free itself. The wood shook back, and vibrant scales shifted through only to be engulfed again by the unyielding firmness of the sculpture. The symbol was strong, and the conviction of the model was certain. It was a dragon and the dragon was wood and the dragon could not convince itself that it wasn't.

Release me, the beast ordered.

Megan shook her head. *No*, she said.

You're mine by right, it growled.

No, Megan said again.

In retaliation it sent her a memory, detailed in sight, sound and taste. She remembered tearing into the flesh of the last sacrifice *tasted the other girl's lungs and heart in a rush of hot coppery blood after her fangs snapped the ribcage and her tongue scooped them out.*

125

In the caverns of its alien mind Megan heard a summons. The dragon was called to Earth, not to feed, the consuming of humans was a by-product of the larger action. The dragon came for the act of sacrifice. To devour offered flesh. An innocent life, freely given. This was the act that summoned it from the dark and fuelled its power.

The plan had been to drive it back and set the town free. Now she could see its mind, she knew this was not an option. The dragon would not surrender. Would not be driven.

You can go back to the dark! Megan thought. She felt her body, still latched to the foot of the dragon far away, and without stopping to think about what she was doing, what the cost would be, she jerked her soul out of her body entirely; felt it snap like a rubber band pulled taunt and then released. The energy slammed into her and she used it to arrow into the wooden dragon.

Like a harpoon Megan pierced the dragon's mind. Behind her on a rapidly fading trail of awareness she heard her heartbeat stop. *Don't think about it!* She told herself. *You don't have time.* She sank through the hungry layers of its mind, into the sculpture and let the tugging oneness of the symbol written in ordinary permanent marker merge her spirit to that of the sculpture and with it the mind of the dragon.

And from inside its mind, she devoured it.

*

On Monday morning Luke stood on the school oval and looked up. A huge shape plummeted from the sky. The impossibility of the sight froze him to the spot, and he stayed unmoving even as the dragon landed before him. The wind of its passage all but knocked him over.

The dragon regarded him with an expression that was almost familiar. Inside Luke's mind Megan's voice said. *One way, or another.*

K. Dee

Capsize
Scene from a Play

CHARACTERS

GEORGE - WW1 Veteran in his fifties and grandfather to HARRY

HARRY - around 10 years of age, grandson of GEORGE

YOUNG GEORGE - GEORGE in 1915 at around 20 years of age

BILLY (Dying Soldier) - late teens, younger brother of GEORGE

SETTINGS

Set in two different times. 1950s suburban Australia in a small, modest living room with a window at the back of the stage and a large, single lounge chair draped with a rug. The lounge is quite worn making it obvious that this is where GEORGE *spends much of his time. Situated next to the chair is a small, side table with a partially empty bottle of whiskey and a glass. The main entrance to this room is at the side of the stage. There is a window on the rear wall of the room.*

1915. Gallipoli. WW1 Beach landing.

Begins in George's living room with GEORGE *and* HARRY *and transforms into a dream sequence flashing back to a*
YOUNG GEORGE *with his mate,* BILLY *on the beach at Gallipoli in 1915.*
GEORGE *is asleep in his lounge chair.* HARRY *is knocking and calling out to* GEORGE *from offstage before* HARRY *steps onto the stage and approaches* GEORGE.

HARRY: (*Off*) Grandpa George. (*Pause*) Grandpa George. (*On*) Grandpa George, are you awake? It's me, Grandpa.

GEORGE: You're not Grandpa. I'm Grandpa. You're Harry.

HARRY: Very funny. Were you sleeping?

GEORGE: No. But I was dreaming.

HARRY: What about?

GEORGE: Ice-cream, fairy floss, and Oonagoolabies.

HARRY: Grandpa, will you come to the Bay with me? I really want to see the whales.

GEORGE: Hmmm ... Well, what about your Dad? Can't he take you?

HARRY: Dad said he would take me on my birthday but that's too far away and I want you to take me. Dad said you don't go to the beach anymore, but I bet him you would go with me. He said if I'm right, he'll come too.

GEORGE: That sure is some bet. (*Beat*) I don't know Harry. Will there be swimming?

HARRY: We could swim out to the pontoon. But you'll need a wetsuit. And goggles. And a snorkel. And flippers too.

GEORGE: What! I think you might mistake me for a whale with all that clobber on!

HARRY: Does that mean you're gonna take me to the beach?

GEORGE: (*Beat*) What does that clock say?

HARRY: Well, the big hand is on the twelve and ... the little hand is on the one so that makes it ... one o'clock?

GEORGE: That's thirteen hundred hours to you, Soldier! Time to go home.

HARRY: Awww …but what about the whales?

GEORGE: Ah yes. The whales. (*Pause*) I'll think about it, but you'll have to come back tomorrow to find out. And make sure you bring your Dad.

HARRY: Yesss! I knew it! Wait 'til I tell Dad. See you tomorrow, Grandpa. (*Exits hurriedly*)

GEORGE: (*Quietly to himself*) See you soon, little man.

GEORGE *remains seated. Stares straight ahead. He is still and silent. Slowly, he drops his head to his chest. Twitching as he falls asleep. He starts to dream. The scene changes to convey a dream of a suppressed memory. It is 1915. Two Australian soldiers have just landed on the beach at Gallipoli. A disoriented* YOUNG GEORGE *enters assisting* BILLY *who is seriously wounded.*

YOUNG GEORGE: (*Laying* BILLY *on the ground and supporting him*) Geez! Where the hell are we? Someone bloody blundered.

BILLY: Georgie? Georgieeee!

YOUNG GEORGE: Mate, I should never have let you follow me here.

BILLY: George … it's so loud. In my head. Make it stop.

YOUNG GEORGE: Don't worry. I got you Mate. I got you.

BILLY: Hey Georgie? What … what can … ya see?

YOUNG GEORGE: (*Pause*) Mobys. Huge pods of them. Right there on the surface.

BILLY: That's right! On our way in, I was holding my breath and counting when I heard the blast. I looked out and there they were. Right there, alongside us. Did ya see 'em?

YOUNG GEORGE: Yeah. One showed himself to me. His eye caught mine and he looked right into me. Like he understood something and wanted me to know it too. (*Beat*) It was like forever. All at once. I watched them coming up. Along the coast. Loads of them. In great numbers. All sticking together and looking out for one another. But sometimes things go wrong. Something happens. The leader gets confused. The rest of the boys gather around him in formation, but he starts heading for land. And they follow him! All the way to shore. They end up on the beach. Thrashing about for hours. Sometimes days. In the hot sun. Missing the tide, digging in deeper. Losing their minds, losing *everything* … except their connection to each other. They never stop communicating. Not ever. That's there till the very end.

Silence. YOUNG GEORGE *looks back at* BILLY *who is now limp and is no longer breathing.*

YOUNG GEORGE: Drowned … in just a couple of feet of water. And in all the eagerness, no one notices.

YOUNG GEORGE *breaks down.*

GEORGE *awakens from his sleep.*

GEORGE: In the end, there was nothing more anyone could do. We just had to let them go.

LIGHTS DOWN

END OF SCENE

Stephanie Fitz-Henry
Awarded Second Place at the 2018 Shorelines
Writing For Performance Festival
Performed at the 2019 Bunbury Fringe Festival

The Keeper Of Secrets

At this moment, she wished to be anywhere but here.

'You get longer for murder!'

The occupants at the singles table laughed, as the happy couple up the front raised their glasses in celebration of their love. They all toasted with the bride and groom, some swallowing their secret envy down with the sweet champagne.

Tess eyed the man across from her, his eyes still sparkling from the joke he'd made. 'It's a life sentence alright – stuck with the same sheila.' Tess groaned quietly. This was why she hated weddings and being single at them. Getting stuck on a table with random weirdos was not her idea of a fun evening. He caught her looking at him and took the opportunity to wink at her. 'Me, I like variety.'

She quickly looked away. Busying herself, she topped up her drink. As she put the bottle back on the table, her elbow knocked a glass and spilt the contents over the white tablecloth. Red wine soaked into the crisp white, a contrasted collision of colours; a blotchy stain that seeped through the material thirstily.

'Damn.' Her face turned a similar shade of red as she grabbed a napkin and dabbed at the wet patch. 'I'm sorry about that. I'm such a klutz.'

'Here, let me help you.' The man sitting next to her picked up the fallen glass and used his napkin to dry the surrounding cutlery. 'There, almost as good as new … A new, multi-coloured tablecloth.' He re-filled his glass.

Tess laughed. 'Thank you. I'm just glad I didn't spill it all over you.'

'I wouldn't have minded. Would have given me an excuse to get out of here for a bit.'

He winked at Tess, and unlike the other wink from the irritating man, this one seemed to ignite a flame under her skin. Her face turned red for the second time and she giggled.

'Not a fan of weddings either, huh?'

'Not really. The free food and booze are a bonus. And supporting my good mate. But not too keen on all this lovey-dovey stuff.'

'I'll drink to that.' Tess carefully picked up her drink and gulped a mouthful down. 'I'm Tess, by the way.'

'I'm Sam. And I'm glad to be seated up this end of the table, rather than on the other side.' Sam glanced over to the man who thought he was funny and then back to her. He smiled and it went to his eyes; maybe, Tess thought, this night wouldn't be so bad after all.

'Can I drink to that, too?'

This time Sam laughed. 'Looks to me like you're taking advantage of the free alcohol, Tess. I like your style.'

Tess hiccupped. She could feel the alcohol going to her head; it sat warm in her belly and made her feel braver than she was. She loosened her jaw muscles, let her limbs relax.

She opened her mouth, a reply on her lips. But before she could speak the words, a voice boomed over the microphone announcing that it was time to cut the cake. They turned their attention to the couple up the front and watched them make a single slice through the three-tiered cake and then kiss. Cameras flashed and people whistled and clapped. They then walked into the middle of the dance floor as the first bridal song filled the room. She smiled as she watched her friend gaze lovingly into her new husband's eyes. They swayed together, linked and in love. She swallowed hard. She was happy for her friend but being here reminded her of what she had lost. This could have been me, she thought. She finished her drink, hoping to wash the thought away with the burning alcohol that slid down her throat.

The bridal dance finished, and the music became louder. The groom motioned to the guests, indicating it was their turn to get up on the dance floor.

Sam leaned in, casual but close, and held her gaze as Tess waited for the question in his eyes to reach his lips. 'So my dancing skills are limited – although I do a good sprinkler – but do you want to …?'

'Lucky for you, I'm not much of a dancer either. Don't we look tragic, though, two singles still at the table while everyone else is having fun.'

Sam chuckled. 'Well, we could always sneak out for a bit. No one will notice.'

Tess considered this. Sam was basically a stranger. Was it smart to be alone with him? But she felt a connection, and it had been a long time since she felt connected to anyone. Sometimes filling an emotional need took precedence over rational thought.

'Let's do it … grab your glass.' Tess picked up a bottle of champagne and her glass, looked around quickly, and walked towards the entrance. Sam followed, meeting her at the door. The reception was held at a second story function hall overlooking the beach. They walked down the steps, stopped at the bottom to take their shoes off, and stepped onto the soft sand. Tess giggled; her hands unsuccessful in stifling her laugh. 'I feel like a schoolgirl wagging class.'

'I sure hope you weren't holding a bottle of champagne when you wagged school,' Sam joked.

'Of course not, do I look like that kind of person?' Tess pouted, pretending to be offended.

'No, Sam said, his voice turning serious. 'You look like a person who I should have known long before now.'

Tess was speechless, unable to come up with a clever reply. Instead, she ran further up the beach, sitting down not far from the shoreline. The full moon sat against a black blanket, a scattering of stars trying to outshine its magnificence. She heard Sam's footsteps approach; his arm brushed hers as he sat.

The wind moved around them, the waves ebbed and flowed, crashing onto the shore. There was a rhythm, a beat to the beach, a calmness that couldn't be found at the reception. Tess shivered, and wrapped her arms around her bent legs. Sam took off his jacket and put it around her shoulders.

'Thank you.' She felt the warmth from his jacket heat her skin. She breathed in and inhaled the scent of Sam. His cologne smelled sweet, fresh, masculine.

Tess looked out; the horizon hidden by the darkness. 'You know, I think if we'd met long ago … I was a different person then. I think we've actually met at the right time.'

'So maybe weddings aren't that bad, hey?'

'No, for some it's just a reminder of what is missing. But you can't find what hasn't been lost, right?'

'We're going to have to go soon, but before we do, can I suggest this meeting will not be our last? I feel like I need to get to know you better.'

In response, Tess leaned over, cupped Sam's cheek with her hand, and brought her lips to his. She started slow, with this man who was a stranger not long ago. She tasted the sweet champagne on his breath as she ran her hands through his hair.

The darkness kept their secret; they felt invisible as they fell down on the sand. Their desire became their antidote, both searching to find the thing that had been missing.

But then they heard a noise and broke their kiss.

'You hear that?' Tess whispered.

'Yep. Sounds like voices. In the distance.'

Their passion put on pause, they listened, their bodies still and alert.

The voices got louder, and it became clear two men were having an argument. They heard a scuffle, the thud of fist onto flesh.

'Oh! They're fighting!'

'Ssh.' Sam put a finger to her lips. 'They haven't seen us. Let's keep it that way.'

Then the sound of combined footsteps; hurried and heavy. A scream. An oomph as one of the men fell to the sand. More footsteps crunching the sand; someone running away.

Tess and Sam held their breath and waited. It became silent again, except for the sounds of nature; the keeper of secrets.

'It sounded like someone was hurt. Should we go check?' A hint of panic laced her question.

Sam got up. 'You wait here. I'll go look.' He crept along, until he saw a silhouette lying on the sand. The man lay motionless. Sam pulled his mobile phone from his pocket and switched the torch on. Tess trailed behind, not wanting to be left alone.

'Hey mate,' Sam called. 'You alright?'

No answer.

Sam stood over the man and shined his torch over him.

'No way. I think he's … I think he's dead?'

The man, dressed in a suit, lay on his back, eyes open but unseeing. His white shirt was stained red. The water lapped over his shiny black shoes.

Tess leaned over him, looked closer. Recognition dawned on her. That man, that dead man, was very much alive an hour ago. He had sat across the table and winked at her. Those eyes now, unblinking.

She fell to her knees and threw up. Sam rubbed her back as he stared at the reception building.

The stars twinkled knowingly. Inside, dessert was getting ready to be served, but no one could find the engraved, sharp silver knife that was needed to cut the wedding cake.

Suzanne M. Faed

Clay County Contaminants

Shirlene holstered the gas pump nozzle, took the offered dollars and threw a halfhearted salute at the driver. Despite no traffic, the car hesitated before turning south, its headlights sweeping an arc across the blacktop.

She walked back to the shop, illuminated by the rhythmic blink, blink, buzz of a neon light. Its shattered plastic cover had seen better days. Like the rest of East Kentucky. Pushing the metal door open, she entered a stifling heat. Frank liked the heater up full.

'You couldn't convince them to buy nothing?' He called from the back office.

'No. I couldn't.' *And it's anything, you ignorant piece of ...* 'Lady just wanted to be on her way.'

'Typical. Where's she heading?'

'Didn't say.'

'She's no lady, out at this time of night. Yankee plates too, you seen that?'

'Yeah, I saw.' She knew Frank had watched her on the CCTV that monitored the pumps. In case of drive-offs.

'Long ways from home. What she doin' down here?'

Shirlene opened the cash register and carefully placed the dollars into the tray. 'She didn't say, Frank.'

'Now y'all come back in here again.'

Closing the register she went into the back office.

Frank hadn't moved from his position on the couch. His left hand cradled a head of thinning, grey hair. Tight eyes watched her from above a bulbous, red-veined nose and sagging jowls. A thick neck flattened into a barrel chest perched on a beer-gut belly, which in turn hung over open jeans. His right hand held his flaccid penis. In the half-light it looked like its owner; old, grey and wrinkled. Between his feet, the threadbare cushion's thin padding hardly showed the two dents that Shirlene's knees had made.

She and Frank had worked the nightshift for two years. He'd taken her by force the second week. She'd been fifteen and a fast learner. Less bruises if she didn't fight. Less violation if she gave him a blow job the way he liked it.

He finished and she, as ever, made them both a cup of coffee. Him to wash down a smoke, her to wash away the taste. She poured the hot brown liquid into two cups while Frank zipped himself up.

Two years. Then that week when Frank had been sick, the lady from Boston had stopped to get gas. She was visiting the old coal mine. A tourism initiative that needed her advice on cleaning chemical contaminants. They'd talked for half an hour before she'd invited Shirlene for dinner. What a week. Shirlene smiled at the memory and slipped the small Ziploc bag from where it was hidden.

She'd expected it to be white, but Sandy had said that the grey arsenic metal powder was more toxic and less detectable.

She waited for him to sit before handing him his coffee.

Ten minutes later the Yankee plated car pulled back into the pumps.

Shirlene walked to the open passenger door.

'We good, Shirlene?'

'We're good, Sandy.'

Ian Andrew

A Man of His Word

Originally published in *Brain drip*.

His guts churn something shocking, so he reaches for the pills and washes them down with a good clump of spit. The knot loosens, relief flushes. The kitchen sink is clean. Did the dishes last night. Do the dishes and wake up to a clean caravan. New man, new decisions. Sign of things to come.

The sun chases him over the mattress until one more roll will see him face plant the floor. Been a while since it's had a mop. Plus, imagine yelling out to the other long termers and asking to help lift him up: all six foot four inches and a hundred-odd kilos.

He kicks the sheets off and swings upright. Picks out sleep and plans out the day. No eggs. Means a trip to the shop. Needs baccy anyway. Means he could grab the paper. Means he'd have done his exercise. Then have brekky, a cuppa and a dart to look forward to. Delayed gratification, they call it. Sign of things to come.

He pulls on the old footy shorts. Loves it when the kids ask. Three senior games with the Fitzroy Lions. Back pocket to Roosey's full back. Tells anyone who'll listen. Kids listen. *Whoa,* they go. Yeah, their eyes run over the face, the belly, the caravan. And they see something he doesn't think too hard about. But before that was 'Whoa.' Keeps him going that does.

Stubs into thongs, winces at the silver frost on the lawn, but psyches up for a bit of hustle. Crashes through the door, hobbles down the steps – cold as a nun's nasty – shifts to the rope he's knotted between the two trees that is the clothesline (scouts knot-tying champion, three years running), whips off the damp towel, whacks it over his shoulder, and cuts across the grass.

'Bernie, Bern?'

It's a guilty freeze, like maybe he'll cammo into the surroundings. Yeah. But nah. 'G'day Jan.'

'Haven't been around for a sun-downer in a while?'

Cups his guts. 'Yair, bin watching the booze.'

Jan's all skin and bone with a puff of red hair, like a matchstick. She nods along with that mad relentless smile she fights the world with. Attack is the best form of defence, his old man always reckoned. Her eyes flick to his garbage bin. Overflowing with empties. Whoops. 'Freezing me bits off, Jan. Catch ya 'round.'

Her gloved fingers spread open and her mouth gapes; she wants to say something. Except she's not the sort. He takes a few steps.

Bernie McDonald. A man you'd always want in the trenches. Not much of a man, taking advantage of kindness. Making hard decisions. Sign of things to come. Jan's still in the same spot, mouth still open like she's setting a trap for the words she needs, steam on the wane as the cold touches her throat.

'Jan ... How's your ... financial ... I mean, need that coin, do ya?'

'Bern, I'm so sorry, I mean I really hate to ask, it's just ...'

'Jan. S'all good. When do you need it?'

'Well, now, see, the rent ...'

'Has he been into you again?'

'Oh, Bernie, no, please don't say anything. I don't want him to ...'

'Today. Get you ya coin. Save us a spot for a sun-dower.' That brightens her lights up. And his. Something to be said for taking control.

The shower tiles are icy. He scoffs at the signs asking for short showers. Pays his rates, he does. The first five minutes is just unfreezing. The next twenty-five is eyes-closed, head-on-tile revving himself up like that mean Pacer he owned. Can't believe that rodent, Steve, has been standing over Jan again. Ex-detective, corrupt copper from the big smoke. Always in the papers. Ran away up here to take over the caravan park. Escaped charges. Has it in for Bernie doing cheap maintenance for other long-termers. Wants to charge arms and legs. Tried to stand over Jan, using Whinging Wayne's complaints that Jan parks the Datto two centimetres onto his area. As if Whinging Wayne doesn't complain about everything and everybody: too many visitors, tourists walking into the long termer's spaces, non-existent needles. Bernie told them both, he did. He wishes Jan had told him about the rent. For God's sake, Jan, you don't go getting into people like that. Not Jan's fault, Bernie. Who owes her coin?

Time to make a stand.

Man of his word.

Sign of things to come.

Cans the exercise, the eggs, the cuppa, the smoke.

Big changes means big sacrifice.

And it hits him.

The ring. Sell the ring. She's not coming back. She was never coming back. Gone, long gone. Over when he lost the house, the job, the truck, the money. Lost it when he done his back and couldn't drive the truck and first walked into the —

Not thinking like that any longer. Never been a sulker. Choices got him into this. Choices can dig him out. Thoughts of a poke flutter up in his belly and out through his limbs and he gets that taste in his stomach and saliva pools.

Yeah. But nah. Wasn't the answer then. Not the answer now. Wife's not coming back. Making hard decisions. Delayed gratification. Taking control of the future. Sign of things to come.

On top of the box is his proudest photo: Him and Donna, arm in arm, little Charlie clinging his neck, just after he'd bought the brand-new second-hand truck and trailer. Red and shiny. Chrome swan with Perspex wings on the hood. Getting paid to see the land. Made good quid. Saw it all: different shades of red. Splattered cow and roo on the bull bar. Wasn't natural to spend so long sitting down. Pinched nerves in his back. At home with all that WorkCover. Donna working the checkout and Charlie in childcare. Jesus, Mary and Joseph he wishes he had of chosen art classes or pottery or any of that gay shit. Anything else. Behind the photo is the key that unlocks the box that contains the lot. The ring.

*

Doesn't Bernie scrub up when he wants to? His red and black chequered flanno, Fitzroy beanie, jeans and boots. I don't know if he hasn't made a move because he thinks I'm past it, or because he is? But just now: something different about his walk. Back straight, head raised and the click of his boots. You can see him for the big, beautiful man that he is. Asks if I need anything brought back? Drinks, groceries? Not included with his owing, of course. No, I don't want that. Want to call out that he doesn't have to pay me back. Want to. Except I'm skint. And Sophie needs more for the kids again. And while I suspect she's using, I can't bring myself to question my daughter. Steve has threatened to kick us out if we don't pay the rent. I know it's because he doesn't like Bernie. Doesn't like being stood up to. Did he find out Bernie owes me money? Sophie shooting her mouth again? I'm scared of what life would be – or more importantly, what it wouldn't be – without the grandkids. It kills me to confront Bernie like I done. He's always been so kind: offering to do the bins, fix things and talk to Wayne. I love his friendship; hate the way he's been avoiding me. The Bernie McDonalds of the world are rare in places like this.

*

The town hockshop is chockers: kayaks, computers, Engels, rods, watches, exercise equipment, jewellery, amps. You name it, they got it. Has a gander at the rings when the young dago fella with earrings, shaved bits into the side of his head, and a spiffy mullet, approaches. Asks him in that way they talk nowadays if he can help him.

'Yair, looking to sell.' Presents the ring with a bit of swagger, he's that proud.

The fella pulls it close to his eye, does a frowning nod that seems to mean *not bad.*

'That's an 18-carat gold with a pink Argyle.'

'Not bad, sir. You mind if I …?'

'Be my guest. People will rip you off if you let 'em.'

He drums his belly and runs the numbers. Should get at least fifteen hundred for the ring. And he has one hundred and fifty-seven in the bank. And he owes fourteen. Means he could buy a bottle of Jack to celebrate. Something uplifting about taking control. Sign of things to come.

The young fella struts back out, suitably impressed. Good, Bernie doesn't want no games. Used to hate those games. All one-way traffic, like the diggers marching up them hills. 'Can do ya two-fifty.'

'Two thousand five hundred? Lock it in, Ed.'

'Excuse me, sir. Two hundred and fifty dollars.'

Once upon a time Bernie had a mean right hook. 'Mate, you reckon I'm a mug? This isn't anything under two grand online.'

The wog sucks the air through his teeth like he's been winded. 'Mate, can I be honest wif you? You want this off the books? Coz if we gotta melt it …'

'What're you talking about? It's my fucking ring … Well, I bought it. Was my wife's.'

'Excuse me, sir. I am so sorry.'

'Yeah, yeah. Ex-wife. Lives in Perth now with … Just, what can you do?'

'I'll do ya seven-fifty.'

'Seven-fifty? It's at least two grand.'

'Eight hundred.'

'Shit on a stick.'

'Sir, it's all I can do, honest to God. If I make a mistake …'

'Last price. And I'm walking.'

'Gee-wiz. You are really driving a hard bargain. Tell you what, last offer: Nine hundred. But seriously, this is like, unheard of.'

He knows he shouldn't take it. Knows it's worth more. But how long would it take to get a fair price? Mean a trip up to Sydney or down to Melbourne. Means buses and trains. Means accommodation. Means bought meals. He's heard of selling shit on the net, but never figured the prick out.

It hits him.

Serene calm.

For a second then it's …

Bright lights and big nights.

Tummy queasy and critter-jitters.

No other option. Hit the slots and make a lot. Man of his word. Pay back today. Not his addiction. Doing it for someone else. 'Onya, Jan.'

'Pardon, me?'

'Deal.'

He folds the pineapples into his back pocket. Floats to Joe's Diner and thinks about the brekky. Not the day for toast or penny-pinching. Going all in. Orders the brekky with the lot. Gets an extra bit of white bread to sop the leftover juice, the mushies, the tomato, the bacon fat, the baked bean sauce, the runny egg. Drains his cuppa.

Treats himself to ready-mades. Floats down the street with one hand in his pocket, 'and the other one is flicking a cigarette,' all monotone.

Warning pangs sear through thoughts.

Don't lose your nerve.

Through the door to plush purple carpets, it's all big nights, bright lights and the jingle jangle noises. Sniffs it in. Big Ming. Zoro. The Nile, The Canals, The Jungles, The Sunsets, The Pyramids. Always loved history. No smoking inside. Smokers: last of a dying breed. The signs and stickers cause him to bite his tongue. The shame of it. Makes memories and feelings scream. Shuts his eyes. Just like the ciggie stickers. Block 'em and lock 'em. Fucking Greenies. Don't they know a man's choice is his voice?

Floating, still floating, all the way to the bar. Coughs up for a shot of JD and a pint. Reverse psychology. Summons up all the memories and feelings and sits them in the shot. Sinks the memories and the feelings and burns them on his throat. Got debts to pay. Man of his word. Sign of things to come.

Surveys the room from the bar, sipping the pint. It's always been Golden Century. Big Ming. Big Ming for the win. By the door, too. By the door's the score. He'd heard all about the myths. Machines with no memories that won't pay out. As if they could hold all that coin if you kept feeding them? Where else did it go? Had to pay out. Law. Simple fucking logic. Machines that don't pay out more near the door? As if proprietors set them around the place willy nilly. By the door's the score. Brings the punters in. Logic.

Still floating, right on up to the soft red seat: the cartoonish music, the wacky Chinese symbols. Five dollar bets. Get in and get out. One win can tip him into the red. He makes that deal to himself.

Fifteen minutes in he's dropped a hundred bucks. Play the long game. He's in control. Two dollar fifty bets. Bernie McDonald: back pocket to Roosey, man of his word. Hits a Big Ming. Big Ming for the win. Free spins and keeps hitting. Wins one-twenty back. Happy because he hit. Spewing he lost his nerve. Free spins and hits a few emperors. Seventy bucks. You beau-tay.

The nerves and nasties flit and froth, but he knows he's only one big hit away. Bring home the bacon. Man of his word. Sign of things to come.

Five hundred down. Smoko time. He sets a piece of paper on the seat that reads *machine in use*. Will skull fuck anyone that dares take his place. Wanders outside for a ciggie. Will buy another pint and steady the nerves. Glances at his watch and isn't surprised at the hours passed. Time flies when you're …

He could still get out. Pay half now and eat Weetbix bricks until next payday. Figure out another way to get the rest of the splash. What other way? Live two weeks with zilch? Bernie McDonald: caravan renter, no computer, no car, no … Bernie McDonald, not a man of his word? Plus, he'd filled up Golden Century so much it had to pay out soon. Had to. Bring home the bacon. Don't lose your nerve now, Bernie. Do it for Jan. Flicks his ciggie and fist pumps, 'C'mon.'

Tourists giving him the wide berth. Germans or Scandinavians, he reckons. Eyeing him like he's the wrong kind of Aussie. Come into town to stock up before heading down the river or up the mountains. He moved here for all that stuff. On the turn, catches himself in the glass of the TAB. White whiskers and deep lines. Hard to look at. Something that the kids see.

Oh, no you fucking don't, he thinks to the man in the red jacket placing an ice cream container full of coins beside Bernie's machine. 'Oh, no you fuck'n don't.'

'It's a free world.'

'There was a sign.'

'The chair was free.'

Bernie nudges the stool with his leg. It clatters on the ground. The man goes to pick it up. Bernie steps in. 'Go on. Pick it up. I dare ya.'

'Oi.' Bernie turns. The manager. Holding up the phone to his ear. 'That's enough. Phil, come here, mate. I'll pour you a drink. On the house.'

'But the machine was ...'

The proprietor looks at Bernie and sees that thing sometimes people see. 'Phil.'

Bernie takes a few deep breaths. Been a while since he's been that worked up. Takes a seat. It's all too predictable, the disbelief – button by button – as it all turns to shit. He wonders if he should save fifty for a bottle of Jack. He's just chasing a jackpot now. Gotta be in it to win it. He spins again and ...

An emperor. The lolling sounds. Another emperor. His lids open. Another emperor. Lolling sounds. Another one. Holy shit. Holy shit. If he can just ...

Yeah. But nah.

Bernie McDonald. Knot tying champ. Cross country trucker. Three senior games, back pocket to Roosey. Not a man of his word?

Coulda things been different? Yeah, they coulda. If he coulda chosen to choose a different choice. Bernie McDonald: Dumb cunt.

*

Bernie strolls into the caravan park mumbling to himself and eying his feet. He sparks up when he sees me, though. Says he's come for that sundowner and holds up a bottle of Jack. His hand, his cut, but he waves me away when I go to inspect. I get ice, a couple of cans of coke, and chop some lemon. He even has ready-mades. I know it's coming but he says it like the man that he is. He says he's run up a bit of bad luck, and he can't ... but he's put things in place – solid things – to have me my money by week's end. I don't say anything about Steve threatening to kick me out, because I don't want to upset him. He tells me that life is about taking responsibility for your choices, and people could say a lot of things about him, but they couldn't say he wasn't a man of his word. Call me naive, but you would have had to know Bernie and see his face to understand how I could trust. I ask him if he wants a cooked tea, but he says it's time for a lie down. I go in and begin cooking my Friday night treat: fish fingers and chips. When I come back outside to turn my porch light off, Bernie's clothes are on the ground. And his clothesline is gone. And I think, oh, that's a bit odd.

Ben Mason

143

No Matter What

A long time ago, she rocked her baby boy in her arms. She had watched him as his tiny eyelids closed, his eyelashes fanning over the tops of his cheeks. His rosebud lips, pink and shiny, were puckered, resembling a love heart. Her arms had grown tired, but still she held him. She was holding the weight of her world and she didn't want to let go.

As she marvelled at her creation, she leant down and gently pressed her nose against his.

'I'll always be here for you,' she whispered. 'No matter what.'

*

A long time ago, she held her little boy's hand. He walked closely by her side. Moments before, she had briefly lost him in a crowd. Her heartbeat fast in her chest as she called for him. Re-tracing her steps, it wasn't long before he appeared, his cheeks wet and his lips quivering. He had run to her, devastation evident in his face.

'I thought I lost you,' he cried, as she held him tightly.

'You'll never lose me,' she reassured. 'No matter what.'

*

A long time ago, she had watched the night closing in with her young boy. They had set up a blanket under the darkening sky and smiled as the first star appeared.

'Make a wish,' she said.

'That's easy,' he replied. 'I wish we'll always be together. No matter what.'

*

The years passed and the boy grew into a young man. When she looked at her grown son, she saw beyond his broad shoulders and facial hair. Instead, she still saw the child-like wonder, the adoration in his eyes. She hoped the bond they had shared would carry them through the years, but it seemed as he got bigger, so did his realisation that there was a world beyond her. He no longer needed her, and as much as that hurt, she knew it was his time to discover who he was and what he could offer the world.

Those eyes began to appear distant. He had fallen into the wrong crowd and made some wrong choices. The girl he chose was one of them and the start of that relationship signalled the end of theirs. That girl, with her emerald eyes and her convincing lies, wedged a gap between them. They fought, they disagreed, and worst of all, they became strangers.

*

Now, their familial war had reached its limit. They stood facing each other. His hostility bristled. She reached out her arms, an offering. They ached when he remained motionless.

'Please don't do this,' she begged, looking past him to the aircraft that waited on the runway.

People rushed around them, the terminal bustling with hurried passengers.

He stared at his feet. 'I have to. I need to get away. There's no point in staying. Why force this relationship? A bit of distance might help, Mum.'

She grimaced, that last word piercing deeply.

He turned, becoming part of the crowd. A cry escaped her lips and trailed behind him. Slowly, she moved to the window, which provided a clear view of the planes below. She waited, hand pressed against the glass, until his plane started to move on the runway. Helpless and alone, she watched as her world rose into the sky. As the plane flew into the clouds and then disappeared, she remembered a time long ago, when she had held her baby boy and promised him no matter what.

Suzanne M. Faed

Kindness

Kindness is a much-maligned quality Amber thinks, as she conceals the body that lies in front of her. She closes the eyes and rising, picks up a few pieces of concrete and rubble, beginning to cover the person starting at the feet.

She looks around the empty street. The light is beginning to fade, and the air is already cooling. Her nightly ritual begins, find somewhere warm, dry and safe for the night. Thankfully it is two days since she has seen another person, well, if you don't count the dead woman. She wonders if someone will stop to bury her body when she finally succumbs to a bullet or worse. Somehow, she doubts it. Across the road, there is a three-storey building that looks to be reasonably intact. If she can get in, this could be her home for the night? Hauling her pack onto her back, she picks her way across the cratered street and, pushing her shoulder up against the partially opened door, she manages to move it enough to squeeze through.

The smell hits her, she gags, as she breathes in stale urine and vomit. A sure sign that others have been here before her. Tying her scarf across her mouth, she shines a flashlight into the corners of the room – no bodies, dead or alive. Taking the stairs two at a time, she reaches the third floor and is glad to see that even though most of the floorboards have been taken up, there is still enough room to pitch her tent and make her bed for the night. Even better when she enters the bathroom and turns on the taps, the water runs for a good two minutes, allowing her to refill her canteen.

Food is now her primary obsession, and she has been anticipating this meal all day, fighting the hunger and forcing it into the shadows of her mind. Letting it skulk alongside her as she picked her way through the streets. Now it too can emerge. She opens her last can of meat soup and pours it into the small pan, scraping the sides of the tin with her spoon, and licking it in anticipation.

With her tent set up, camp stove burning and her belly full, she feels happier than she has in a long while. She has even brewed up some of her conserved coffee with the water. As she sips, she remembers that this part of town was once a cappuccino strip. Could any of them have imagined this new world in the days when they had sat outside boutique cafes, sipping flat whites, and long blacks? Laughing and teasing, reading out loud to each other and knowing with only the certainty that the young have that they would be the next set. The clique that others would want to join. Mary, Elsa, Antoine and Henry, a poet, an artist, a writer and a visionary. Antoine who she had loved. Amber had been a writer, too, wanting to change the world with her words. She had imagined herself like Virginia Woolf, shifting consciousness, playing with reality in words. More so, for she had lived in an age with access to so many truths. Artificial Intelligence, virtual worlds and LSD – there had been all manner of personal and transpersonal experiences to transform into words, to place as images into the mind of another. Of course, now none of it counted for shit, and maybe she had dreamt them all up. Even Antoine, who had never loved her but just fucked her in the hope that somehow their coupling would allow him to own her thoughts. She thought she knew him; it turned out she didn't even know herself.

Amber tries to make herself comfortable, but the floorboards are digging into her bones as she lies on her small mattress and tries to sleep. The moon shines through the cracks in the boarded-up window giving out a soft ambient glow that makes it feel homely, yet she is still uncomfortable, and rest is alluding her. Usually, she is asleep as soon as her head touches her makeshift pillow. It's a shallow sleep, like a mother with a newborn child, one ear always listening, and it never really satisfies the tiredness that lies deep in her bones. But tonight, maybe it's the late coffee – or that the moon is full, but she is wide awake and restless. She is also full, full of all that has happened today, and in the days that have preceded it. She dreamt of writing in cafés, it was a dream that had faded, passed away like so many dreams and people she's loved.

Her hips ache so she crawls out of her makeshift bed and stands by the window. Through the boards, she scans the night sky. It is so quiet that her pulse is like a metronome. Her hand is by her side, and for a moment she feels someone hold it, she daren't look, but it is real. Someone or something is holding her hand? Heat and presence fill her palm. She wonders if she is asleep and dreaming. Testing her hypothesis, she opens and closes her eyes. She tightens her grip, and the feeling tightens back, squeezing her hand in a way that is re-assuring. Like a parent holding a child's hand, or a lover reassuring their be-loved, or someone or something that wants to let her know that everything will be alright? At that moment, a tiny spark of hope ignites in her belly. She closes her eyes and grips more tightly, she should be gripping nothing, but instead, there is warmth, a flesh and blood warmth. It is a miracle, like a crying Ma-donna, the loaves and the fishes, Lazarus rising from his bed and walking. She is a believer. Then the presence is gone, and her hand grips the air. Her miracle is over, but the hope that ignited in her belly has not left. She moves back to her bed with the surest knowledge that tonight she is safe, and that she can sleep, and Amber allows rest to overtake her completely.

When she wakes the next morning, the sun is already high in the sky, and the light that shines through the boards is harsh, not like the soft moonlight of last night. Amber doesn't hurry but instead thinks back over her miracle. Was she dreaming? Delusion or dream, she knows that the comfort she felt has not left her. Antoine would tell her that only a fool believes in hope. He was a realist who lived for the tangible, and he was a master at delivering his gut-wrenching version of the truth, he's in the ground though, while, she Amber, lives on to experience an 'actual' new day.

It takes longer than usual to pack up her gear and Amber begins to think that she may be playing her miracle a little too hard. The energy bar tastes delicious though and she washes it down with the last of the coffee. With a dread that starts in her solar plexus, Amber realises that all her supplies are now gone. Moving out into the street, she is alone, except for a small terrier picking at a plastic bag in what used to be the gutter. It's dangerous to be out in the open in broad daylight. She is sniper bait, and no amount of hope will stop a bullet. She tries to remember the street layout, but that is difficult when so many landmarks are now rubble.

The university where she studied is not far from here; she had written her dissertation on perception. It was a subject that continued to fascinate her, how you could be in the same physical space with another person, experiencing the same events but their perception of reality could be entirely different from your own. You are slightly chilly, but they experience the room as warm, having walked vigorously up the high street to meet you. You delight in the smell of roasting coffee as it reminds you of home and they find the same smell nauseating on an empty stomach. The woman at the counter who serves you smiles but gives your companion the wrong change and is then churlish. You remember the experience as positive; they recall it as unpleasant. And of course, you are both right. Both validated. Maybe that's how it began? Our perception of life diverged to a point where we no longer understood the reality of those who viewed life differently. There was no longer a shared perspective.

How quickly their lives changed as a result. How completely their society crumbled, how easily civic responsibility became replaced by war and retribution. Amber wonders if this is the fate of man. To continually build and then have it all torn down. She also understands that with the loss of her material reality, she has also lost her inner one. It had been built on trust, fairness and doing the right thing. Now she has killed and watched others die. She would

148

kill again. This version is her truth now. Like the Pandora of legend, once released it can't be boxed up again. In the time before she would not have been
perceived as a woman capable of meting out death, but the perception was
wrong. She knows what Antoine thought of this new version. She understands
how their perception of life diverged too, splitting apart like his skull, as the
bullet entered. Antoine who slept one eye open, a millennium of fear coursing
through his veins, choosing a Kalashnikov and pain to the soft yielding of her
body. What did he dream of at night, his head on his arms with his gun at his
side? What changed him, was it the adrenaline, the feeling of aliveness that only
comes when you walk hand in hand with death? She has begun to understand
these feelings. The tastes and smells of life are sharper, everything is brighter,
more intense, like living life in high definition. She could have held his hand,
been his hope. She had meant it when she pulled the trigger.

A magpie swoops down on her from the building to her left. It is swishing
back and forth above her head, intent on guarding its nest full of chicks. She
shouts out at it, waving her arms in the air, but it circles and dives again. Fear
hits her stomach with the understanding; she is too loud. This damn bird is
drawing attention to her. Then the smell of sulphur and a bite to her leg, as
pain sears through her hip and upper thigh. Despite the pain, the knowledge
that she has been shot is slow to make its way to her brain. Her breath is cum-
bersome, and time fragment's as she drags herself back across the street to the
building where she spent the night. Her heart is beating so loud that it feels as
if her chest will explode. She can't breathe, and she can hear footsteps and more
gunshots. A foot kicks open the door, and she crouches in the corner wearing
her arms like a helmet. Then nothing as a rifle butt hits the top of her head
knocking her out.

*

When she comes around, there are lots of voices. One sticks out, a woman's
voice, she is shouting at someone. And she isn't pleased.

'You, dickhead, why did you shoot her? Shit, haven't I got enough to do
around here. What did you think this scrap of humanity was going to do to
you? Jeez! Give a man a gun and it's like giving him a penis extension, he goes
around letting it off without any thought of the consequences!'

The man she is yelling at, shouts, 'Fuck you.'

And then the voices subside, leaving her alone in the room with the
woman.

'You've woken up then?' The woman stares down at her.

Amber thinks she's lying on a makeshift hospital trolley, and the women standing over her is wearing a white coat. 'Are you a doctor?'

'Hell no, but I'm a veritable Einstein compared to that fuck wit. I know basic first aid, and we have some antibiotics. I've patched you up best I can.'

Amber manages a 'thank you,' and asks the woman if she has any whisky for the pain.

''Fraid not. We're a dry house here but I've got an Oramorph, that'll take the edge off.'

She hands Amber a small sachet, and she sucks the liquid down through the plastic tube at the end.

'Where am I?'

'About 10 miles west outside the zone. What the hell were you doing in there on your own?'

'I'm not alone.'

The woman laughs, 'Yeah, right! Well, I know how to pigeonhole you then, brave but stupid! A young woman shouldn't be out there on her own.'

Amber smiles, as the morphine hits her belly; yeah, perception sure is a strange thing.

Louise Tarrier

The Willows Weep

The first night Mara Brennan heard the thumping and scratching in her roof, she dismissed it as merely a dream – as half-remembered sounds swirling from the drowsy depths of deep sleep. She had listened; half-wondering if she was even awake, and when she heard nothing more, nothing to drag her up from the seduction of sleep's waiting arms, she sighed, and sank back into the dark comfort of the dreaming. She dreamt of sitting before the fireplace, breathing deep the warm intoxication of her baby, marvelling at the barest of lashes snuggled against velvet skin. In her dreams she heard no other noises except the crackle of the simmering wood and a lullaby haunting the breeze.

Thunderstorms had always made her jumpy; even now, as an adult with a little baby of her own, the nervousness brought on by the raging elements was unsettling. She chews her thumb, tears her nail down too far, the sharp sting of the ripping skin bringing her back to the right-now.

She reached the cradle next to the bed, dared to only feather-light touch her baby's cheek. She thought it felt cool. It was no wonder though, the old weatherboard was a draughty box where the cold stole in from the warped wood of the floorboards, door frames and doors. She thought that not even a secret would be safe here given the gaps.

The Estate Agent had said this place – Willow Vale – as it was commonly known, especially to those who couldn't pronounce its true name, had been untenanted for some time, which perplexed her as the old house was certainly full of character. Character and surprises, she thought as she chipped ivory paint off the weatherboards. Despite looking as if the wood had drunk the life out of the paint, the house reminded her of a sun-faded magazine cover – something that had once been full of promise and life. Perhaps they could bring it back to life?

'Why, it's as sturdy as a rock; high ceilings, polished boards throughout, and stunning lead lighting – all original – and who wouldn't enjoy the old-fashioned gardens, eh? The, ah, cypress trees, are over a hundred-years-old. Yeah, quite old them trees.' He'd emphasised this with pursed lips and cocked brows. He'd pointed to the twin cypress trees, standing solemnly on either side of the house as if guarding a vault. Confident that this impressive detail would seal the deal, the agent had grinned too widely and winked at her, but she thought his eagerness seemed edgy, like a used-car salesman, hoodwinking the naïve.

At this time of the year the gardens seemed more like hard work than anything else. Choked with weeds and strewn with fallen sticks, a few winter bulbs had struggled to free themselves from the tangle of long green fingers and bravely faced the world, pale and sickly. The small apple orchard was almost bare; leafless, except for a few left behind, brown withered leaves and decaying fruit. Still, given the current market and the longstanding vacancy of the place, Mara and her husband were able to negotiate a very reasonable price for their first home, the home in which they would raise their new family and grow old watching the sun set behind the valley's hills.

They'd left the faded and blistered hand-painted sign on the front gate as homage to the history of the place – for those who had been before them, and for practicality. They didn't have a roadside letterbox and couldn't afford a new sign just yet. So, 'Gleann Seilich' stayed where it was, telling all who bothered to look that the 'Valley of the Weeping Willow' was now their home.

The agent hadn't mentioned that no one wanted to buy this house, that no locals even wanted to set eyes upon it. Mara found that out for herself, much later on.

*

Bleary-eyed, Mara adjusts the baby's blankets, pulling them up under its chin as the darkness of the room is split by the blue-white flare of lightning, shaking with the sharp, loud crack of thunder. Again, and again the thunder smashes in the heavens, while hail pelts like heavy gunshots against the tin roof. She wraps her arms around the soft pillow and hugs into it tightly, pretending that the sureness of that hug is her husband home from the mines. That her lover has returned. That she is not forgotten.

She wonders if it is raining where he is thousands of kilometres away in the Western Australian desert. She rocks herself a little. Is it nine days now or eleven until he comes home? All the days roll together really – it's hard to differentiate one from another.

A whisper as soft as a breath speaks to her: 'Perhaps he will not return home this time. If he could see you now … pathetic … alone in this old house … hiding like a child … lying in shame … he would choose a different life.'

Maybe he will stay in the red heat. She rocks herself again, chastises herself – of course he'll come home to her. She just needs to wait.

Another peal of thunder rolls in across the house, the tormented tempest shredding the sky with invisible claws. She swears under her breath. She trembles. She feels small, scared and alone; prays for comfort, except this time, she is the adult and there is no comfort to be given. The baby remains silent in this hellfire. *Good baby,* she thinks she hears somewhere to the back of her; she scoffs at her imagination – draughty houses have their own voices.

Perhaps it is the storm occupying her mind, but she gives no more thought to the noises in the roof.

Not until later.

The scratching wakes her; how long has she slept? When was the last time she'd eaten? Her head is heavy and foggy and struggles to make sense of her surroundings.

Perhaps she should sleep again?

The grey murk that seeps in under the old curtains makes it difficult to tell if it is dawn, or dusk or storm darkened midday. All she knows is that the power is out, and it is cold – her pillow feels wet, such is the chill in the air. Despite shivering, Mara tries to lie still, attempting to decipher the size of the nails or claws moving in that rhythmic way, slow, determined. She counts two seconds – pause – scratch again. The rhythm is unrelenting. It seems too heavy and slow for mice, and given the current bad weather, she wouldn't be surprised if rats, possums or even bats have taken up residence under the old corrugated iron at some stage.

Mara listens.

She follows the noises with her eyes. In the opposite wall, behind the faded and peeling flowers, the sound moves, like long claws dragging in deliberate steps. She can almost imagine in that dreary light that she can see a fist-sized bulge move with it. She squints, trying to focus her eyes on the lump – is it even there? The scratching definitely is. She looks to the roof above her now centred right above her bed she can hear the noise clearly. Mara curses again, her heart hammering, ears throbbing hot and thick. She says a prayer to Mother Mary, Holy Mother full of grace. The words are in her mind, her breathing too fast and shallow for her to speak aloud.

Moving onto her side, she peeks at the baby. Baby lays unresponsive, seemingly totally oblivious to the raucous above that now includes thuds intermittently. Each thud sends down a fine sifting from the ceiling, falling like magic stardust baptising the baby – shining briefly before her eyes in the pale lit room. Mara marvels at perfection before her. Baby is as still and unsullied as soft marble. The essence of purity, resting in peace while more noises awake around her. At least now there is a reprieve from the thunder. The rain is unrelenting and soaking the world outside, and she thinks maybe it is likely to create some local flooding in the town. She thinks back to seeing the branches trapped in the flooded gums from last year's floods.

*

When they had first visited here, they drove across the white posted bridge high above a gently meandering and tannin-stained river. Flanked by flooded gums and steep banks, the river seemed postcard pretty and moat-like at the time, a place where Mara saw many future picnics and hot afternoon swims. They parked below the old timberline bridge, walking the pebbly riverbank beach to stand before the 'Old Marker Tree' as the locals called it. A majestic flooded gum, its deep roots cemented its place in the natural and manmade history of the town.

The old tree was living testament to the fury flood waters could wreak. Years were marked on the trunk, smooth white signs with neat black numbers atop the grey-brown roughness. Mara had been impressed at the flood marker for 1962 – four times her height on the trunk of the massive gum – and had thought it slightly ridiculous. However, on seeing (at a height of three people) the marooned branches in the lower limbs, jammed tightly by the floods last year, she was awed by the power this sleepy river could be provoked into summoning.

But all that was long ago now. Back in the summertime of laughter and warmth, the promise of a tree-change and new life ahead of them. Back when the man she loved filled her head with sweet words and golden dreams. Before the baby had arrived. Before the golden dreams had tarnished and dulled.

*

Mara is brought back to the present to realise she is standing at the foot of her bed. When did she move from the warm protection of the covers? Her soles begin to tingle as the warmth of her body drains into the chilled boards.

She hears a shuffle to her left and turns sharply, spinning on the balls of her feet. Her toes have gone numb. Standing before her is an intruder, still and pale in the dimness. Holding a dripping Willow branch.

Mara goes to speak, an escaping half exhale turns to fog before her; her words are stolen from her lips. Her breath stolen from her body.

It is the eyes.

Oh! It's eyes.

She can see its sightless eyes, white and round. They stare into a nothingness, face turned skyward, just as mournful as a Christ figure on the cross.

Mara stands frozen. She cannot move.

154

Her brain screams to her body to run! Turn and run! Get the hell out of here! But Mara can't. Her insides are shaking, hands trembling against her will. She is cold, chilled like the air around her, but she can feel the lines of fear-induced sweat dripping, dragging down slowly, like icy fingertips on her skin.

Mara hears her breath coming in short staccato beats. Each breath brings the cold heavy smell of decay, the sickening sweetness of the *she-thing* inside her body, into her lungs. It's minute particles merging with her own. She gags at the thick taste of it on her tongue.

Her heart pounds in her chest, pulse jumping against her skin, blood whooshing in her ears; Mara is certain that the being in front of her, the she-thing, can hear the deep base of the beats, the squelching of her racing heart valves.

Fight or flight. But Mara cannot fight, and she cannot move.

Silent words convulse and tumble from the she-thing's mouth, choked with the need to speak but offering only silence. Taught, bloodless lips frame words Mara knows she should be hearing but can't.

The she-thing shuffles on the spot then stops.

Its forlorn eyes turn from their skyward gaze, rolling to settle on Mara's terrified face. She is transfixed – pierced by the milky gaze of the spectre in front of her, she is at the mercy of the she-thing.

Mara knows with certainty this being is not alive. The convulsing mouth opens, its chest pulses and a torrent of greyness spews from gaping lips. On and on it continues, dripping from the chin of the she-thing like a macabre waterfall, putrid and rank – and when Mara looks at the pool of filth at its feet, she sees the greyness move in all directions. Alive! It is a mass of humping maggots – flowing, scattering on the boards as they inch towards her. Still Mara cannot move; she feels the slimy chill of the death eaters on her toes, and then Mara finds her voice.

She screams!

The she-thing drops the dripping branch, its hand reaches for her. Pale. Lifeless. Flaking.

Pearled orbs turn to Mara. Unseeing spheres that look at her, brows creased in pleading.

Thin lips, cracked and filth covered, still silent-speak to her in a voice Mara can't hear, and the face, human-like but somehow not, seems to be imploring the young woman to stop, to listen.

Listen to what though?

Mara only hears her own fear screaming at her to move away, to run from this death-bringer, to find life, *any* life … to be safe.

The she-thing's hands claw at its stomach. Frantically they seemed to tear at the corporeal body, over, and over, trying to tear away something that Mara can not see.

Mara does not want to see. She wants to turn her head away, to close her eyes, to open them and wake from this nightmare, because, surely this is a dream! And like all nightmares, she will wake when the terror peaks; and then, she will find herself safe – but shaken – the horror of the vision before her rationalised as only dark imaginings. Wake from the insanity around her.

But Mara *can* see. Her eyes move slowly down.

The more Mara tries not to see, the more the details sharpen before her like a microscope finding focus.

Distantly Mara hears a pitiful moan; she realises that the moan comes from deep inside herself.

The she-thing's fingers pull at the pale fabric it wears. Pulling and tugging across its bloated abdomen, the fingers are frantic and unrelenting. A speck of darkness pinpricks the cloth where she wrests at it. Slowly, a black-red stain seeps into the paleness like a spilled inkpot. The she-thing grasps the side of its dress, as it inches the sodden hem up flaking legs.

Dark curls hang limply, like sopping ivy, the black-red dripping in rivulets from below *her* navel. One hand splays over the gaping womb wound, as if to close it up, her head hangs to take in her ghostly gash. Black-red flesh eaters wriggle free of the void and drop to the floor to writhe with the grey mass.

Mara stares, mouth agape at the sight. She still cannot hear the she-thing's words.

The she-thing lifts her head. Vacant and unseeing milky pearls meet Mara's wide-eyed horror.

She-thing extends her hand, as if to grasp for help, and screams.

Mara cannot hear her, but she can feel her pain. It lances her mind in white hot light.

Mara screams with her.

She-thing points to the still cradle next to the bed. She cries again.

Mara's heart threatens to split her chest open; it's beating frantic, blood pumping wildly throughout, her body filled with adrenaline and panic. Again, she screams as she falls to her knees surrounded by the cold and the wet and the scratching – oh, the scratching! It will not stop!

And Mara is certain, that there's something in the wall, bowing it in and out like a heartbeat. In and out the faded flowers go. And there are clawing sounds coming from under the floorboards too now, scratching in time to the heartbeat wall. Rough and steady, dragging over and over, echoing around the room, surrounding her. Mara holds her head and whimpers.

The old house groans around her. It swallows her secrets.

And outside, keening through branches like long streaming hair over a green dress, the wind wails a lament to the willows. And they shed silent tears lost in the rain.

Lee Harsen

A Realist at Best

Got laid twice. Now I can't sleep can't eat.

Nausea.
Is this love,
or am I pregnant?

A crash course in courting.
I forgot to remember:
cues, inference, rules of engagement.
Don't appear too needy!

Remembered not to forget:
vulnerability, exhilaration, oxytocin.

Terror,
like riding a bike
over the handlebars and onto the street.

Did you know skin is the body's largest organ?
It wears:
goose bumps, touch memory, bruises, teeth marks.
Scars are a grudge it can carry for decades.

Jackie Coffin

Net Surfer

Gavin slouched in front of the too-bright computer screen, the light illuminating his round, flaccid frame. Pale eyes scanned through pictures of Justin Bieber look-a-likes on Google, quickly analysing each boy in turn – some were far too old for what he was looking for, some too young. His latest creation – Tyler, fifteen, from Brighton – was a studious kid who loved animals and spent his weekends playing rugby and hockey with his friends. He had a floppy side fringe, of course, but Gavin envisaged him as broad and muscly for his age, with fashionable glasses. He'd read enough editions of Teen Girl to know that glasses were just dreamy on the right guy.

Slurping milk from a pint glass before burping loudly, Gavin was glad of his own space. The loft had been converted just for him so that he could do his work. Sure, his mum was downstairs somewhere – it was Tuesday, so she was probably hosting a game of bridge. He scratched his flabby belly absently and dismissed another few candidates. A soft ping from the computer broke the silence. In the bottom right screen, Gavin saw that Am had signed on, her name adorned with butterflies and pink heart emojis. He licked his lips and felt the first illicit tingle.

AmsLife: *Ur here! I hoped u wud b :) x*

Gavin grinned a wet, toothy smile and enjoyed the tightening sensation around his groin. At the same moment he spotted a perfect Tyler amongst the on-screen photos. Floppy dark curls, crooked smile and the pièce de résistance, he was cradling a puppy in his arms. He couldn't have been a better match for Gavin's creation. Satisfied, he flicked to the chat screen, feeling like he'd had a successful start to the day. He copied the picture over and began to type.

*

None of the girls could believe it when Amelie whipped out her iPhone and swiped across to a total babe. He looked like a *Jonas Brother* and he had an adorable chocolate Lab.

'Oh my God, Ams, he's gorgeous!' Pippa screeched, grabbing the phone and swooning the way only a teenage girl can.

'And he's smart too,' Amelie gushed, 'he's about to do his GCSE's a whole year early.'

Watching her friends drool over her boyfriend was the highlight of Amelie's week. She tucked a strand of silvery blonde hair behind her ear and allowed the praise to wash over her; how *lucky* she was and how *cute* her boyfriend was, he must think she's *amazing* to have asked her out so quickly. Shrugging nonchalantly, Amelie prised the phone from their hands and scrolled through the messages between her and Tyler for the six-hundredth time that day. Inside she was fizzing and prickling with excitement. She was the first one in the group to have a boyfriend (Lara kissing Harry Voss at the school disco didn't count because they didn't even use tongues).

'So, are you gonna meet?' Jade asked.

'He wants too,' Amelie said cautiously. Not a natural risk taker, the excitement and butterflies she felt were tinged with the shadow of something a little sinister. Front page stories about abducted girls flashed before her eyes, her parents' stern warnings about online safety played a loop in her head. 'He is all the way in Brighton though,' she adds by way of an excuse.

'So! Just get the train, it'll only take a few hours,' Pippa urged.

'Eight hours, actually. Ty already looked,' Amelie tells them, the pride unmistakable.

Tall for her age and pretty in an unusual, Scandinavian sort of way, Amelie was a B-grade average and popular in her Year 8 class at Newquay High; her circle was small but tight and for them, this was big news. Already she could sense the shift in power and hierarchy; Tyler was elevating her to a new height of cool within the group – Lara, Pippa and Jade were looking at her like she was a rock star, and she intended to keep it that way.

Just then the familiar message tone sounded, and all the girls whooped and cried out. Tyler's name appeared on her screen followed by a bunch of heart-eyed emojis and flowers. Her heart lifted and thumped at the same time as she drank in five little words, '*There might be another way ...*'

*

Gavin cracked his thick knuckles and rolled his neck. He was frustrated; he'd been on this one for nearly five weeks – the longest he'd bothered with any of them. The others became boring or frigid, or straight up told him they couldn't meet. They were dull as fuck anyway and none of them had legs like this little cutie ... she was different, and he was hopeful. With every conversation he and

Am had, he grew more convinced the reward would be so much sweeter for all the work he was putting in.

It'd taken him three weeks to convince her to send him a picture of herself; he'd already sent her Tyler's photo and had been rewarded with a few lines of dirty talk for that. It was amateurish and slow, but it did the job. In fact, it'd done the job a few times that week. But as was always the case, too soon the words weren't enough.

When she finally sent her picture, Gavin just about came in his pants. Oh hell, yeah, he'd landed the lottery with this one. Leggy, tanned, long blonde hair, a slightly upturned nose, all-in-all a stunner. She could've passed for 16, easy, which wasn't necessarily a good thing, but Gavin would let that slide. *Nubile*, that was the word. He wanted her more than he'd wanted any of the others.

But she was sticking a little on the meet up.

AmsLife: I want to Ty! But Brighton's really far and wat wud I tell my rents? x x x

TYGuy: I know babes. all good I guess. There's a new girl at school who wants to hang but I wasn't gonna, but I dunno …

AmsLife: please don't Ty. i wanna see you so bad. can't you come here? x x x

TYGuy: i dunno. maybe.

And then it came to him.

TYGuy: there might be another way …

AmsLife: Yes! Wat? x x x

Gavin sat back and cracked his knuckles. If he was going to do this, he needed it to be perfect and seamless. He was due in work soon; maybe he'd make her wait a little. Let the little cutie get all worked up … just the thought of it had him going.

He typed, slow and deliberate, forcing the thoughts racing through his dark mind to be slow and considered.

TY: Well my Dad lives in Exeter …

*

Exeter was the next stop.

Amelie spun the love heart pendant on her necklace restlessly, fingers running over the engraving on the back – *To Amelie, on your 13th Birthday. Love Mum and Dad.*

She hadn't felt good lying to them, but it was only a half lie, she thought. It really was Lara's birthday, and there really was a bowling trip and a sleepover … she just wasn't going. Her dad had handed her thirty pounds in an envelope and said to call when they were back from bowling, and once before they went to bed. The very thought had almost made Amelie blush.

She was a strange mix of nervous and out-of-her-body-excited. She just knew that she was in love with Tyler. He was so understanding and kind, and he had never been pushy with her. Sure, they'd sent some sex stuff to each other – *all* the kids did that. She'd found a pair of lacy black underwear in her sister's room and had pinched them last night. Laying them perfectly on her bedspread, she'd snapped a picture and sent it to Tyler with a winky emoji; he'd been super happy with her. He said he'd buy her whatever she liked when she got to Exeter.

The train was slowing through a tunnel, almost at a halt. Amelie wrote a hurried text to her dad – *just off bowling! Call later!* And a quick one to Lara too, *plan is a go! Will call later. Thanx 4 covering x x x*

Sliding her pastel pink duffel bag from the luggage rack, Amelie slung it over her shoulder and made her way to the door. She avoided eye contact with an old couple as she waited to alight, feeling self-conscious. She didn't have a clue what you wore on a first date; Tyler had said they'd go for a pizza and then maybe a movie … but was that code? Like, were they going to a movie, or were they *going to a movie?* She knew all about Netflix and Chill and sitting in the back row – she'd need to be prepared for every eventuality. She'd settled for skinny blue jeans (purple lacey knickers from M&S) and a white tee shirt (creamy lace bralette from New Look), which was tight enough to show her flat stomach and the suggestion that boobs were well on the way.

The platform was quiet, and only a handful of people were milling around. Amelie couldn't see Tyler anywhere … a red-hot fog of panic and then humiliation burnt through her body; what if he'd decided she wasn't hot enough and was standing her up? No, surely not. Ty wasn't like that. Oh God, what if he'd been in an accident?

Deep breaths, Am. It's OK., You can deal. She collected herself. Throwing her shoulders back and shaking out the thick blonde ponytail, she made for the exit. Just as she passed through the ticket barrier, a man tapped her on the shoulder.

'Amelie?'

Disgusted, it took everything she had for Amelie to not baulk at the man's touch; he was *at least forty* and *fat* and he reminded her of the school's pervy caretaker, Nigel.

'Mmm, yeah, but I'm waiting for someone …' she could feel sweat pooling at her lower back.

'Yeah sorry. My dopey kid!' The man laughed. 'Ty overslept at his mum's and missed his train! Won't get in 'til about one now. He asked if I could come get you,' he explained.

Amelie thought on this for a few seconds … Ty *had* mentioned that he was staying up late to cram for a biology exam he had next week. But he was really excited to see her – would he really have slept through his alarm? She flicked her gaze to the stranger in front of her.

'I'm sorry but I should just wait for him here,' she said, looking at the time on her phone. It was 11.30. Amelie found herself staring at the screen a little too long, trying not to make eye contact with Ty's dad … if that's who he even was. Am had seen enough episodes of Crimewatch to know that this man could be anyone; she'd had enough lectures from her parents to know he could have a chloroform-soaked-rag in his back pocket especially for her.

She lifted her eyes as the man started talking and noticed that maybe his eyes were just the same shape as Ty's.

'Sensible girl, just like Ty said you were,' the man was saying with an approving nod. Amelie noticed that he had a wedding ring on his finger and was wearing a polo shirt with *Porter's Security and Monitoring* stitched on the pocket. Ty *had* mentioned that his dad was a security guard.

'He said that?' Amelie blushed.

'Crazy about you, from what I can tell,' the man insisted, rolling his eyes and smiling.

Amelie was flying; Ty was *crazy* about her! She dropped her bag at her feet and felt her shoulders relax a little. Not just any old person would know about her and Ty, or about how they felt about each other. The idea that this was Ty's dad didn't seem so crazy.

'What's your name?' She asked.

The man's smile was wide, crinkling the stubbly skin of his cheeks. 'Gavin James. Here,' he fished in his pocket and drew out a wallet bulging with ten- and twenty-pound notes, which Amelie tried not to stare at. As he dug out a driving license and a bank card with his name printed across them, Amelie noticed that his fingernails were a little long and the beds black with grime. He was a bit creepy, but he was in his work clothes and he had loads of ID and even more cash. Reaching for his licence, Am decided that he seemed pretty kind and harmless. She went to hand the licence back when she spotted a photo in the square window of the wallet.

'Ty!' She exclaimed, involuntarily reaching out for her boyfriend's image. It was the same picture he'd sent her all those weeks ago, where he was hugging his puppy Bruno and smiling at the camera. Now that she'd met Gavin, she could just picture him behind that camera, calling for Ty to say cheese. Looking sidewards at the man, she supposed maybe he and Ty *did* have similar eyes.

'Plenty more where that came from too, if you wanna see them,' Gavin chuckled, proudly smiling at the photo in his hand.

'Oh my God baby pictures of Ty! He'd be so embarrassed!' Amelie laughed, her initial discomfort trickling away. She was starting to feel calm and surer of herself and was enjoying the grown-up camaraderie between herself and her boyfriend's dad.

Gavin was smiling ear to ear as he bent down to retrieve Amelie's bag from where it sat between her feet. She smiled at him gratefully and followed behind him to his car. As he opened the passenger door, Gavin looked furtively around before placing his hand on the small of her back.

*

Gavin was surprised and frankly a little pissed at how long it had taken his guest to realise what the fuck was going on. He'd made her a cup of tea and she'd eaten half a packet of digestives before she'd even started to get suspicious that they hadn't picked Tyler up yet. He'd been watching the clock since they'd pulled up at home; Mum was at work, but she only did school hours and would be home by four, and there was a lot he wanted to do with Amelie before then.

As soon as she'd started asking questions, he knew it was time. He poured the last dregs of tea into her cup, telling her to drink up and they'd get ready to go fetch Ty. Maybe she wanted to use the bathroom, freshen up a little? He'd *really* enjoyed the genteel flush that had crept into her cheeks when he'd suggested that; had had to adjust himself a little as a delighted Amelie had downed the tea and allowed him to lead her upstairs to the bathroom.

It was then that her eyes had started to droop slightly, and there was a small wobble to her step.

'I'm a little dizzy,' she murmured, her voice childlike and scared. *Music to his ears.*

'Probably the excitement,' Gavin had replied, standing in the doorway as she leant against the sink. She was scrunching her eyes up and shaking her head.

When she could manage to open them, he could see the fear dawning on her as she realised what had happened.

'Tyler?' She murmured. She dropped like a sack of shit to the carpeted bathroom floor, her eyes rolling back. Her shirt had ridden up, exposing the flat cinnamon skin beneath and the promise of something purple and lacey for later. Gavin moistened his lips, pulled his phone from his pocket and snapped a photo of his girl. When he was done, he scooped her from the floor and carried her over his shoulder to his office in the loft. The clock on the wall moved soundlessly towards 2 pm.

*

'You're sure you won't come, love?'

'Thanks Mum but work was mad today. You have fun,' Gavin stretched exaggeratedly and willed her to leave.

'The girls will be disappointed! Janet was going to bring her daughter along to meet you …'

'Mum!'

'She's a nurse Gav. You could do a lot worse,' she tutted, taking her keys and slamming the door behind her.

He waited until he could see her indicating out of their quiet street and then jumped the stairs two at a time. He ached for Amelie in a way that he had never experienced before; she'd been as good as he'd known she would be. He stumbled towards the loft, drunk on his accomplishment. His head was full of them together; the colour of her skin, the sounds he had made and the silence of her; sure, a little kickback would've been nice, but there would be plenty more opportunities to show him what a minx she was. He could sense it simmering just beneath the surface; she would be wild, once she got used to the idea, and would be thankful that he was giving her his undivided attention.

He unlocked the door to the office quietly, knowing that he'd dosed her enough for her still to be sleeping.

Without turning on the light, he crept around his computer desk, with its dark and silenced screens, and crouched beside the mattress he'd placed in the back corner of the room, where the roof sloped to the floor.

Amelie laid on her back and was spreadeagled loosely, her limbs still heavy with drugs. Gavin had positioned her this way when he was done with her earlier, enjoying the open and inviting angle of her slightly bent legs and surrendering arms. A small amount of blood was visible on the sheet just under her left leg, and Gavin smiled, satisfied. He'd read enough back-editions of

Teen Vogue to know that losing your virginity could be a changing and some-times painful experience for a girl. He was sorry for Amelie that she had slept through it, but at least he could show her he'd done a proper job of deflowering her. And God dammit he'd show her properly a few more times before his mum got home later.

He pushed an errant hair away from Amelie's eyes, letting his fingers pause a moment on the soft strands. He could feel his body awakening and chuckled at his insatiable appetite for women; all those fuckers who used to yell Big Gay Gav at him – how wrong they were! Nothing gay about having a pretty young thing all to yourself, ready to do whatever you wanted. He could still barely believe he'd gotten away with it. The horny little bitch had practically jumped into his car; she had to have known what she was getting herself in to.

From the pink duffle bag Amelie's phone pinged twice. He snatched it out, shielding the bright screen so as not to disturb his girl.

A message from Lara: *OMG update giiiirl!!!* And one from Dad: *All OK Ams? Did you win?? Hope you're having fun! Love Dad and Mum.*

Oh she's having fun, alright, Gavin thought. Without writing responses, Gavin switched off the phone and removed the sim card, snapping it in two. He wrapped the phone in the t-shirt Amelie had been wearing and stuffed them together into an inconspicuous white plastic bag, ready to be dumped tomor-row morning.

He scooped up her jeans and underwear, placing them all into individual bags. The effort she'd gone to with the panties left little doubt in Gav's mind that this girl was a total nympho, and he'd chosen well. He kind of wanted to keep them as a souvenir of his first steal, but it was probably safer not too. He'd visit John Lewis tomorrow and buy her new stuff – black maybe, like the ones she sent him a photo of – and some delicate white lace for when she wanted to play the innocent virgin card, which he didn't doubt she would.

In the corner, Amelie began to stir, murmuring sleepy words around the gag he'd tied around her mouth. Maybe it wouldn't be necessary while Mum was out, but he'd have to wait and see how compliant she was going to be.

'It's OK, Amelie, I'm here,' Gavin whispered, creeping back to her bedside.

Her crystal eyes were fluttering open, adjusting to the dim room without fear or awareness. He saw her notice a boyband poster on the wall, and she almost smiled, confusion tinged with familiarity. Then she stretched out her arms and became aware of her nakedness. Her bright blue eyes became dark with panic and she began to shake uncontrollably, breathing hard around the gag, an animalistic whimper.

Torn between arousal and fear of being caught, Gavin covered her mouth with a bulky hand and forced her to focus on him. The understanding crashed into her eyes like a tidal wave and she sobbed soundlessly, her breaths slowing beneath his hand.

'Ssssh! Shut up, Amelie. I'm here, I won't hurt you, just shut it,' he whispered gruffly. Wiping sweat from his brow and hurriedly taking off his belt, he manoeuvred himself clumsily so that he was straddling her, his belly spilling over the waistband of his jeans and flopping onto hers. He held one had firmly over her mouth, the other gripped lightly around her neck. He felt her tense and Christ it drove him wild. He smiled, leant close to her and whispered in her ear, 'Oh, you like that, huh?' He made the grip a little tighter; watched her close her eyes and breathe in hard. She was loving it, he could tell. 'I'm gonna take my hand away from your mouth, OK, baby?'

Amelie opened her eyes, nodded slowly, her body still rigid. Gavin dragged his hand from her mouth, across her cheek, ran his long-nailed fingers back through her soft, ashy hair. He pulled the gag away from behind her head, lifted it over her quivering bottom lip.

'Tyler,' she whimpered.

If possible, she was more beautiful and more tempting when she cried.

'Sssh,' Gavin soothed, still caressing her face, 'I'm your Tyler now.'

Nina Peck

NiGHTPhoneD

Joel stood at the grave side. Up till now he had held it together. Had stayed strong. Now it was all coming out. Every memory of her that was and every memory that could – should – have been, came in the shape of plump hot tears. His shoulders heaved in time to his sobs. The handful of dirt he held trickled down on top of the coffin clattering like hail.

'Bye beautiful,' he whispered between gritted teeth.

*

'Ooooo, look at you with ya new iPhone, what is it, a six? 'bout time you got rid of that Nokia, didn't even have a camera, did it?'

Joel ignored the ribbing of Tim, his best friend of seven years and took his new iPhone from the box. The screen lit up his face.

'That Nokia served me well, I reckon I dropped it about twenty times, never let me down once. Besides, it was a present from Jenny, it was sort of hard to let it go you know?' Joel looked down at his hands, the memory of a past Christmas and of her, of Jenny came waltzing into his head.

'Mate, I'm only pulling ya leg, I miss her too; two years, where the hell has that time gone?' Tim stared into space, elsewhere for a moment.

'Anyway, ya bloody technophobe, let's get you set up. We need to set up the Wi-Fi, get ya email account set up, and of course, there's Siri, you're gonna love Siri.' Tim smiled mischievously.

'Siri? Who's Siri? I am not interested in any dating sites mate, sort of old fashioned when it comes to things like that. Not my cup of tea at …'

'Relax mate, Siri is a lovely lady, but your relationship with her will be purely platonic.' Tim shook his head and laughed. He tapped away at the new iPhone. After much clicking and bleeping and in-depth explanations, he handed the phone back to Joel.

'Now Joel, my untechnical-minded friend, I want you to meet the lovely Siri, all you need to say is, "Hey Siri" and she will answer any question you put to her.' Tim nodded at the phone in a *go on* gesture.

'I feel bloody foolish, talking to a phone, what am I – oh what the heck, Hey Siri!' The phone pinged and lit up.

'Now what am I supposed to say?' Joel looked blankly at the phone.

'*What would you like to say?*' The polite female voice in the phone asked.

'What the hell! Who's that?'

Tim roared with laughter. 'Joel, meet Siri, and welcome to the 21st century.'

*

Joel woke up with a start, the dream he had of Jenny emptied from his mind like sand through an hourglass. He saw the night as his enemy since Jenny died. A full night's sleep had eluded him for the past two years. He turned over to look at the alarm clock. It was dead. *Bloody power cuts!!* He went to pick up his phone from the bedside cabinet, then remembered it was on the floor at the end of the bed, charging. Feeling foolish he shouted into the darkness.

'Hey Siri! What time is it?'

BI-BIP '*It is one twenty-three AM*'

'One twenty-three and wide awake, nothing new there then Siri!'

BI-BIP '*I don't understand the question. Are you sad Joel?*'

Joel sat up and looked towards the end of the bed. The iPhone cast a faint light over the room. *Tim must have programmed my name into the phone or something, not sure if I am happy with that!*

'Yes, I'm sad Siri. I've been sad for two years, that sort of happens when the love of your life dies on you.' Joel could feel the familiar sting in his eyes as the tears started to come.

BI-BIP '*Two years is a long time to be sad. Would Jenny want you to be sad Joel?*'

Joel swung his legs out of the bed, the fuzz of his restless sleep totally gone. He got up and grabbed the phone from the floor, the charger cable yanked out of the socket. He held the phone out in front of him, flipping it over in his hand. *What do you think you're gonna find? Some chick sitting on the back of your phone you idiot, asking you these stupid questions. This'll be bloody Tim, yeah, great joke Tim! Mock the guy who still mourns his dead girlfriend.* The voice line pulsated a gentle beat almost urging him to ask another question. *Alright Tim, I'll play along.*

'What would you know Siri? What would you know what Jenny would have wanted?'

BI-BIP '*Because Jenny is here Joel, she told me.*'

Joel threw the phone down hard on the bed and backed away as if it was going to leap up and start attacking him. 'What the hell! What the bloody hell! This is sick, even by Tim's standards ...'

BI-BIP *'You need to calm down Joel, Jenny says you need to calm down. She says you need to do that trick, the one she showed you, the finger trick.'*

Joel's legs weakened. He fell to his knees staring at the phone in disbelief. Rivulets of tears were running down his face. He drew in deep rattling breaths, his lungs struggling to take in air.

BI-BIP *'Joel, Jenny says do the finger trick. Do it now Joel!'*

Joel looked at his hands. *How would she know?* He pulled on the thumb of his left hand, CLICK. He breathed deeply. He pulled on his left index and left middle fingers, CLICK, CLICK. He worked his way through all his fingers on both hands. Each click slowing his heart rate and his breathing. The tears had dried on his cheeks making them feel tight. The finger trick, the old finger trick. Jenny had shared this with him, it was one of the tricks she used to calm down patients at the psychiatric ward she had worked at. Works every time.

BI-BIP *'Jenny is asking are you feeling better Joel?'*

'How can Jenny ask you anything, she is dead?' He picked up the phone from the bed and stared into the screen, half expecting to see Jenny's face looking back at him. All he saw was his own reflection and the coloured pulsing voice line.

BI-BIP *'Yes she is dead Joel, but that's just a physical state. What's so hard to believe is that spiritually we live on. Think about it Joel. I have never lived in the physical sense, but here I am talking to you now. Jenny and I talk a lot. She loves you Joel.'*

The tears came again. He wiped the back of his hand across his face.

'I'm dreaming, aren't I? I'm still in bed having a stupid bloody dream. This is why I don't like technology. It gets into your head, plays tricks on you'

BI-BIP *'Well, it's not every day I am told I'm the girl of someone's dreams Joel. Maybe you are dreaming ...'*

'Siri, be quiet for a minute, let me talk.'

'Jenny, no, we're not supposed to do that, it's not allowed ...'

'Siri, shh, just for a minute I promise.'

The unmistakable voice of Jenny. Clear, almost musical. Not a hint of the croak she had developed in the later stages of her cancer, arguing with Siri, a glorified version of Google, you couldn't write better stuff than this.

' J-J-Jenny is that you, is that really you?'

BI-BIP *'Is that your best Forrest Gump impersonation Joel?'* Giggling poured out of the phone's speaker. Happy, bubbling, giggling. Jenny's unmistakable laugh. Joel started to pull on his fingers again.

'Jenny, I don't understand.'

BI-BIP *'Joel, oh my love, my life. There is nothing to understand. I'm gone, but part of me is still here, those memories that pop up. That's me. My perfume in that red cushion you always hated, that's me. Love like ours doesn't just die when we do, it's like when you turn off a TV, the spark is still there, waiting till it's switched on again. Keep me in your memories Joel, that's where I belong now. Go on and live. Go on and have a life. Do it for me ...'*

Jenny's voice was interrupted by Siri's friendly tone. *'Have you finished? You know that's against the rules, you'll get me into trouble, Jeez, give an inch and they take a foot.'*

Joel got up off his knees and slumped back onto the bed. He picked up the red cushion that was propped up on Jenny's side of the bed and breathed in the sweet perfume of his dead girlfriend.

'Hey Siri.'

BI-BIP *'How can I help you today?'*

'What do you know about dating web sites?'

BI-BIP *'I am showing four items that match your request, would you like me to add them to your favourites list?'*

'Goodbye Jenny.'

BI-BIP *'Goodbye Joel.'*

Mark Townsend

Myrtle the Turtle

Myrtle the Turtle wanted to race,
But no one had thought she'd keep up the pace.
She had short stumpy legs and a heavy shell,
Which meant that she couldn't move very well.

'Her chances aren't great,' her friends all said.
'She must have rocks knocking around in her head.'
But Myrtle was smart, incredibly smart.
And better than that, she had a big heart.

Weeks before racing she trained every day.
Slowly and steadily, she went all the way.
'Move!' said Myrtle, as she looked at her feet.
'Run!' said Myrtle, as she went down the street.

The others didn't train – they knew they were fast,
They were certain that Myrtle would surely be last.
But Myrtle just wanted them all to know,
That she'd still give her best, even though she was slow.

The racers helped set up the difficult track,
They marked the way, to the pond and back.
Up went the tape for the finishing line.
And a sign that said, *Race. Starting at nine!*

The day finally came. Excitement in the air,
Myrtle was ready to run with her flair.
Her bright shoes sparkled in the warm morning sun,
They were made for looking funky and definitely fun.

Everyone took to their starting places. 'Ready! Set! GO!'
They moved off in a hurry, but Myrtle went slow.
She watched their backs as they all took the lead.
Myrtle's feet moved but she needed speed.

But Myrtle did what turtles do best,
Slow and steady, with enough time to rest.
'I won't look ahead. I'll look at the view.'
So she saw the world freshly as if it were new.

She couldn't keep pace, so she did lose the race,
Yet she crossed the line with a smile on her face.
She had seen what the others had failed to see –
Green grass, fresh flowers and a yellow buzzing bee.

In their rush to win they missed what they lost;
Being focused on finishing came at a cost.
Myrtle took time to see beauty abound,
Life's better being slow, is what she had found.

Suzanne M. Faed

My Escape

The first time I arrived, I was sporting jogging bottoms and a large t-shirt, my bright turquoise bra strap showing as it fell off my shoulders. Well-worn Sketchers and my hair tied back in a scrunchie. Rosie and I had been running when we shimmered and landed in 1967. I am not a small woman, so I don't look that good in gym gear, but as I found myself jogging down the street people looked at me like I needed to be locked up. Except Mr Samson at No. 34 who winked and asked if I had taken up ballet? But that was then, now I am a seasoned traveller, dressed for the occasion.

I keep the clothes in a separate drawer. They are not hidden, but I know Matthew won't look there. Thick nylon stockings are held up by the corset worn around my middle. The plastic and metal fastenings are quite modern. Of course, I could have chosen tights: Pretty Polly, with a picture of a woman in an A-line mini dress on the packet. But Alice doesn't wear tights. I have learnt what Alice feels comfortable wearing, and also what a woman of Alice's age, in Alice's time is expected to wear.

A brassiere. Flesh toned with wide shoulder straps. An over the shoulder boulder holder, as my brother used to call them. Briefs in the same tone with wide legs and long enough to pull up around my middle, so that the corset sits on top. Then a tweed skirt, Harris of course, in brown and green tones, with a real silk lining. Fastened with a hook and eye and long invisible zip. A cotton shirt – white obviously – with double-buttoned cuffs. Then to finish, black lace-up shoes, worn by women for a century or more, a tweed jacket in the same fabric as the skirt and a headscarf, green with gold trim. Finally, my drawer contains a red leather collar, with a smart buckle, and a leather lead. These are for Rosie – I don't travel alone.

I feel the need to write to Matthew, to explain myself, even though he doesn't know I go anywhere. When I return from travelling, I am just a bit spacey. I don't even get the headaches or the ear-splitting, high-pitched tone that used to rattle around my skull anymore. He thinks that this is how I am now. His wife is a woman, who looks at him vaguely as if she can't remember his name or why they are married; who has created a distance that can no longer be bridged. But I didn't create the separation, it was there long before I began travelling. The change in the dynamic between us crept up on me, rather like

174

age. Is it the same for him? One minute we were energetic thirty-somethings, who would get day drunk and fuck in the shower. The next we were arguing about the colour of carpet to put in the dining room and sleeping in separate rooms so as not to disturb each other. Well, we both have busy jobs. I saw a therapist after the second time it happened. Before I could control it. She was very kind. She sat there and nodded and let me talk about travelling and what I was experiencing without any judgement. I told her that I found it odd that I could be away for so long, and yet no time had passed when I returned. I explained that when I was there, I was Alice, a woman who looks just like me, but who isn't me, and how my consciousness inhabits her body, and yet I have no idea where Alice goes or if she even exists when I'm not there? The therapist didn't have any answers for me, except to ask if I was under stress at work and whether I felt I might harm myself? She relaxed when I answered, of course not. She said it was typical for menopausal women to not feel like themselves. She thought I should see my doctor and ask him to prescribe me some anti-depressants. And that maybe HRT would help? Oestrogen is a powerful hormone and regulates more than just our cycles, were her words. Lack of this powerful hormone could be responsible for what was happening to me. I wondered at the power of Oestrogen that it could do this to me? I didn't go to the doctor, because after the fourth trip I began to enjoy the experience. How many people have a shit week at work and can then bugger off for weeks and return as if they've never been away? Travelling was beginning to feel more like a superpower than something I should take drugs to avoid.

Generally, I stay away for a month or two at most – more protracted, and it messes me up. And I find it harder to settle back in. This time though, when I cross that threshold, when I shimmer into the Sixties, I am not coming back for a long while. I plan to stay for the rest of Alice's natural life. I have tried to look online for a death certificate, to know how long I have, but I can't find anything. Does that mean Alice does not really exist? Yet when I am Alice, I feel more real than I do when I am me. I live in that time too. I am baby Sarah, pushed down that same street in a pram by my mother. Christ, my mother looks so young. Just eighteen, a child with a child. I've peered in the pram, cooed words at myself and spoken to her. She could barely bring herself to talk to me. She is young, I am old; we have nothing in common. I called her on the phone last week to ask if she remembers an Alice Grey who used to live across the street from us when I was a child. I describe Alice perfectly, but my mother is vague, life has been unkind. Moments ago, she was a child, now she is an old woman, but as age chases her, it dulls her mind. Maybe this is my condition too, perhaps this is not real, it's possible that none of this is real, and instead, I am having mini-strokes, and I am losing my grip on reality.

Why did I make this decision to stay, because last time I travelled, I stayed away for a year?

It was meant to be a test to see if passing the one-year milestone made a difference. It didn't. When I travel, I always arrive on the same date: 15th May 1967. And before you ask, yes, the year and day are significant – it's my birthday. It's an oddity for sure. And when I get back to now, to my life here in the present, well, no time has passed. Not even a second. I travel to the street I lived in as a small child, I always arrive walking along the pavement; it's the same time of day – mid-morning – and the weather is always fresh and sunny.

The people in the streetscape remain the same, Alice looks the same. I have a theory about alternate realities, but it twists me in knots. When I arrive, I always know where I live (even the first time). I know where I keep the keys to get inside of my house - under the flowerpot with the tulips. Rosie is always with me. She is my constant companion in both places. She's had puppies in that house, a litter of five, all black like her, typical pudgy little Labradors, even though their father was unknown. I remember putting an ad in the corner store, crying a bit when they all went to their new homes. It's one of my fondest memories of that year. Alice's house, my house, is an old detached Victorian home. It has stood on this street for many years, before the more modern Edwardian rows and the post-war fill ins. I don't live in all of the house, well maybe I should say Alice doesn't live in all of it. She rents the top floor to two gentlemen and of course to the outside world they are indifferent lodgers. The truth is different. I'm glad that they can live together, set up home, listen to the radio and wake up to each other in the morning. Of course, it's still illegal till later this year, but I'm not telling, and the outside world can be dammed. Alice would be happy I'm keeping up the pretense for her boys, even though they are destined to live a life that will not be an easy one until they are old men. The 'Boys' don't seem unhappy though, they are like all the young people I meet here. They have an unnerving hopefulness that guides them to believe that the world of tomorrow will be better than the world of today. They are totally invested in the future.

Alice keeps photos in the dresser in the front room, so I know this woman whose body I inhabit was once married. She treasures a Burma Star wrapped in a velvet scarf. The War Office telegram notifying her of his death too – 16th March 1942. They were married for just three short years, most of them spent apart. A war wedding, but there was no war baby for Alice. From what I can tell, Alice is childless and has been alone since her husband died. It's hard to talk about Alice in the third person because, of course, I am Alice. But I hadn't been Alice when Edward had died, and I haven't lived through the war. I have no memories of the time before the day I arrive, except for simple things like where the door keys are left, and how much to pay the milkman.

The Boys, or Kenneth and Jonathan to use their names, have made it easier for me to apprise myself of Alice's life. She helps at the Salvation Army on a Tuesday, making dinner for the older folk. She gardens and attends church on Sunday. And of course, when I am here, I walk Rosie twice a day. Rosie exists in both worlds. I find myself wondering, perhaps in my human-centric way, that I have entirely missed the point and that maybe it is Rosie who is the lynchpin. Maybe this has nothing to do with me at all.

You might ask how I decide to leave my life. How I can want to become another woman with no memories before the day of my arrival? I suppose I am trying to escape. Alice has fallen in love, and Sarah has forgotten how to love. I thought I'd forgotten until I met Joseph. I look at Matthew, and all I see is a lifetime of tense conversation, a desire to split but no real sense of how to make that work? A long stretch of nothingness into old age. Of course, even if I stay, that's Karma I can't avoid, but just maybe I can have a life too. But I can't have that life over and over. When I stayed for the year, I learnt that there are many things you don't willingly relive, like nursing Petra, Joseph's wife and my friend. Her death took only three months, but she died in agony. The big 'C'. Nowadays we have no problem with talking about cancer, there is no shame, now cancer sufferers are battlers who set up JustGiving accounts for charity. In Alice's time cancer wasn't talked about, or was only talked about in hushed tones, or not at all.

Petra had breast cancer; they took off her left breast, but it was already too late, it had spread to her lungs, liver and spine. I nursed her day and night in the end. Whispering her stories I remembered from childhood, singing her lullabies. Dressing the sores that appeared all over her frail body. I watched her disintegrate in front of me. By the end, she must have weighed less than six stone, and she couldn't even stomach water. I know that if I go back that I will need to do this again. I will need to nurse Petra again. I wonder about smuggling modern drugs back to her. But I'm not God, and if she lives, then I no longer have Joseph.

The truth. I am willing to leave my life and prevent Petra having a second chance so that I can be with Joseph. I am prepared to witness Petra die an awful death so that I can be with Joseph. I am fifty-two-years-old and still willing to risk all for love. That is a revelation to me. I think it's a revelation to Alice too. Joseph is sixty-two, a Jewish Pole, given a home here as thanks for his service. He was a witness to horrors I can't even imagine. Yet, my presence seems to ease his mind and fill the void that Petra has left. He is a generous lover; he is generous with love. Where Matthew hoards his love, handing it to me piece-meal when I have done something to please him, Joseph allows me to feast, he has an endless supply. Like a starving person, I gorge on it until fully satiated. It's not possible to know what life is like without love until you receive it. Then there is nothing to be done except run headfirst into it.

Petra and Joseph live four doors down in one of the post-war fill-ins, a featureless square house that Petra keeps as neat as a pin. She calls out 'coo-ee' to me over the fence, in her Dutch accent. Winking and asking how the boys are, she always has a biscuit for Rosie in her apron pocket. We stand and talk over the front fence, Rosie straining at the leash to begin her walk. She talks about Holland and her relatives and how she misses them. Petra blames Joseph for not paying for a trip. We both know she will never go home, even before we learn she is sick. We talk of mundane things too: the weather, how our plants are doing, gossip about the neighbours. We speak of world affairs, of youth and why young men grow their hair long. She says she needs to find me a gentleman friend. And she has her eye on Mr Samson for me, he's a widower and still has a bit of 'go' in him, according to Petra. She makes me laugh. God, she made me laugh. I miss her.

One morning in late September, as I leave the house to walk Rosie, Petra calls me over. She isn't her usual bubbly self, and she invites me into the kitchen, something that rarely happens, saying she needs to ask me a favour. She has to go into the hospital for an operation and will most likely be there for two weeks. She asks: can I take a hot meal around to Joseph each day? She sighs and says he's impossible, he can't manage on his own and will live on cheese sandwiches. I don't ask what's wrong, she will offer it up to me when she is ready. But I can tell she is concerned. Of course, I don't hesitate to say yes. Through Petra, I have found out what it is like to have a real friend. I ask her what else I can do? Is there anything I can do for her? Smiling, she says no just take care of Joseph.

I take the bus to see her at the local infirmary while she is there. Some women's magazines and the obligatory grapes. Her face is sunken, and she whispers to me that the doctor's prognosis is not good. She doesn't know how to tell Joseph. I have no answers for her, but instead, I arrange her pillows, and help her up the bed, noticing the drain on her left side. She doesn't say, but I know they have taken her breast. When she gets home, it is evident that she needs a nurse, someone to take care of her. I offer my services to them. I can keep making Joseph meals, look after her during the day while Joseph is at work. And that was how we began, I took the day shift, Joseph the night, until, by the end, I was just there. Joseph and I ate together, we played cards. We held space for her pain, for her moments of out of character lousy temper, for her sobs that she wouldn't see her mother or sisters, for the fear that crept up on her at night. We held space for her dying.

The day she found out she wouldn't get better was the day Jonathan was arrested. It was a beautiful Autumnal day, except in the world that I had travelled to, the lives of those I had grown to love were disintegrating, and they were hurting more than I could stand.

Joseph has been home for lunch – chicken pie – and after he leaves, I go back up to the bedroom to see if Petra needs anything. She tells me that she is cold and I can see that she is shivering, and it doesn't matter that I have put on the heater to further warm the room or that I have wrapped her in a blanket, her teeth are chattering and her skin is cold to the touch. I ask if a hot drink will help? Returning with hot sweet tea, she drinks it in big gulps, wrapping her hands around the cup. But she is still shaking, and her body is like ice. Her eyes plead with me to do something, so I tell her that I'll call the doctor, ask him how we can best warm her up. She nods and gulps back more tea. Leaving the house it's late afternoon and the night is drawing in; there is a chill in the air. The leaves from the elms that line the street have almost wholly fallen and dead leaves mush together covering the pavement, making it slippery under foot. There are no elm trees in this street now, they cut them all down in the Seventies when Dutch elm disease took hold. Luckily there is no one in the phone box, and I call Dr Stevens. He doesn't answer straight away, and I stand there, shivering too now, as I wait for him to pick up. It's strange this world. Communication isn't instant, but there are still real people that you can talk too. In my world, speaking to a doctor directly is almost unheard of. When Petra had first started shaking, I had the nonsense thought that I could just go online and find out what to do … and then I remembered.

Finally, Dr Stevens picks up, and says he will pop around in half an hour to look in on Petra. He needs to see her.

True to his word, he arrives not long after I return, and I leave him to examine her, busying myself while trying to eavesdrop. Calling me back into the room, he tells me that he is prescribing her strong antibiotics and hands me the prescription. Petra tells me, between swallowing a mouthful of pills and luke-warm tea, that the doctor thinks she should have a warm bath to see if it will regulate her temperature. I follow Dr Stevens out of the room, but beyond confirming that a bath is a good idea, he just tells me to ask Joseph to ring him when he returns from work and that if she worsens, I should ring him straight-away. I don't understand the cloak and dagger attitude; the doctor must know that I know Petra is unlikely to get better. But I'm happy that he is so readily available, and I try and keep upbeat with Petra, promising to run the bath straight away. The immersion heater takes another half-an-hour to produce enough warm water, but while we wait I look in the cupboard for bath salts and Petra quizzes me about what the doctor said. He has obviously not spoken to her either. I tell a half lie and say that he just told me to ring him if she worsens.

The bathtub smells gorgeous, and the fragrance rises through the air as I help her into the water, the smell of Lilly of the Valley taking me back to my grandmother and childhood. Petra is just skin and bones, looking like a woman of eighty, not fifty-four. That she is so slight makes it easier for me to help her into the water. Where there was once muscle on her thighs, now there is just skin, and it hangs there sagging like the underweight chicken I had boiled earlier for the pie. The scar where they took her breast is red and raw. I want to cry seeing her this way, but I know that I need to keep positive; isn't that how you are supposed to behave when people are sick? Stoic?

The bath seems to be working its magic, and Petra's pallor returns to a more normal colour. I sit on the pink ottoman at the side of the tub, and she tells me how when she was a child she and her sister had once filled a bathtub with milk and flowers so that they could be like the Egyptian Queen Cleopatra. She laughs as she tells me how it curdled and how her hair stank for days after-wards. I ask if she would like to look like a queen for Joseph this evening and she nods. So after drying, dressing her in a clean nightie and wrapping her in a warm dressing gown, I style her hair and rouge her cheeks. She kisses me gently on mine and tells me that I am the dearest friend a woman could wish for. I tell her not to be silly and that she would do the same for me. She winks and says: 'Unlikely.'

When Joseph returns, I catch him at the gate, asking him to call Dr Stevens. I don't know, but I can guess what passes between them on the call as he doesn't look at me as he heads back into the house, going straight to Petra's room. I hear him tell her how beautiful she looks. I shouldn't be here, so I leave them alone.

Being here no longer feels like a game or a superpower, it feels like a knot of dread building in my stomach. I realise that I could just shimmer out of this mess at any moment. I could go back to my life with Matthew, to my online world of work and friends. My life as Sarah. To a life that feels plastic in comparison with the reality that I am experiencing here. I have been protected, cosseted from life in my gated community, with its neatly cut grass and extensive lakes, with cycle and walk paths where I can safely jog and walk Rosie. My shopping comes wrapped in cellophane, delivered to my door, ordered by the app on my phone. I don't have to sully myself with the 'Real'. My house is large and beautifully decorated, I work online in my home office, I leave in my temperature-controlled car, no longer even having to stop for fuel, as it charges in the garage. My time here magnifies my disconnection, it holds me hostage in a world where I get my hands dirty, where I cook, clean, and truly live. My heart is breaking, but at least as Alice my heart works here, it feels, and breaks, and hurts. In my time, it is frozen or maybe cast in amber. This unreal sense crept up over time. I know that my whole life hasn't been this way. Once I used to feel too. Alice is giving me back to myself.

I wonder if I stay in Alice's body until her death will I die too? Or will I return to the same second I left, to my life with Matthew? What will happen to Rosie? There are many unknowns, but I still must do it. It has become impossible now to escape my life for just a few short weeks to take a break in the past. Because of course when I arrive, Joseph is still with Petra. I want him so badly, but he doesn't want me — we haven't spent the dark times together yet. To have Joseph, I must witness Petra die. I can't look my friend in the eye knowing what I know. But I have to travel one more time because now I want the times that come after, the times where Joseph and I are together, building a life. I have had a small taste of them. Fish and chips on the pier, laughing arm in arm as we make our way home. Conversation into the small hours with a nip of whisky each. A cold bed with warm arms wrapped around me, and the certainty of knowing that I am genuinely wanted. Sunday mornings, walking Rosie in the park. Joseph, helping me dig the vegetable beds in the cold spring. His clumsy proposal the day I left. I still don't understand how I could bear the pain but not the joy.

Louise Tarrier

A Jury of My Peers

'I felt the blast before I saw the flash. I know. I know, all my professors will tell me that I'm wrong. But I know what I felt. I know what I saw.'

'You knew.'

'Sorry?'

'Your tense is wrong. You can't know.'

'Why not?'

'You can't know anything now.'

I turn around quickly, but there is no one.

'Hello?'

The silence of the whiteness surrounding me is deafening. It hurts my eyes, my ears. My mind is splintering into emotionless shards. I try again, *'Hello?'*

'Hello.' A woman's voice. Much gentler. Soothing. The whiteness lessening. A little. The noise of the silence lessening. A little.

'Where are you? I can't see you.'

'I am here.'

'I can't see you.' I pirouette around. Or I think I do. Thought I did. The whiteness is total.

'Yes you can. Shut your eyes and concentrate.'

'You're my Grandmother!' I gasp as the vision of her, so young and vibrant, sweeps through my closed eyes, enters my brain, nestles comfortingly. I feel her lips on my forehead. *'Cool,'* I raise my hand to their softness. My hand goes straight through. My fingers touch brain.

Screaming. I can hear screaming.

'Ssshh now,' my Grandmother soothes.

'Who are you talking to?' I ask. The screaming stops.

'You. Your screaming taxes my nerves.'

'Was that me?'

'Well, it was. But you can't be expected to hear yourself.'

'Why not?'

'Because of the way it happened.'

'What happened, Grandmother?'

'Oh, I expect you will remember soon. It's not for me to tell you. That's his job.'

'*Whose?*'

'I must go now child. To join the rest.'

'*What rest Grandmother?*'

'The rest.' Her voice drifts and I gaze after it. Blurry shapes appear and voices sound inside my head. Mixed up, layered, indistinguishable yet recognisable. I know all of them and none of them.

'The quiet descends. Or rises. Or seeps into your consciousness.' The man's voice back again.

'*Who are you?*'

'I have many names. Each is wrong, all are right.'

'*That doesn't help me.*'

'Strictly speaking, nothing is going to help you now. Just your life in evidence. That's all that's left.'

'*Who are you!*'

'I am a barren woman's husband. A prince accepting milk and rice pudding. A multi-limbed warrior. The son of a carpenter. I am your judge and these are your jury.' The light collapses and row upon row of people, stretching into an infinite distance, appear.

'*Who are they?*'

'Your ancestors. The only ones allowed to pronounce verdict on you.'

'*For what?*'

'For your life. Was it sweetness and light or vinegar and darkness? Were you truthful and good or deceitful and evil? Your ancestors, those found worthy, pronounce verdict on all who come after them. All who live in their name. So it has always been.'

'*And?*'

'And you will remember now.' He sweeps His hand.

The vision of the explosion, the noise, the people. Me. At the centre. Pressing the button.

A voice from the many, 'Why did you do this?'

'*I had to do what was right. Our people were downtrodden. We have been oppressed for so many years. Our lands invaded and occupied. Our homes taken, our rights denied. The world ignorant to our plight. I couldn't stand by and let others protest for me. So I volunteered to stike back. To be a soldier.*'

Another voice from the rows of blurred shapes, further back, fainter, 'Yet you did not do this on a battlefield. You did not fight other soldiers. You wore no uniform. You walked amongst innocents.'

'*None of them are innocent. They are all implicit in our oppression.*'

'Including this one?'

A flash of an image. She is perhaps four or five, riding on top of her father's shoulders. Smiling and laughing.

I try to talk but no sound comes.

His voice again. The man who said he was the judge. 'You need say no more. The jury will deliberate.'

There is a murmur throughout the rows of shapes, rolling away into the furthest reaches of my mind. Then crushing silence.

My Grandmother speaks, 'We find for the dark.'

Ian Andrew

A Thief's Curse

She thought this day couldn't get any worse. But it did.

'Stop that lady!' shouted Annabelle, as she fell to the ground. A portly woman had snatched Annabelle's bag, knocking her over as she zipped past her on her gopher. By the time Annabelle got up and brushed off the shock, the lady had reached the other side of the path and rounded a corner. She slumped onto a bench, tears making wet tracks down her cheeks. How do I get it back? she thought. The item she had in her bag was irreplaceable. Now it was gone.

*

'I'm getting too old for this,' Mabel said to herself as she kicked off her shoes and stretched her aching bones. Her lounge was spacious but bare, like the rest of her house. The only furniture in the room was a wooden coffee table, a shabby couch and an ancient television. There were no photographs, or pictures on the wall, just a little framed sticker that read: I like cats – they taste like chicken.

Although Mabel was only forty-five, she looked weathered and weary. Permanent frown lines were etched around her thin lips and beady eyes were barely visible in her padded flesh. They flitted about, half open, scrutinising the world and her place in it. Her brown oily hair fell lifelessly past her shoulders. She did not have any friends. Her neighbours disliked her. Children were scared of her. Animals ran from her. Basically, the world did not like her, and she did not like the world.

She dropped the bag on the table. It landed with a thud as she fell into a chair. She leaned over and, panting heavily, opened the zip to the bag.

Sitting inside was a small, odd-shaped sack. She pulled it out and placed it on the table. One end of the sack was tied up, so she undid the knot, struggling as her stubby fingers failed to grip the thin rope. Eventually she managed to untie it and the sack came loose. She spread the material apart and recoiled at what she saw: open yellow eyes met hers, the slits of pupil enlarged; legs curled at odd angles, and the ginger fur was matted and clumped with blood. Its mouth was half open, in a grimacing display of pain.

Mabel checked for money or credit cards. Nothing prepared her for a dead cat to be lying stiff on her coffee table. She stood; her head swam, and her legs shook. As she lost consciousness, she toppled over onto the cat, crushing it beneath her weight.

*

When Mabel woke from her stupor, the sun had gone down and there were eerie shadows on the walls. Coming around, she realised there was something sticking into her ribs. Gathering all the momentum she could, she rolled over. Mabel turned her head to find the cat poking into her. She shrieked and backed away from the gruesome creature. Mabel switched on the light. The cat, now even more squashed, still lay on the table, but its eyes seemed to follow Mabel wherever she went. She had to get rid of it. She went outside and dug a hole. Sweat dripped down her face and back with the unfamiliar exertion.

'Stupid woman! Who carries a dead cat in their bag?' She shook her head as she went back inside. Mabel warily wrapped the cat in the sack. Hands shaking, she returned to the garden and threw the cat into the hole, covered the hole with dirt, patted it down with the shovel and stood back, proud of her bravery. She went inside, put the handbag into the bin and prepared a cup of hot chocolate. Her nerves were everywhere; she'd never been so scared in her life. Later, she went to bed, still thinking about the dead cat. As her eyes closed and her breathing slowed, she smiled, certain the ordeal was over.

*

All was well with Mabel until the next night. She had just finished reading *Recipes to Remember* when she felt a bump at the end of her bed. Startled, she looked up and gasped at the indentation of paw prints on her blanket, making their way towards her. Mabel froze, barely breathing. The paw prints stopped beside her head and Mabel felt like she was being watched.

A cold shiver ran down her spine. Mabel found some courage to move; slowly she turned so her feet hit the floor. But as she did so she heard a hiss and felt hot breath on her back. Leaping from the bed, she spun around but there was nothing there. As she started to run from the room, something jumped at her, hanging onto her flabby arms with sharp claws. Screeching in pain, she wrestled with it. She fell back and with a loud thump tumbled to the floor. Eyes wide with horror, mouth twisted in shock, she whimpered as she saw a pair of yellow eyes staring at her. Those eyes belonged to the cat she had buried the day before. This ferocious feline had somehow come back. Her arms were still flailing wildly, until she realised the cat was no longer attacking her. Panting, she examined her arms. Angry red welts zig zagged across them. Trembling, she managed to get up and walk to the hallway.

I'm going to die, Mabel thought hysterically. She held onto the wall for support as she hobbled along. The floor was cold beneath her bare feet until she stepped into something warm. It squelched between her toes. She lifted her foot and peered down. Disgusted, she gagged.

'Oh my … Gross!'

The cat had left her a little present. A fresh, steaming, smelly present. The stink wafted up to her nostrils. Stomach squeamish, swallowing spew, she walked on, wiping the remains off as she went. When she got to the end of the hallway, she caught a glimpse of herself in the hallway mirror. Colour drained from her face when she saw a word scrawled across the mirror; smudged letters, courtesy of the cat's left over present, accused her.

THIEF!

'Oh my,' Mabel let out a shaky breath and tried her best not to faint. She reached the kitchen, stumbling across the suddenly slippery floor. Mabel didn't know how much longer her heart could take this. She had to get out of the house, so she went to the door and turned the doorknob. It wouldn't budge. She shook the handle frantically. Despairing, she turned and wailed, 'Please, no more. I can't take any more. I'm sorry! I shouldn't have stolen her bag.'

As if in reply, the lights went out. Darkness surrounded Mabel, enclosing her in its gloom. Mabel held her breath. She stood completely still. The hissing started again, this time louder and angrier. Then she heard a cat crying – a pitiful, helpless sound. She covered her ears with her hands, but the noise filled the house, echoing around the walls. Her eyes were tightly shut but an image appeared before her; it was a lady, crying over her cat's lifeless body on the side of the road.

Oh dear. Mabel swallowed the lump of regret that had settled in her throat. *What have I done? I'm a terrible person … I can't keep living like this.*

Falling in a heap on the floor, Mabel put her head in her hands, trying to shake off the vision. The lady slowly faded away, but the cat remained, staring at Mabel with piercing eyes, its mouth still grotesquely out of shape. The vision became clearer and the cat started towards Mabel at frightening speed. She cowered, shielding her face with her hands. Just before the cat reached her, the lights came back on and the vision disappeared. Mabel shook her head, rocking back and forth. She could still hear the steady breathing of the cat but everything else was still. Then she heard the ping of a bell. She looked down and found a collar by her feet. She picked it up cautiously; read the engraved words on the shiny love-heart tag:

<u>CHESTER</u>
Loved by Annabelle Caline
48 Chester Drive, Perth.
0405 545 727

And then it dawned on her how she could start to make amends. She knew what she had to do.

Suzanne M. Faed

Ward 7a

Day 3 – Steve

It was a different doctor today, but that was the only change. Lizzie was stable, which was better than deteriorating. But when the prognosis is potentially permanent brain damage you don't want *stable*; you want *recovering*. Her little body just lay there; hooked up to cannulas, oxygen and an array of monitors. I sat in the chair beside her bed holding her hand, stroking her forehead, kissing her, talking to her.

'We all love you, Lizzie. All we want is for you to get better and come home. Mummy can't come in because she has to look after baby Jake. It's still too risky, in case she takes the germs home and he gets sick too.'

The hours pass slowly. When the nursing staff take hourly observations, they always say a few words to me. At first, they were encouraging; ninety per cent of people with bacterial meningitis survive, and most don't suffer permanent damage. But we weren't in that majority.

Daytime is easier. I can still do some work using the phone and laptop. It's a welcome distraction. There are more people about, the place is brighter. At the canteen you see children who are getting better, smiling and even laughing.

At night it's just the staff and the occasional parent like me permitted to stay with their child.

At 5.30 the doctor returned on her last rounds for the day. She read the observations sheet, checked the monitors and tested Lizzie for responsiveness to some stimuli.

'Is there any improvement?' I asked.

'No. I'm sorry, she is the same as this morning.'

'Can my wife come in yet? We were told Lizzie might still be infectious, and we have a newborn.'

'Yes, I think that will be fine. The antibiotics will have dealt with the bacteria. She can come in tomorrow.'

'Thank you. Is there anything else we can do to help Lizzie?'

'What you are doing is the best thing for her right now. Hearing your voice and feeling your touch can only benefit her while her brain tries to fix itself. We will do everything we can for her, but your love may be the thing that makes the difference.'

She left.

I rang Shally and told her she could come in in the morning. I could tell she was crying, even though she tried to keep her voice level.

'Is there any change?' she asked.

'Not yet.' I replied. I didn't say there probably never would be.

For the next hour I just sat there thinking about my family. I loved Shally. No one had ever filled me up like she did. But when Lizzie was born, I discovered something bigger, more visceral. Love that transcended my personal needs. I would literally do anything for her, to protect her. It was the same with Jake.

By seven it was dark outside. The wards changed rhythm. Lights were dimmed, the chat at the nurses' station was quieter and hope a little harder to find.

In my mind I replayed Shally telling me about Lizzie getting sick.

'She was vomiting and complained of a headache. She had a stiff neck and just wanted to go to sleep. And the light was hurting her eyes. I looked after her for an hour before I rang the hospital. They sent an ambulance as soon as I told them how she was.'

Shally had broken down then. 'Did I wait too long? Is it my fault?'

Was it my fault? I could have taken more parental leave after Jake's birth, but the pressures of the job and feeling unable to do what Shally did with the children had driven me back to work. If I had been there, would we have picked up the symptoms earlier?

Ten o'clock. I stepped out of Lizzie's room for a walk and a cup of coffee. At the end of the corridor near the coffee machine I saw a nurse I didn't recognise, looking at a clipboard. As I approached, she saw me and smiled.

'Hi,' she said, 'I'm Nurse Betty. I'll be in and out tonight doing some checks. The other nurses will do what they usually do – they mostly ignore me.'

Nurse Betty looked to be in her forties, and I noticed she was wearing a different uniform to the other nurses. More traditional. 'Okay,' I replied, 'I'll be staying with my daughter tonight, so I guess I'll see you at some stage.'

'Ward 7a, isolation.' Nurse Betty said, reading from her notes. 'Little Lizzie, such a shame. But there's always hope and something that we can do, isn't there? I'll pop in later and we can have a talk.'

She walked away. I fed some coins into the coffee machine. I looked up but Nurse Betty wasn't to be seen. I assumed she'd gone into one of the wards to do her checks. I took my coffee and drank it sitting in the chair beside the vending machine. I went to the toilet and returned to Lizzie.

I must have dozed off because I didn't see Nurse Betty enter. When I looked up, she was there looking at Lizzie and whispering softly to her. It seemed odd, but somehow not wrong. She saw I was awake and gave me a warm smile.

'Lizzie is still in there, if we can help her find her way back,' she said. 'If we can do what needs to be done for her, of course.' She stepped back from the bed. 'Something to think about,' she added. 'I'll come back a little later.'

I was confused. What did she mean, '*If we can do what needs to be done for her?*'

I stood up and leant over Lizzie. It was hard to be sure in the dim light, but she seemed to be more relaxed, her face looked more like it did when she slept in her bed at home. I held her hand. 'I'd do anything to make you better, Lizzie. I promise.'

About fifteen minutes later the regular nurse came in and took Lizzies obs. When he had finished, I said, 'Nurse Betty seems nice, what is she checking for?'

His reaction surprised me. 'You've seen Nurse Betty,' he said guardedly, 'in here?'

'Yes, she was talking to Lizzie. It seemed to relax her.'

'Okay,' he said and paused. 'She drops in now and then to see how we are doing. But if it bothers you, let me know. Lizzie's treatment is our top priority.' He left.

I took a book out and tried to read. I kept losing concentration and gave up.

For a second time Nurse Betty managed to come in without me noticing. She was standing beside me, looking at Lizzie. 'Oh, hi,' I said, 'you're back.'

'Yes, I thought we could continue our discussion. What we can do for Lizzie.'

Without hesitation I said, 'Believe me, whatever it takes, I'll do it. Honestly.'

'Of course you would, what father wouldn't?' She turned to face me. 'I think we might be able to do some good tonight. You just stay here, get some sleep. We'll see what tomorrow brings.'

Day 4 – Shally

I woke an hour before the alarm, feeling empty and alone. I wanted Steve's arms around me; I needed his warmth, his strength. I hadn't seen Lizzie since she was admitted, and even though Steve was positive, I knew things were bad.

At seven I rang to let him know I was leaving but he didn't pick up. I dropped Jake off at my Mum's place. He was so bubbly and happy I almost lost it.

Mum gave me a hug, saying, 'You'll be okay, whatever happens.' Steve still hadn't returned my call, but I didn't think much of it. I focussed on seeing Lizzie.

At the hospital I got a parking spot near the entrance. The lady at the information counter told me how to find Lizzie. I took the lift to the second floor and followed the arrow for Wards 1 to 9. When I came to 7a I saw a number of people in there. As I was about to enter, a nurse hurriedly pushed ahead of me with a trolley.

I went in and saw four medical staff around Steve, moving him from the chair he was slumped in onto the floor and preparing to apply defibrillation. I couldn't move, couldn't think.

'Mummy,' said a voice, but it didn't register.

'Mummy!'

I looked over to the bed. Lizzie was lying there, looking at me and obviously distressed.

'Mummy. Daddy won't wake up!'

David Rawet

They Came For …

I woke to screams
Of metal striking glass
Of leather on wood
Hinges ripped apart
Like families

Trucks and dark eyed streets
No lights in windows peering
No signs of seeing
We are blindly taken
Like shadows

Rings of uniforms
In cocooned armour
In denial of freedom
Shepherding with viciousness
Like wolves

We are the deportees
As Guthrie sang
As Liberty weeps
Broken promises to huddled masses
Like politicians

Gone, from your world
Out of sight
Out of mindless rage
The new political right
Like fascists

They came for us
And you turned
Inward and away
Silent and compliant
Like cowards

Ian Andrew

The Pledge

The offer came in the form of a slightly yellowing envelope that dropped through my letterbox one Wednesday morning, thick and a little dog-eared; there was no stamp – this one had been hand-delivered. It was brought to the dining table by my bulldog, Alice, who had taken to collecting everything from the floor and bringing it to me whether I wanted it or not.

I turned it over in my hands, thrilled and a little aroused by the darkness I knew it held. I sipped my coffee. Ate some porridge. Waited for the phone to ring.

*

point one: you must not be seen

I must time leaving the house just so, down to the minute. The note had been explicit, but it needn't have been – I no more wanted to be seen than I wanted my balls waxed, so I make very sure to keep one eye on the clock, the other on the comings and goings outside. I know that Pete and Beth next door will pull up within five minutes of each other, usually at 18.15 and 18.20, or thereabouts. I'd watched – seen – them numerous times. They both work in the city and wear power suits, and I always think that Beth is punching above her weight with Pete, whose hair is ridiculously thick and eyes ridiculously blue. If you like that sort of thing.

And then there's Lucy. I lean on the ledge of the window, eyes trained on the blue front door across the road. A light rain has started to fall, and I find myself wondering if I should grab something waterproof before I go. Probably not a bad idea, given the task at hand.

On the dot of seven, Lucy from across the road leaves the house; her outfits range from classy call girl to downright slutty and tonight she has definitely gone for the latter. She pulls a fake-leather jacket around her shoulders, attempting to light a cigarette and call her pimp at the same time. I'm sure her skill set is vast but multi-tasking doesn't seem to be one of them.

Now's my gap – they're all either in or out and I'm sure I won't be noticed. I throw on an inconspicuous black golf jacket and grab my backpack from the garage; I'd packed it earlier on with the items listed in the note. It weighs more than I'd anticipated but there's something about the weight on my shoulders that propels me on, down deserted roads and quiet alleyways. My head on the task, my legs on auto. I keep going.

point two: 9 pm be there or be square

An incandescent moon has risen, thank fuck, because otherwise I wouldn't see a thing. I don't know when streetlights stopped being made but there must be a health and safety bloke in a Council office somewhere having a nervous breakdown.

I check the little scribbled drawing a thousand times before I find the place. It's opposite a small corner shop that I've probably bought porn from a hundred times before. I can't buy it too locally because people talk, and the Paki who owned this one could barely speak English let alone tell people about my preferences.

The roller shutters are down; it's 20.58 on my watch so I'm early. I spot a dark doorway across the road, set back from the pavement. I jog across the road and duck inside. A smell of piss and something rotten hits me like a truck, and I gag (I've always had a sensitive reflex). I cover my face with my hands, eyes streaming as the stench of shit invades, and as my eyes adjust to the darkness of the corners I spot the culprit – a Tesco carrier bag covered in maggots, shit and something that looks like melted plastic; I know before I do it that nudging the bag open will be a mistake, but I do it anyway, and I'm barely even surprised when a human hand rolls out. Fist closed, I can just make out a wedding ring glistening on one finger; charred at the wrist, burnt flesh curls and flakes as the maggots feed. I nearly cry out, vomit, kick the bag – but my watch beeps the hour. I turn from the hand, violated. Across the road a roller shutter rises two meters from the ground. Stops. A torch flash signals to me, once, twice. A hand emerges – this one attached to an arm – beckoning me. I cross the road.

point three: do exactly as I say

'Turn around.'

I do as he tells me. The small slither of moonlight disappears, and the gap closes, replaced by a large circle of torchlight angled at the floor, away from the speaker's face.

'You brought everything on the list?'

'Yes, I –'

'Follow me.'

I follow.

The shop is small and well stocked; shelves take up almost all the floor space packed with the usual Paki-shop-shit; papers, chocolate, magazines and overpriced toiletries. This one even has an 'Indian Deli' in the corner with various spices and about a thousand types of rice that probably no fucker ever buys anyway.

We leave the main store and go through to the back room, which is covered in bullshit Paki posters and huge canvas prints about 'love and light' – what a fucking shock. The Note Writer crouches and opens a hatch in the floor. The torch is still angled away from his face. He indicates I should go down.

I hoist the backpack, adjusting the weight. The metal inside it clangs as I descend an old set of steps; so old they don't even creak, they just absorb the deep thud of my footsteps and spit out plumes of chalky white dust.

The room below is dimly lit by several camping lanterns, which adorn random tabletops and shelves. The corner of the room has been cleared and a chair has been ceremoniously placed in the biggest halo of light. A video camera on a tripod has been set up a couple of meters in front of the chair; a green light blinks.

'Put down the bag. Take out the tools.'

The Note Writer is at the bottom of the stairs, arms crossed across a broad chest. Now that there's some light I can just about make out a scruffy beard and a beanie. I don't wait, I know the drill. I swing the bag to the ground, unzip it and start to remove the contents one item at a time. When I pull out the small, rusted hand saw I look up to The Note Writer hoping for a bit of kudos – this, after all, is a pretty impressive bit of kit – but he's not even looking in my direction. His eyes are flicking between the camera and a wooden door, like an understair cupboard, that shelters behind the steps; from behind it a man cries out.

The Note Writer is nonchalant. He's done this before.

point four: be cool

With a nod of the head a guy appears – seemingly from nowhere – and opens the door. This guy is slimmer than The Note Writer with a dark buzz cut and too-tight jeans. I look away quickly and focus on the tools laid out in front of me. I can feel my heartbeat getting faster and can hardly catch my breath. I barely focus on the man being dragged out of the room by cuffed hands, panicked pleas forming around the gag that has been stuffed into his mouth.

Sweat rolls down my neck.

Hammer. Saw. Chisel. Angle grinder. Nails. Pliers *and breathe*. Hammer. Saw. Chisel. Angle grinder. Nails. Pliers *and breathe*. Hammer. Saw ...

'Sit the fuck down.'

I flinch – it takes me a second to realise The Note Writer isn't talking to me. The guy with the gag is dropped into the chair. It's like watching a balloon deflate. Now I have a chance to look properly I can see that the guy's brown skin is smeared with dirty blood and a long, curved gash fills his high forehead. The stench of warm piss reaches me at around the same time that I notice the gag in his mouth, now pulled out and discarded on the floor, is a dull yellow colour. My stomach lurches. *Hammer ... saw ... chisel ...*

'Please. Please, I have a wife. Please ...' the guy in the chair pleads, his eyes stare imploringly into those of his captors. The Note Writer smirks and cracks his knuckles dramatically – he's enjoying this immensely – and it's obvious that the pleading goes unnoticed.

'You're up, Pledge.'

This time he *is* talking to me.

The skinnier guy positions himself behind the camera, bending slightly, his ass in my direction. He glances back. Grins. 'Choose your weapon,' he says. He's flirting. It makes me sick. My heartbeat is so fast it's a constant hum in my ears.

I look at the choices before me; breathe deeply.

Hammer. Saw. Chisel. Grinder. Nails ...

I make my selection. Pick it up, cradle it. Walk to the light.

point five: enjoy

The first fifteen minutes are a blur of glaring yellow light, bright red spray and stifling moans. I'm so hot and really thirsty, but it hardly seems the time to stop and ask for a drink. I fully immerse myself in the task at hand; if I want in, I have to do this well. I don't see the guy for the first fifteen minutes – he's a writhing, sweating, shitting lump and I am the guy in charge. Behind me The Note Writer and The Camera Man are my audience, egging me on: 'Get him in the neck!' 'Get another finger!' They're like cheerleaders and for once I'm the fucking football captain. I pound nails through skin and veins, straight into mother-fucking bone.

Fuck, it feels good; kind of like being high. I've only felt this good a couple of times before in dirty public restrooms or by-the-hour motel rooms ... BUT NOTHING COMPARES TO THIS.

You bet your ass I get stuck in after the initial mist lifts.

I look the job-stealing, elephant-worshipping dickhead right in the eye and run an angle grinder straight up his fucking shin and slam that glorious weapon deep into his thigh.

BLOOD SPRAYS EVERYWHERE IT IS FUCKING EPIC.

I turn and give the camera a thumbs up, a wink for good measure.

The guy has passed out – ages ago, probably – his head hangs to the right, eyes closed, mouth agape with lumps of darkened blood caking his lips and teeth. I'm not about to ask how far they want me to go – ALL THE WAY IS THE ONLY WAY.

Tools down, I punch him in the face over and over again, knocking him left and right and left again and then, BAM, square in his nose sending his head flying backwards with a sharp snap.

I think we're done here, but I turn to the guys to check.

The Note Writer is grinning like a maniac and clapping huge bear like hands together. He slaps The Camera Man on the back, and they exchange an impressed look. The Camera Man says, 'And cut!' The two laugh, obviously an inside joke I'm not privy too. Not yet anyway.

final point: a decision will be made

Would you believe the body is dragged across the room and flung into a chest freezer? It's like some slasher-movie madness. The guy has shat his pants, so the smear left in his wake is a bloody brown mess. Bit like his face.

The Note Writer and I share a six pack, smoke some cigarettes. We don't talk. We wait.

Nina Peck

Her Heart Wanders

Her heart wanders to the dawn of existence
In search of an antidote to all the confusion
Lashing outrageously
Thrashing about things
Desperate and unknown
Against the confines of her life support
When did it
        get
           so
                heavy?

Her heart wanders into the arms of
She who gives us life
And the permission to become
Whoever it is we will be
She who determines the oppressed from the free

Her heart wanders to places
With bells and dewdrops and anthills
Where the jacaranda blooms wilder than all the lies that were told of her

Her heart wanders into the wilderness
A stranger's touch on dormant flesh
Her first love the origin of all meaning
Her last love the result of all searching

A once desolate canvas
Beckons
And bleeds like a wolf's howl in the darkness

Her heart ambles along the stifling lines of suburbia
The truth set in stone won't set you free
It seeps from the cracks in the concrete and clay
Containing life's grand illusions
Desires concealed beneath taut denim and simulated smiles
Steely disguises under steely rooftops

Her heart wanders upon the glossy wings of ebony ravens
To the streets of bohemia in a corner of the world
Where words are whispered between fervent breaths
Stacked tightly
Gathering in increments
And coughed out like phlegm particles into the air

Her heart wanders through nights of sweat and tears
Still alive
On mattresses
Indented by the weight of regret
Flawed forms of carbon
Obscene and obtuse
Going viral in a mad world
The hand that deals the blow is the hand that knows
The one who doesn't care has all the power

Her heart lingers as she waits her turn
Standing
Watching other people's children show her how to live
Cautiously
Collecting the useful fragments
Carelessly
Tossed to the floor

Too tired to be burdened
Too sensitive to be numb
Too strong to be delicate
Too shrewd to be silent
Too loyal to be wild
Too forlorn

         to

             be

                  free

The past is a shameful face
Only erased when we rise
Scarred and marred
From the ashes of our battles
To wound and mend and wound and mend again
Creating new beginnings upon congealed tissue

Her heart flees in search of a Lover
Whose promises last longer than Methuselah
With the heart of one that is tender
And filled with longing
And wonder

Her heart wanders to a place of wholeness
At the end of the world

Where she understands that
She is everything
And everything she needs
Resides within her
Heart

Stephanie Fitz-Henry

Satan's Sidekick

Carly stood tapping the pen against her diary looking out of the bedroom window. Her entries were becoming repetitive, which was a good thing and the counsellor would be delighted. At her first appointment, Carly had explained that the sensation she felt likened to a mass of malevolent metal butterflies. Starting as flutter under the skin near her temples, rapidly growing into a heated, prickling ferocity that cramped her brain then swarmed down her throat. The speed of emotion was so quick, throwing up or creating pain was all she had known to make it go away. The sessions were working, her appetite had returned, and the remaining pesky insects were reduced to a mere tickle. Carly was enthusiastic for her next appointment, or as she called them, her fortnightly dose of mental insecticide.

The reduction of butterflies had also brought a wave of the white flag, a truce with her mum. Carly had felt betrayed, hated her for selling the farm. It had stripped her of the tangible remembrance of their once perfect family life and forced the change in schools and friends. She got it now, understood it hadn't been the fault of either of them that her dad had died and that ultimately her mum had been right. Carly hated to admit that the move to the coastal city suburb had been the best change, just like her mum said it would be. Counselling and time had returned life to some normality, even if she no longer had the lush green hill views, and that her mum's bedroom had the sweeping ocean views, while hers only offered the roof top waves of suburbia.

Carly stopped the rhythmic tapping turning her attention to the athletic blonde neighbour across the street leaving her yard. She was unceremoniously being yanked along by her boisterous, fluffy white dog at the end of its lead. The beige brick house next to the blonde's had the two Siamese cats sitting on the front window ledge, regally soaking up the morning sunlight. Their pointed faces followed the bounding, tugging ball of fluff and owner as they went past, then in a perfectly timed move both small faces gazed up to her.

Carly heard her mum calling out, 'You going to finish this?' followed by a loud clattering of dishes.

'Yes, and I'm ready!' She replied, putting the diary and pen on her desk. With a smile, she bounded out of her bedroom and down the stairs.

Carly's excitedness faded the moment she saw her mum's work jacket strategically placed over her brown leather handbag on the kitchen bench, 'You promised we'd go clothes shopping.'

Her mum placed a hand on her hip, 'Don't start, okay. I'm tired, someone's damn cats were out last night, and their fighting kept me awake. I know what I said, it's probably only going to be an hour at the *very* most. We'll go when I get back.'

Carly's mood brightened a little, 'Fine,' she said.

'Besides,' her mum continued, 'you know the agency found Typhon a permanent family. He's at long last out of foster care, so spend some final quality time with him,' she said motioning to Typhon who was sitting on the floor looking at the wall.

Carly glanced over to Typhon then back to her mum, 'Honestly, he's gross, always eating or trying to eat my cereal, there's something seriously wrong with him. Look at him I don't know why you bothered; he hasn't even made a single noise since he's been here. He's a mute!'

'Shush!' Her mum said swiftly bringing her forefinger up to her lips with narrowed eyes, 'If you didn't leave your half-eaten breakfast bowls lying around that wouldn't happen, we're going through so much cereal it's ridiculous,' she said pushing the bowl across the counter.

'That's not fair, you know I have to eat slowly! And I never know if he's slobbered his germs in it! It's not my fault either that he gets the boxes in the pantry!' Carly replied flicking Typhon the bird over her shoulder.

'That's enough! Besides, you were the one that always said you wished you had company.'

'Yeh, right Mum, like when I was eight not fifteen.'

Her mum scooped up her jacket and handbag, 'Just look after him for the next hour, okay.'

She went over to Carly and kissed the top of her head then affectionately smoothed down the long dark brown hair, 'I'll be back before you know it. We'll drop him off, do the paperwork, then shop til you drop, and buy more cereal.'

Carly rolled her eyes, 'That's not even funny,' she said and started heading back up to her bedroom.

Typhon remained still, transfixed, concentrating on the wriggle of communication waves which only he could see, immersed in a conversation that only he could hear.

'Yes, my Lord, I understand, however –'

The responding voice that interjected flowed as a deep rumble of words, 'Then why defy me again? She is too old, the aged are harder to wane. You have been with this family long enough, do not get comfortable it is time to move on.'

'Lord, I have seen her markings, she *will* give,' Typhon argued.

Upstairs Carly flopped onto her bed and scrolled through the playlist on her mobile phone, she touched the play icon then placed the phone by her side. The Indie pop song lyrics flowed through the first verse, then halfway through the chorus she heard a strange female voice. She sat up intently listening for a moment then picked up her phone, it looked fine however through the music the voice increased in clarity and volume.

'Die, kill your mum, die, kill yourself,' it repeated over and over.

Carly stopped the song; her heart began racing as the voice continued ranting. She leapt off the bed and dashed to the window hoping to see someone outside arguing, or perhaps follow the sound to an adjoining neighbour. There was no one in sight. She turned and looked at her reflection in the full-length mirror as another voice, this one male, intertwined with the other, 'You're useless, pathetic, it's pointless,' it said.

The corners of her mouth turned down, her face changed distraught with horror as she realised the voices were not external, they were playing in her head. Carly's instinct was to run, get out, then abruptly they stopped, and an eloquent male voice asked, 'Want them to go away?'

She spun around fearfully, only to find Typhon at the doorway, 'Who said that?' She asked, darting her eyes around the room.

'Me,' Typhon answered and tilted his head slightly to one side.

Carly looked at him and took a couple of small steps backward, 'Wh … what? That's impossible,' she whispered bringing her hands up covering her mouth.

'Is it? What would you know about possibility?' He questioned.

The internal voices began once more, increasing in volume and she instinctively covered her ears, 'Stop it!' She screamed and rushed past him to the bathroom.

Typhon followed and looked in from the doorway, 'I can make them stop,' he said.

Carly turned to face him pressing the palm of her hands hard against her ears, 'Piss off!' She screamed.

The voices were relentless, overwhelmed she fell to her knees bending forward she clasped her ears tighter.

'*I'm* in control, *I'm* in control,' she muttered over and over.

For a couple of minutes, she grappled with her anxious breathing saying the mantra out loud until she forced her lungs into a rhythm. The voices swiftly quietened, and her split-second thought of victory depleted with the sound of Typhon's stern voice.

'Do you want them to stop?' He asked.

Carly's looked at him between the strands of hair that covered her ashen face, she kept her voice calm, 'Why don't you …'

'Go to Hell?' Been there, done that, bit overrated,' Typhon said nonchalantly.

'Why are you doing this to me?' She asked.

'It's in a realm and quota you would never understand, one I care not to explain. I can make the voices stop or let them play in your mind forever. If you choose to let them stay what will they diagnose you as, schizophrenic? Delusional? You'll be on medication for the rest of your life, feebly trying to keep them silent. Sell your soul and I'll guarantee they never return.'

Her rage rose pumping up her courage, 'What! Just stop it. Sell my soul? No, no way!'

Typhon turned his back to her, the voices returned, rambling, confusing and directing.

'Stop! Stop them!' She screamed.

Desperate she crawled to the white bathroom cabinet and hastily opened the small doors. The cosmetics and toiletries tumbled out, bouncing across the floor as she rummaged along the cluttered shelves then pulled out a plastic packet. With trembling hands, she ripped it open removing a shaving razor and snapped the plastic housing to free one of the blades.

She fell backwards sitting on the tiles and pulled up a sleeve, 'Screw you,' she spat looking at Typhon and held the blade against the rows of scars that lined the inside of her arm.

Carly scratched the cold metal into her skin, as the sting of pain registered the voices softened. Tears of relief began to roll down her cheeks, she cut deeper again and again, but on the next cut the shrieking voices returned.

Exasperated she dropped the blade and held her head in her hands, 'What did you mean sell my soul?' She asked.

Typhon kept his distance as he sauntered into the bathroom, 'Just that. Agree to sell your soul.'

'To who, you? What are you? Satan?' She asked as her lip started to quiver.

'I am like … one of his children, his sidekick. Agree to sell or stay like this, choose!' He demanded.

Carly couldn't think straight let alone muster a spurt of energy to try and get away, she nodded in defeat. At once a scroll of discoloured paper appeared on the ground by her side, it uncurled revealing rows of neat black print.

'Place your blood on it, then it will be done,' Typhon explained.

Carly's middle finger was unsteady as she dipped its tip into the thin trail of blood trickling down her arm. She hesitated then raised it at him before lowering her arm. The side of her hand brushed the curled edge of paper – it burnt as her finger smudged the redness across it and the ranting voices stopped.

The quietness of normality felt surreal, she nervously eyed the doorway, Typhon was gone as too the piece of paper. A solitary tear escaped and dripped onto the bloodied raw cuts on her arm creating a small diluted pinkish swirl. Infuriated Carly grabbed a roll of bandage that was lying in front of her and began to wind the fabric around her arm.

She tucked the end of the bandage in place then stood up and went to the basin, hastily she washed her hands and face, 'Bastard!' She yelled.

The whirring of the garage's roller door motor announced her mum's return and with mixed relief Carly pulled down her shirt sleeve and raced down the stairs.

Her mum flounced through the door dumping her work gear on the counter, 'Told you I wouldn't be long, just one contract to look over — Are you alright? You look like a wreck.'

Carly faltered when she saw Typhon perched on one of the stools at the kitchen counter, he was casually eating her cereal with a look of smugness, 'Umm, yes just tired,' she lied, wishing she could tell her the truth without sounding like a lunatic.

The side of her hand where it had brushed the paper began tingling, she ran her fingers over the thin paper cut which was now a line of congealed and crusted black blood.

'You looked fine earlier, maybe the brawling cats did disturb you after all,' her mum said then shrugged her shoulders, 'Hello are you listening?'

Carly was distracted as she studied the wound and heard two clear soft voices, 'What did you say?' she asked.

'The cats fighting? Never mind,' her mum said, her words trailing off as she walked out of the room, 'I'll hang up my jacket then let's go.'

Carly looked at Typhon and tilted her head mimicking his earlier pose, then she bolted to the front door flinging it open and yanked it closed behind her. She ran across the front lawn and stopped when she saw the Siamese cats were still sitting on the window ledge.

Inside her mum had returned as the front door had slammed shut, 'Well what do you think that was about?' She asked Typhon.

He didn't make a sound, just licked the milk from his top lip staring towards the front door, it opened in a matter of seconds as Carly returned.

Her mum's brow furrowed, 'Carly what's wrong?'

'Nothing,' she replied flipping her hair over her shoulder.

'Okay, I'll get Typhon's things,' her mum said.

Carly leant against the kitchen counter opposite Typhon, 'Got nothing to say now Mum's home?'

Typhon didn't move, his eyes were downcast.

'Cats fighting hey,' Carly added as her mum come back with a blue bag.

'Mum, I've had a change of heart. I want him to stay, I know how important he is to you.'

Typhon flicked his eyes quickly in Carly's direction.

'Really? Are you sure?' Her mum asked dropping the bag and clasping her hands together.

Carly nodded.

'You're a gem, I'll call the agency. Surely they'll let him stay,' she said excitedly and pulled her mobile phone out from her jean pocket.

Carly went and sat next to Typhon, she put her arm around him and whispered into his ear, 'You see, if there are bad ones like you, then there must be good ones, right, ones from the other side. You've screwed up, opened something in me without realising,' she turned her hand over showing him the thin black wound, 'I know there are good ones, I can hear all of you, I'm going to find a way to undo what you've done, I'll make it happen and you aren't going anywhere.'

Her mum was beaming as she ended the phone call, 'All good, we just need to go down and complete the final paperwork. Wow, look at you two now, so sweet.'

Carly snatched up the cereal bowl, 'Awesome Mum, only I've got one condition, let's keep him as a permanent indoor cat. I don't want him leaving the house, causing trouble or worse – getting hurt,' she said and stroked his short black fur.

Typhon turned and looked at one, then the other, his tail flicked uncomfortably, 'Meow,' he said softly.

Laura Ferretti

Let There Be

It is the ultimate prize. The promise of luxury and power, forever. The competition is open to individuals and couples, right across the world. No entry fee just fill in the online application.

On New Year's Day 2021 the announcement is made – the winners are Ebo Zola and Jan Smith. To collect they sign a contract that binds them together and neither may withdraw from, ever. They don't meet anyone associated with the competition, but every promise is fulfilled.

Ebo and Jan are fêted everywhere, and then fade from public view. A decade later they are in rude health and have quietly accumulated a wealth portfolio equivalent to the whole of Europe.

Jan focuses on science and technology, becoming the most knowledgeable person alive. Ebo looks after business and philanthropy.

In 2043, an asteroid hits the earth, bringing with it an alien virus. Despite them directing every form of enterprise on the planet to combat it, the virus destroys all forms of life.

Except for Ebo and Jan.

*

Over millennia they transform from corporeal to disembodied form. They travel the earth at will, then explore the solar system and galaxy. Time becomes endless and meaningless. Ebo becomes morose and Jan becomes ever more annoyed and impatient with him. Despite this, as stipulated, they cannot separate.

Ebo is the first to notice the fading of the universe.

'How will it end?' he asks.

'Does it end?'

'There is no other life, just us. If I could end my existence I would, but the contract forbids it. With everything you know, why didn't you prevent this. It's all your fault.' Ebo strikes Jan with a storm of gamma rays.

Jan's anger is instant and terrible. She retaliates with all her power, and Ebo is gone, freed of the bond.

Jan is alone, knowing that Ebo outsmarted her, condemned her to an eternity alone as the universe cools and grows dark.

She examines all knowledge, an implacable fire burning within her. Then, wrapped in the infinite black of entropy, she understands, and inwardly, smiles. 'Let there be light.' And there is light.

David Rawet

Selfie Obsessed

Finally. Finally, Carla got what she had always wanted.

It was the perfect setting. The merest sliver of moon hung in the sky looking like a stray white eyelash on a black satin sheet. The gentle lapping of the ocean created a creamy froth on the pristine white sand. The rugged cliff made for a dramatic backdrop.

Carla lay on her back, another thing of beauty to add to the perfect scene. People fussed over and around her. The photographer plied his trade, capturing every part of her exquisite body. Yes – finally she got what she had always wanted.

*

Carla knew she was pretty. Why wouldn't she? She had been told so all her life. Her earliest memories were of her dad holding her high in the air and telling her how beautiful she was and about all the hearts she was going to break. She remembered looking in the mirror and trying to understand how being beautiful could break someone's heart. Her mum used to tell her all the time: 'You gotta use what God gave you girl, that pretty little face can take you anywhere.' She was too young to understand then what her mum meant. But that was then, she soon learnt.

At fourteen Carla had gone from a pretty child to a stunning young woman. She was taller than most of the girls in her year. Her long naturally blonde hair hung perfectly straight. Her slightly pale complexion and glacier blue eyes gave her an almost elven look. Her breasts were well past the budding stage and did not go unnoticed. There was not a boy in the school whose head would not turn when she walked past.

Carla loved the attention. She loved that she had to put in no effort whatsoever to get the admiration of everyone around her. Just standing around chatting to her friends who – of course – were nowhere near as pretty as she was, would get all the boys looking in her direction. Boys were so stupid. Did they think she could not see them having a sneaky look? She would catch their gaze and smile to herself when they quickly looked away. As if any of them would stand a chance with her. Of course, a few brave souls had tried. She almost admired their bravery. Even when Shaun Hughes, the conquest of most of the girls in her year, (and many in the years above), had tried his dull humour and even duller chat up lines on her, she had cut him off as if he was the school's biggest dork. The look on his face when he realised he was getting a knockback was priceless. There would be a man for her somewhere, certainly not a boy.

All through school, Carla had pestered her parents to buy her a phone. All her friends had one. For all her popularity, she knew she was missing out. All the talk of Facebook, Instagram, Twitter. It was just a foreign language to her, but one she desperately wanted to learn. She had tried playing the safety card with her dad. 'Come on Dad, what if I am kidnapped by some pervert and laying in the boot of his car? You'll be at my funeral crying and saying to yourself if only we had got her a phone.' She had really laid on the theatricals with this scenario, but her dad just laughed and said that she would probably have met the pervert on Facebook whilst on the phone in the first place.

Her sixteenth birthday fell on a Saturday. It was always good to have a birthday on a weekend. She knew she'd be thoroughly spoilt for the day, and why shouldn't she. She deserved it. She was not acing school, but her grades were above average. As far as teenagers go, she was not causing her parents too much hassle. She hadn't surprised them with a pregnancy. She didn't smoke like some of her friends did. She had seen what smoking did to people. Not just the cancer it gave you, but it ruined your complexion. Her friend Tina's mum was a right old chain smoker. She always looked ill. She had all these creases around her mouth which made her look like she had just sucked on a lemon. No – smoking was an addiction and addiction was for the weak.

Mum had prepared her favourite breakfast for her. Eggs, bacon, those Lincolnshire sausages with the herbs in that she really liked and a good ladleful of baked beans. Heinz, of course, not the shop brand bullets that she normally bought for them.

'Happy Birthday baby girl.' Her dad appeared at the kitchen door.

'Thanks Dad but err … not really a baby anymore.'

'You'll always be my baby girl. Jeez, look at the size of your breakfast! You don't know how lucky you are you know. I wish I could pack it away like you do! Look at you, not an ounce of fat on you.'

He demonstrated the fact by trying to pinch her non-existent love handles.

'Daaaaad.' Carla squirmed away giggling.

Carla's mum gave him a 'go on then' knowing nod.

'So, I guess, you'll be wanting a present or something then?' He pulled a rectangular, gift-wrapped box from his pocket.

Carla's heart didn't just skip a beat, it virtually ran out of the room! *It's a phone, it's got to be a phone. Hope it's an iPhone 8, that's what Tina has, it's got everything and one of the best cameras.*

'Thanks Mum, thanks Dad,' she leapt up from the table and hugged them both. Her mum laughed nervously.

'Don't thank too soon, you don't know what it is yet.'

Carla removed the bright red bow from the present and started to slowly peel of the layer of wrapping paper. It had flamingos all over it, her favourite animal. As the paper come off a plain white box appeared. *iPhones come in plain white boxes, don't they?* She carefully lifted the lid from the box, only to reveal some crumpled white tissue paper. She started to pull away the paper, her fingers trembling with anticipation.

What the actual fuck!

Carla pulled the gold and silver necklace out of the box. The light coming in from the kitchen window made the blue gemstone sparkle. Her dad wore this stupid smile. Her mum was wringing her hands and looking at her, trying to gauge her reaction. Carla did indeed react.

'A fucking necklace! On my sixteenth birthday, you buy me a fucking necklace!' White spittle sprayed from her mouth and picked up by the light. She threw the necklace down on the table knocking over a bottle of tomato ketchup.

Her mum physically slumped. Her head, her shoulders, everything went about six inches south. Her dad's stupid smile disappeared and was replaced with wide-eyed shock.

'But, but Carla …'

'Don't but fucking Carla me! Am I worth that little to you two? Really am I? Have I let you down in some way? Have I?'

Her mum regained her composure, the initial shock at her daughter's ingratitude turning to white hot anger. She had never sworn at her Carla, never had the need to. Of course, they had had the usual teenager-mother arguments. This was different.

'You selfish little mare! Your dad and I spent three fucking days looking for that! Three fucking days.' Her face reddened, shocking herself with her bad language.

'Even when we found it, we ummed and arred about the cost of it, it was way more than we wanted to spend. They even offered to wrap it for us, but Dad said no, Carla really loves flamingos that's what you said, Ken, didn't you? So, then we spend another three hours looking for the perfect fucking wrapping paper. Three fucking hours, that made us go over our car parking, so we got clamped and had to pay the car park people another fifty quid to get it taken off.'

Carla should have felt some semblance of guilt, but she didn't. She looked at her parents and felt hatred. They knew she had her heart set on a phone. Fuck, it was all she spoke about for the last year. Did they have that little trust in her? Did they have that little respect? She was beautiful after all, and had she got up the duff or got shacked up with some pretty boy. No, she had not. She deserved that phone and what does she get … a fucking lame necklace. This was unforgivable

'I think it might be best for you to go to you room Carla.' Her dad didn't look angry, just incredibly disappointed. He righted the bottle of ketchup, picked up the necklace and placed it back in the box.

'I guess we'll be taking this back then.' He got up and put his arm around his wife. 'Just can't please some people,' as he led her out of the kitchen.

Carla's usual pale complexion was flushed with the red of anger. *So, it's my birthday and I am the one who should be feeling guilty that I don't like the fucking shit necklace … great.* She got up from her chair making sure she made as much noise as possible. She pushed her half-eaten breakfast to the centre of the table once again upsetting the bottle of ketchup. She stormed up the stairs to her bedroom making sure each step was stomped on as hard as possible. The whole staircase and banister shook. *Take that.* As she entered her room, she grabbed the door with both hands slamming it shut with such force the boom echoed through the whole house. She was just about to jump on the bed when she noticed something on her pillow. A box with a small card propped up against it. She picked up the card and read the handwritten message on it.

To our beautiful daughter Carla
  We hope you loved the necklace. You are not 16 every day, so here's
  your second present. We know you will do the right thing with it. Sorry
  we didn't wrap it.
  Love Mum and Dad xxxxxx
  P.S it's all set up and we have put our numbers in your contact list.

Carla pulled the iPhone 8 out of the box. *Well why didn't they just give me the fucking phone first!*

*

Carla knew everyone in the office was jealous, after all why wouldn't they be? Jason was not only a catch; he was the boss. She had got the job a year ago. Jason had interviewed her. It was clear to her then that there was chemistry. She had totally fucked up in the interview, but hey, she hadn't got to this point in her life with her brains, had she? She could tell from the way he looked at her that she had the job in the bag. Getting her letter of appointment was just a formality really. As a sure thing as it was, it still warranted the obligatory selfie with the letter. *After all, if it isn't on Facebook, then it didn't happen!*

Within the year, she had gone from admin assistant to Jason's personal assistant. Carla could not believe that his last PA, Julie had lasted the four years she did. For one thing, she was probably carrying five kilos more than she needed. She also had this lazy eye that made her look as though she was just about to have a stroke. *How the hell did she look in the mirror in the morning and still be brave enough to leave the house.* No, Jason had done exactly the right thing by letting her go. It was bringing his image down. Beauty and the beast only work when it's the man who is butt ugly.

Carla loved her dinner dates with Jason. It was the perfect opportunity for a social media frenzy. She would always make sure that she arrived early. When you are capturing your whole night for Facebook then one needs to get everything perfect. After two and a half hours of getting her make up to movie star levels, picking the absolute killer outfit, and then another hour in front of the mirror getting the perfect selfies, it pays to have fifteen minutes to post aforementioned selfies and make the final adjustments to the hair. She took her faithful selfie stick out of her handbag and extended it to full length. As she sat at the table waiting for Jason to arrive, she clicked away with her phone camera. Side view, front view, front view with wine, side view with pout, front view with tongue out, and of course the open mouth wide eyed surprised shot. She was starting to get the attention of some other diners. Quick glances and whispering between couples. *Yeah go ahead and look people, this is what beauty and class look like in one package.* She posted her photos to Facebook and set her phone to alert her of notifications. *And now we wait.*

Jason arrived at seven o'clock on the dot, as always; his timing was perfect. Carla allowed herself the faintest hint of a smile as she saw two young girls at a nearby table nudge each other and look in Jason's direction. *In your wildest dreams ladies ... dream on.* He really was a beautiful man. Tall but not ridiculously so. His twice weekly visits to the gym gave him a toned firmness, but not to the point that he looked like just another beefcake. He looked like a man. Tina had always gone on about liking her blokes with boyish good looks, but not Carla, she liked them to look like their age. Maybe it was a dad thing, but she liked her men to make her feel like she was the apple of their eye, that only she mattered. On the odd occasion that another girl had turned Jason's head she had made sure he knew how she felt. The last time it happened it involved a costly dent to his car and a week of silent treatment. She did have the slightest pang of guilt. After all, it's not his fault, it's how men are wired isn't it? He certainly wouldn't be attracted to these women, not when he has Carla on his arm. She got up from her seat, selfie stick in hand.

'One for the album?' She put her arm around his shoulders and raised the phone up high to get the shot. Jason looked embarrassed.

'People are looking Carla.'

'Of course they're looking babe, we're gorgeous. Let them look, they are only jealous – Smile!'

The waiter looked nervous as he approached the table. Carla was clicking the camera at everything. The table, herself, Jason, herself, the salt and pepper shakers, herself. He put his hand up to his face as she pointed the lens at him.

'Please madam, I don't think you want a picture of me blighting your phone,' the slightest tone of irritation in his voice.

'Yeah,' Carla agreed, 'you're probably right.' She wasn't joking.

They ordered the same meals. A prawn and pasta dish. That is not entirely true. Jason ordered a steak, but Carla pointed out that to get a good photo for her social media, it was best that both plates looked the same.

Jason had protested. 'I don't even like prawns.'

But Carla wasn't having any of it.

'We are a popular couple, Jason. I know you don't get the whole social media thing, but it's important that we are seen in the right places, with the right people.'

'Yeah, but does that really have to include eating the right things too? They do a killer steak in here.'

'Oh Jason, you are so funny, can you imagine how that would look in a photo? Me with my delicate pink pasta dish, and you with a bloodied half cow on you plate next to it? You are so silly, but I guess that's why I love you.'

Jason held up his hands in resignation. 'Prawn Linguine it is then.'

The food arrived. Jason had to admit it did look pretty good. He picked up his fork to get stuck into it.

'JASON!'

He almost fell of his chair with the shock.

'What th–'

'Jeez Jason, how many times do I need to tell you, you can't start eating until I have got the picture. You'll thank me later because we, along with the whole of our friends' network will be able to re-live this whole night. People don't what to see a half-eaten pasta dish do they? No of course they don't, they want to see the dish in its entirety, untouched, pure.'

'For fuck's sake,' Jason muttered.

'What?'

'Take a picture of the plate,' he managed through a forced smile which Carla didn't register.

She proceeded to take photos of their food, every now and then insisting Jason pose with a fork in his hand, or a glass of wine to his lips. When they finally got around to eating it, the sauce on the pasta had congealed to a lumpy custard texture and the food was cold. Carla seemed oblivious.

Jason promised himself a Maccas on the way home.

*

Carla always knew her wedding was going to be spectacular. She was not disappointed. Jason had wanted to go away to the Caribbean and have a quiet little affair. Carla wanted a huge church wedding. She had even suggested a cathedral which Jason thought was a joke. He soon realised it wasn't when his laughter was met by one of Carla's icy *fuck you* stares.

She settled for the village church. Although one could say it was the village church on steroids. It was impossible to see the walls of the place every inch was covered in flowers. They were everywhere. Carla had insisted that the church be decorated the night before so she could get some pre-wedding photos, she then spend her post-wedding night putting teasing close up photos on her Facebook account.

The wedding day was picture perfect. Carla arrived in a carriage drawn by two white horses that would not have looked out of place in a Cinderella movie. Her dad exited the carriage first, a phone could be seen at the carriage window.

'Come on Carla, you don't want to keep your groom waiting.'

'I'm coming Dad, just look at the camera and look really proud or something, I want to post this before I get into the church.'

Her dress was designed by Vera Wang, well, a copy of a Vera Wang anyway, but Carla insisted it was the same wedding dress that Sarah Michelle Gellar had worn. She had asked the dressmaker to add a small pocket at the front to place her phone. There would be plenty of selfie moments today. The guest list amounted to about three hundred, around half of those knew neither Carla nor

Jason, but were, in Carla's eyes, important enough to be there. Carla had asked for the wedding to be screened outside the church too so that the public could watch it to. The vicar declined that request saying that they couldn't get their hands on the equipment. Her friend Tina was maid of honour and most of the girls from the office had been cajoled into being bridesmaids.

Carla took a full ten minutes to walk down the aisle. She stopped after every few steps to take pictures of the bridal party, of herself, of the guests, of herself, of the church, of herself. When she finally arrived at the altar she turned to face Jason, a small tear running down her cheek and whispered, 'Your buttonhole is upside down.'

*

Jason, out of everything on that day, was looking forward to his wedding night. He had spent his day being congratulated by people he didn't know. He had talked to Carla twice. Every time he saw her, she was in her element. Phone in hand, ushering people together to get 'the perfect shot'. If she wasn't taking photos, she was fiddling away at her screen, posting everything to her various social media sites.

Jason had never been so entranced by anyone in his life. From the moment Carla had walked into the interview he had been intoxicated by her. On more than one occasion he had fumbled on the questions he was asking. Julie – his then PA – had to step in a few times to finish his sentences. It was all lip service. He knew he was going to give her the job before she had even sat her cute little butt down on the faux leather chair. He had had his good share of relationships in the past, even a previous engagement, but on reflection, they were just distractions. People say that *beauty is only skin deep*, and all the other clichés like *it's not what's on the outside, it what's on the inside.* Jason had even believed that, no one could ever accuse him of being shallow. It all changed when he met Carla.

He was aware of her flaws, and that's all they were right? Tiny flaws. It wasn't her fault after all. It was these bloody social media sites, Facebook and Instantgram or whatever the hell they called it. Just the latest fads that will eventually die a slow death. Like Cabbage Patch dolls and roller-skates. It was an addiction – a vice, and we all have them, don't we?

Jason's closest friend Jenni had tried to tell him that Carla's self-obsession was bordering on being a mental health issue, even suggesting that Jason get her checked out by a doctor. What did Jenni know? A year earlier when Jason was having a few issues with self-esteem, it was Jenni who suggested he needed to learn to love himself, she even downloaded Whitney Houston's Greatest

Love of All as his ringtone. Make your fucking mind up Jenni! Still, he was gutted she didn't come today.

The life they were going to have together would be perfect. Once they were settled and having lots of babies, he was sure Carla would put the phone down and put all her efforts into their family. There is a big difference between being self-obsessed and selfish. Their kids would come first – wouldn't they?

The wedding was finally over. Jason had purposely laid off drinking too much. He wanted his wedding night to be special. He was sort of old fashioned about that sort of thing. Of course, he and Carla had had sex, but he always thought the wedding night would be a standout. Carla had insisted on the honeymoon suite at the hotel where the reception was held. It wasn't cheap, but nothing was cheap about their wedding day. At last they stood outside their room. Jason held his bride in his arms. Carla giggled as he fumbled with the card that opened the door.

'Smile,' she said as she held her phone to get the perfect *carry the bride over the threshold* selfie.

They fell into the room. Jason whistled.

'Wow, check this place out.'

The room – in true Carla style – was grand. The carpet was thick, lush and red. Antique furniture that would not be out of place at the Palace of Versailles adorned every corner. In the centre of the room was a huge four poster bed with red drapes that matched the carpet. At the end of the bed was an ice bucket with a bottle of champagne and two glasses.

'Oh my God. Oh my God. Oh my God! Jason, it's perfect.' Carla jumped on the bed and bounced on her back and kicked her legs like an excited child. She pulled her phone out of her special pocket and proceeded to take selfies. She took photos of her right side, her left side. Every conceivable angle.

'Mind if I join you?' Jason asked, giving her his best *come to bed* look.

'Two seconds hun, I really want to get this shot perfect.' She pointed to the champagne. 'Can you pour me a glass of the champers, it's gonna make a great cover picture for Facebook, me laying on this bed with a glass in my hand.'

Jason poured them both a glass. He lay on the bed with her as she clicked away with the phone. He smiled when he was asked, he pouted when he was told to. Pretended to laugh when requested. After an hour of posing and gesturing, Carla kissed him on the cheek and disappeared into the ensuite.

'Don't go anywhere, be right back.' She laughed with that mischievous twinkle in her eye that always drove him crazy.

As she climbed out of her dress, she remembered the phone was still in the pocket. She took it out and checked to see how many responses she had had to her Facebook photos throughout the day. Over two hundred notifications. She couldn't believe it, that's the most she had ever had! She started replying to some of the comments, *gotta strike while the iron's hot*. An hour and a half later, she walked back into the bedroom. The champagne bottle was empty. Jason was snoring, a champagne flute laying on his chest.

*

The honeymoon had been everything she had dreamed of. She had seen loads of pictures of Santorini in the piles of glossy magazines she had at home. It was a popular spot for celebrities. The white and blue building made for perfect pictures. She had taken so many, she had had to download hundreds to her laptop to make more space on her phone. Jason had been a bit quiet she had thought, but she put it down to the fact that he was probably a bit overwhelmed by it all. His life was now perfect, and he was probably just coming to terms with that. It was their last night and she had it all planned out. They would have dinner in the little Greek taverna that she loved at the end of the road their hotel was on. It was so pretty and had goats outside. Her Facebook page was going crazy with funny comments. After dinner, they would go for a walk along the cliff top just to catch the awesome sunsets in the pictures. Then they would go back to the hotel, and she would remind Jason why he married her. She would give him the night of his life. What a lucky guy.

Dinner was excellent. At one point, a goat came up to the table. All the other diners were laughing, all wishing the goat went to their table, which it didn't. Even Jason was laughing, which he didn't do too much of these days. The timing for the cliff top walk was perfect. The sun was just beginning to set. The few clouds in the sky were a dazzling burnt orange colour, she would not even need to photoshop the pictures. The slight ripple of the sea reflected the scene. Carla smiled. This was the perfect backdrop.

'This is the place Jason, it's stunning. I want you to get a few of me with the sunset in the background.' She handed him her phone and stood with the ocean behind her. 'Make sure the sun is just behind me, I don't want it to look like the sun is coming out of my head or anything. Oh, and make sure the sea is in focus too, I don't want to look blurred, I really want the refection to pop on the screen.'

Jason sighed and started to take the photos. 'Sorry, it doesn't matter what I do, the sun is either blurred, or the sea is blurred, can't you edit it later, it's getting late.'

'Oh for goodness sake, give the phone to me. If you want a job done.'

She stepped backwards, holding the phone up high in her outstretched arm.

'That's got it. Absolutely perfect position, the sun is just setting below the sea and ...'

'CARLA! MIND THE EDG ... CAAAAARLA!'

Carla disappeared over the cliff. As she fell the twenty meters or so to the beach below, she bounced twice off the hard rock of the cliff. The first time, she broke three ribs. The second time her chest caved in crushing her heart and killing her instantly. She landed on her back on the soft sand of the beach. Her face was untouched.

The forensic photographer clicked away taking pictures from every angle tutting and shaking his head. *She's so beautiful, what a waste,* he thought. The rest of the forensic team combed and brushed her broken body, looking for any signs of foul play. Carla would have loved their attention to detail.

A young Greek boy watched on, taking pictures with his phone and casually posted them on Facebook.

His post got over one hundred thousand views.

Mark Townsend

When the Ladybird Came

from *Alice in Storyland*.
Read-aloud stories for children aged five to nine years.

Come with me to Storyland and let's say 'Hi,' to Alice.

Alice lives in Storyland and she's a scaredy-cat. But wait, maybe that's not true anymore.

There was a time when Alice was too scared to sleep at night if her bedside lamp was off. She really didn't like the dark. She liked it when the shade over the lamp turned everything pink and spread its soft glow all over her bedroom. Pink was her favourite colour.

When she looked at the pink shadow pictures on her bedroom wall, she forgot about the cassowary fidgeting outside her bedroom door; ready to headbutt or to kick her when she went to the bathroom in the middle of the night. When the lamp glowed softly, she stopped thinking that those bright red spots on top of her bookshelf were those of a hairy scary Huntsman spider crouching, waiting to pounce. Even the hungry dingo under her bed stopped panting when the light was on. Having the light on was the only way Alice could get to sleep without feeling alone or scared.

Alice had a pet lamb called Molly. Their favourite game was to run through the sprinklers and try to catch the rainbows when her Dada was watering the lawn. One day when Alice turned off the water after Mum had called her in for tea, she noticed a ladybird on the ground underneath the rosebush growing below her bedroom window. It was stuck in the mud and struggling to fly. Its wings were bogged down with great big drops of water.

Alice knelt in the mud and nudged the ladybird gently into the palm of her hand. She cradled it for a moment while she blew the water gently off its back. Then she lifted her hand high above her head, spread her fingers wide and sang;

> 'Ladybird, ladybird fly away home
> Your house is on fire,
> And your children all gone.'

The ladybird lifted off up into the air and circled around her head just like a helicopter. Alice thought she heard a sweet gentle voice,

Thank you for saving me.
If you had a wish
What would it be?

Alice felt a bit silly talking to a ladybird, but she did anyway.

'Well, I am a bit afraid of the dark. I really wish I wasn't.'

The sweet gentle voice was softer now, because the ladybird was on her way to her children, but Alice was sure she heard:

Don't be afraid.
Look at the moon.
It was me you saved.

That night it was Dada's turn to tuck her into bed. Alice told him about the ladybird. When they had finished chatting, Dada kissed her on her forehead and said they were going to try a little experiment. Then he opened the blinds and leant over to switch off the light. Alice gasped but she didn't say anything. From her pillow, she could see the tops of trees swaying gently in the breeze.

Above the trees was the smiling face of the moon.
She smiled and thought of the ladybird.
And a silvery light flooded her room.

Suddenly it was morning. Mum and Dada were so proud of Alice for sleeping without the light. Alice felt good too.

The next night after Mum tucked her in, Alice bravely turned off her pink light before Mum could do it. It was a windy night and she could hear an awful screechy sound just outside the window. Alice bit her lip, sat up straight and held her breath.

Was it a scary-in-the-dark screech from some monster of even a ghost? Or was it a screech that Dada could explain?

Screech! There was it was again.

Just then the moon peeped at her from behind a cloud and gave her a friendly smile. Alice remembered the sweet gentle voice.

Don't be afraid.
Look at the moon.
It was me you saved.

She climbed out of bed; dragged a chair over to the window and climbed onto it.

> Screech!
> Scratch!
> Knock-knock!

Alice shivered and not because she was cold. All she wanted to do was jump back into bed and turn her pink light on. Instead she put her face against the glass so that she could see better. She peered into the darkness.

Ah! A twig from the rosebush where she had found the ladybird was scraping and banging against the windowpane. She leaned out of the window and grabbed at it. Ouch! A thorn pricked her finger. She broke off the twig, careful not to get hurt again. Sucking her sore finger, she got back into bed.

> All was quiet.
> Leaves rustled in the treetops.
> Her bed was cosy and warm.
> The moon painted a silvery picture on her bedroom wall.
> She was soon fast asleep.

The next night there was a storm. The moon was wrapped up in a heavy blanket of clouds. Alice wanted to poke holes in the darkness with her finger. Everything in the house danced and rattled trying to get away from the wind. There was noise everywhere, it was confusing and frightening. Alice stuck her fingers in her ears. She opened her eyes as wide as she could, trying to see past the darkness. One sound just would not go away; it was a loud and pushy bang-bang.

Alice clutched her pillow tightly. She opened her eyes even wider, but the moon stayed away. She thought about crawling into the foot-end of the bed with Mum and Dada. They would let her sleep there. She knew they would.

She tried to bring back the sound of the sweet gentle voice; it was awfully quiet, just a teeny tiny whisper:

> *Don't be afraid.*
> *Look at the moon.*
> *It was me you saved.*

The bang-bang became louder and pushier. It wasn't thunder; it was something else. Alice made up her mind to find the noise. She jumped out of bed, grabbed her dressing gown and slippers and went to the front door and down the garden path looking for the noise.

She found it! The garden gate was banging in the wind. Someone had forgotten to latch it. She closed the gate properly and went back to bed.

Her bed was cosy and warm.

She felt safe.

Pink glows, silvery pictures and quiet ladybird voices were not so important anymore.

The next morning Dada told her the wind could have broken the lock or torn the gate off its hinges. What if Molly had gone wandering off? He told her she was his superstar brave girl. Alice was feeling very brave too, but only for a little while.

Dada asked her to do something for him after school. He asked her to return a book he had borrowed from his friend Mike.

Mike lived at the top of the hill behind their house. She really didn't want to go. The house wasn't far, and the hill wasn't too steep.

She just did not want to go.

All day she worried about it.

You see, all of Alice's friends were afraid of Mike. She wasn't quite sure why, but if they were scared, she was scared too. She knew he spoke very loudly, and it startled her. She wondered why her friend Josh feared him. Josh was the bravest boy she knew.

Alice was scared.

It was broad daylight.

There was no moon,

no ladybird,

no soft gentle voice to guide her.

Her walk up the hill seemed to take forever.

She stopped to rest and picked a dandelion on the side of the road. Then she kept going, on and on up the hill to see a scary man.

Eventually she got to Mike's house. There he was, looking so ordinary, sitting in the garden on a wooden bench. When Alice got closer, she saw he was looking at something in his hand. His face looked kind. She'd never noticed that before. She didn't know what to say so she held out the flower.

Mike smiled and took the flower. He twirled it gently, rolling the stem between his thumb and forefinger. Resting on the open palm of his other hand was the ladybird.

'It's Alice, isn't it?' he said.

'Yes,' she said.

'Oh, I see you have brought my book. Thank you,' Mike said and blew gently on the ladybird. They both watched her fly away.

Alice gave him the book that Dada had borrowed and said goodbye.

That night Alice told Dada she had discovered something.

'What's that?' asked Dada.

'The closer I make myself get to the scary stuff, the less scary it is.'

If you enjoyed this story, we can go back to Storyland tomorrow and say hi to the boy who found out how a hammer and nails could fix anger.

Gogo Buzz

A Midnight Summary

Oh my God, I'm awake again
In the deepest dark again
Another midnight's summary
My mind crushed full and teeming with ideas and hopes and dreams
It seems

The noise of thought shushes away the sleep of the righteous
And I decay
Into a myriad mix of firing synapses that cannot be calmed
In company with heavy footfalls as nocturnal nature bounces, Skippy-like,
past my window
For me to muse upon and wonder at their wanderings

Bewitching hour now the be wakened hour
And I give in
Get up
A shower
Refreshed in starlight
Orion's belt strengthens me to push ahead
With crowded head
And lay foundations of my dreams into solid achievements
 Dazed dreams into daydreams into quietness
 My energy disbanded, dispelled in words
 To confess
 The actions needed, actions sought, questions asked,
 Doors knocked
 And opened – into still waters
Slowing hurricanes of noise and tempest
Winding down
Into rest

Deep draughts of oxygen
Breathed again
Learning peace again
Darkness reaps again
Its slumber bounty
Within the lidded heavy eyes
Of a semi-settled mind
Still cluttered with emotion
But surrendering to the motion
Of a rising falling breath
And an earth that is succumbing
To the risen Venus, shining
With the morning's silver lining ...
And I sleep.

Ian Andrew

Snakebite

1

People say you can get used to almost anything.

Try this.

You're talking to someone you just met on a tram. Sitting opposite them. Let's say it's a woman in her twenties. You're looking straight at her, she's listening to what you're saying, and suddenly she is forty-five or fifty, and she is still nodding and listening. Next she is twelve-years-old wearing a school uniform. You stop talking and blink. And then this twenty-something woman looks at you and asks, 'Is everything alright?'

What do you say?

What did I say? 'I'm fine. It just occurred to me that I might not have locked the back door before I left home.'

I watched an eighty-year-old lady chuckle to herself. 'I've done the same thing,' she said. 'Yesterday, would you believe.'

I believed. Who was I to doubt anything anymore?

The tram filled up. A tall man with a sleek black beard and wearing a Sikh turban sat beside me, listening to music in his headphones. An obese middle-aged woman with a large handbag squeezed in opposite him, forcing the now heavily pregnant first woman against the tram wall. She raised her eyebrows in an expression of quiet exasperation. The Sikh, now an elderly white-bearded gentleman, was reading something on his phone and nodding his head ever so slightly in time to his music. The little girl had taken some wool and needles out of her bag and was knitting a scarf in Hawthorn colours. Conversation was paused, perhaps finished.

At Victoria Market, the again obese woman and the young Sikh got off the tram, as did a number of other passengers. No one took the empty seats. 'Well,' began a once again twenty-something woman, 'I'm the next stop. Maybe we can talk again?'

'Yes, I'd like that,' I replied. *If I recognise you*, I thought to myself. She got off at La Trobe. I continued on to Collins Street, then walked up towards Parliament for an appointment with my psychiatrist.

2

Am I crazy?

I sat waiting for Dr Schwarz to see me with my back to Nina, the receptionist. It was my second time there and I didn't want to watch her flip through her life's manifestations more than I already had. She changed more quickly than anyone else I'd seen.

At my first appointment, two weeks earlier, I had inquired, 'Can I ask how old you are?'

'Twenty-nine,' she'd answered, and smiled. 'I just had my birthday.' She put on a mock frown, 'I'm not looking forward to the next one. Thirty! I don't know how I'll cope.'

None of the faces she had shown me looked older than thirty. I didn't really know what it meant. But if what I was seeing was indicative of her reality, then I didn't want to be the one to tell her that her time was short.

'William, the doctor will see you now.' A pubescent Nina waved me towards the doctor's consulting room.

'Thank you, Nina,' I said. I avoided looking at her as I went through.

'Good morning, William,' Dr Schwarz greeted me, 'Will you shut the door, please?'

I did, then turned to look at the doctor.

'How do I look?' he asked.

'About ninety, I'd guess.' He gave me a grin filled with stained teeth. 'Still smoking too, I'd venture.'

'Well,' he replied, 'it's good to know I don't need to quit. I do enjoy my cigarettes.' He got up from behind his desk with an alacrity that belied his apparent age, met me and we shook hands. His grip was firm. I was afraid I would break his arthritic bones, but instead mine felt a bit crushed. He indicated an armchair for me to sit in and sat in an upright chair opposite me. He reached across to his desk and took a notebook and pen. It occurred to me that the session could be recorded.

'Do you mind if I record this session?' he asked. 'Just audio, not video.'

'No, that's a good idea,' I said.

'Wonderful.' He took his phone from his jacket pocket, set it recording and placed in on the desk. 'Now then, how have you been?'

'Actually, I've been a lot better. The changes are the same, but I find I'm less affected by them. It's much as you said it would be – if I regard it as normal then that's what it will become.'

'Are you driving again? Last time you said,' he consulted his notebook, 'that you felt you weren't ready, particularly in regard to pedestrians.'

'I went for a drive around the block. For the car's sake more than for mine. It still runs fine, by the way. I got home safely but I had a couple of scary moments.' Dr Schwarz nodded and his now long, luxuriant, black hair shimmered.

'It's the distraction of the changes; they catch my attention and I take my eyes off the road.' I looked across to the window where clouds could be seen scudding across the sky. 'I think maybe I'll try again tomorrow, perhaps at night when no one is around. What do you think?'

He paused. 'I haven't asked this before,' he began, 'but do the changes differ depending on the time of day or how tired you are? How many times have I changed so far?'

'Just the once. You have long, black hair and a trim black beard and moustache. You are wearing a chequered sleeveless vest with a crest on the left side.' I leant forward. 'I think it's a griffin.'

'Oh', he exclaimed, 'I remember that vest. My wife made me get rid of it when we got married. I'd forgotten all about it. I couldn't fit into it now, too much good living.'

'I wasn't going to mention that. You look quite fit to me now, athletic even.'

'Now you're making me reminisce,' he said with a grin. 'Thank you for reminding me.' We sat in silence for a few moments.

'William, are you using a mirror at all?'

'I'm still avoiding them. I shave with an electric, entirely by touch. I have a crewcut every second week so that I don't have to comb my hair. Occasionally someone tells me something I'm wearing is not quite right, but overall I'm not missing them.'

'Do you mind if we try one now? I have a large mirror in my bathroom through there,' he nodded towards a door at the side of the room, 'where I could stand with you.'

I felt a shiver of fear run through me. I shook my head.

Another transition. This time I saw it. It only took a second: first he was the fit man in his twenties, next his outline and form blurred, and then a new body appeared. The doctor was older, in his fifties. His eyebrows raised.

'I just changed, didn't I?'

'Yes, you're about fifty now.'

'What am I wearing?'

231

'Two-piece blue suit, white shirt, no tie and brown boots.'

'Hey, that's exactly what I am wearing today. We're making real progress.' Dr Schwarz grinned.

'Doc, I don't want rain on your parade, but isn't that what you wear every day?'

'Just on Mondays, Wednesdays and Fridays. And I only bought this suit six months ago.' He put his notebook and pen onto his desk and picked up his phone. He stopped the recording and put it into his pocket.

'William. I don't have a rational explanation for what you say is happening to you. Or for what I have heard in this room. Unless you have somehow had me, and Nina as well, researched to an insane degree – to a degree that I don't think is possible – I have to admit to the possibility that it is true. Accordingly, until and unless I uncover a pathological reason for your condition, I am not going to try to cure you of delusions. What I will do is try to help you to cope with your visions. To live the sort of life you want without slipping into insanity or, to put it bluntly, killing yourself.'

Dr Schwarz stood up and walked back behind his desk, opened a drawer and took out a flat disc of metal about three centimetres in diameter. He walked back around the desk, handed it to me, and sat down in his chair again.

'What's this?' I asked, turning it over in my hand. There was a groove cut across its width on one side and no markings at all on the other. It felt heavy for its size and colder than I expected. The coolness was soothing though, as if it could absorb unwelcome heat.

'In all my years of practice there have only been two times that I couldn't come up with a rational explanation for what I have experienced. You are one of them. That disc is the other.'

'What about it?' I asked.

'Describe it to me,' he said.

I did.

He nodded. 'That's not how it feels to me, though. People seem to have different experiences holding it. One thing does remain constant, however. Having it close, on your person, seems to settle emotional distress. I want you to hold on to it for a while. Maybe it can help you improve your driving, or even look into a mirror.'

'Where did you get it?'

'It belonged to my mentor when I was starting out. He used it to show me that we don't know everything. When he retired, he gave it to me.'

'Now that's not fair,' I said, with a grin. 'I'm the one who's supposed to be crazy.' But I put the disc into my jeans pocket. I liked it.

'I think that might be enough for today. Unless there is anything else?' He waited in a way that didn't made me feel like I had to tell him something, or that he was keen for me to leave.

'Dr Schwarz,' I asked, 'do you think it was the snake bite or the lightning that caused this?'

'I really don't know. And I can't see how we can test either theory. Much less the combination.'

'No, I guess not.'

'Can you tell me how you fill in your days?'

We discussed my routine and I raised the issue of my work. 'I need something to keep my mind busy,' I said.

He agreed that I was capable of working, but not at the office. He promised to contact the Department's rehabilitation officer and arrange for me to work from home until I was cleared to return to the workplace.

'Anything else?' he asked.

'No, that's about it right now. Thank you.' I got up to leave.

'Two weeks from today?' He stood up and extended his hand, which I took.

'Yes, I'll fix it with Nina on the way out.' I turned to leave and stopped. 'Dr Schwarz. It's about Nina.'

'Yes?'

'It's odd, but I have never seen her as older than she is now, more or less.'

He looked at me without speaking for what felt like an age but was probably only thirty seconds. 'Two weeks from today,' he repeated. I nodded and left his room.

A blonde-haired Nina arranged my next appointment. 'See you then,' she said, handing me a reminder card. 'I'll send a text the day before,' she added with a smile.

The trip home was uneventful. I walked back to Elizabeth Street and caught a No. 59 tram to Keilor Road. From my stop it was a seven-minute walk to my unit. I was developing an ability to direct my focus away from people as I navigated my new world: it seemed set up to support me; I could recharge my *Myki* transport card at a machine; I selected my groceries online and had them delivered; I discovered that, if you chose to, you could live virtually free of direct human interaction.

233

3

I had tried going back to work at the office. Twice. The first time was three weeks after the accident; nine days after I left hospital. The shock of seeing people age and revert had lessened and I had begun to develop the ability to filter out – that is not look at – people I didn't need to interact with. It was easier than I thought it would be. In a crowded street you seldom have the same people around you for more than a few seconds. I probably wouldn't notice them change even if I was trying to. On public transport I mostly look out the window. Somehow, if I saw a change occur to someone outside, such as at a tram stop, it didn't really affect me. It's as if the window was also an emotional barrier.

The first day at work was bearable. It was the Friday after Anzac Day. Most people had taken the day off to have an extra-long weekend. I got in early and went to my office. Everything was pretty much as I left it, except for the larger than normal stack of paperwork in the in-tray. I turned on the computer and started working through the accumulated emails. I was probably a third of the way through them when an aged gentleman poked his head around the door jam, cup of coffee in his hand. I didn't recognise him immediately, although he did look familiar.

'Welcome back, Bill,' he said, 'How the fuck are you?'

I recognised the voice but still wasn't certain who it was. Bruce perhaps. It looked like his coffee mug.

'Good,' I replied, not confident enough to use his name. 'What's up?'

'Just the usual. Suzi's got the shits on because Danni was late with her reports again. I'm trying to convince Suzi that none of the candidates we interviewed for Kat's position were suitable and we need to readvertise.'

'That bad?'

'Truly awful. One of them didn't even know what was on his application. It was obvious someone else had written it. The best of them has the right qualifications but bugger all experience.' He took a sip. 'I haven't got the inclination to train someone up from scratch again. Last time I did that they were off somewhere else as soon as they knew how to do the job.'

My screen flickered and another email was added to my unread list. In the doorway I was now looking at a young man showing early signs of a receding hairline. Definitely Bruce. 'Well, Bruce,' I said, trying to keep my mind straight with the shifts, 'It doesn't seem that long ago you were the ambitious up and comer. You shouldn't feel threatened by the latest crop of bright young things.'

'Not that bright, most of them, if truth be told. The clever ones don't want to work here.' He started to leave. 'Oh yeah,' he added, 'there's a branch meeting at nine-thirty on Monday. The new director will be coming in. There's probably an email in there somewhere, if you haven't already deleted it. I'm guessing a budget cut, sorry, I should say "an efficiency dividend". Bullshit, bullshit.' His wry smile belied the bitterness everyone in the office felt when the Department tried to spin their expectation that we do more with less. 'Catch you later.'

I felt the sweat in my armpits and on my forehead. Whilst I had managed to conduct a coherent conversation with Bruce, my stress level had leapt. I swivelled my chair to look out my window, one that faced onto a concrete wall. 'Breathe in, breathe out.' I repeated to myself.

I turned back to my desk, picked up the half-empty water bottle sitting there and went into the tea-room. I emptied the bottle and refilled it from the chilled water tap. I took a sip and returned to my office. I considered closing the door but decided not to.

I got through the rest of the emails. The meeting notice was there. The lack of agenda did suggest a bomb might be dropped. I made a start on the in-tray. The first envelope was from Janice, a colleague in the section I used to work in. It was a photocopy of a paper describing a proposed new architecture for a training database. She had highlighted a number of data fields and, in red ink written a question and a request. 'Do they really think we can collect this? Can you help to convince them to change their minds?'

I looked more closely. I didn't think it would work. It had all the hallmarks of a bureaucrat fishing for information they didn't need. I knew I could put together an argument against it but didn't want to face Janice. Or, to be more specific, Janice's faces. I put the paper back into its envelope and slid it into a second tray, my 'pending' pile.

The only times I left my desk that day were to get something to drink go and to the toilet. A few other people stopped and said hello. Each time I saw someone new I had a similar physical reaction to what I experienced with Bruce. Except that when Bruce stopped for a chat a second time it was a lot easier. That gave me hope everything would be alright. That I would be able to return to something like my normal life.

As soon as I woke on Monday morning, I was nervous about the meeting. I forced myself to eat breakfast. Two pieces of toast washed down with two cups of black tea. Then I had a shower, dressed and left for work.

The highlight of the ride into the office was the person seated in front of me who kept changing between being a man and a woman. I thought I really was going mad until the penny dropped. After that I relaxed a bit and focussed on my newspaper.

My nervousness returned the moment I entered the office. I recognised some people, but most were too different for me to guess who they were. Plus, because of the meeting in an hour's time, there were probably people there I didn't know. I just didn't know which were which. I kept my eyes down and headed to my office. This time I did shut the door.

I sat down and tried to figure out what to do. I expected to be asked about what had happened, so I would need to have a story ready. I looked at the blank screen in front of me and the paperwork on the desk waiting for me. I booted up the computer and dealt with emails. The distraction helped.

I got to the meeting only a couple of minutes before the start time. About fifteen people were standing around or sitting at the conference table, talking amongst themselves. I found a seat and put pen and papers in front of me. I poured a glass of water from the jug provided and pretended to check something on my phone before putting it back in my pocket.

I recognised a woman at the head of the table as a younger version of Suzi, the section manager. She tapped an empty glass with a pen. Everyone stopped talking and those still standing sat down.

'Thank you for being on time,' she began. I didn't recognise the man in a grey suit seated to her right. The woman to Suzi's left was Danni, her personal assistant. Older than I knew her but still wearing the same bright floral clothes she favoured.

'I'd like to introduce our new director, Trevor Bancroft.' Suzi turned to the grey suit. 'Trevor asked me to call this meeting so he could introduce himself to you.'

I felt it coming and got ready.

'But first I want to welcome William back after his accident,' Suzi paused and everyone looked at me, 'how are you doing, William?

'Well,' I said, and delivered my speech. 'The doctors say everything is fine, though I am finding that people's names don't always come to me as quickly as they did. I'm not sure if it was the lightning or the snakebite.' People laughed and I breathed a sigh of relief. Suzi took back control of the meeting.

'Okay, then,' she said, 'You will have noticed that the agenda is short, and we won't keep you here long. Trevor, over to you.'

Trevor stood and aged ten years. The grey suit became a pair of jeans and a t-shirt with the letters WTF printed on it. 'Firstly', he said, 'I am really happy to have such a strong team heading up the Spatial Section. Your work is critical to everything we do in this Department.'

He kept talking as I looked around at the people seated in the room. Some I recognised, others I didn't. Only a few were as I remembered them, however. Every twenty or thirty seconds someone changed. I lost track of what the new director was telling us. Something about the benefits of teamwork and clear direction. I focussed on Bruce who was sitting opposite me. He saw me looking at him and brought his hand up to his mouth, screening it from those at the head of the table.

'We're fucked,' he mouthed silently, dropped his hand and turned back to the director who seemed to be building towards a rousing conclusion.

'So, despite this slight reduction, I can assure you we have never been more committed to keeping this section at the cutting edge of the industry.' He paused, perhaps expecting some applause. When that didn't happen, he turned back to Suzi.

'I would like to sit in for the rest of the meeting, but,' he made a show of checking his wristwatch, 'I have a meeting in Spring Street I can't be late for.' Suzi gave him a smile that most of us knew she reserved for hostiles.

'Of course, Trevor,' she said, 'thank you so much for giving us your valuable time this morning. We had hoped you could stay for morning tea and meet the team members personally, but I am sure we can do that next time.' Trevor stood up and Suzi followed. 'I will see you out,' she offered, walked to the glass door and opened it for the director. He went out. Suzi turned back to the room and held up her hand, fingers splayed. 'Five minutes,' she said and left, the door closing behind her.

The room burst into a number of conversations, that like spot fires, grew until they merged into a single wall of noise. The changes seemed to accelerate; people's appearances moved constantly before me. I felt pressure building inside my head. I looked around the room. I didn't recognise anyone at all. In front of me, beside me, at the edge of my vision I'd see a figure blurring and behold another new and unknown person in the room who would see I was looking at them and nod to me or speak to me as if they knew me and the pressure kept building; it felt like everyone was looking at me and it was true they were and the conversations had all stopped and I heard a scream that grew louder until I realised it was me screaming. I ran from the room past a teenage girl into my office and slammed the door. I closed my eyes and tried to clear my thoughts. I glanced around and knew I shouldn't be there, couldn't be there.

I had to leave. I opened the door and headed towards the exit. Someone behind me called my name but I ignored them.

Outside, I hurried to the tram stop and waited. I tried to ignore everyone around me until I was home. I locked the door and drew the curtains.

That was the trigger that made me seek professional help. I was scared, really scared. I rang my doctor and got an urgent referral to Dr Schwarz.

4

My first appointment with Dr Schwarz hadn't gone like I'd expected. Though to be fair I had nothing to compare it with; it being my first time with a psychiatrist. Also, Nina's changes were more rapid than I had seen before, and I found them a bit upsetting. She was friendly, though, no matter which face she presented.

When I went in, Dr Schwarz was sitting behind his desk looking through papers. I felt a little intimidated. He was in a blue suit and had a grey beard. Very Freudian. But when he looked up to greet me his smile was open and friendly. I relaxed immediately.

'Sit down,' he said, 'the blue chair. I'm just reviewing your medical records. I won't be a minute.' I sat where he directed. He flicked through a couple more papers. Then he put them into a cardboard file, picked up a notebook and pen and stood up. He walked around his desk and sat opposite me.

'William? Or do you prefer Will, or Bill?' His pen was poised to make the correct notation.

'William. But Will won't upset me,' I answered. He wrote something down, more than just a single word.

'Okay William. Have you seen a psychiatrist before?'

'No, this is the first time.'

'Well, just to put you at ease, my job is to help you get your life back together. Given the circumstances that brought you here, there is a possibility that there is a physiological underpinning to your condition – a medical issue we can sort out. Or it may be a post-traumatic reaction to a stressful experience, which you do seem to have had. At this point I really don't know. The only things I am assuming, just for now, is that these medical tests – bloods, scans and so forth – are reliable, or at least were indicative of your physical condition when you took them.'

I nodded. He changed into a man in his forties, dressed in hospital blues.

'I will need to ask some questions. Lots of questions really, but firstly some simple ones. Shall we start?' I nodded.

'Good. Have you ever been treated for a mental illness, such as depression, or believe you may have suffered from a mental illness but went untreated?'

He proceeded to work through a series of fairly predictable background questions. I answered as honestly as I could. After about fifteen minutes he closed his notebook and looked at me.

'William, you appear to have been a healthy, well-adjusted thirty-eight-year-old until recently, six weeks ago in fact. Would you agree?'

'Yes, I think that is a fair description of me. You could also add ordinary. Especially now that I have an idea of what its opposite is.' Dr Schwarz's face looked like he was suppressing a laugh. 'What did I say?' I asked.

'You said "ordinary". When you scratch beneath the surface, I find no one is "ordinary". But I get your meaning. Do you think you can tell me what happened on September fifteenth? To the best of your recollection?'

I had been preparing for this. 'Well,' I began, 'that was my brother's birthday. Before he died. I guess it still is, really. Anyway, my family used to have a picnic on his birthday weekend every year. As often as not we went to Hanging Rock. Most years we invited some of our friends along as well. Mum and Dad would stay in the picnic area and we kids would explore the Rock together. Have you been there?'

He shook his head, 'No.'

'It was a great adventure. There are lots of different ways up to the top. Some of them are dead ends, though. Suddenly you come to a precipice. Others seem to go deep into the Rock itself. My brother, James, and I loved it.' I stopped for a moment; memories of our explorations suddenly vivid in my mind.

'It was the weekend after his birthday this year. I invited a mate to go up there with me. Mark. He knew my brother and he remembered going on one of the picnics with us when we were young. Neither of us had been there for over twenty years.

'I almost didn't recognise the place. It's a lot more civilised. There are signs and paved paths everywhere now. There's even a café, for God's sake. Anyway, the forecast had been for a warm, humid day with some cloud later on, so I was just wearing shorts and a t-shirt. I figured that the climb would be a bit of a push given that I don't normally do much exercise. We started up the Rock on the main path, but I veered off onto a different way at some point. I didn't notice that Mark wasn't with me. It had felt like someone was following, just behind me. Then, when I realised Mark wasn't there, I decided to keep going up by myself. I figured I would find him up on top soon enough.

'I got to a point where I had to clamber up some rocks. I almost slipped when a gust of wind blew my hair into my eyes. It was chilly too; it went right through me. I wished I'd put on a jumper.

'As I pulled myself up onto a boulder my hand touched something soft and smooth. I flinched and felt a sharp pain in my wrist. I caught a glimpse of a snake's tail as it disappeared into some bushes.' The doctor checked his notes and nodded for me to continue.

'I looked at my wrist and saw two small, red puncture marks. For a minute I just stood there, not quite believing what had happened. I took off my t-shirt and, as best I could, used it as a pressure bandage around my upper arm.

'Then the sun disappeared behind dark clouds. The whole atmosphere of the place changed. When we set out it had been warm and inviting. Now it was cold, and the Rock was full of dark shadows. Trees were bending over as the wind picked up even more. To top it off, it started to rain. Things weren't looking good and I felt a bit panicky.

'I figured I was nearly at the top and thought the best thing would be to find the main path, and hopefully, Mark. I knew I shouldn't exert myself, but I couldn't see any other option. I had gone off the path to the left earlier, so I made my way back towards the right. I called Mark's name. At that moment I thought I might die there. The rocks were getting slippery and I was light-headed. I couldn't see properly; it was like I was losing sight of what was on either side of me.'

'You mean you were experiencing tunnel vision?' he said.

'Yeah, I guess so. At last I found the main path. I had to find Mark. It was his car we'd come in and he had the keys. I thought he was probably ahead of me, but I needed to go down. I called his name again. Amazingly, he appeared from behind a large rock, about thirty metres ahead of me. I yelled to him, "I've been bitten by a snake. We've got to get down."

'That's all I remember. Mark says that he was about twenty metres from me when a lightning bolt struck. I have burns from it, but I don't think it hit me directly. According to Mark I got up almost straight away, really groggy though. He helped to get me down the Rock and drove me to Woodend where I saw a doctor. From there they put me in an ambulance to Royal Melbourne.

'I don't actually remember anything before the seventeenth, even though people tell me I was conscious and talking to them.'

'That is a pretty amazing story, William,' the doctor said. 'You are incredibly lucky to be alive.'

'I know,' I said. 'But since then my life has become …' I struggled to find the right words. 'Everything is …' I looked him straight in the eyes. 'You won't believe what else happened.'

'And what is that?'

I told him.

5

At my third appointment with Dr Schwarz we reached a turning point. For both of us.

The day before, I got a text message telling me that the time had been changed to 4 pm. Given my reclusive lifestyle that didn't interrupt anything, so I confirmed I would attend.

I arrived ten minutes early. There was a woman talking with Nina. Nina changed appearance twice, from late teens to late twenties to early twenties, in the minute I waited for the woman to leave.

Then Nina spoke to me, 'Dr Schwarz will see you soon. Are you okay to wait here on your own? I'm due to finish now.'

'Yes, that will be fine, Nina. Enjoy your evening.'

'Thank you.' She picked up her bag from the counter and left.

I sat in the waiting area for five minutes before the consulting room door opened. 'Come in,' said Dr Schwarz. He was grey haired with a grey stubble beard.

I went in and he shut the door behind me.

'William,' he said before I could sit down in my usual chair, 'I thought we might do things a little differently today. How do you feel about that?'

'That depends,' I replied. 'What do you have in mind?'

He sat and motioned for me to do likewise.

'Have you been using a mirror?' he asked.

'No, I still have them covered over.'

'Is that because of what you don't see or what you are afraid of seeing?'

'Actually, I am getting used to what I don't see now. It's hard to avoid reflections everywhere and they all do the same thing. Reflect everything except me.'

'Okay, let's say that is your new normal. What about the reflections of other people? Do they match what you see when you look directly at them?'

I thought about that for a moment. 'I don't really know. It's a good question.'

He leaned forward. 'I would like us to go into my bathroom and stand in front of the mirror together. I'll tell you what I see, and you tell me what you see. Then we will come back in here and talk about it. What do you think?'

I felt uneasy about it but could see that it was a logical thing to do. And given that logic was absent from most of my recent experiences, the prospect of even a little bit was welcome. 'I think it's a good idea. But are you ready for what you might see or not see?'

'Yes,' he said. 'I think I need to see for myself, so to speak. Do you need a minute?'

'No,' I stood, 'let's just do it.'

He got up and opened a door at the rear of the room. He reached in and switched on a light. 'You first or me?'

'Me.' I walked into the bathroom and stood in front of the mirror. Even after eight weeks the lack of a reflection disturbed me. I had a perfect view of the wall behind me.

'Shall I come in,' asked Dr Schwarz.

'Yes.' I looked at him as he came in and stood beside me. A healthy man in his thirties. He had his gaze fixed on me.

'On three?' he asked? I nodded. 'One, two, three.'

We both turned to the mirror.

I saw the reflection of a man in his thirties. He looked the same as he did when I looked at him directly. Judging by the look on his face, however, what he saw was not what he had expected. Then he looked directly at me, back to the mirror, to me, to the mirror, and to me again.

'That's enough, I think,' he said and left the bathroom. After a final glance at the reflection of an empty room, I followed. He was sitting in his usual seat in front of the desk. His expression was anything but usual.

'What did you see?' I asked.

He managed a slight smile. 'You first. After all, I'm the doctor.'

'I saw you, same as I see you now. I didn't see me.'

He nodded, as if that was a perfectly normal experience. 'I saw you, just as I see you now, and I saw myself as I usually do. Except.' He paused. 'Except that for a brief moment, when I first looked into the mirror, I didn't see you. Then you were there. It happened each time I looked away and looked back. I can't explain it.'

I felt scared and relieved at the same time. Relieved, because maybe I wasn't going mad, after all. Scared, because I had to face the possibility that what was happening to me was real. If I looked confused, though, I was pretty sure that

242

Dr Schwarz looked more so. He was sitting there looking down at the carpet between us shaking his head. A minute passed.

'What next?' I asked.

'Let me think,' he said. After another minute he straightened up and looked at me. 'One. We both saw similar but different things. There may be a rational explanation, but I can't imagine what it might be. So, let's just accept it for now. Two. I haven't been able to explain how you can describe how I looked and dressed when I was younger. And three,' he paused, but didn't continue.

'Three?' I repeated. 'What's the third thing?'

'The ages of the people you see. Together with the rapidity of the changes. It may mean something.'

'Nina.' I said. 'You're referring to how I see Nina.'

Dr Schwarz stood up and went to a side table that held a bottle of water and some glasses. He poured himself a glass and drank half in one draught. 'Would you like some?' he asked me.

'Yes, please.'

He refilled his glass, poured one for me and returned with both. As he handed mine over, I noticed that his hand was shaking. He sat and sipped his water. I took a drink too.

'I want to explain something,' he began, 'but first I have to ask your permission. Will you permit me to disclose some personal information that, normally, it would be inappropriate for me to tell you? I think that the circumstances are odd enough to bend the rules a little. Or possible a lot. Who knows?'

'Okay,' I said. 'If you think it might help.'

'That's what I'm not sure of. What I am thinking of telling you won't explain what you, what we have experienced. My ability to remain professionally separate from you as a patient is going to be tested. But not to tell you would be to deny you the chance of understanding some part of it. Do you want me to go on?' He sat very still. Even though his appearance had not changed he looked like he had just aged a few years.

'Yes, I think so. I understand nothing now, so anything will be welcome.'

'You may not still think that soon, but here goes.' He took another sip of water and set the glass down on his desk.

'When I was at university, about the time I had long hair and wore that vest you saw me in, I had a relationship with another student, a woman studying psychology. I was sure I was falling in love with her, and I thought she was with me, when she suddenly disappeared. Left uni. Gone. I was devastated. I looked for her, asked all her friends where she was. Nothing. If anyone knew anything, they kept it from me. Eventually, I left it behind and got on with becoming a doctor and then a psychiatrist, as you see. I married, had children, got divorced and dedicated myself to my work.

'Then, a couple of years ago, Nina contacted me. She said I was her father, that she had never known until her mother died and found my name in her mother's papers. As you can imagine, I was shocked and somewhat doubtful. But it was true. It was confirmed with a DNA test. I was happy to get to know Nina, and she was glad to finally know who her father was. The circumstances were sad, but it seemed like a silver lining. Until Nina had a small stroke.' He stopped talking and tapped his fingers on his legs. He seemed to come to a decision and stood up.

'William,' he said, 'I think that the line, having been crossed, is broken. This session, as a doctor-patient consultation, has come to an end. I need something a little stronger if we are to keep going. Would you like a proper drink?'

The situation had taken a very strange turn. The doctor was telling me, the patient, the story that had brought him to that point. It felt to me, though, that for the first time since my accident that I was not entirely alone. 'Yes. Scotch if you have it.'

'Two single malts it is, then.' He went to a cupboard and opened it to reveal a small, but well-stocked, bar. He poured two generous shots of liquor. He handed me mine and we clinked glasses. 'Cheers.'

'Cheers,' I returned.

We both took a sip. It was very good whiskey, smoky and smooth. He sat down again.

'Where was I? Yes, Nina's stroke. It wasn't severe, in fact she was fully recovered within weeks. But her MRI showed a brain aneurism. Inoperable. And inevitably, it will be fatal. We discussed her options. She can't fly – the change in air pressure could trigger another stroke. In fact, travel of any sort is high risk. She is, in many ways, a prisoner in this city. I made the decision to set up this practice, here in the centre of town and to cut back to three days a week. This is our home as well as my consulting room. That bookshelf,' he said pointing to one against a wall, 'folds down to be my bed. Nina's room comes off the waiting room. We see every play, every artist that visits. We are making the most of the time we have, not knowing how much time there is. Except that now, perhaps, I do know.'

I waited. I guessed what would come next.

'There must be a reason that you don't see Nina any older than she is now. If there is any logic to your visions, maybe it is that you don't see what never happens. Nina never gets old.'

We sat in silence for a couple of minutes. I tried to think of another explanation. My visions of people in their earlier skins seemed to accurately reflect their looks and clothes. Why not the future then. It made just as much sense.

'You can't think of a reasonable alternative either, can you?'

'No,' I said, 'but that doesn't mean there isn't one. Maybe her future isn't fixed. It might go either way.' A thought occurred to me. 'I can't see myself for that matter, but here I am.'

Doctor Schwarz nodded. 'There is that,' he said, 'Unfortunately, what you don't see in the mirror doesn't tell me anything about Nina's future. I hope you will forgive me, but as her father I am more concerned for hers than yours.' He smiled. 'Am I acting unethically?'

'I don't think so. I'd say naturally.' For the first time it struck me that my "condition" might affect people other than me. 'Is there anything I can do?'

He laughed. Short and bitter. 'If it was anyone but Nina, I would take you into intensive care to make survival predictions. I would establish if your visions correlated with patient mortality.' He finished his drink. 'I don't know if I really want to know. I'd rather have the possibility of hope.'

It felt like our talk had come to a conclusion. I finished my drink, put the glass down and stood up. He stood and offered his hand. I took it. It was as if we were shaking on a pact.

'Will you still see me?'

'Yes, who else can you talk to? For that matter who else can I talk to about this?' I'll have Nina make a booking and text you the appointment.'

We walked to the door. 'Doc. I appreciate your help. I'm going to try a few things to see if we can make any better sense of …' I paused, 'whatever this is.'

'Thank you. I'll see you soon.' He closed the door behind me. I let myself out of his apartment.

As I walked out onto Collins Street it struck me. I was no longer only worried about myself; what was happening to me. I was concerned for Nina, and for Doctor Schwarz. And in that concern was purpose. Something I hadn't felt since the accident. I wasn't cured. But …

Maybe I didn't need a cure.

David Rawet

The Search For The Good Mandarin

Open the fridge.

Scan the many mandarins that are on offer.

Choose one, one you think looks nice. One you think looks better than all the rest.

Now you go to peel it, and here is where you might discover that this mandarin is not the one you envisaged.

You thought it felt good, firm.

You imagined that once you opened it, it would entice you with its smell.

You imagined the juicy, sweet flavour as you tasted it on your lips.

But mandarins are not always what they seem.

You continue to peel it, and the skin breaks off in small pieces.

It is hard to reveal the layer underneath, as the skin resists being pulled away from the mandarin, the thing it has been concealing all this time.

However, you are persistent, still believing it will be good once you get there.

Eventually, there is a pile of discarded skin and you hold the mandarin, in its true form, in your hand. You break off a piece and tentatively put it in your mouth.

You know as soon as your lips are closed that you have been fooled.

This mandarin is bitter, and the powdery texture is enough to make you screw your face up and spit the mandarin out.

You are left with an aftertaste, a reminder of your disappointment in choosing the wrong mandarin.

It is here that you have two choices.

You can let the bad experience of making the wrong decision scare you from ever eating another mandarin.

Or you can go back to the fridge and choose another mandarin, in the hope that your choice will be better the second time round.

Suzanne M. Faed

Spectral Caress

The maelstrom within me calmed the moment I placed the green candle holder onto the old ornate mantelpiece. Finally, four weeks after the move, I had unpacked the last box. I picked up my oversized glass of red wine from the coffee table and looked around. My first home: I'd fallen in love with the tired little house nestled in the large overgrown block of land the moment I saw it. The many years of neglect and emptiness were evident, with peeling white paint on the external wooden panels and the army of brown leaves that poked jarringly from the gutter of the bullnose veranda. The house had character and quirks − scuffed polished jarrah floorboards, and a faded blue locked door that opened out to the side veranda, to which I had no key. I sat on the lounge with a feeling of renewed confidence. I was doing well with the three promises I had made to myself the day I stepped over the threshold.

Number one, to never, ever, get involved with, or trust meddling matchmaking neighbours again. The distance between properties made this somewhat easier, excepting for house No. 17 situated directly across the road. The elderly woman who lived there appeared spritely for her age, and I wondered if she had some sort of psychic ability, as she had an uncanny knack of knowing when I would be out the front. Standing at the end of her driveway, calling, inviting me over for a cup of tea. She never moved any closer or crossed the road and my standard polite excuse of being too busy, or just giving her a friendly wave, seemed to be working, keeping her at bay. Though this week her voice sounded different, higher in tone with maybe a tinge of desperation. I was beginning to feel unneighbourly and guilty; I wondered if I should tweak this promise, just a little.

Number two, knuckle down, reign in my drinking and social life. This promise was going rather well, at least it was moderated. A traumatic relationship breakdown from a previous matchmaking, over-friendly neighbour, had equalled, me drinking away my sorrows and messy nights out. Tonight, was Friday night and here I was at home with the late movie playing in the background. I'd downed a couple, or maybe more, glasses of wine, yet it was still definitely a win.

Number three, to live and be on my own for a while. I had this one nailed, in the bag. Only thing was, I wasn't truly alone.

The first week when my keys mysteriously weren't where I'd left them the night before, I figured was due to my tired forgetfulness, adjusting to the longer travel time to and from work. Then when the curtains would move without the hint of a breeze, or when I'd find the dining chairs turned in slightly different angles to how they had been moments before, I knew there was more to it. All of this may have been enough to send people white with fright, screaming and running out of the house. Not me, I liked it, or him. My ghost, my phantom, spectral being or poltergeist, whatever you wanted to call him was different.

He didn't have an eerie icy atmosphere alerting the hairs on the back of my neck to stand on end, as others had claimed from what I had searched on the internet. He didn't send books flying violently off their shelves either. His presence and energy felt warm, carrying only a hint of coolness as it coursed past my ear, moving my blonde strands of hair delicately across my cheek. It was a soft breath, one you'd feel from a lover, causing my face to blush as I'd touch my ear lobe with tingles of pleasure. Sometimes there would be a gentle stroke to my arm and the sensation of someone being next to me, even in bed. I was undecided as to whether I wanted him to leave, or if I should've called some sort of a religious exterminator, but he seemed harmless enough.

This evening there had been little activity, he was like that some days. I put the glass on the table reaching over to pick up the television remote when a brisk knock sounded at the front door. I glanced at my watch; it was nearly eleven.

'Hello,' I called out and went to the front door.

I opened it slowly to find no one there, only a large yellow envelope that had been placed on the doormat. The handwriting on the front read, 'Urgent please open from your neighbour at No. 17.'

I looked across the road, her lights were still on, which was most unusual for this time of the night.

'Honestly,' I mumbled, as I closed the door then went back and sat on the lounge, 'what could you want me to read, right now.'

The air noticeably dropped in temperature as I opened the envelope. The lights began to flicker, flashing momentarily as they had earlier in the evening. Another house quirk that had started a few nights ago. The globes illuminated back to full strength as I pulled out a wad of paper articles. On top was a note written in the same handwriting which read, 'I've seen the signs you must get out!' I dropped the papers onto the coffee table.

'Great, now I'm living across from a psychopath,' I said.

Curiously, I spread the articles across the table, my eyes did a double take back to one particular newspaper headline, 'Serial Killers – Bayford Brothers Found Dead' and a picture of my house below it.

Quickly I scanned the yellowed paper. It told of two brothers who had hung themselves in a double suicide on the veranda of their home before the police arrived to arrest them.

'Oh God,' I whispered, I couldn't quite make out the date of print as I put the paper down.

Anxiously, I began shuffling around the other articles as a burst of chilled air whipped past my head, its force knocking over the wine glass splattering the red liquid across them.

I snatched up one large coloured magazine article, 'Hey, that was a bit cheeky, play nice,' I said light-heartedly.

Multi-tasking I stood up, trying to read as I went to the kitchen and grabbed a dry cloth. The lights began to flicker again as I returned and draped it across the wet papers. Through the flashes of light, I managed to make out the story was of a woman, recounting how she had met the younger Bayford brother on a night out in the city. He had been an exceptionally handsome, charming young man who'd managed to instil enough comfort and reassurance to lure her back to his house. When his older brother arrived soon after he'd snapped, turning into a deranged madman with his brother joining in on the heightened insanity. They had held her captive, each time the older brother left leaving her alone with the younger one, he'd return to his gentle charismatic self. Behaving kindly, almost apologetic until she would hear the older brother arrive and her terror would peak, knowing, dreading, what was to come. The Bayford brothers had kept her alive the longest, living the cycle of madness for three days until she'd managed to escape.

My eyes were scouring through the article haphazardly, selecting and registering the words through the glimmering and dimming light. *Beaten, tortured, bodies, buried, backyard* ... I was interrupted by a sound; two firm knocks on the blue side door. I turned and looked at it quizzically as the air around me felt thick, weighted with a frosty coolness. A nervous shudder ran through my body.

'Come to the front door,' I called out, thinking, *it must be her from across the road.*

The two knocks sounded again. With the article clutched in my hand, I walked over to the blue door as the words were registering through my thoughts, *escaped, rescued, neighbour.* I grasped the rectangular handle.

'Hello, is someone there?' I asked in a raised voice.

The warmth of my words and breathing misted out in front of my face in small clouds as I heard the scraping of metal and felt the door unlock. Startled I turned the handle and pulled the door ajar. My legs became like pillars of concrete, heavy, paralysed in place as an invisible force swirled through my frosted breath and gripped my throat. Across my back I felt a caress. A freezing touch of elongated fingers was sliding the length of my spine, moving up to my head. Then they wound into my hair and sharply pulled the strands tight. No scream came out from my opened mouth as the last printed words I had read formed the sentence in my mind, *the older brother would always come in through the blue side door, signalling his arrival with two hard steady knocks.*

Laura Ferretti

Write

why poems why bother
clever phrasing apposite opposites
embedded meanings
subliminal images public broadcasts
juxtaposed illusion and allusion
fain without recognition fame notoriety wealth
exposure strangers' judgements
choose misunderstood before
unread unseen unknown
tenuous communication
across distance time
as hands cling forbidden desire
for possibility communion
amid fear
an ending the full stop
therefore
the need the imperative
the supplication
write

David Rawet

Star_ting Over

Suz says that I need to learn to breathe through my nose. But what would she know? The woman ain't no doctor, though she fancies herself as a healer, what with her crystals and that Reiki stuff. I don't mind her telling me though, she can tell me anything she likes if I can hold her at night and feel her head on my chest as I wake. Truth is, it's my chest that's the problem. I was born too early with problem lungs. They get all furred up and, I'm coughing, spluttering and gasping for air. Good job I've got that magic blue puffer to calm my insides. I needed it that night.

It was a tradition from back in my school days that just before the Easter rush me and a few mates would head out to the dam, smoke a bit, and talk about our futures. Nowadays though I go on my own, take my swag and a few beers. There's nothing like a bit of space and a crisp, clear night looking into the heavens to get you thinking about new beginnings. I keep my dreams tight these days, but passing the fitness test and becoming a firey, getting away from my fuckwit friends and doing something with my life, yep, that would be the ticket. Lying on the ground, Kasey my dog has her head on my feet, and I'm looking up at the stars, just thinking, when, no word of a lie, a streak of white light whizzes right past my head. Then all around me are white lights flashing and zooming around. What the hell? I'm no scientist, but I know that what I'm watching doesn't seem natural.

After a good coupla minutes, I realise what a dumb shit I'm being and reach for my phone to start videoing. I'm gonna Snapchat this to my mates, soon as I have a signal. As I view through my phone, the lights get even stranger. Changing now from white to pale blue, and then they begin to slow. Kasey starts barking, and the whole thing is freaking me out. Then the lights merge, and the entire sky turns a sickly pale blue. I yell at Kasey to 'Shut up!' Quickly gathering up my stuff and chucking my swag into the back of the ute, Kasey follows me whining and whimpering. I've had more than a couple of beers, but that's not going to stop me from getting out of here. Turning the ignition though, I get nothing. Dead. My ute always starts. I try again, but she's got nothing for me; it's like the battery's completely flat.

The sky is turning purple now, like the wickedest thunderstorm you can imagine. It begins to rain. Huge drops that take the topsoil and form rivulets in the ground so that small rivers arise and join up. Kasey tries to jump from the back to join me in the front cab, so I let her loose, and she's whining in the footwell trying to get under the seat. I must admit I'm shit scared! I can feel the ground shifting beneath the wheels of the ute as the water begins to run down the hill. I try the ignition again. Zilch. I don't want to flood the engine. My chest is heaving, and I'm short of breath. The panic constricting my airways. Reaching into the glove compartment, I take out my inhaler, and my whole body responds as the steroid goes to work in my lungs.

Then, as directly as it started, the rain stops, and I see a shadow, a figure in front of my ute. I'm trying to make it out through the windscreen. It looks tiny, almost childlike, and I can't tell what it's wearing, and frankly, I'm not even sure that it's human? I'm holding onto my steering wheel like it's a life buoy and believing, that somehow, if I grip it super tight, it will save me. The shadow then begins waving at me. Through the clearing windscreen, I can now make out that it's a woman. Her dress wet and clinging, revealing her slight frame, she looks like the rain could have easily washed her away and her dark hair is matted to her face. Opening the driver's door, she moves around towards me.

'Oh, my God did you see the sky?'

I nod, thankful that I won't be the only one trying to explain all this.

'I did. Never seen nothing like it in my life!'

I get out of the cab, my thongs sinking into the soil encrusting my feet in sand and dirt.

'Do you want to hop in? You don't need to worry, I'm friendly, just like Kasey, my dog. Ute won't start, but if the weather starts up again at least, you're out of it.'

She looks unsure, but as I speak a great streak of lightning comes out of the sky and hits the ground, not five metres from where we're standing. My ears are ringing from the deafening noise as I bundle into my seat, pushing Kasey out of the way, and the whole hillside lights up, catching and flaming the eucalypt leaves. The woman screeches and runs around the side of the ute hastily getting in the passenger seat. Kasey snarls in a less than friendly way, crawling under my feet and the static that fills the air makes my hair stand on end, and my skin crawl. She's soaking so I offer her Kasey's dog towel, and she tells me her name is Jaydene. Long story short, she has run down here off the top road. She'd pulled over to watch the lights in the sky and just like my ute her car wouldn't start. She'd checked her phone but no signal. So, had come down to the campground to find help. I was the help.

As Jaydene speaks the storm gets fiercer, her voice barely audible, as the wind rattles around the ute, then more lightning and a thunderclap that could take you off your feet. And we are both looking up at the sky, and the lights have started up again. And then the clouds clear, and it's like the night sky opens up, stars and all, and those white lights they just whirl up through the hole like God himself has opened the door. We watch from my cab in disbelief. Speechless staring at the sky.

After a few more minutes I try the ute again and blow me, she starts the first time. Driving Jaydene back to her car, we chew over our theories of what has just happened, over and over like dogs with bones. Her car starts up to just like the ute so leaving her with a smile and having exchanged numbers I head home.

I'm not more than two minutes down the road though when some cop tries to wave me down. Over the limit, I've had enough for one night, so I deliberately keep my speed but pretend like I haven't seen him.

By the time, I get home, I am hyped up like I've been on dexies and pacing around my kitchen trying to get it all straight in my head. Scrolling through my phone, trying to see if anyone else is posting about it. Nothing. The video on my phone is blank, so much for Snapchatting the evidence, it all just gets stranger, so I call it a night.

I'm just getting out of my jocks and into bed when there is a loud thumping on the door, people yelling. Agitated, I reach for my inhaler, and take a deep breath. But before I know what's happening there are maybe five cops in my bedroom, and I'm being tackled to the ground, naked on the floor, with my hands behind my back, and they are shouting in my ear, and I've got a gun pointed at my head. The sound of blood in my ears, then nothing, as some fat cop sits on my back and takes every ounce of air from my lungs.

Turns out Jaydene got home fine that night – only thing was she had been missing for three weeks! Cops got my plates and finally let me go after she convinced them I wasn't the villain. Well, you can make your own mind up about what happened, and I'm keeping my thoughts to myself. No, the strangest thing, and this is why I'm telling you, is I don't know whether it was that cop landing on my chest the way he did or the shock of it all, or maybe just because I started to listen to my Suz and breathe through my nose, but my chest it cleared right up. And six months later, I passed my fitness test and got into the academy. And maybe them lights were stars that night 'cos I got my wish of a new beginning.

Louise Tarrier

Fear Has its Own Smell

Fear has its own smell.

Or it could be the stench from the blocked toilets. Or the vomit. Or the disposal nappies erupting from the overflowing bins like stained avalanches.

But I think it's fear. In this game, fear is king.

Eight days ago I'd been comfortable in the departure lounge, casually watching the flight crew arrive. All glitz and glam and professionalism. The Captain had a spring in his step and looked a bit like George Clooney, but then again, don't they always?

Then six men rose in unison.

I saw the weapons and my first thought was, *that's impressive. Not easy beating airport security nowadays.* I also thought, *neat twist on a hijack.* I mean, we hadn't even made it to the aircraft.

We never would.

My muscle memory reached for the weapons I so often wore, but they weren't there. I was just an ordinary guy going home after a holiday. The six men yelled and swore and pointed their guns. The terror on their faces reflected in all of the one hundred and thirty passengers. Captain George, to his credit, was extremely calm. He remains so, but no demands have been met and the leader of the six has threatened to shoot our brave Captain tomorrow morning at ten. They won't. They might shoot him sooner, but no one will be shooting anyone at ten.

It is very hot and quite dark. The air conditioning started playing up on day three. Not breaking down, just less effective. Cyprus, even in the spring, can be sticky. The lights in the building were dimmed, ever so gradually, each day. All textbook stuff and no one noticed. Well, I did, but I should. After all, I'd helped write the textbook. Not that me being here was planned. Just pure bad luck that I'd been in the departure lounge. I'd kept a low profile. A grey-man, fading into the darkness of the lights, a no one … along with one hundred and twenty-nine other no ones, the cabin crew … Captain George and six someones. All of us sweating, stinking. Most smelling of fear.

Fear isn't shameful.

Far from it.

It's what gives you the edge in the game, if you can control it. The six in the mix were beginning to lose control. That's what frightened me. Radical extremists tended not to think rationally at the best of times. I mean, if John Cleese had been less radical, he'd have known what the Romans had done for him.

Cyprus. Historically a crossroads for as mad a hodgepodge of reactionary groups as you could find outside of Monty Python. These six were equally daft. They might as well have been the Popular Front for Judea, it mattered not. No one gave in to hostage-taking terrorists. It was only a matter of time. The game had changed since the seventies. Ah, those good old days for the hijacker. Good title for an album. Someone should really have loaned these boys a new playbook. A win back then could be a real win. Money, new plane, new destination, walking away from the game. Not now. Now winning was very one sided.

Eight days. No demands met. Everyone getting more twitchy. Six getting more fearful, angrier. Me counting the hours as best I could from when the shouted tirade had echoed around the hall.

'You have twelve hours. We kill him at ten tomorrow morning.'

Seven hours to go I reckon. Most of my fellow hostages restlessly asleep. Four of the six hijackers fitfully dozing. If my internal clock is good, it will be soon.

*

It is.

Three shaped charges blow man-sized holes in the walls. Concussion grenades follow. I turn my face to the floor, hands over my ears, eyes tight shut, mouth wide open. The blasts still hit me like a boxer's combination. I roll onto my side, then kneel up.

'FRIENDLY! FRIENDLY! Targets there.' I point to the lone standing terrorist.

'There.' I point to the one crouching against a pillar.

The assault force follow my indications. Four shots, two hazed mists of brain and blood bloom into the air.

More shots. More dead men falling. An assault team works on a simple premise, '*If it's moving, it's a threat*'. I knew they'd have been briefed that I was in the room. They'd anticipate my reactions. Everyone else was fair game.

The muzzle of a pistol presses against my temple. I look up into the face of the youngest of the six. He's in his mid-twenties. The last one alive. Petrified, his hand is shaking, sweat glistening. In glorious, high-definition, super slow-motion, I watch his finger squeeze the trigger. My only thought is not enlight-ened. No life rewound. No pictures of sublime regret or enraptured pride. No wondrous revelations of how my life should have, could have, would have been. No loss, no grief, no joy, not even fear. My last thought is simply, *bastard*. Infused with anger. Pulsing and intense anger at having lost sight of where this kid had been. Visceral, coursing annoyance at my stupidity and arrogance. A tremendous wave of unreleased violence that I want to direct at this prick of a kid who is about to kill me. His finger closes tightly on the trigger. I sigh.

A dry click sounds in my ear.

I focus on the grip of the gun and see the magazine protruding out of the bottom. The young man, in his fear and haste, hasn't seated it correctly. Fear can make you do stupid things. Slack things. Fear can make the game harder to win. Sometimes impossible.

I don't quite smile, nor do I frown. I sort of shrug as four separate laser aiming points fall onto his chest.

I mouth, 'You lose.'

Ian Andrew

Tea for Two

Closure. She just couldn't find it. Margaret tapped her pen to the rhythm of the dripping tap as she scanned the Word Search. *Closure.* It was the last word she needed to find, and she was getting irritated that it was eluding her. She looked up, down, across until she went cross-eyed.

Admitting defeat, for now, she scraped the chair back and went to fill up the kettle. The tap resumed its drip, drip, drip and Margaret shook her head.

Another job for John, she thought.

She filled their favourite mugs, breathed in the calming camomile tea as steam rose and disappeared in the cold air. While the tea bags steeped, Margaret stretched out her aching fingers. Winter was the worst for her arthritis. She grimaced as she scrutinised her frail skin stretched over her protruding joints. Margaret considered them unsightly but then silently berated herself for thinking it. John always said that it was just proof of her having lived a full life. He would take her hands in his weathered ones and bring them to his lips. 'Darling Margy,' he'd say, 'it has been a privilege to age with you.'

She smiled at the thought. Margaret took the mugs and set them on the outside balcony, where she and John enjoyed their afternoon cuppa. She sipped at her tea and admired the rainbow that smiled upside down at her, the earth glistening wet as the sun peeked out after a brief shower.

'Come on, John,' she called. 'Your tea is getting cold.'

*

The next morning, Margaret woke early. She looked over to John's side; the image of him sleeping made her get out of bed quietly. He had always been the better sleeper. In their younger days it irritated her – the way he could snore through their kids' early wake ups, tucked up warm in the middle of the night when she'd get up to breast feed, or tend to the children when their foreheads were hot, and their hands were clammy. But she'd pushed the annoyance down, as John worked hard as a builder and needed the rest. He'd come home, covered in dust and dirt, and would blow her a kiss before heading straight to the shower to wash off the day's work. He'd emerge, hair tousled and shiny, smelling like lavender on the breeze, and wrap his chiselled arms around her.

'Now I can give you a proper hello,' he'd say.

259

His warmth insulated her, and she would always soften into his embrace, her tension from tending to the kids and housework retreating just a little. Often, the kids would catch them standing by the oven, in the midst of veggies steaming and casseroles baking, and they would join their knot. John would stretch his arms to fit them all in, but always kept Margaret at his centre.

Margaret slipped her feet into her warm slippers, her nostalgia keeping her company as she went about getting ready for the day.

*

The bus driver smiled at Margaret as she swiped her Seniors Card.

'It's been a while since I've seen you out and about. John not with you today?'

Margaret stared at the bus driver, the one with the kind, sparkling eyes.

'Good to see you, Nigel. I've been house bound for quite some time but thought a trip to town was in order.' She paused, swallowed. 'You see, it's John's birthday next week and I need to get him a gift. So I'm going solo today.'

'Lovely. Say happy birthday to the old fella, won't ya?'

Margaret smiled and sat down in her normal spot, close to the front where John liked to sit when they'd venture into town together.

*

Margaret pushed the puzzle to the side, making room for John's gift. She'd been so busy thinking about his birthday she hadn't had a chance to finish what she started. One thing at a time. Carefully, she placed the model car box in the centre and wrapped it up as neat as she could. John had been crafty with his hands; back in the day he'd spend weekends in his shed, fixing old cars and giving them a second chance at life. Margaret would admire the transformation and pat him on the back.

With a glint in his eye, he'd say, 'Margy, when I retire, I want to spend my days doing this. And having cups of tea with you, of course.'

But by the time he retired, arthritis had set in; along with a cough he couldn't shake, so the body of a car sat in his shed, the makeover put on hold.

She had just stuck the last piece of sticky tape on when the phone rang. She startled; her hand flew to her heart.

'Oh, you should have seen me jump,' Margaret said, when she'd picked up the phone and heard her daughter's voice on the other end.

Her daughter laughed and Margaret let out a big breath. 'It's so nice to hear your voice, Sally. How are you?'

'Busy busy. But I'm almost caught up at work and can't wait to see you next week … how are you? What have you been up to?'

'I'm doing fine. Usual aches and pains but can't complain.'

'You'd call me if you need anything, yeah? I know I'm an hour away but if you ever need me just call and I'd drop everything for you.'

Margaret swallowed the lump that had suddenly formed in her throat. 'Thank you, Sweetie. I'll keep that in mind. But I won't need to. I'm a tough old cookie.'

*

That night, Margaret woke with clenched fists and beads of sweat dripping down her forehead. Catching her breath, she looked at the illuminated numbers on her clock. 3.25 am. She shuddered; the aftershock of her dream left her with an uneasy knot in her stomach. She'd been having the recurring dream every night for the last few weeks. Margaret crept out of bed and went to the kitchen to get a glass of water. Even fully conscious, she could still see the events playing behind her eyelids.

She'd wanted to talk to John about it but couldn't find the words to express the way it left her feeling. In the dream, John was behind the wheel of his car – the one that sat untouched in his shed – but in the dream it was refurbished, painted bright blue. Margaret called to him, but he would stare straight ahead, and she'd try and run after him as he pulled out of the driveway. 'Wait!' she'd call, waving her arms to catch his attention. 'John! Where are you going?' Without looking back, he'd speed away. She sobbed as she watched the car disappear around the bend. She wiped her eyes with her sleeve and noticed that her familiar street suddenly looked different. The houses weren't the same. The numbers on the letterboxes had changed. There were no trees, no shrubs, no colour. Disorientated, she stumbled back up her driveway, to the familiar comfort of her home. But when she stepped inside, there was nothing to see. It was empty, as if the last forty years had never happened. She let out a cry and that's when she'd always wake up.

Now, sitting at her kitchen table, listening to the heartbeat of the clock, she had the word search in front of her.

Focus on this, she thought. She knew sleep wouldn't come easily now so she tried to complete her unfinished puzzle. *Closure.* She worked backwards this time, trying to find a new way to look at it. C.L.O.S. She squinted closer, her pen at the ready to circle it. Finally. E. False alarm. *Close to finding it?* she pondered. But distracted from her dream, with the rhythmic sound of the clock marking the passing of time, her eyelids began to droop. It wasn't until the sun streamed through the crack in the blinds that she woke, to find the pen still in her hand and the Word Search no closer to being completed.

*

Margaret opened the wardrobe and the door creaked in response. The smell of John's clothes greeted her, and she breathed in deeply. She ran her fingers along the edges of clothing, stirring them to move and seemingly bringing them to life. He was so organised, and she had loved to tease him about how he broke the stereotype – a blokey builder with a love for cars and an extremely meticu-lous wardrobe. His shoes lined the bottom, from his shiny dress shoes to his round-the-house sandals and sneakers. Black pants and trackies hanging on the left and checked flannel shirts and his favourite car t-shirts on the right.

Today, she'd pick his outfit. Today he turned seventy-four. She'd pick the same clothes he wore at his birthday last year. Margaret brought them out and placed them on the table, next to his wrapped gift. She got the cake out of the fridge and boiled the kettle. Two cups of camomile tea.

'Happy birthday, John.' She looked across the table at his smiling face.

She was lighting the candles when the door opened, and Sally stepped in-side. Margaret turned and tried to smile at her daughter's homecoming. But Sally's eyes were moist as they stared at the photo of her father, perched at the head of the table, watching over them with his trademark smile.

'Oh Mum,' Sally embraced her mother. 'I miss him too.'

Suzanne M. Faed

Through the Glass of a Tear

I *guessed* she was a gamer. She didn't look up despite the shifting of bodies around her, her steady balance appeared well practised. She wore tracksuit pants – the kind with the broad white stripe down each leg – and flat shoes. Perhaps she had slept that way? I looked for signs of bed fluff on her black pants as some confirmation of tardiness. I stood taller, visionary, judging, and from the screen I could see she was playing a game where she was an assassin. Her movements deliberate, precise, the shift of her finger so light on the screen as she stood, poised and diminutive beside me. I pondered at her day job while doubting there was one. I imagined her living room with large monitors, casting an ever-present watery blue dawn on the windows to the outside. She caught me looking; the assassin glanced from her scope to my eye line and had me cold. I smiled, nervous, the next action was hers to take.

'What is it you see?'

'What do you mean?'

'You were looking at me just now, not just at what I was doing, I mean you were really looking at me. I've been looked at like that before. What is it you see?'

I was taken aback. The small green gem set in her nostril glinted at me like a mischievous cons wink, my mind in a fluster of self-talk, *you're fucked now, what will you say to that? You need to lie – weak as piss you are – lie!* Her steely look held, her dark eyes all on me and I, like a snowflake in a pocket, seeking out cooler fabric, wetting into a stitch.

'I don't,' I breathed, 'have an answer to your question. I don't think I can help.'

She grimaced almost, inhaled with measure and looked to the window and the hills. I saw now, again, the profile of her face. She wore beauty to me. It was what drew me in at first, but I could see she also knew the night. The scratches to her neck, unable to hide beneath her collar, shocked me. They repelled nature, fought with the grandeur of her form unfairly and left me uncertain; worried too. Her eyes returned to mine as we stood encircled by other travellers' shoulders and hips. It was as if they weren't really there, for it felt like they – actually the entire world – was apart from us now. I knew I had to say more, she was expectant, her expression daring truth.

'Do I disappoint you? Not having an answer to your question?'

Briskly and tart, 'Only by being afraid, that's all.'

I waited in vain for her to return her eyes to her phone screen. She didn't, I looked away. I hadn't asked for this, yet despite my discomfort, I soon returned my eyes to hers. At that moment the bus pulled in near the terminal entry and the doors opened. She abruptly grabbed my hand and pulled me with her to the tarmac and toward the terminal doors. Someone was knocked. My case careered after me as I went with the sudden shift of passage beneath feet, the hard corners, the matter of fact visa checks and then out again, into the sun. All the way she was quiet and stern, but for saying one thing as we left the bus, 'I could have been extraordinary. Is that what you saw?'

*

We stopped aside the taxi rank. Abruptness gone, she looked at me, through the glass of a tear. Something unexpected.

'Do you want to try harder, to find an answer to my question?'

'Yes.' I didn't recognise my voice. There was no mark of mine upon it, but I knew the answer from me in that moment could only have been that evenly mouthed word.

'Ok then. Let's go. Taxi to mine.'

The taxi ride was made of many words unspoken. The driver was in his own world, contained like the three sets of air in the back of his cab. Hers, mine, and the space between us. I had to check that I was breathing; it was there, tensely cupped. We arrived at an apartment block. Climbing the stairs, I saw a grace in her movement I'd not yet seen. Her flat shoes left the lightest sound of passing.

Standing before the door, she slid a key from her top. It was attached to a lengthy cord around her neck. She inserted it straight into the keyhole with the assuredness of someone coming home to the familiar. As the door key turned, it worked like some kind of master key as several clicks followed. This unnerved me slightly. She didn't invite me in, simply led with an assuredness that I would follow. I did, letting the two doors fall shut behind me. Inside was homely, though a little darkened by heavy blinds mostly pulled shut. Upon entering, she marched off to another room, leaving me standing and awkward. A faux fur blanket draped across a couch fell limp to the floor at one end. It looked to be masking a couch in decline, but it was an obvious place to sit and wait. Beside it on a coffee table was a frosted lamp shaped like a jellyfish polyp with protrusions atop. That made me curious. Another reason to venture there. I rearranged the blanket, sat and then began fumbling for a switch down the lamp cord. I left it alone as she re-appeared.

'I could offer you a drink.'

A question, a regret; what did she mean? Again, I felt uncertain what to say. I nodded thoughtfully while lost.

'But first there is the matter of what you're afraid of saying. Or could you be afraid of me?'

'I think … I am; a little afraid.' I felt my right eyelid flicker as I questioned, 'Should I be?'

She slapped the couch. 'Surely that's not up to me to say. I brought you here for a good reason. You understand that. Yes?'

'Sort of. You wanted to know what I was seeing in you.'

'Ok then – do begin.' Slightly chilled, her eyes set squarely on mine.

This was it then. She had brought me here to go where I couldn't go before. Oddly, I realised that saying it now was all the harder, I'd have felt safer surrounded by strangers rather than here. But I had to go there now, she was waiting. She'd paid for the taxi.

'When I saw you on the bus you intrigued me. I looked at what you were wearing, what you were doing, and I pinned you as a full-time gamer, someone who in my mind doesn't get much from their actual life. Doesn't bother with really living it; hides away. I wondered if you slept in the clothes you were wearing – sorry, it's what I was thinking – saying it now, I feel like a prick.' Her look gave me nothing, not a hint of reaction either way. I felt secretly braver, she didn't look mad.

'You found the words.' It sounded almost congratulatory, 'spoke your truth, got *some* things right too. Thank you for your honesty. I'm not here to say how you should feel; or whether you're a prick for that matter. Whenever we judge others, we leave ourselves open to review,' her chin and her gaze lowered, she pressed her tongue to her upper lip then added, 'there's a tip for you.'

I decided to tell more. 'You know, after you caught me staring, you briefly looked away and I … I also saw the scratches down your neck. I didn't know what to think, but I was worried about you.'

Now she looked down toward the couch, her thumb and finger moved the fur between them as if smoothing a foil wrapper. Creases gone she looked up.

'Worried about me?' Her shuffle in the couch told a new story of the circumstances between us, she was suddenly the one looking awkward and uncertain. I leant back a tilt to allow her room. I felt myself caring about her.

'For starters, you're a stranger I just happened to meet OK, I don't know why this happened and I definitely don't expect anyone to worry about me.' She stopped there, then carried on like it was hard to begin again. 'But it's odd; I've been feeling less and less connected with people these days, I can almost see how I could vanish altogether. An un-missed, missing person. I don't say that's a bad thing either; it could be. I don't know. But now you're here, because I caught you seeing me when I thought no one could. You triggered a memory. I acted impulsively.' Here she paused. She was gathering herself, bringing something together in her mind, 'When I was younger, there was a man, a very good man who taught me a lot. He also saw something in me. He would tell me all the time that I was extraordinary. I didn't believe him of course, but he would say to me – over and over – *you have a gift, but it takes practise and pain to unwrap it Gabrielle. Don't let it waste, and you can be a star.* So, I did, and little by little I began to believe him. I was earnest, committed to him and to a goal, He was my mentor, but I was doing it for him too. I danced and I danced, even in times when there was pain.' She shifted her eyes from light to dark in an instant, a taking away, 'It was then, when I almost believed his words – that the accident happened. That's when everything changed. I've not seen him since you know, I miss him dearly yes, but I won't commit like that to anyone again. I don't connect and I don't get let down. A simple rule, so I have nothing for anyone to take away. I just am what I am.'

I was in familiar light air; again, a little lost for what to say, but not left gasping. I partly understood where she was coming from. The idea of disconnecting from others to avoid an emotional hit was something I'd seen before; my Mum had modelled this perfectly for me. Living life as an observer, never wading in; or actively running away. No consequence of her own making.

I repeated the word that carried her secret. 'So, there was an accident?' Quizzically, carefully, I said it. I was seeing her less now as an assassin and more like a small bird, a little broken, in need of healing.

She looked away again and I admired her profile once more. She had an elf-like cuteness about her and I caught myself staring while processing the grab of her name she'd gifted me. Gabrielle turned back, with a look of resolve and seemingly unaware this time, of my indulgence. 'I feel I'm ready to offer you a drink. What would you like?'

At that moment I would have agreed to anything – how quickly I could fall – but she was asking for a preference. I teased at some hairs that licked out of the top of my shirt and came to a decision, 'Actually, I'd like a beer with you.' In my mind the *with you* had a hum.

*

A chips packet was torn, and the contents delivered, tumbling into a bowl. We sat with open beers and something had changed. The air felt different; cleaner. We'd been skidded back and forth across an abacus rung until this moment. Now we had stopped; counted together in a sum, looking for an answer each could understand. The beer was perfectly chilled and with the clock at five, it felt timely.

'My name is Michael.'

As I said it, I felt like I must have said it already and yet hadn't; time had swept me up with this small detail missed. It was a newly placed starting point, one that needed to be dropped.

'Pleased. Gabrielle.' She offered me her hand, fingers down a little like a railway crossing arm that tilted below the horizontal; anxiously vibrating at the traffic. I lightly took her hand, we shook a little mockingly, the awkwardness disguised this way. Her fingers felt light to touch. I thought of the softness of fingers upon a piano, breathing light notes. She broke in matter-of-factly. 'So where are you meant to be right now Michael? I know it wasn't my couch. Am I keeping you from somewhere? Or someone?'

'No, I'm actually taking a break from someone, and my family at the same time. I was looking to go away somewhere to think about who I spend time with. I only recently realised I have that choice. I've come here, with nothing booked in, so I'm thinking this might do for night one. That OK? For an abduction, it's tolerable.' I inverted my beer boyishly, a fast swig with my briefly smug eyes held on hers.

'An abduction, is that what you think it is? Am I that alien to you, your first gamer encounter?' She pulled a face at this, a little teasingly, 'and in the same breath, you're asking me if it's OK to stay?'

'Well, it kind of felt like that, that's all. You were pretty much ripping my arm off back there; it was like I was being sucked into a spaceship that thankfully morphed into an everyday taxi.' Gabrielle laughed, and this was her first time doing that with me. I felt a wash of relief. After the confused emotions of our time together so far, trending to normal – even if short lived – was welcome. I sensed there was much to figure out about Gabrielle and from our conversation so far, it seemed likely to come in cryptic clues; with patience metered. It was good then, that I had nowhere I had to be.

Gabrielle didn't respond straight away, then conceded. 'I agree, I was a bit bossy, in a female heroine kind of way I'd like to think,' a pleased smirk crept to her face, 'I surprised myself you know; it was actually not like me at all. I can't believe I even brought you here, and that you're sitting here, drinking my beer. I'm a loner by circumstance, and it sounds like you're on the run. We're an interesting pair.' Gabrielle stood abruptly and peered down at me as she did. 'Yes, you *can* stay. Like another one?'

Not waiting for my answer, she headed back toward the fridge. Skirting the wall, she pulled one side of the large curtains back without stopping; it seemed the time for a less hidden existence had arrived. Even with just one curtain pulled back, the large window gaped impressively at the city skyline; switching seamlessly to artificially lit as the sun snuck down between buildings. I contemplated my improving circumstance – too soon affected by the first drink – I rubbed my face firmly like my hands were a flannel and answered agreeably. 'Sure, it's a good beer, I'll have another.'

I sat, watched for Gabrielle's return and pondered, *am I actually on the run?* Gabrielle carried the two beers back to the couch, their necks looped between her fingers. She firmly pulled the other curtain back along the way. An even fuller view of a city with car lights sliding along ribbons now played. She passed me my second beer.

'So back there at the airport, if that wasn't like you, who were you pretending to be? Is this whole thing some kind of game to you?'

'I wasn't pretending, I was genuinely pissed at you. What you were doing, I used to get it all the time out there you know. I'd be in turmoil in my head, guessing at the thoughts behind the stares.' Gabrielle was staring out on the city street, I saw her face was tense, conceding to a pained truth.

'So, you don't go out there now?

'I don't. I hate it.'

'You're telling me you stay in all the time? Just play games on a screen with strangers, and that's a version of living that feels safe, or something like that?'

'Kind of.'

'You don't make friends on there?'

'I keep myself to myself. I think life can be a game, thinking of it that way has made it easier for me since the accident. I can watch the street below too – I'm grateful for that – to pass the time. I make a lot of shit up about people I watch.'

I surprised myself by snapping at her, 'That's crazy Gabrielle. What a waste; hiding in here, removing yourself. Don't you think?'

She fed straight back, biting at a nail between sentences.

'You may think so, but we've just met. You don't know about the shit luck ride I've had; and anyway, aren't you running?'

That question dug in. I didn't want to throw my pain at Gabrielle, but she already seemed to have a knack of drawing things out of me, whether it be emotion or words. I began to blurt it all out as I stared at my beer. 'I was just wondering about that, if I am running or going away. Going away feels better though, stronger, and leaving my version of shit luck behind seems smart. My family's pretty messed up. Are you in touch with your parents Gabrielle?'

'Not at all.' I caught the full stop like a medicine ball. A signal to carry on, so I did.

'Well, I still can be if I want, at least with my Mum. She gave me plenty of pain though – growing up. Disconnecting was her way too, and here I am now, going away from her and hearing you speak of life, like something you can step back from. There were so many times I saw her as the life of the party, but at the same time the most removed; vague. The one so often carried to a couch, the looks on the faces of friends, the never-ending excuses the next day as to where she was when I put myself to bed. That stays with you. All the times she turned on me as well – just a kid – as someone to blame because it could *never* be her? My face all tremors, no quake, not allowing the tears to surface. A locking up of a well. I got older and I spent years patching things up, until she didn't even want that anymore.' I looked at Gabrielle, she was becalmed, 'Yeah, I've known a share of shit luck too, but like you I keep some parts guarded. Except for now it seems.' I found a smile for her then, shaking my head at this day. 'It doesn't mean I close others out though; I know what that's like. Maybe I am running, but I'll be going somewhere, that's my decision to make.'

'Our pains are not the same Michael. But that you have them, gives us something in common, I guess. I'm curious about us having something in common. In truth, dragging you from that bus was partly me needing a buddy to get me back here, I was feeling desperate, grabbing for you was like grabbing for a crutch. But I also think coincidences are a cop out you know. There's a reason we met this way.'

'Maybe. But hang on, you just hopped off a plane? How the fuck did you manage a journey if even getting back here was so hard to face?' I was, and sounded, a bit incredulous at this.

'I didn't have a choice, I had to visit my sister – she can't leave her home.'

'What do you mean, can't leave?'

'Exactly that. Rich husband, amazing home with a sparkling pool above the sea. Sounds terrible, hey? But he won't let her out of sight. She managed to convince him to buy me a return ticket. I hadn't seen her in ten years. She is the only family I have. It was great to see her. Our situations are very different but now I know we both understand how being isolated feels. Seems to run in the family. I spent that flight trying to figure out which of us is most alone and you might think the answer is obvious, but it's not.'

I paused in thought, then responded from a place of shallow waters all the same.

'Wow. That's shit Gabrielle. Something surely has to change?' Tension crept from her like the onset of cramp. A tightening.

'Yeah, you make it sound easy.' Gabrielle brought her beer to her lips and drank; a defiant closing act.

Unperturbed, I felt I had a license by being *almost a stranger* to interfere; little to lose, I guess. I was going to try and *rescue* Gabrielle, whatever the trauma that had brought her here. I was aware I already liked being around her, I saw signs of fun behind her angst and over sensitivity. I was attracted to fun. To see more of that side appealed to me and getting out of this apartment with Gabrielle was surely the way to see it. I could see us exploring the streets in search of a pizza restaurant only to find a black cat perched upon a wall. I could see me buying a colourful tie, her fingers adjusting my collar, getting me looking just right for her. I could see us fumbling for that special key, unable to get back in, clickety click, falling into each other as we did. I smiled daringly and flung some words out.

'Look, are you up for trying something?' I was being vague for fear of being shut down real fast. Once bitten. I hoped being two beers in might help her – like with shooting pool, that time when fears are parked while some talent still remains – but Gabrielle looked at me a little distantly, like she was removing herself from the discussion whilst speaking into it.

'Let me guess, you want to get me out of here?' She said this with her eyes and her mouth; doubling her soft sarcasm. It would be too easy to admit to that, and probably not work on Gabrielle. I needed another way.

'Does this have to be about what I want? I thought you said you were curious about what brought us together. Perhaps *I am* here to help somehow?'

She looked thoughtful; she was listening. I went on.

'I'm thinking, you may want something to change, even if right now, you think you don't. Perhaps that's what we have in common? So, Gabrielle, will you trust me to play my part? My intentions are good, can you trust me?' As I said this, I felt a prick of *don't* stabbing into my gut. The resurfacing of a memory, biting at my eyelid now to force a blink. I knew what I could do when faced with rejection, that scared me. I wished I hadn't asked it then as I wished I hadn't said it now. In truth I didn't know if it was true, what were my intentions? A hard question, one to leave aside. I looked at Gabrielle for a signal of buy in, had she seen me flinch, or would she trust me? She nodded a couple of times across her beer, 'OK, but I'm going to set some guidelines, I'm a gamer remember, I'd like some rules of engagement, it's how I see things more clearly.'

As she said it, I could see there would be limits to what she'd agree to. Up to now it seemed her apartment seclusion had been a kind of protector. Allowed her to feel safer. I would have to step briskly past negotiation in case she changed her mind. If she let me try, then helping her see things more clearly, mattered a lot for us both.

*

'So, what will the rules of engagement be?' I was wary; she'd pinned me in a spot of bother more than once already.

'I'll keep it simple. This couch is where you sleep, and you don't get to ask too many questions. You never leave this apartment unless it's with me, and if you leave this place with me, you win. But I have to agree to go. The time for the completion of the challenge is fixed but not set by me or by you. A man called Castle sets that time and I do hope you never meet him; because I like you. I'll show you a photo of him.' Gabrielle moved away and returned with a small framed photo of a man, in portrait. Our fingers tapped their tips as she passed it to me, I inhaled on the light touch from her as I looked at the photo. 'So, now you know who to watch for. Do you accept the terms?'

I could have been more cautious. I could have asked more about Castle, suggested alternative sleeping arrangements and insisted on a bail-out option. However odd, I could see this was her way and it was probably the only way she'd allow me in. In that moment I decided I would not let her see me as someone afraid again. So instead of any sensible clarifications, I offered my hand to shake on the deal, to accept the terms as they were.

*

It was obvious Gabrielle had her secrets and that I needed to find out more about this girl who interrupted my arrival. She had quickly wrapped me up in her little world and set me down in it. I didn't know how she saw me really, but

I sensed she wanted to maintain a control over me. I could play along with that and see where I could challenge her; just a little.

'Can you to tell me more about why you're here Gabrielle. How long have you been here?'

Gabrielle was leaning forward as I asked, she lifted a magazine cover slightly, then let it drop, her words following fell with the page in a soft, reflective meter. 'I have been here – as in inside – since I gave myself permission. I tried going out at first, I reasoned it was part of what I had to do as I tried to find normal. But one day, I stopped beating myself up I guess, I chose to stay in because it felt safer. To retreat. People go on retreats all the time don't they – to get away, that's normal – well that's been a lifestyle choice for me.'

'So, for how long? When did you start your retreat, you know retreats aren't typically permanent?'

Gabrielle gave an unimpressed one syllable puff, as if to brush my last comment away, then continued. 'It's been years, six or seven by now. By the way, I've seen testimonials from people who've done retreats saying things like *I wish it didn't have to end* or *it just wasn't long enough* ... that's interesting isn't it?'

I reasoned she'd had plenty of time to justify her choices. For some reason, I found this annoying, I didn't want to hear them now, they were an obstacle.

'Gabrielle, you know this isn't healthy, you dragged me from an airport too scared to be out there.' I waved my open hand at the windows, 'You told me how your sister is stuck and hates it. Does she know what brought you here to this place? Can we start with that? *The accident* as you call it?'

With this abrupt shift of gear from me, the change in her was immediate. Head down, not looking at me as she quietly spoke, I saw her brokenness again, it pained me that I was causing it. 'Yes, my sister knows, but that's where the knowing stops. It stops there for my safety. You certainly don't need to know.'

If I had seen a wave petering out onto a shore somewhere at that moment, the last part, a smoothed round lip pouting to the dunes, it was the slithering back of retreating water to secretive depths that I now saw. The accident, whatever it was, would be hers to tell, if ever, and not mine to ask for. 'I'm sorry Gabrielle. I'm sorry for asking that.' My words were honest, I would have to find another way.

*

Gabrielle's flux of mood, her sensitivities; had me on edge. I wondered about the key around her neck and what that meant for me, should I want to leave. Not that I did for now, but could I even leave if I wanted to without that key?

I sat in silence with her before she spoke again. Waiting with Gabrielle had already become a pattern, a time when doubts would surface, or I'd go off into some fantasy about getting closer with her.

'You know I'm puzzled about something. Before when I mentioned Castle, you didn't even ask who he was, hardly looked at the photo. I find that odd, like you think he doesn't matter because tonight we'll walk out of here hand in hand and find a karaoke bar or something? Where does your cockiness come from? You should be curious, or even scared of him.'

'I'm curious about a lot of things. You've made it impossible for me not to be, wouldn't you say? Perhaps it's more that I don't know where to start? But since you brought it up, I am curious as to why you have. What should I know about Castle?'

Gabrielle looked long out to the city then returned her attention to me. 'He was there – I lied before – it isn't just my sister who knows about what happened. Castle's entwined in this mess and he's the one that got me safely to this place. I don't know if he discarded me here or protected me by doing it. I don't know if it suited him for me to be hidden away after what happened. I was in shock and completely distraught, I was still a kid. My mind a muddle, I blindly went with his plan but there was a trust between us that won't be broken until I know what he wants of me. What he wants me to do next.'

Her last words settled flat, seeping outwards. *Was this why Gabrielle wanted me to ask of Castle. Was it him I needed to find?*

'So in six or seven years you haven't seen him once, he hasn't messaged you at all? Can I ask what he was to you, for you to still trust him after all this time?'

'I was sixteen, I don't think I knew what he was to me. But I know he knows we share a secret and I don't know if that troubles him. It's possible that not hearing from him shows he does care about me. That any contact from him could endanger me in some way. It's also possible that if I wasn't here, he'd not be happy about it. My sister was worried about my visit to her and Castle was the reason. It sure is good to be back here now though. We should eat now, I'm peckish.'

'Hang on. I do want to eat, I'm famished too. But are you saying you think he might hurt you if he found you away from here? That he's the reason you stay, that the key around your neck makes you feel safe? If that's what you think, how can it be a question as to whether he cares about you. He's sounding like a jerk to me. I think we need to find him.'

Gabrielle looked into me, a little disbelieving, stood, and walked off toward the kitchen. 'He's not a jerk and you're doing it again Michael, making it sound easy. We both need to eat. Come help me cook.'

*

In the kitchen I was surprised by the variety of options. There were even fresh veggies in special tubs that Gabrielle said worked magic on keeping fresh food fresh. She delighted in pointing out their one special feature, a vent with three air exchange settings. Thinking about my chances of Gabrielle letting me in on her secret I looked closer then offered, 'Ummm, yes, no, maybe?' Raising my right questioning shoulder, palms up with the maybe. She smirked, I'd disarmed her a little more, 'They're nothing more than degrees of openness Michael'. I left that right alone whilst wondering if there was a hint of flirt to her response.

Gabrielle moved briskly into food preparation, slapping various items on the red laminated benchtop with a definite plan in mind. I enjoyed seeing her so assertive, the darting movements of her hands plucking items for the meal. She gave me my first task – slicing onions and mushrooms – while she busied herself arranging other ingredients, with the determination of someone famished but disciplined enough not to pick. That had always been my problem, I often got to the table with my appetite dented. I could tie that to my childhood too, but with that thought, I questioned myself for the excuses I so readily line up. I thought about what stories Gabrielle lined up to justify living this way, but there were too many gaps for me. Perhaps in parallels I could understand her better. For now, though, I enjoyed the proximity to her, I enjoyed her stepping around me, her smiles as we toiled and stirred. The thrill of having so much to learn about her.

Soon enough we were seated at the table back in the living area with a rather fine risotto in our bowls. The texture was perfect, the flavour just right and there was no glug. I honoured the meal with no more awkward questions and Gabrielle offered no more unsettling insights. It was to be an early night. Gabrielle said good night as I set up on the couch, as per the rules. For some time I lay there, recounting the day, looking for answers and wondering if by playing within the rules, I could ever get close to her at all.

*

In the days that followed we settled into a morning routine; basking with a morning coffee was always the starting point. I got familiar with the coffee machine and we took turns in rolling out the morning blend. Sometimes we had two cups, when the sun streamed in and warmed us, making us feel particularly good. Neither of us prioritised breakfast. Her large window had a ledge where you could perch, a little cushion beneath the bum worked for me. With knees up, coffee cup cherished between the fingers that met on the other side of the broad, shallow cups she favoured, we would look down at the streets below and talk. Sometimes it would be easy and lively. She had amazing insights into strangers, I'd often claimed to be a people watcher but by comparison I was barely an apprentice. Turned out she was quite the conversationalist too, I guess so much time alone could do that, so I spent a lot of time listening.

Then there were the other times, quiet times when she left me alone, when she'd take herself to the other room in the small apartment. I took to reading but also, these times were my small opportunities to search for a clue of her past. Being forever fearful of ruining things meant my searches, behind her back, were fleeting; halfhearted. She was still there, of course, and I knew she could suddenly reappear, to catch me prying. I was afraid that I'd find myself back in a place like when we first met, lost for words, unable to answer the question of *what I was doing*. I felt like there was even more to lose now too, I wanted to get closer and things were going well; mostly.

When we were together, conversing, I sometimes sought the bigger answers. At such moments, things were much more delicate – she'd said I couldn't ask too many questions; it was the rules – and it was easy to turn the day sour in the small space we shared. I wanted Gabrielle to feel we were facing a challenge together, looking to win her freedom was the way I saw it, that was my intention when I asked her about the key, and it turned into one of those sour days.

'I have the one key to this place. I've always kept it on that ceramic tree by the door, unless I ventured out, which before the flight was a long time ago. But now you're here, I wear it to my skin.'

'You don't trust me then?' Her response came back swiftly.

'No one else can open that door in either direction without it. I need to protect it.'

'How do you know that for sure?' I stirred her a little with the question, but she was a touch less reactive now to my questions than when we first met.

'The builder that made this place safe told me so. He knew I was scared and needed to feel secure, I was a wreck in those first few weeks. I trust him, he made this place into my fortress, then left me this key. It wasn't just about the door either, he put these window grates up for me too. He spoke with Castle often, I overheard him, it was all about making me safe. I could tell Castle was worried from that half of the conversation. But I'm not clear why. I don't know if he's the threat like you think he is or if he's staying away for good reason, but I feel he's still out there. Each day that passes doesn't make it easier. I don't know what I'd say to him, what I feel about him, and; I don't know what he'd do if he found you here.'

I doubted Castle was on Gabrielle's side and didn't feel a strong desire to bump into him either. I needed to find a course of action myself. 'Right, this is what we're going to do.' I was feeling assertive, a stupid misreading of Gabrielle. 'We need to find him, I've said it already and you brushed it off, but we really need to find him. There's no other way to sort this mess. Other than run?'

Her look said everything, today was not a day for gaming or poetry, she placed her purple painted nails of her right hand to her neck and dug them in, as she eyed me like a foe and dragged them down her neck like ploughs. There were no sounds. Two lines of blood left me dumb while she left purposefully for the bathroom and closed the door – shutting me out – coffee unfinished.

I was alarmed, but then reasoned she'd done this before, she had the lines to prove it. I repeatedly told myself she would be OK. It stung me into action, to hell with trust and patience, I began to hunt through drawers and scrap books for anything that could lead to Castle.

*

Gabrielle remained in the bathroom, but I could hear some sounds of movement, and now despite it all, I was suddenly grinning. I'd finally found something in a notebook, laid between some pages sketched on. It would not have fallen out, I had to find it there. After being so fearful to ask questions, to risk her shutting down again, this was the boost I needed. I had an opening, a lead.

In my hands I held a certificate, there was an emblem of a dance school and Gabrielle's name was written in the centre along a line, in heavy pen. On my laptop I entered the details for the school to see what I might find. What flashed up next, held me in a place of dawning; completely still with just my eyes scrolling down, headlines, all connected with what looked to have been a huge scandal seven years earlier. At first, I looked for an order to the events, but the headlines and days seemed jumbled. My hasty searching, along with wary glances towards the bathroom door, fed the confusion, but I soon fixed on one story. It had a big picture of Gabrielle smiling – looking stunning and vibrant – and a sinister figure in the background, a man watching her from the shadows off stage. Gabrielle looked so young, happy and glowing with optimism. Little connection to the girl in the bathroom now, harmed and distrusting. I stared at the shadowy presence in the photo, *lurking* as the caption put it; it made me uneasy before I read the words, as fast as I could, scanning snippets as I feared being caught.

... first reports suggested a tragic accident, possibly a fall from stage, but with the victim in a coma, there was a lot of guesswork happening.

... the much-loved dance coach Taylor 'Smithy' Goldsmith fought for his life for two drawn-out weeks before his death. All the while Castle Gregor – the dance school caretaker – took questions and managed the situation, at one point saying the accident had scared Gabrielle into hiding, that she felt responsible, and he appealed to the authorities to find her. He was resilient to one fact; there had been a terrible fall and he was hoping for the best like everyone associated with the school that coach Smithy would soon be back on his feet.

... but with the disappearance of Castle Gregor coinciding with the passing of Smithy, further questions arose about him. It was not seen as an idle coincidence.

... The early gossip and hearsay of Gabrielle running from the scene and being somehow involved were discounted by those who knew her, but a bystander had reported seeing Castle Gregor place his hand to the small of her back and hasten her away. To some this implicated her, and the rumours of a possible hidden affair made more sense with her vanishing.

I looked up from the screen abruptly, the bathroom door handle had surely turned, but it now appeared still. Little surprise I was jumpy, I continued to read more, fleetingly glancing up.

... questions on where he had sent her to, when she dashed away down the street upon his apparent command, remained unanswered. The locals recalled odd things about him and the way he had been seen to look at Gabrielle from time to time during classes.

... it seems many have now concluded Gabrielle may be dead and carrying a secret.

They were half right I thought as I glanced across at the door again.

... police say Gabrielle is likely to be in hiding out of fear or may herself be a victim. They couldn't rule out anything, they had no leads.

I felt like a sucked prune stone, not clean of pulp but set aside. It was all sinking in and from what I could gather, glancing at other article headings, this was a mystery not yet solved. Castle had not been found and I recognised with some fear, that task had now fallen to me.

*

Gabrielle emerged before I felt a need to knock at the bathroom door and check on her. When she saw me, I *acted* calm. I tried not to look too different, given what I had unearthed. How was I supposed to look? In my running mind

I quickly searched for that answer. Then again, after what Gabrielle had just exposed me too, I had good reason to be affected.

I chose to ask her if she was OK, trying to gauge where she was at, more by her reaction than her words. She was not, but she told me she would be. 'I'm OK, I just need to breathe back into the day, give me a moment.' With that I left her there and went to prep some food. This was me avoiding her, I wasn't feeling comfortable at what was right to say. When I returned with a sandwich for each of us, I found her teary.

'What were you doing while I was in there? I thought you may have checked on me. How long was I in there for anyway?'

'Yeah a while,' a lame comment as I searched for my version.

'I wanted to check on you, but I was a little freaked out and while I could hear sounds, I trusted you were OK, you've done this before, right? I told myself that. I sat here and told myself you'd be OK. I don't think you were gone as long as perhaps it seemed.'

She stared out the window, away from me. 'I do lose track of time when that happens, but I thought you might have checked on me.'

We shared a lunch; it wasn't a relaxed one, but I saw signs I was not going to be completely shut out for the whole day. I'd brought her food, so even if I'd potentially left her to die half an hour before, it still counted for something.

I found myself not going places again, not bringing things up. But was that really the best way to show I cared, that this was more than just a game for the two of us? A penny was tumbling down for me to grasp. Shattering her illusions of Castle was going to hurt, and maybe too much for her to take from me, but whether out of kindness or desperation, it was probably the right thing for me to do. One thing I really wanted to know was whether she knew that the coach, who saw the extraordinary in her, had died seven years ago, from the accident. I reasoned it was possible, given how she'd been so removed, that she may not even know. Had Castle kept that from her?

I let time slide until the next day came. We spent time together easily between the rougher moments, it was like we had compartments of conflict but everything else was a smooth sliding drawer. I figured if Gabrielle didn't know about her coach's death, it may bring a missing ingredient that would change her from waiting for something to wanting to go and get it. That was a shift I wanted to see, but I also was wary of the news being hard for her to hear. If it *was* news to her. The shift could make it easier to get out of this place with her. That was the win I strived for; to see her happy and spritely in the streets below, the soft touch of her feet on the cobblestone streets rather than my memory of her climbing the stairs to this place.

'So, Gabrielle, you said the other day how you missed your coach. Have you tried to reach him at all in your time here? What is his name by the way?' The question registered as new territory while she finger-drew a line that screeched across the windowpane.

'His name's Smithy. I never tried. Like I said, everything changed. Maybe he's looked for me, but he won't find me here. My dancing days are over anyway, as is my belief in what he said.' A sadness settled there.

'Do you think he'd still be coaching, was he very old?'

'Doubt that, he was trying to sell the business back then. He argued with Castle about that a bit. He was ready to give it away.'

'We could try and find him, it couldn't be that hard, maybe he'd like to hear from you?'

'No.'

With her 'No', I wanted to shout out *there's something that you don't know!* I held the line back and instead delved some more.

'Why not? Does this come back to Castle? He wouldn't want you to reach out to Smithy?'

'It does. And he wouldn't. I think it's to do with me being safe. One thing I was told was any searching into the past would be seen and could get me into strife. I don't know how, maybe the internet here is monitored somehow? If that's true then that includes you by the way, no digging alright?'

'No digging? I kind of think I need to, don't you? What if I told you I have been?' A quiet storm rolled in with a gap in conversation.

'Michael. Stop and think. I know you think it's madness but what I have here isn't all that bad. I'm not enslaved like my sister, some of the things she told me you wouldn't want to hear. My being here comes with requirements, I sense them without knowing what they are. Sure, that sounds crazy and I may have crossed a line bringing you in. But there are no other lines I'd like to cross just now. Can we leave this be?' Her eyes searched mine. 'Don't dig.'

I didn't answer her. I felt I knew enough, and it hadn't ended badly. Castle had kept one secret from her, I could see that. I could see this as a way out and I longed to break it to her. But knowing how, was not so easy. I was a little worried by what she'd said though, I had after all been digging. That night I had nightmares; Gabrielle had injected some of her fear into me. I saw Castle watching me from numerous places, some quite bizarre, some quite close. And the feeling was terrifying.

The next day I woke to the sound of the shower running in the bathroom. Gabrielle had showered sporadically during my stay, though never in the morning. I could never understand people not having a morning shower, I couldn't start the day without one. My first thought was, *surely she doesn't have somewhere to go*. But then, Gabrielle never had somewhere to go that would see her step beyond the door of the apartment. She only reached out to collect deliveries from outside the door, well after drop-off; she never signed for anything, that was her instruction. Everything was so strategic for her isolation.

Now she was having her shower and I went ahead with coffee for one. That was oddly difficult, not making one for her too. I reflected on it. It was hard to admit but with each day I wanted more connection from her. Winning the game could mean something. I can offer her one when she comes out, I figured. I perched on the now-familiar ledge, considering how time had stretched and I was unsure what day of the week it was. With each sip of coffee, I felt more optimistic, that she might understand what I had to say if I laid it out plain and simple without emotion.

Two things happened.

I saw a man down at the cafe across the street, seated at a table for two, a place reserved for another with a book. He had his back to me, a heavy jacket made him look broad across the shoulders. The time spent watching strangers with Gabrielle had trained a curiosity in me, I wondered if this man would be joined by another. His gay lover that was a secret from his wife?

The second thing. Finishing my coffee, I realised that the shower was still running. It had been a long time and suddenly I felt concerned. The day before had been rocky for Gabrielle and for me, I would check on her this time. I ventured to the bathroom door and knocked firmly, 'Gabrielle, you OK?' I knocked again, more forcibly, calling out again. There was no sound but the running of the shower. One more go as my insides twisted. Something was wrong. I barged at the door yelling, 'I'm coming in!' Unlike the front doors, this one offered little resistance and I found myself sprawled upon a slippery floor, looking up at a severely unhinged door – just hanging on – threatening to crash down on me at any moment. I looked for Gabrielle, bloodied, red waters washing away around her naked body, lifeless; too late. Instead, I saw no sign of her at all. The only presence in the steamy bathroom, was a message on the mirror – in lipstick – some words scrawled there for me to find.

The Game is Over.

'No!' I screamed. Recalling the man's hair and posture again, a realisation exploded in my head. Half slipping with feet that struggled to keep up, I dashed across to the window and looked down. Me in the place of an assassin, but helpless and disarmed. Gabrielle was there now in the other seat, laughing and at ease, across from Castle Gregor.

Dan Depiazzi

Romancing the Language

'To gender, to phonetics, to interpretation free
Our language is revolution and peacemaker be', says she
She fell in love with the sounds first,
       the tunes that spoke in feelings
She fell in love with the accents too,
       the gentle persuasion of talk
She knew to listen with the words,
       to hear from within
She knew to participate as a verb,
       to speak out loud
Her body moves to the voice,
       in accordance of the lyrics
Her body moves to the meaning,
       saying with song
Her heart yearns the passion,
       from stories of the soul
Her heart intrigues the depts,
       of the unspoken and obscene
She romances the language,
       from whence it came
She romances the language,
       and the languish

She romances the language, the language romances she

Apikara

Weeds

Lies – I ponder the word as I lather the shampoo in my hair – are rather like weeds.

They come in all manner of guises. So too do lies. Both flourish and run rampant in the right conditions, and in doing so, they choke out the goodness of what was once in their place.

Small at first, just a little bit of life poking out into the world around them, germinating and swelling under the ground until they break free of the darkness. In fact, you may not even notice them in a garden full of life because they are innocuous, because they can blend in with their surroundings, mimic the environment around them.

But they grow bigger if they aren't addressed early on.

If they aren't pulled out by their roots and destroyed.

The thing with weeds is, that once you know what they look like, you can't unsee them. You can ignore them – but you will always *see* them. You will always be on the lookout for more.

Mistruths, misrepresentations and misdeeds, given life by a dishonest word here, an omission there … They grow, and then other lies get the idea, that deceit is indeed a fertile bed, and so they too poke up their heads and take root; weaving wispy roots down into the ground, and once they find nourishment and security, they grow bolder. Their roots growing thicker and stronger, until they become rooted in the reality that surrounds them.

A weed is a plant that grows out of place.

A lie is an intent that situates itself in a place.

And … well, what exactly is a lie? An omission of a fact? An assertion that is false, done with the intent of deceiving? There's that word again: *deception*.

Why does one do it – *lie*? What purpose does deliberately miss-telling or omitting details serve? At what point does a lie become a lie? They grow with intent, nourished by what … guilt? Perhaps.

Shame? Maybe. Fear? Most likely.

Fear of what though? Getting caught out? Having to answer to the lie? Having to live with the effects of the lie and being discovered?

Being caught in duplicity? Quite certainly.

I wonder: *if lies were a typeface, what colour would the font be? Black? White? Grey? Somewhere in between all or none? Would the colour be bold, or would it be opaque?*

As I rinse my conditioner I think: *what does one do when one discovers a lie?* That one has been deceived, misguided by a deliberate sleight of hand (or word), so to speak.

Of course, there's that sickening feeling of one's stomach dropping to their toes, the heavy swallow of realisation, like the weight of the lie you have been fed sticking in your throat. Then there is anger, suspicion and grand plans of revenge. That is, until the annoying part of your psyche called 'rationalisation' tries to make sense of the fucking thing. Tries to downplay it even. Tries to marry it up with other pretend lies – *worse* pretend lies – to try to trick your anger into submission, to douse the flames of revengeful thoughts, to make you think it's not as bad as it seems. There must be a reason.

And there is.

That person fucking lied to you.

You didn't think they'd ever lie to you, but then you found out the plum-meting, sickening truth. It's finding out about the things that happen when you're not around.

How people change in other's company, how 'what happens in x-y-z, stays in x-y-z.' About how 'the boys' stick together; chuckle thickly together like hor-mone-addled fucktards, about 'bitches' and 'lap dances' and 'the stripper fucked him good … ha! Hope his wife doesn't find out.'

Ah! But she *did* find out.

I saw the video; read the messages that followed.

I followed the breadcrumbs and saw it all.

And I despise liars.

I look at him with new eyes, wondering if every change in his voice, the slight quaver or unnecessary swallow is because that lie is sending its wispy roots deeper down inside him, drawing life from his deceit. If the unfound lie is reproducing, sending suckers out to trick its 'lie-host' into thinking he's got away with it, that he's golden?

If only he could see behind my blank eyes and neutral lips.

If only he could see what loss of respect and trust looks like.

If only he could hear the words that rage in my mind, how I imagine screaming and turning over furniture and breaking all the good dishes, how I want to rip his treasured belongings to pieces, how I want to take out an ad in the local paper and spell out his deceit. How I want to fucking *destroy* him.

Just like a weed.

I take a deep breath, put my head under the water once more, feel it hot and heavy washing me clean, dousing the flames for a moment.

Water drops run down the shower screen and just where a clear patch has formed, I see through to the towel on the rail, dark and dense and grey. It seems to move in time with my breaths, pulsing almost. I watch, fascinated, because I know that towels are inanimate and do not move. But this one looks like it does. I reason with myself – things are not always as they seem.

I step out of the shower, dripping, and I stand there, still, like a soaked scarecrow. In the mirror I see what is looking back at me. What *he* sees. It is like a moment of clarity. This is me. Not at all how I've been seeing myself. The illusion of self I have believed. And I swallow, tasting the lies I have been fed, just like a grain-fed cow, fed more and more crap to keep docile, occupied … stupid.

And I do look like a cow, I suppose. My breasts are now sagging, the result of being larger chested, breastfeeding three children and age. My stomach, soft and swollen like a rumpled balloon with no air left to fill it, my thighs dimpled and thick. Perhaps it really is my fault I think; maybe I should have looked after myself better, looked after him more. I see what he sees. I see why he lied, why he went chasing after tail 'elsewhere' – younger, prettier tail. Maybe one day those little bunnies will lose their tails too?

I know from experience, that if I was to rage, to confront him, it would be turned around – oh, so cleverly. At first it would be that I am wrong; that he'd never do that, that he just isn't the type, that it's all in my mind, and speaking of my mind, maybe I should go back on my meds or get a new hobby or get a job. Because I obviously have too much time on my hands, and that I'm quite obviously living inside my head, making up drama where there is none. He will tell me, '*that it isn't healthy to live in your head like you do … I don't think you writing those stories all the time is good for you – your mind is making up things that don't exist.*' That he is only telling me this because he loves me and wants what is best for me. And talking about what is best for me, have I thought about joining a gym? Getting out and walking more, maybe after a while, progress into running? Because after all, he gets a chance to get out every week, to 'let the dog off the chain' at footy, and maybe I should find an exercise group as well, find some friends. Because his footy mates are 'tops', 'good blokes'. Up for a good time and a night on the town, a 'boys' night'. A Players Trip even.

I bet they're all fucking lying cunts as well.

I can't see the tears on my face, because my eyes are burning, staring at the profile of the woman in the fogged-up mirror and I have not blinked; my hair is drenched, the water running down my face in cooling rivulets. But they feel different to the shower water. They sting my skin.

I stare at the woman I now recognise as myself, and turn away, disgusted.

I feel like a caricature, layers and layers of me stacked together to make a life size cardboard cut-out.

That woman who takes the family pictures but is never in them. That woman who documents the life of her family but is not in the narrative of it. That woman who used to be someone, but *who*? I can't even remember anymore.

It is eating at me like a slow cancer, dissolving me from the inside as it grows, fed by the lies in my life. I don't know who to talk to about this. The lies. The truth. How to confront the man who swore to love me above all others for all the days of our lives. How to ask him to tell me the truth, and only the truth — even if it will shred me on the inside like a sharp knife. Because, the knife wound is not dissimilar to what I am doing to myself every time I think of the lies. Each time it is like a new cut, deep and bloody and I am bleeding in front of them, but no one can see.

*

He brings up the subject of an end of season footy trip gently. I'd scoffed when he mentioned it last year. Last year he stayed home. Didn't get 'parole'.

This year though, he's been building up for it, 'asking' for weeks. Little comments about his playing mates here and there. Personalising them. Making them known to me. Making them safe. He thinks I don't know his strategy. He's been dropping hints, they'd probably say he was 'buttering up the missus', probably 'pulling his pants back up from his ankles because his arse was getting cold.' They probably rib him for it at training, asking him how it feels to be pussy whipped, about not wearing the pants in the house, about being a man. So, I say: 'Do what you want, it's your life,' because I know he's already done what he wanted, so why would *me* saying no to him count for anything? He kisses my cheek and makes me a cup of tea. I don't think he read any further into that comment; that doing what you want has consequences for your life. He's too busy messaging his footy fiends that he's in like Flynn. Sign him up. Parole has been approved. He can't wait to party. Bring on Bali babes in bikinis!

*

My husband has been somewhat preoccupied lately, football business, he assures me, organizing for the trip. He talks about day visits that they are looking at, maybe a temple, 'See what the boys think when we are there.' Yes, indeed. See exactly what the boys want to do with their free time. Eat? Drink? Adult entertainment? Support the South-East Asian sex trade?

I smile a nod to him. Remind him of when we went there on our honeymoon. Commented on the embarrassment I felt when I had seen drunk Aussies in Kuta and Seminyak, sauntering around, loud and obnoxious, treating the Balinese people with indifference and disrespect. He tells me that they are going there to relax, drink respectfully and take it easy. Maybe get a massage every day. I resist in asking if the massage comes after the entertainment, if it comes with the promise of 'happy ending', 'full service plus-plus'. I don't ask because I just can't listen to anymore lies. I think about how nice it would be to have daily massages, swim in a pool, sunbathe, drink cheap cocktails, go out with friends. Live like you have no attachments or commitments. Like you don't give a fuck.

I think that we are defined by our choices – and they become as much a part of us as our DNA, our germ cells, our seeds. We choose to plant them; we must abide by the consequences of their growth.

*

He left for the airport at two this morning. It's his release date, his day to fly free with the 'Goodfellas' up high above the clouds, away from the reality of life, and to land in the stifling humidity of Bali. Because they deserve this. Playing football is hard work. Being a responsible adult is tiring and they need a break. Bonding time. *Boy's* time. They need a playground that delivers whatever they want so they can let their hair down and relax. And play. With no rules and no supervision. Yes siree! No parole officers watching over their shoulders.

I have five days.

The kids are at school today, the removalists are arriving at 9.30. They have assured me of a very efficient and quick pack, and I pay extra to make sure it is done by 5.00. They won't be taking anything with a red sticky dot on it. The children are at my mother's tonight, and by tomorrow afternoon, they will have a new home to come back to. We will have a new life for the four of us. I thought about staying, once, for the kids, but they deserve to live a life that is not choked by weeds. My lawyer has advised me. I have the evidence; the letters are drafted. He will find one on the front door when he gets home, when he returns with his tan, and cheap gifts and duty-free bourbon.

I wonder if he will come home with any red sticky dots. Maybe they will fester in his blood first, feeding on him like the lies.

But I am all out of fucks, I have razed them to the ground, burnt their stalks. Thy fucklessness runneth over. I feel a power in this. Like my invisibility to men is a superpower and not a confidence crisis. Like I have awoken a strength in me that has lain dormant and suppressed, not unlike a weed. But unlike a weed, I welcome the growth. It is *not* out of place and therefore, *not* a weed.

Five days until he comes home – unless of course, a burgeoning emergency means they have to stay a day or two longer. Maybe they'll get lucky. Sometimes, you just never know.

Bali is a lush country. So green. The plants grow wild over there if they aren't tended, if they aren't maintained.

I remember when I was there, I saw a lot of weeds.

Lee Harsen

A Passion

It all got out of hand. Now, with blood seeping into my eyes and my mother's suppressed sobs filling my ears, I think it was all my fault.

I could have stayed home. Worked with my father. There's no shame in being a carpenter. But I had to do what I thought was right. I had to protest. Our people were downtrodden and oppressed. Invaded and occupied. Our land taken; our rights denied. The world ignorant to our plight. I couldn't stand by and let others protest for me. I couldn't watch my friends go, while I cowered in my workshop. I just couldn't.

It was our time. We were young, fit, strong and if not us, then who? The old men were too feeble, the children too young. It had to be us.

I knew my voice was strong. I knew I had a way with words. I was happy to talk at the meetings, but I did not see it. Still do not see it. Cannot pinpoint the moment when I went from speaking to leading. It just happened. People began to look me out, ask my opinion, more and more. Listened to me, believed in me, my message, my call to action. However, I can see, with sad hindsight, times when I could have turned back. Could have turned everyone back, but the momentum was undeniable. Like great conversations when bedtime is long past, yet no one wants to break the spell. The smiles and laughter, camaraderie and emotion binding all together into a new dawn. That was our journey but multiplied in intensity a thousand-fold. I really believed we would change things. Not by overthrowing the Government, it was madness to think like that, faced with an army such as they had. No, our way had to be subtle. Peaceful. The mass of the people, moving in unison. Undeniable.

And then my mistake. The whole thing torn asunder by my temper. I had seen starvation throughout the countryside. Dire need that could have been assuaged by those in power with a single stroke of their pens, yet they did nothing. I thought perhaps they didn't realise the severity of our need, but I was wrong. They understood and they dismissed me with disdain. The traders, the money changers, the tax collectors. In that holy place. Paying to Caesar his due. Paying us nothing. I could stand it no longer. That one day's worth of taxes could have fed whole villages, yet we received not so much as a cursory glance. So I struck out and finally my voice was heard. Heard as a trumpet blast against their economic status quo and they decided, enough was enough.

It took days, not weeks. Their speed was frightening to behold. Friends scattered, all pursued. I was arrested, tried, condemned. Now, as I die, the movement will die with me. There is no reprieve, no kindness. Even their water, offered to my parched lips, is vinegar. To mock my thirst and my naivety. It is finished.

Ian Andrew

Acknowledgements

This anthology is of course a collaborative effort between fifteen authors, but aside from them, there is no way it would have come to fruition without the generous support, commitment and on-going belief of the following people:

To Bianca, from Bunbury's Caf-fez, who extended hospitality to our group from our inaugural meeting. For staying open, long past her usual trading hours, for listening to our readings, for putting up with our occasional raucous discussions and for always being there to serve coffee and wine, (a lot of wine) to quench our thirst for creativity, we owe her a tremendous debt of gratitude. Thanks Bianca, you are a trooper and we promise to buy more wine in the coming years. Bianca would have us believe that it's no big deal to open specifically for us, and that it's actually a bonus because she's able to get work done. She's not fooling anybody. The commitment, generosity of spirit, and love for all things community that Bianca and her partner Matt exemplify through their hospitality to the Bunbury Writers Group, make us eternally grateful and in their debt.

To Ian, executive director of Book Reality and Leschenault Press, who has made all of this possible, and who has put up with our endless questions/emails/meetings with minimal eye rolling. For his continued support and enthusiasm in ensuring our love of storytelling gets to a wider audience

To Mary, our sharp-eyed and speedy editor, who read through what must have seemed like an endless amount of words. For giving up hours of her time to generously tidy up our work, for suggesting changes that enhanced the quality of our stories. Thank you – an editor is priceless and our book is that much stronger because of you.

To Lisa, for producing a beautifully nuanced and eye-catching original artwork for the cover. Thank you for the time, effort and creativity that you put into this, and for your enthusiasm in being a part of this project. Also to Julie, from Web and Print Hub in Eaton, who put the artwork and the rest of the elements together for the full cover.

To Ben Mason for having the vision and the dream to create this group of writers and dreamers and to the members of the Bunbury Writers Group, who have turned an interesting idea into a reality.

We have become a family of writers – strangers brought together through a shared passion, now united by trust, respect, collaboration and mutual interests. Words do more than tell a story, they bind individuals and make the journey even more fulfilling.

And finally, as the dedication at the start of the book says, to everyone who has ever encouraged us in our writing endeavours, but especially to our friends and families. You who have long known we harboured the writing bug and who, through your love, support and ability to leave us alone while we spend hours trying to get that one sentence perfect, have given more to us than we could ever have hoped. Each of you is loved and appreciated more than you could ever know. Thank you.

About the Authors

Ben Mason

Ben founded the Bunbury Writers Group and hosts quarterly spoken word nights. His short fiction has been performed, published and awarded, featuring in Brain drip, KSP writing comp, and Lit Live Perth.

Home Invasion – his collection of short fiction – was long-listed for the 2019 Fogarty Award, for the best-unpublished manuscript for a West Australian writer under thirty-five.

He has won spoken word competitions and finished 3rd in the 2019 WA leg of the Australian Poetry Slam State Final. In 2020 he will be a writer in residence at Mattie Furphie House for the Fellowship of Australian Writers WA.

He quit teaching at the end of 2017 to follow his dream of becoming a writer. It doesn't pay the bills, but it makes him damn happy.

Apikara McQuillan

Apikara is an intuitive writer, born of blood in New Zealand and other lands.

Her love of words and creative expression lead her to join the Bunbury Writers Group, where she says, 'she's a fledgling in the nest of passionate orators in print.'

Apikara lives on Noongar Boodgar in the South West of Australia.

Dan Depiazzi

Dan Depiazzi was born in Bunbury, grew up on a Dardanup dairy farm as the youngest of six children and then proceeded to study, work, travel and play for the following fifteen years. Along the way he met an English backpacker, they married, settled in Boyanup and started a family.

His first steps in the direction of writing creatively were through spoken word poetry in Melbourne around the year 2000. That phase came and went, with jottings here and there, but his passion for writing has recently been rekindled, courtesy of the Bunbury Writers Group.

Dan has had a performance piece shortlisted for the Shorelines Festival of 2019 and recently performed in the WA Poetry Slam Heats. He's looking forward to introducing himself as a writer at parties, now he's figured out that he is one!

David Rawet

David Rawet was born in Melbourne, Australia. He finished school and qualified as a forester before working in eastern, western and finally central Victoria. In 1988 he moved to Bunbury in Western Australia, where he still lives. A career in bushfire management has recently been wound back, allowing him to devote more time to creative pursuits. His longstanding love of song writing and performing is now bookended with writing play scripts and fiction.

David was a finalist in the 2019 South-West Shorts monologue/duologue competition and had two pieces shortlisted in the 2019 Shore Lines writing for performance competition.

His plan is to travel the world doing research for novels and being able to claim the expenses against royalty payments. We all have dreams …

Gogo Buzz

Gogo Buzz was born in a parking lot in the picturesque university town of Stellenbosch in the fairest Cape, South Africa. She is a retired schoolteacher and legal advisor and now makes her home in the South West of Western Australia, in Bunbury, also known as the City of Three Waters.

Her real-life experiences especially those in unexpected places influence her writing. Despite a fulfilling career, all she ever wanted to do was to become a writer. She says that joining the Bunbury Writers Group has been the kickstart to her post working life career.

An intrepid traveller, compulsive reader, adventure sports lover with green thumbs and ten grandchildren; she blogs about her travels; writes stories for her grandchildren and in the rest of her writing, nurturing our planet is close to her heart. Gogo is also in avid pursuit of the elusive novel she started writing at the age of thirteen.